(JFK & Mona Lisa)
"Seeking Mona Lisa"
by Joseph A. Harriss
pg. 54-64
Smithsonian magazine
May 1999

Reference:
① "Mona Lisa: The Picture & the Myth" by Roy McMullen, Houghton Mifflin, 1975
② "Mona Lisas" by Mary Rose Storey, Abrams, 1980

MYSTERY OF THE MONA LISA

MYSTERY OF THE MONA LISA

Rina de' Firenze

Translated and expanded from the Italian edition by the author

HASTINGS HOUSE
MAMARONECK, NY

To my beloved son Renato, my thanks for endlessly encouraging me to write this book. And, most of all, for so graciously giving your final editing touch to the manuscript.

All rights reserved under the International and Pan-American Copyright Conventions. Published in the United States by Hastings House, 141 Halstead Avenue, Mamaroneck, NY 10543. No part of this publication may be reproduced, stored in a retrieval system, or transmitted, in any form or by any means, electronic, mechanical, photocopying, recording or otherwise, without the prior permission of the copyright owners or the publishers.

Library of Congress Catalog Card Number 96-077682

ISBN 0-8038-9381-7

Italian edition Copyright © 1988 by Rina de' Firenze

English language edition translated and expanded by the author © 1996

Printed in the United States of America

10 9 8 7 6 5 4 3 2 1

CONTENTS

Foreword · vii
Prologue · 1

PART I YOUNG LOVE

1 The Mission · 11
2 The Most Beautiful Corner of the World · 34
3 The Gift · 53

PART II MATERNAL LOVE

4 The Wonders of Creation · 75
5 Shattered Illusions · 92
6 The Separation · 107
7 La Bella Fiorenza · 132
8 The Forced Surrender · 150
9 The Lovely Abode · 178

PART III ETERNAL LOVE

10	Sweet Exile	209
11	Broken Enchantments	238
12	The Portrait	259
13	Flowers and Revelations	272
14	Herbs, Mechanics, and Angels	299
15	A Call from the Past	314
16	Lilium Candidum!	328
17	Leonardo's Epilogue	345
18	Together at Last	352
	Author's Note	354

FOREWORD

Adapted from the author's lecture on the origin of the painting of the Mona Lisa *by Leonardo da Vinci at Fordham University at Lincoln Center in New York City on April 29, 1989 to commemorate the publication of the Italian edition of this book.*

This is the story of Caterina, an extraordinary woman whose existence was unknown for three hundred years until the 18th century, when Leonardo da Vinci's birthdate was authenticated. It was on a paper discovered in an assessment of property belonging to Leonardo's grandfather, the *notary Ser Antonio da Vinci.

The document, dated 1457, records that Leonardo was born on a Saturday at three in the morning on April 15, 1452, the illegitimate son of Ser Piero da Vinci and a peasant girl called Caterina, in Anchiano, a village near Vinci, where the established family of notaries originated.

It is understandable that no folklore or legends have ever referred to this woman who gave birth to one of the great geniuses of all time. The discovery in the 20th century of Leonardo's Codex (writings) stimulated an ever-greater awareness of his universally prophetic works.

Several years ago, I was seized by a sudden inspiration to write a book about Caterina. I knew almost nothing about

---

*Notary—an official appointed by the pope in medieval times whose duty was to record transactions, certify the authenticity of documents, certify deeds and other writings by affixing his official seal, and to take affidavits and depositions.

her and the early life of Leonardo other than what was mentioned in the birth certificate document. Faced with the problem of writing about Caterina and overwhelmed by this powerful inspiration, I didn't know where to start. At the time, I was living in London and was hard at work researching material for a historical novel set in Italy during the 19th-century revolution called *Risorgimento*. I certainly had no time to consider another project, but some strange events changed the course of my life.

One afternoon, I was resting with my eyes closed when I suddenly felt the presence of a man dressed in a long coat and dark hat standing in a corner of the room. His piercing eyes seemed to direct a sharp ray toward my forehead and another to the forehead of a veiled woman who had suddenly appeared in another corner. From her, a third ray was directed toward me, forming a kind of luminous triangle. Somehow I knew that by joining the woman to me he was telling me she was his mother.

By now I realized I was not dreaming but was awake. I opened my eyes and was surprised to find that both figures had disappeared. Though it all happened in an instant, it seemed so real that I could not dismiss it as a figment of my imagination. I had never before experienced a psychic encounter.

At a party not long afterward, a man I assumed was an Englishman came up behind me and said softly in my ear, "A powerful spirit is urging you to write the story of his mother." Somewhat startled, I tried to turn my head but couldn't.

Out of the corner of my eye, I could see the man staring at the wall as if he was witnessing a scene. Then he whispered that the man lived during the Italian Renaissance and had painted the *Mona Lisa*. "I know you are not ready to undertake the task immediately, but in time you will be prepared."

I was speechless and a little frightened, so I nodded and walked away. Though overwhelmed by the extraordinary announcement, the idea of writing about such a historically important woman was too absurd, as I didn't know where to start. Yet as time went by, during odd moments startling visions and images related to Caterina flashed inside my head.

And I gradually became aware that the seed planted in my mind had taken root and had begun to grow.

The third incident occurred the following Easter, when I was visiting Paris with friends. One afternoon, as we drove by the Louvre, I suddenly felt compelled to go in. It was almost closing time when I got out of the car, went up to the guard at the old entrance, and told him I just wanted to see the picture of the *Mona Lisa*.

He politely pointed at the grand staircase, which, he said, led directly to it. When I got up there, the room was empty, as the last of the visitors were going down the stairs to the exit.

Alone, standing before the painting, I wanted to drink in every detail of the masterpiece, trying to understand the mystery of the dark shadings and wondering what feelings had induced the great artist to create such a magical work of art and whether this was really a portrait of his mother.

Suddenly, I saw a heavy veil drop in front of the picture. It seemed like a protective panel that covered the painting at night. The lights began to dim. I looked incredulously as a corner of the veil seemed to be lifted by an invisible hand.

As the picture reappeared, the background became brighter, like a color slide, and in place of the Mona Lisa there was a dainty figure of a very young girl.

I was puzzled by the sudden change when I was distracted by the voice of the museum guard, who asked me to leave as he passed by to clear the museum. When I looked back at the painting, I was amazed to see that the original portrait had reappeared. Somewhat disconcerted, I made my way toward the staircase and as I descended I felt two hands gently touching my arms while a voice repeated:

"*Vaya con Dios! Vaya con Dios!*"

Startled by the Spanish phrase, I turned, but there was nobody there. By now I was totally confused and I rushed back to my friends.

The following summer, the gnawing thoughts about Leonardo took a new turn. I went to Florence, where I was certain that in the *Culla delle belle arti* (The Cradle of Fine Arts) I would learn more about Leonardo's origins. During my formative years in my native Italy, I had studied the great masters of the Renaissance, yet little was known of Leonardo da Vinci's private life.

Browsing one day in a small bookstore called Libreria Vittorio, I spoke to the bookseller. It turned out he was a great admirer of Leonardo da Vinci and had collected many books on the artist's life. He could tell of my interest by the many questions I asked.

He pulled out a rare book that revealed a picture of Leonardo that looked exactly like the man who had appeared to me on that fateful day in London, even down to the shape of his hat.

I asked if he had a book on the life of Leonardo's mother. He said regretfully that nothing had ever been written on her life except for what appears on Leonardo's birth certificate. Then he showed me a brief description of her in an anonymous compilation of short biographies of famous people written at the time Leonardo was still alive. It said, "The mother of Leonardo da Vinci was *di buon sanque* (of noble blood)." It was a revelation that excited me because it confirmed that the scene of Caterina's birthplace I had seen in one of my visions had been just another true glimpse into her mysterious past.

As the bookseller explained this lack of information, it became clearer to me that this was the reason why the great master wanted to uncover the mystery surrounding his mother's identity. I decided then that I had to go where it all originated to see what I could find.

Following my instincts, I found myself in the small town of Vinci, visiting the museum in the medieval castle where, thanks to a generous contribution by the IBM Corporation, there is a permanent exhibition of Leonardo's inventions.

The next pull inside me was to go up the hills of Anchiano to the place where Leonardo was born. The taxi driver was doing his best to convince me that according to historians and architects from all over the world, the little house still standing up on the hill of Mount Albano, was in fact where Leonardo was born.

As the car climbed the winding roads, I looked out at the dreamlike countryside, trying to take in as much of its beauty as possible. The figure of a girl about ten years old standing in a field caught my eye. She was wearing a long, faded blue dress and a white bonnet. Next to her was a white goat. It was a beautiful pastoral scene as I watched the girl raise her hand to greet me.

As I waved back, her smiling face reminded me of the girl who appeared in the painting at the Louvre. I turned around to take another look at her through the rear window, but she was gone. I asked the driver to stop, and I got out to look around, but she and the goat had vanished.

We finally reached the house and the keeper showed me around. I was astounded by the familiarity of the place. When she mentioned the brook in the valley behind the house, I had an urge to go there at once.

The sparkling brook runs along the bottom of the green Mount Albano, a place of utter enchantment. I sat on a rock drinking deep of its beauty and listening to the sound of the water. Enraptured by the mystical aura surrounding the valley, I pondered the real meaning of what one might call the "eternity" of the soul.

From that day on, I knew I could no longer avoid my assignment.

I made notes of my trip and when I returned to London, I studied the notes and my experiences. I concluded that I still didn't have enough historical data to write about the subject. Discouraged, I put away my notes and once again tried to forget the whole matter.

But as time went by, more inspirations, too many to describe, kept reviving my interest. Meanwhile, fate had other plans in store for me. One of them was to take me to New York. It was a trip organized by the Woman's Press Club of London, of which I was an active member.

Stimulated by the frenetic pace of New York, I found that this was a place more suitable to my temperament. I made plans to return here even though New York has a way of testing newcomers by making their lives a kind of challenge. If you have dreams, you have to learn so much before you can even dare to try to make them come true. I, too, had to abide by that rule in my endeavors to make a living.

In the following years, I worked as a freelance journalist and designer in New York, but Leonardo and his mother were tucked away in a corner of my mind. Five years ago, the sudden urge to write the book once again took hold of me. It haunted me.

Where was I to get the information I needed to write the life story of the mysterious Caterina, a woman I had only glimpsed in visions and impressions? How was I to describe her feelings and the events of her life?

All writers have some peculiarities. One of mine is that when characters give me a hard time fitting into a story, I force them to open up and tell me their stories.

One evening, with paper and pencil in hand, I tried an experiment. I concentrated on Caterina and made her tell me who she was and what really happened to her after Leonardo was taken away from her at the age of five. My effort was rewarded when I heard her response in my mind. Then and there the manuscript was born.

I felt a surge of excitement as I wrote down every detail as she described it. The electricity was frightening, and yet, as I wrote, a kind of peace came over me. The revelations came out in random episodes as if they surfaced from the deepest recesses of Caterina's memory, and curiously, in the rhythm of an ancient language.

The complete manuscript, with hundreds of handwritten pages, took one year to complete. At this point the hardest part of my research started. I went back to the reference libraries both here (New York) and in Florence and resumed my annual pilgrimage to Anchiano. It was imperative that I verify to my satisfaction the plausibility of the events, the locations and their chronological order so that I could feel more confident when I began to write the book.

To my amazement, in almost every case the details coincided perfectly with the historical data. Of course, there was no way to verify events that took place in Caterina's private life and in the lives of some of the people she encountered.

Nevertheless, I would not leave anything out as long as it did not contradict historical facts, because it was an integral part of the story she had miraculously revealed to me.

Once that was established, I now faced the most demanding part of the work—organizing all the information that she had given me and writing it in book form. This took another eighteen months.

Finally the book was completed and published in Italy in the fall of 1988 under the title *Caterina—La Madre di Leonardo*.

Looking back, I became increasingly convinced that the reason Leonardo wanted this book written was not only to make known the story of his mother, but also to reveal the truth about the portrait.

The *Mona Lisa* was the only work of art with which he never parted, either to the husband of the woman who allegedly posed for it, or to any of his influential patrons. For as long as he lived, he kept the painting with him wherever he went. It represented the image and soul of his mother, whose real name was Lisa.

Over the last hundred years, there has been speculation that the painting is the master's self-portrait. Of late there have been highly publicized computer theories about the painting.

With great reverence to the young woman who gave birth to the greatest mind and talent of the Italian Renaissance, I bowed my head and humbly obeyed the bidding of psychic phenomena that used me as an instrument to lift the veil of time and make known to the world the true story of Caterina.

RINA DE' FIRENZE
1996

PROLOGUE

FALL 1438

Distant flashes of lightning flickered ominously behind the battlements of an old medieval tower, the only remaining part of a small castle, almost completely hidden by the tall trees of the hilly Tuscan countryside, not far from Florence. The rest of the building was a rather grand and obviously new country villa, bridging the gap between the tower and the stables, which were renowned for the breeding of the Italian peninsula's best thoroughbred horses.

A guard in soldier's uniform strolled the wide cobblestone path leading from the iron gate of the estate. He walked around a huge polished marble fountain. The smiling marble cherub in its center held a cornucopia from which water spouted into a deep, round basin. The gentle gurgle of cascading water mingled with the sounds of occasional thunder reverberating somewhere far away in the starless sky. Loud spasmodic screams came at intervals from a lighted window in the tower, piercing the night.

Inside the tower, on a silken frilled canopied bed lay a blonde girl giving birth with the help of a country midwife and a young dark-haired maid. After the delivery, the maid hastily straightened up the room, while the midwife bound the baby in swaddling clothes on the edge of the bed. She then carefully laid the baby in the finely crafted cradle, picked up her shawl, and left the room. At the foot of the stairs, she was met by a page, who furtively handed her a small bag of coins.

Quiet seemed to have returned inside the chamber. The mother's pretty head sank back into the soft, lacy pillows as the maid held up the baby girl, wrapped in a warm blanket, for her to see. Still somewhat dazed, she smiled at the tiny face, but her sweet maternal gaze dimmed with tears.

The maid, conscious of what was troubling her mistress, laid the baby back in the cradle. "Rita, does my father know that the baby is born?" the young mistress asked feebly.

The maid shrugged her shoulders, her drawn face showing signs of strain. "I don't know, Monna Alicia. After he arrived today and spoke to you, I think he stayed in his room in the new west wing," Rita said in her warm Spanish accent.

Behind the pond-green silken drapes, the shutters rattled insistently as the wind rampaged outside the ancient tower. Rita patted her mistress's hand reassuringly. "Don't worry, my *principessina!* He won't make you leave for the convent on a night like this. Rest now! I'll watch your beautiful baby girl."

Alicia reached to touch the cradle. "Rita, I want you to come with me to help me take care of my baby. I'm sure Father will agree to it."

Rita forced a smile. She felt close to her mistress, but the idea of confinement within a convent stifled her. With concern, she looked down at Alicia's wan face and patiently waited for her to close her eyes. As she gently moved a lock of golden hair from the moist forehead, she glimpsed the page entering the doorway and beckoning her to come out. Content to see that the mother and child were resting now, she carefully tiptoed from the room.

In the master bedroom, dressed in a sumptuous crimson robe, the tall, robust master of the house was pacing the floor. He was a Frenchman in his late forties, with a sunburned face and strongly marked features offset by piercing blue eyes. His long straw-blond hair was the color of his thick wavy beard. He stopped pacing to look at the stormy sky from the large window draped with heavy dark-red velvet. Hearing a timid knock at the door, he jerked back, irritated. After a few moments, he shouted in a French accent, "Come in, come in!"

Rita appeared at the door. "*Condottiere*, you called me? I'm at your service, *signore!*" she said, her eyes cast downward.

He turned abruptly. "Yes, come here and listen to me carefully," he said imperiously. She advanced slowly, trembling with fear. "You must do exactly what I say. *Compris?*" She looked up at him and gulped. "As soon as Principessina Alicia falls asleep," he continued brusquely, "you will place the baby in a basket and take it to Fernando, the stableman."

"But *signore*, what ... what will I tell the *principessina* when she ... when she wakes up and asks for the ba—"

"You won't see her anymore," he interrupted. "She will be leaving for the convent as soon as she is able to travel. Meanwhile, you stay away from her quarters, or you'll be out for good! *Compris?*" He motioned her out. "And now, *vite! Vite!*"

Shocked, the girl backed out of the room. In the hall, she went straight to a service-door entrance, slipped through it, and ran down a winding staircase that led directly into the stables.

In a corner of the stablemen's room sat young Fernando, holding his head in his hands. As Rita laid her hand on his shoulder he jumped up.

"Nando, the master ordered me to bring you the ba—" she blurted, suddenly feeling his hand over her mouth, while he looked around to make certain that the other stablemen had not overheard her. "I must come with you!" Rita insisted. "And if you care about me," she continued in a forceful whisper, "you'd better tell me where you're taking her!"

"To the convent—didn't the *condottiere* tell you?"

She stepped back. "Without the mother? That's terrible! Why, since she already agreed to go there?"

He shrugged his shoulders. "But ... you, darling, cannot

come!" he said, his voice weakening as she ran her fingers through his black, curly hair.

"Well, we'll have to do something to help her," she said resolutely. Then, mellowing, she murmured, "And we'll do it together, darling!" She looked seductively into his eyes, moving back up the staircase, and he covered his face in confusion.

It was dead of night when the guard grudgingly drew open the iron gate for the heavy coach leaving the villa. Inside the coach sat Nando, looking pleadingly at an unrelenting Rita, who under her short blue mantle jealously guarded the basket with the sleeping baby girl on her lap. "Nando, where are you taking this baby?" Rita suddenly burst out. "You must tell me the truth now!"

"I told you—to the convent. But you're not coming, so please get out now while you can still walk back! You know what'll happen if the master finds out you came with me," he said, leaning out to call the driver.

She jerked his sleeve smartly. "And do you know what'll happen if you don't tell me the truth? Yes, let me tell you, you'll just have to forget all about us—our love and our wedding!" she bluffed, clutching the basket as the coach went over some uneven ground.

His jaw dropped in dismay. "Well ... well ...," he mumbled, overcome by Rita's merciless anger. "Well, I'm supposed to take her somewhere and ... Oh, you know I couldn't kill a fly! That's why I stayed in the stables all these years, instead of becoming a soldier in my master's army."

"*Dios mío!* Kill this innocent creature? I knew it! I felt it! I'll take her to a Spanish gypsies' camp. At least they treated me better than this! I'll get money from my mistress and buy the baby back later. Now let me out!" she cried, tightening her grip on the basket. "Go back and tell your master whatever you want!"

"How can you find a gypsy camp in this pouring rain, my dearest?"

As the coach took to the open road of the countryside, they entered directly into the storm-bitten area. The coach driver cracked his whip, and the two horses, blinded by the fierce rain, pulled the coach off the main road. Soon the rumbling of the wheels became overwhelming, and the baby started to cry.

Rita lifted the curtain to look out the window. "Look, there's a little house over that hill. Let's see if anyone lives there. Maybe we could leave her with some countrypeople." Nando put his head out the window and yelled at the driver to stop. The coach came to a jarring halt.

As they got out, fierce, slanting raindrops hit their faces like darts. Nando sheltered Rita under his cape as she carried the basket. They scrambled up the muddy slope, but could no longer see the little house. But, as a powerful lightning bolt brightened the higher ground, it reappeared before their eyes. It was a small stone house, humble but well kept, in the benign shadow of a tall elm tree. Peering through a small hole in the door, Rita saw the light of an oil lamp and knocked.

"Who's there?" called the tired voice of an old man.

Rita placed the basket on the doorstep, adjusting the folded linens around the baby. She wrapped her snugly in the soft blanket and placed a loving kiss on her forehead. Then, filled with anguish, she cried, "I'll be back, my beautiful angel! I'll find you again, I promise you! Now, *vaya con Dios!*"

Touched by Rita's deep concern for the baby, Nando took out a purse with gold coins given him by the master and slipped it into the basket. "Now we have to go, darling," he said, tearing her away. He drew his cape over her again and led her back to the coach as she moaned, "*Vaya con Dios,* my little one, *vaya con Dios!*"

The old man inside the little house opened the door, his foot bumping the basket. As he bent to pick it up, the baby cried. The old woman standing at his side flung her arms up and burst into a cry of joy. "A miracle! A miracle! My prayers have been answered!"

Wet, angry, and anxious to get home, the coachman whipped fiercely at the horses as they took the downhill road, galloping out of the storm.

Inside the coach, Nando tried hard to calm Rita's sobbing, but she turned her face away, distraught by the ugly situation awaiting her back at the villa. She pulled the curtain aside to breathe fresh air and to still the upset caused by the bouncing carriage.

Dawn was breaking, but the sky seemed much too red to her. There was a strange burning smell in the night air. "Nando," she said, leaning out of the window, "there's smoke rising above the estate! It looks like a fire!"

Nando called the drowsy coachman, who started yelling, "The villa, the villa is burning! The whole building is on fire!"

"Stop the coach outside the walls!" shouted Nando.

In the tower, the crackling noise and heat from the fire had awakened the young mother. She staggered to the window and saw the flames below. Frantic, she rushed to save her baby. At the sight of the empty cradle, she screamed for Rita, but nobody answered. She ran through the hallway into the maid's room and seeing no one there, she started down the narrow tower staircase, screaming.

As soon as the carriage drew up outside the estate, Nando leaped out and forced the iron gate wide open. Then, leaving his cape with Rita, he dashed toward the stables, while she stared at the blaze, paralyzed. She gasped when she saw her mistress stumbling out of the tower. She was narrowly missed by a heavy flaming beam that crashed to the ground, catching her nightgown on fire. Alicia kept running along the path, engulfed in flames, until she tripped and fell into a flower bed. Rita rushed to her and smothered the flames with Nando's cape. Alicia looked up and cried, "Rita! Where's my baby? Where's my Lisa?" Rita was at a loss for words. "My father ... he must have taken her!" Alicia screamed deliriously. "Find her, Rita! Find her for me!" Overcome with pain and despair, she fell back again, clutching the cape in her arms.

"My *principessina,* don't die! I'll find your baby, I will! I promise you!" Rita cried, but her mistress was already unconscious! She called out, but her screams for help were lost in the surrounding chaos. As she ran this way and that in search of Nando, through the blinding smoke, all she could see was that the worst part of the fire was closer to the stables. She shrank back as the familiar voices of those trapped inside shrieked with terror. Suddenly, horses, maddened by fire, neighing in full cry, bolted out of the stables.

Nando, who had been trying to lead the frightened horses, blindfolded, two at a time toward the gate, saw her. "Rita, stay back! Don't come any closer. The roof on the new wing is going to collapse at any moment now!"

"Nando, come! Come quickly!" she cried in a shrill voice, "Monna Alicia's over there, lying by the path. She's badly hurt—maybe dying."

"Go back to her and wait for me!"

Terrified, she made her way back through the thick smoke, searching for the spot where she had left her mistress.

In the master chamber, the *condottiere* was unable to open his heavy door. When he finally forced it, the flames in the hallway overpowered him, igniting his robe. He called for help, lunging toward the grand staircase. As he bravely ventured down the blazing steps, the staircase caved in, plunging him into the chasm below.

Outside, as Rita approached her mistress again, she observed through the smoke the large figure of a man bending over her. His huge back, covered by a heavy black cloak, shook with sobs. As she drew nearer, she overheard him say, "Forgive me, Alicia! Forgive me!" When he saw Rita, he pulled his hood over his face and stepped back.

"Who are you?" Rita cried out, quickening her step. But when she drew nearer, the mysterious stranger, although limping heavily, had swiftly crossed the garden and disappeared into the dark bushes.

Then, looking around, she was relieved to see Nando sweeping up Alicia's limp body in his arms. He carried her toward the gate, and Rita followed him. As Alicia was being lifted, her gold chain slipped off her neck, unnoticed, and fell among the flowers.

Outside the walls, the air was clearer and the changing colors of dawn were tinting the distant golden horizon.

In a nearby field, they gently set their young mistress down on a bed of amber leaves. They tried to revive her, promising to find her baby, but to no avail, for as they struggled, she gradually sank into an eternal sleep. Yet her last gasp had been a happy one, for she still embraced a thick fold of the cape that, in her last moments, she had managed to gather into a bundle, holding this illusion tightly to her breast.

The story you are about to read is the story of an unsung heroine who led a simple but charmed life in a time and a place of fable. All that remains in memory of her is the most enigmatic portrait ever painted, one of the greatest works of art ever to touch the hearts and minds of all mankind. This is her story.

PART ONE

YOUNG LOVE

1
THE MISSION

SPRING 1448

The small stone house set on the slope of a hill became the home in which I spent the first ten years of my life. To my child's eyes, it seemed as if the topmost branches of the tall, majestic elm tree that sheltered the little house reached to heaven. In springtime, it turned into a birds' paradise with nests hidden all through it. Its lower branches hung down gracefully, caressing the flat ground surrounding our humble home. The velvety wind from the high hills of Mont'Albano blew gently on its leaves, creating a sweet rustle that harmonized well with the timid sound of my flute. Yes, I owned a little flute my father had carved for me from a rare piece of cane. It had been my favorite pastime through those years I spent with my elderly parents.

I never wondered why my parents were so old. I didn't know that their white hair was a sign of old age, because they both were very active. We lived in an isolated part of the countryside and, except for a young couple who only lately had moved into the abandoned house on the hill above us, there were no other young families with which I could make a comparison. Every morning at dawn, I got up with my father. He went to work on his small field, and I sat under the elm tree and played my flute for the baby birds while their parents went to find food for them.

One day while I was gathering firewood, I saw a white nanny goat, lost and frightened, hiding in a small cave. I took her to the well, gave her some water, and stroked her back. From that day, she followed me everywhere I went. My father showed me how to milk her. I named her Jasmine, because of her snow-white coat. Not only did she become my steadfast companion during my search for firewood, but also a devoted listener to my music.

Those had been the happiest days of my childhood, but new circumstances were about to put an end to my carefree life, compelling me to grow faster into adulthood. First, my old mother became ill and had to stay in bed all day. Then I noticed that my father's legs were troubling him. At the end of his long day's work, he seemed to be in pain, dragging his feet as he walked all the way back to the house. I made my mother drink Jasmine's warm new milk, as it seemed to help her, but I didn't know what to do for my poor father.

One day while I was washing clothes near the well, I saw him sitting on the doorstep, pounding the wall with his fist. I rushed to him. "Father, what happened? Is it Mother?" I asked, but he didn't hear me.

He kept pounding and muttering to himself. "No, it can't be ... it can't be the end. My God, you cannot take her from me!" he pleaded. Then, looking up into the sky, he pointed at the house and cried, "You know that we found this house together and rebuilt it together. Now you must take us together! I don't want to be left here alone!"

I touched his arm. "But, Father, I'm here with you, don't you see? Don't be afraid, I'll take care of you!" He turned to me, almost surprised. With my fingertips, I dried his wet, tired cheeks.

"Caterina! Caterina!" We heard my mother's frail voice calling from inside the house and rushed to her bedside.

Grasping my hand, she said, "Come ... come here, dear daughter! Come! ... I feel that God is calling me back." Then turning to my father, who stood motionless at the foot of the bed, she implored, "My dear husband, it's time we told her everything, don't you think?" My father didn't reply, but looked at her with pleading eyes, his shaking hands grasping the bedpost. "My dear, I cannot leave with this on my mind."

"Tell me what, Mama?" I asked, confused.

Acquiescing to his silence, she grasped my other hand. "That ... that I will soon have to leave you both. But, my dear daughter, I want you to remember that I love you very much and will always love you, because you are my beloved daughter ... and always will be, even when I won't be with you any longer! Now, please ... take care ... of my dear hus ... band...." Her voice soon failed her, her eyes closed, and her head sank back into her pillow. Her features seemed suddenly smoother, as a faint smile moved across her lips. It was the smile I had always loved to contemplate since I was in my cradle. That sudden recollection seemed to give me the strength I needed to hold back the bitter lump that had risen in my throat. I knew, though, that she was dying, as her hands were growing cold and lifeless, yet I didn't want to break the silence of that precious moment in which the human spirit passes into another life, that mysterious life my mother had recently talked about to me. So I just stood there feeling as if I were suspended in air.

A pain in my legs made me realize that my knees had slipped onto the cold stone floor. I looked at my father, who was still holding on to the bedpost, staring absently into space. I got up and brought him a chair. He fell into it, exhausted and ashen, and I quickly covered his legs with a blanket.

A low ray of sunshine brightened the room. Jasmine had pushed her way in, flinging the door wide open. The warm, luminous sun ray reached my mother's bed. I went to stir up the fire. Jasmine came close to my side and rubbed herself against me as if trying to comfort me.

Suddenly, the room fell into complete, almost blinding

darkness. The ray of sun had gone behind the hill, and the votive lamp was out—out for the first time since I could remember. That was the lamp that only my mother tended. "It went out in sorrow!" I told myself.

I moved swiftly through the dark room, carrying a lit taper from the fire. I took out the oil bottle and went to refill the lamp. With trembling hands, I poured the oil into the glass chalice in the terra-cotta bowl hanging from an iron hook in the ceiling next to the bed. As I relit it, the light reflected gently on my mother's serene expression. I smiled at her. Then, gazing around the shabby room, I could only hope that she had left this world remembering nothing but the happy times of her life.

With the first light of day, I climbed up the hill to ask the couple living there for help. They soon appeared at our house, followed by the old priest and his sexton. I watched in dismay as the two men dug a hole right under my beloved tree. "Your mother's grave, according to her wishes," they said. I glanced up at the birds perched silently on the tree branches, and my heart ached at seeing my favorite play corner turned into a place of mourning.

The death of my mother not only broke my father's heart, but also struck him physically. He seemed to have less control of his body, and his legs had weakened so that he hardly moved anymore, something that my child's mind could not understand. During the following summer, he only managed to get to the kitchen garden with a cane just to teach me how to care for it so we would not lack vegetables. But as fall came on, it became too painful for him and soon he lost interest in that, too.

One sunny day, I managed to make him sit outside, while I went to find some grapes. But, alas! The vineyard that had been my father's pride was completely depleted. I felt tears in my eyes. Then I found a few clusters of large grapes on a pergola next to the well. Most of them were infested with worms, but I picked the few that had survived, placing them carefully in a small basket.

I dried my tears and went back to my father.

When he saw me, he looked up and smiled. "Ah, Caterina, you're back. What have you got in that basket?"

"I brought you some nice grapes. Look!" I said, forcing a smile.

"Oh, my poor vineyard! It must be in a terrible state."

"No, it's not! Don't you see how good these grapes are?" I lied, setting the basket down on a stool next to him. He touched the grapes with the tip of his finger and stared at them in anguish.

Golden leaves from the elm tree had fallen all around. I brushed them off the steps so I could sit down and, with the corner of my apron, I polished the marble slab lodged on the top step. I wasn't able to read the mysterious writing engraved on it, but the symbols representing the sun, the moon, and the stars, carved around those words, never failed to fascinate me.

"Father, I really do love this slab!" I said brightly, hoping it would take his mind off the grapes.

"Yes, I know, my dear daughter," he said still absently. "That slab represents the origin of our little house!" Then, silently, we both admired the smooth marble slab as if we were seeing it for the first time.

"Was it really left here by a saint?" I asked.

"Of course," he replied, with his eyes again on the grapes.

"Was it already on the doorstep when you found it?" I continued to ask, just to keep him talking.

"Oh, my dear, it's a long story. One day, when I feel better, I'll tell you all about it."

"Why don't you tell me now? Please, Father, please!"

"Well, all right, my little one," he said, stirring himself. "Come here and I'll see what I can remember." I quickly got up and crouched on the ground next to his feet. He shook his head and, as if suddenly amused, he began his story.

"Once upon a time, there was a nice young couple," he said with a sly wink. "They were madly in love! The young man knew that his rich parents wouldn't let him marry the girl he loved, so he decided to elope with his pretty blonde sweetheart." He smiled, pretending to be coy. "Taking her on his horse, he rode far and deep into the countryside. They rode for days and days, looking for a place where they could make their nest. Finally, they rounded this hill and stopped right in front of this little house!" he said, brightening.

"And they were you and dear Mama!" I said, imitating his cheerful tone of voice. He laughed, his eyes twinkling as he looked at me. Then he sat up and straightened his shoulders. Suddenly, he looked younger.

"Why wouldn't they let you marry each other?"

"Ah, because she belonged to the class called *'il popolo minuto'*—those people who have to work with their hands. She'd only handled the finest silk yarns, though, and she was a lady at heart, but for my parents, it wasn't enough!" He paused and shook his head, still embittered by the memory. "Ah, my beloved daughter," he then said, "if only you knew how cruel rich parents can be! Anyway, as I was saying, we stopped in front of this little house—it must have been abandoned for over a century—and got off the horse. Its walls were weather-beaten, and the roof seemed on the verge of falling to pieces, yet to us it was the loveliest house in the world. 'As lovely as a palace!' your mother kept saying. When we tried to open the old door, it fell back into the dark room. And as we stepped inside, we found ourselves wrapped in veils of cobwebs," he said, laughing heartily, and I laughed with him. "In the middle of the room was a long, narrow, altarlike table. There, on top of it, was this unusual marble slab! Later, we discovered a pile of old parchment under it, entirely covered with strange writings. When I looked at them, I saw that they were written in Latin, like the writing on this stone. That's a language no longer in use. But somehow I knew they were written by a great wise man, maybe even a saint. When we finally finished fixing the house, we saved the parchment and I placed this magnificent stone on our threshold to remind us of the grace of God! Well, the day we were ready to be married, we went to the church of Sant'Amato, high up on that hill, to ask the young priest to bless our happy union. When, after the marriage ceremony, I told him about those mysterious manuscripts we had found," he chuckled, "he couldn't wait to see them. In fact, he got so excited that he followed us back to the house on his donkey and loaded the precious papers in his packsaddle." The old man was silent for a while, reminiscing. "He was a bright young scholar then," he commented, "deeply interested in these kinds of mysterious writings."

"Could he read them? What did they say?" I asked anxiously.

"It was hard for him, too. But with his knowledge of Latin, he was able to grasp a lot of their meaning." He smiled as he recalled. "Every time he discovered something new, he came back here and we spent many hours on the porch, discussing the true meaning of the wise man's revelations. Now he's as old and tired as I am and he doesn't talk about it anymore." Then, shaking his head, he added, "I wonder if he forgets things like I do these days...."

"Do you remember what those revelations said?" I persisted.

"Oh, my dear, I can't remember all the details, but I know they were strange revelations about the formation of our earth and its position in the universe, insisting that the earth was just another star floating in the sky. Very strange! The rest of them were mostly prophecies."

"What are prophecies?"

"Prophecies, my dear, are discourses of a man who knows about the past and about what will happen to our world in the distant future, and we call such a man a prophet."

"Do you think the saint, the prophet, carved this stone himself?"

"And why not? If he's a saint or a prophet, he might also be able to engrave something as beautiful as this. When a man has the gift of God to write about the mysteries of the universe, he might have other talents, too! My master always said, 'When one is God-gifted, he can do anything!'" he exclaimed, flinging up his arms. "Ah, my dear child, you've brought back memories of the years I spent at the studio!"

"What's the studio?" I asked.

"Well, the studio is where the sons of rich families go to

learn a profession. Unfortunately, the father always chooses the profession. Only *he* can decide on his son's future," he said, sighing deeply.

"Where do the daughters go to learn?"

"Girls are not allowed in any studios because their place is at home. They're only taught how to raise a family. Except for some of the girls belonging to the nobility—they're taught by private tutors."

"Then all the others don't know how to read or write—like me!"

"That is so, my dear. Like you, all the others can't read or write."

"But I want to learn. You can teach me, Father! Now that you don't work in the fields, you have the time."

"Oh, my dear, I wouldn't remember how to do it. Don't you see? If I'm not working like I did before, it's because I'm too old ... which is what upsets me most, my dear, because I realize that I cannot give you enough time to grow up and be independent."

"But, Father, I am grown up. Don't you see how tall and strong I am? Don't you see that I can do everything around the house? And the garden, too?" I added rather boastfully.

"Yes, you're tall for your age, but you're still a child. What are you going to do when I am gone? When you are left alone in this, in this ..."

"Father, dear, you won't leave for a long time! I'll take care of you. And you'll be here, telling me beautiful stories, like you did today."

But he wasn't following me anymore. He kept looking toward his poor vineyard, pursing his lips tightly, trying to control his grief.

My father's premonition was correct. When the good weather was over, he had to stay indoors all the time, sitting in front of the fireplace, which was usually cold, since I could no longer provide enough firewood. Our food reserve was ending, too, and very soon we would have no flour left for bread. The miller who used to come around with his cart hadn't shown up since he found out we had no more fresh produce to give him in exchange for flour and other basic necessities.

Aware of our plight, when I stepped on that special stone on my way out each morning, I prayed and implored our good prophet for help.

It was almost dark when I was on my way home one night. Cold rain kept falling on my face, blinding me as I struggled against the fierce wind. My chapped hands were blue with cold as I held a few precious fire sticks. Before going in, I lingered again on the doorstep, knelt, and, with my head bent, stared at the slab, begging desperately for a miracle.

I heard my father call from his sickbed. When I went in, I found him muttering to himself. I rushed to the fireplace, warmed up the leftover soup and brought it to him. After he settled down again, I went to the cupboard to look for some food for myself, but except for a slice of dry bread and some flour at the bottom of a jar, it was empty. My father woke up and started mumbling again, more agitatedly this time. "Caterina! Caterina, my little one, it's your anniversary!" he cried.

Worried and distressed as I was, I did not pay any heed to what he was saying until I saw him waving his arms to catch my attention.

"Caterina, my little one, bring me one of those white linen handkerchiefs!" he shouted. "I must draw your face. Don't you see? It's the anniversary of your ..."

I rushed to his side and stroked his head. "But, Father, there are no more linen squares left. Besides, you are too ... much too tired now."

"Can't you hear, my child? We're having the first storm of the season, just like the night when they brought you to us."

"Brought me? What do you mean? Who brought me?" I asked, alarmed.

"We don't know.... Oh, my God! Mother will scold me now. Where is she? It's dark and storming outside. Where is she? I'm worried about her."

"But, Father, don't you remember? She left us many months ago ... forever," I answered, still confused about what he had just said.

"Oh, yes, I remember now. Well, then, I can tell you the whole truth."

"What truth?" I asked, cold shivers running through me as I recalled my mother's last words. Though well aware that my dress was drenched from the rain, I knew, too, that those were also shivers of fear; fear of finding out something more terrible than my child's mind could ever conceive. Yet I went on anxiously. "Tell me what, Father? Oh, please tell me! What truth?" I repeated, taking hold of his hand as he collapsed onto his pillow. Yet his bloodshot eyes darted back and forth as if searching his memory. Then, pointing at the door, he whispered, "It was a stormy night ... like tonight. Frightful peals of thunder seemed to break down the house! All of a sudden, we heard a loud knock on the door. We jumped with fright. Then I asked, 'Who's there?' But nobody answered. My wife sat up and looked at me as we both heard a woman's voice crying, *Vaya con Dios! Vaya con Dios!*' Then everything was silent. Even the rain had stopped." He paused, exhausted. I held my breath, wanting to hear more, yet dreading the outcome of these revelations.

Recovering a little, he resumed his strange tale. "When I opened the door, there was a basket on the doorstep. But I waited for your mother before I picked it up. Then we heard the sweetest cry. It was your first cry, my dear! A cry that filled our hearts with joy! 'A miracle, a miracle!' said your mother!" I listened incredulously to this story, trying to convince myself it was just a dream he was relating. I sat on a stool and listened as he continued.

"When your mother took you in her arms, you were wrapped in a soft pink blanket. I went to light the big lamp, so we could see your angel face. Your mother jumped with joy as we saw your large deep-blue eyes—two big lakes of blue water! I searched in the basket for some clue, and saw that they'd provided you with plenty of soft linens. Then I found a small purse full of gold coins! I knew then that those who had brought you here were good people. 'God bless them!' I said later, each time we needed to use one of those coins." He paused again.

By now I knew that he was telling me what had really happened. I stood up, infuriated. "Who were they? And if they were so good, why did they abandon me to strangers? Why did my parents allow this to happen? Why were they so cruel?" I shouted out with a force I didn't know I possessed.

"My dear, we were not strangers. We loved you with all our hearts—you know that. We had prayed for years, asking Santa Caterina for a child of our own, and you came along! You were Santa Caterina's answer to our prayers. That is why we named you after her."

"How could my ... my mother allow that to happen?" I went on, regardless.

"My dear, we don't know the circumstances. Maybe somebody took you away from her," he said, moving his hands, trying to calm me.

"But my mother, my real mother, should have protected me, whatever the circumstances!" I cried.

"Poor woman! Perhaps she has been weeping ever since. Perhaps she died. One day you'll find out everything, you'll see."

"No, I don't want to find out about it. I wish ... you'd never told me. I wish ... you hadn't," I said, as heavy sobs choked me.

"I told you so you could look for your parents when you grow up."

"What for? I don't want to find them," I cried hoarsely.

Shocked by my reaction, he sank back again, distressed.

I stood there looking at him, pitiless, unfeeling, as if my heart had turned to stone. Then I felt my wet dress sticking to my skin and slowly started for my bed, which was tucked away in a recess behind a wall, but something made me linger in front of the old trunk, where my mother had kept what was left of my baby clothing.

I lifted the heavy lid and took out a small package, neatly tied with a blue ribbon. I put down the lid and started to unfold the clothing and the bundle of linen squares on which my father had drawn my face at different stages of my life, starting at the age of about one to the present time. It was a ritual he performed yearly. At his request, my mother used to give him one of those squares, which he stretched flat on the floor and, having me sit still, he would carefully draw my face on it using a burned firebrand. Now, contemplating these images, I wondered why he wanted to draw my child's face. I couldn't even recognize myself, as I had never seen myself in a looking glass. My fingers touched a folded square, which hadn't been used yet, and I felt a little guilty. I turned to look at him and met his shining eyes staring back at me.

"My dear daughter," he began with a hint of a smile, "I did it so when you grew up you could see how noble your features were as a child. They still are! Unfortunately, I didn't have the colors to match the blue of your eyes turning green, the gold of your hair turning brown ... and your rosy cheeks...." He stopped talking. Maybe he knew that I was not listening anymore. In fact, my fingers had just touched the elaborate embroidery in the corner of that last linen square. I unfolded it and looked at it in the dimness of the room. There on a monogram was a richly embroidered family crest. My mother had never shown me that linen square, but she had told me what a family crest meant.

It was at that moment that I realized how powerful my parents' family must have been. Yet, they had denied my existence, and for the first time, I really hated them. In a fit of anger, I flung it away from me. Suddenly, the heavy ache in my heart moved to my head and burst into such overwhelming pain that I lost control of myself, wanting only to see those remains of my dishonorable origin destroyed for good. I threw all of the clothing violently into the air. Frenzied, I jumped on those miserable rags, scattering them over the dark stone floor. I stamped on them, hoping they would disintegrate. My world had suddenly become awful, and all I could think of was escaping. I turned and ran out of the door.

Hurtling through the blinding darkness of a thunderstorm, I kept running through the night, which was fleetingly lit with stark flashes of lightning. I didn't know where I was or where I was heading until a long, snakelike bolt of lightning struck the well pulley before my eyes. A roll of thunder followed closely as the bucket plunged to the bottom of the well with such a thud that the ground shook under my feet. Stunned, I tripped backward and fell into large puddle of water.

When I recovered, the storm had already cleared. There was silence all around me, a silence more frightening than the storm because it foreshadowed something beyond my understanding. From the mouth of the well came a stream of voices, which soon turned into a single, deep, thunderous voice saying, "Don't fret, my child. You're protected. Know that your life was saved at birth because you were meant to carry out a great mission, a mission important to the whole world! Now you must go on your way among new people. You will always be guided. Go, my child! Go with God!"

As the voice faded away, a vibrating flame emerged from the well, turning into the bright, slender ray of a tiny luminous star. The small star rose above the well and moved slowly higher and higher into the dark sky until it suddenly disappeared.

I felt Jasmine's warm breath on my face. "Did you hear that voice?" I asked her, flabbergasted. "Did you see that star?" But Jasmine kept licking my cheeks. I suddenly realized I could see everything around me, for the moon had just reappeared. A refreshing breeze was sweeping the dark clouds away as, one by one, the stars pierced their way through the deep night sky.

Jasmine butted me with her head, urging me to get up, and I dragged myself out of the puddles, lifting my mud-soaked skirt.

As I tottered back to the house, trying to digest the incredible events of that evening, I marveled to see that the slab on the doorstep had been washed clean by the rain and was shining brightly in the silvery moonlight. Caressing the perfect surface of the slab, my finger felt the carved star, and my thoughts returned to the shimmering magic star I had just seen rising above the old well. Then I suddenly knew whose prophetic words were those I had just heard. A warm shiver shook my body, and I smiled as a glow of light seemed to radiate through my whole being.

Still dazed, I stepped inside. The squalid room under the votive lamp seemed much more welcoming to me, and I went to my poor father's bedside.

He looked at me with his tired eyes and smiled. Then, with a deep intake of breath, he turned on his side and closed his eyes.

I bent over and placed a kiss on his forehead. My eyes wandered around the familiar room, seeing my mother's old chair and her favorite frayed cushion, still showing traces of her bright embroidery. I was dismayed to see my baby things still spread all over the floor and rushed to pick them up. I folded them carefully in the same way my mother had done for years, tying the bundle with its own special blue ribbon and replacing it in the trunk, the only remaining evidence of my true origin.

In the morning, I found that my father had also left me forever. Later the same day, I watched the two men digging another grave next to my mother's under the elm tree. Holding a small bunch of flowers, the last few frail blooms of our tiny garden, I stood there motionless, watching the old priest go over the same rites he had given my mother. I noticed, though, that he kept glancing at the bundle tied up in an old tablecloth that was lying on the ground next to my feet. When he finally came over to talk to me, I promptly asked him, "Padre, what's a mission?"

He stood back, as if baffled by my question. Then, recovering, he said, "A mission? Why do you ask?" I did not reply. Trying to remain in control of the situation, he searched in his mind for the right words and said, "A mission? Well, a mission is something that ... that is usually assigned by someone, or inspired in some way." He waited for my reaction, but I kept silent. "In either case, it's always a religious task, you can be sure of that." Then, staring curiously into my eyes, he questioned, "Anyway, why do you ask?"

I plucked up my courage and answered solemnly, "Because I know I have a mission."

"Who told you so?" he demanded. Then seeing that I did

not intend to reveal my secret, he went on, "If you have a mission, there's no better place than the church in which to fulfill it. The sexton's wife would be very happy to take you into her home." As he spoke, he pointed at the old digger, who nodded in agreement. I turned to glance at the well.

The priest waited patiently, then said, "In any case, whatever you decide to do, remember, my dear, that the house of God is always open."

My lack of communication tired him, and he walked away with pity in his eyes, shaking his head silently at the others. The old sexton followed him to the cart, carrying the digging tools on his back. Vincenzo, the younger gravedigger, stayed behind, intending to talk to me, but then he seemed to change his mind. After adjusting the heavy bandage around his leg, he waved good-bye and made his way up the hill, dragging his foot.

So there I was, all alone, still holding the small bunch of flowers, staring at the two wooden crosses marking the places where my dear parents had been buried and wondering why such good people had to end their lives under a pile of earth. I remembered my mother talking about the immortality of the soul, and I waited for a sign to confirm her words. But all was silent around me. Even the rustling noises of the leaves seemed to have stopped. I looked up and saw that my brave sparrows were perching quietly in rows on the branches above with their tiny eyes fixed on me. "Oh, my friends, I see that you feel my pain," I murmured, suddenly overcome by heavy sobbing. Soon the tree seemed to come to life as the leaves started to rustle; my friends had begun flying and chirping! I held in my sobs and smiled at them. Then I divided the bunch of wilting flowers, now wet from my tears, into two equal parts and placed them one on each grave.

The sky that unforgettable gray day had suddenly cleared, and there was a glowing sunset. I stopped on the edge of the slope, turning to glance once more at my elm tree and the little house I was leaving behind.

Jasmine, taking advantage of my inattention, twisted herself around the rope I was holding and pulled me back toward our home. Since morning, she had disappeared from sight.

When I finally spotted her, she was hiding in the same cave where I had originally found her. I had always taken her with me wherever I went, but now, for the first time, she was stubbornly refusing to follow me.

When at last we reached the top of the hill, I saw Vincenzo's house. It was bigger and much prettier than ours, with its newly painted windows and red roof tiles shining in the sunset. Vincenzo was washing his face in a large basin placed in the middle of a table on the porch.

When he saw us, he stopped and waved to me. Still drying his arms, he came to meet me. "Ah, Caterina, I'm glad you decided to come and stay with us!" he said in his pleasant voice.

"I'm sorry, Vincenzo, but I didn't come to stay. I came to ask if you could keep my goat for me," I said, still holding her rope tightly.

"Good evening, Caterina! Welcome home!" announced Maria, his wife, as she came out of the house holding their son, a sickly little boy, by the hand. Her pretty face looked drawn, and though her beautiful dark eyes had a touch of sadness, they shone as she smiled.

The moment the boy saw Jasmine, his face brightened and he started jumping up and down with excitement. I patted Jasmine's neck and whispered in her ear, "You see? The little boy loves you already!"

"Why aren't you staying with us, my dear?" Vincenzo asked.

"Why? Where are you going, then?" asked Maria, surprised.

"Thank you, dear friends, but I couldn't give you another mouth to feed. I'm going down to the village to find work. But I would like to leave Jasmine with you. She feeds herself in the fields and gives a lot of milk. I'm sure it would be good for your little boy!"

"But you're too young to go off by yourself!" protested Vincenzo.

"I'm not too young! I'm an adult now. I can do many things. I'm sure I can find work down there."

Having loosened the rope, Jasmine twisted herself out of my grasp and leaped downhill. Vincenzo ran after her and I followed him. As he reached to catch Jasmine, I couldn't help noticing that his leg was unbandaged and that it had no sign of any wound. Vincenzo soon became aware of my gaze and quickly pulled down his pants cuffs, glancing around to make certain that nobody else had seen him. "Yes, Caterina," he confided, "my leg is all right now, but I have to pretend my wound is still unhealed, so if the men of the *condotta* spy on me, they won't force me to go back with them."

"What's the *condotta*?"

"The *condotta* is a legion of soldiers headed by a man who calls himself the *condottiere*. He's always in need of strong young men to fight his horrible battles for him."

"Why does he fight battles?" I asked, shocked.

"To conquer more towns and more territory so he can become richer and more powerful," he said with rage in his eyes.

"Does he know you?"

"I've been a soldier for years. They let me go because I was wounded, but if his spies find out that I've recovered, I'll have to go back to the battlefront. How could I leave, now that I have a wife and a little son who needs a father?" he argued, stroking Jasmine's coat. He soon covered his face so I wouldn't see the tears filling his eyes.

Then we walked back to the house in silence. It was amazing to see how such a strong man could be so sensitive, simply because he wasn't free to live his life the way he wanted.

When we arrived at the house, I stroked Jasmine's head and whispered softly in her ears. "Be brave, my friend! I have to leave you. I have to go on my way. Do you remember what the voice in the well said? I'm sure you heard it, too. Now promise me you'll take care of the little boy like you did for me. He needs your good milk to get stronger." Jasmine's sad eyes looked into mine, and I knew she understood everything I said. I motioned the boy to come over to us. I took his little hand and put it on the goat's back. At the touch of her warm body, he jumped with joy.

"Come indoors—it's getting late. Come, I've made a good meal for you!" called Maria from inside the house. The smell of her cooking and the goodness of her heart made me waver slightly about my plan to look for work in the village, but remembering the prophet's words, my courage returned.

After dinner, Maria took me by the hand like a child and, holding a candle, led me into a room where the only piece of furniture was a bed placed in a corner. "You'll sleep in my little boy's bed tonight," she said. "Vincenzo made it for when our baby grows up! Isn't it beautiful!"

Indeed it was, with its ornate bedposts covered with carvings and reliefs in the shape of flowers and leaves made in different kinds of wood. "Did he do this marvelous work?" I asked in amazement.

"Yes, my husband likes to work in wood," she stated proudly.

"Where did he learn to do this?"

"Nowhere. I think he was inspired by his love for our little son!"

I then remembered seeing Vincenzo bring the boxes for my parents' burial to our house, and was suddenly filled with gratitude for his skill. "Monna Maria," I said, recalling my father's words, "your husband is not only a brave and generous man, but he is also blessed with the gift of God!"

"I know," she said, her eyes glistening in the candlelight.

It was a mild dawn announcing a pleasant autumn day when I went outside to say good-bye to Jasmine. She looked at me so dolefully that it broke my heart. Please don't be so sad. "I'll be back. Meanwhile, they'll take care of you. They're good people!" I kept telling her.

Maria came out, followed by her husband, and gave me a package that I knew contained food. "My dear child, we'll be waiting for you and worrying about you, knowing that you're out alone in the world."

"Don't worry about me—I'm protected, and I always will be! But I'll never forget you, my friends!" And before she could say anything more that might deter me from following my plan, I placed my bundle over my shoulder and backed away toward the path leading to the highway. When I saw the little boy run to Jasmine and hug her neck tightly, I quickly turned away, only to be met with the view of the lovely village standing far away on the hills below. I didn't know the name of that place with the tall towers, but to my young eyes, it looked wonderful, with its small houses surrounding the towers like little children gathering around their mother's knees. I turned to take a last look at my friends, but, alas! their cottage had disappeared behind the chestnut trees.

So, carefree and footloose, I set out toward my unknown future. The delightful chirping of the birds reminded me of my precious musical instrument. I took the flute from my skirt pocket and began to play as I marched through the hills, producing the most cheerful, energetic sounds that had ever emerged from it.

After a while, though, I realized that I had strayed much too far into the higher hills of Mont'Albano. I had been distracted by the gloriously rich vegetation around me, so different from the flat, barren hills I had always known. So I changed my route, following a downhill path leading to the open fields of the lower hills, where the sun had reached the middle of the sky. But to my disappointment, the village was still nowhere to be seen.

Feeling hungry, I sat in the pleasant shade of a solitary chestnut tree and enjoyed dear Maria's food. In the distance, I saw a huge house, the largest I had ever seen, so I got up and followed the path leading to it. Through the slender cypress trees, I could see it had several windows and the grounds were enclosed by a thick wall covered with decorative ivy. Searching for the entrance, I came across an imposing black iron gate with intricate grillwork, through which I saw a stocky man digging around a pretty little tree. When I caught his attention, he came forward, motioning me to stay out. "What do you want? There's no more work—the house is closed," he said brusquely. "The masters have left for the season. Come back next year!"

"Forgive me, but I only wanted to ask you a question," I

said, taking out the embroidered handkerchief from my bundle. "Do you know if this belongs to this household?" I asked, showing it to him.

"I wouldn't know. See that woman over there hanging clothes? She's my wife—she handles these things." He impatiently swung the gate open, directing me toward her.

The woman turned, making a wry face as I approached her. "Who are you? Didn't he tell you we have no work?" she cried in a high-pitched voice.

"I just wanted to ask you something," I said regretfully. "Does this belong to any of your masters?" I asked, timidly holding up the cloth.

"I don't think so. How did you get it?" she inquired suspiciously. Then, pointing to the crown, she explained, "See this? It's a royal crest! It might even belong to a princess! How did it get into your hands?"

"Oh, I found it ... over there ... on the highway," I said, hiding it quickly in my pocket as I turned to leave.

"Wait, where are you going?"

"I'm going to the village to find work."

"But the village is much too far from here. You'll never get there before nightfall. Go back home. Winter is hard in these parts."

"I'm much too far—I couldn't find my way back," I said, hurrying out of the gate.

"Do you want something to eat?" she asked, suddenly concerned.

"Thank you, I have some food with me. Now I must go to look for work. Don't worry, good woman, I'm protected!" I said, turning to wave good-bye, but she just gaped at me. As I tore downhill, I couldn't help reviewing in my mind my first encounter with complete strangers and wondering how I would fare when asking for work. Feeling hungry again, I slowed down and found there was no food left in my bundle. I searched for fruit, but the trees were bare, except for a couple of dry figs, which hardly served to quiet my pangs of hunger. Casting my eyes over the lower hills, I still couldn't see any sign of a village. I started to lose hope, as the sun was already setting on the horizon. Parts of the countryside behind me were turning dark as a fierce wind unleashed itself. For the first time, I was really frightened. I wrapped myself tightly in my old shawl and huddled against a large tree trunk. Exhausted and discouraged, I closed my eyes.

    The sudden rumbling noise of wheels startled me. I sat up. Through the bushes, I saw a big horse-drawn cart, with two men in it, approaching. Another cart with more men soon followed. I concluded that the highway could not be very far. Both carts turned into a side lane, at which point the noise stopped abruptly. A man on horseback, singing loudly, as if with all his heart, followed them closely into the lane until his voice, too, stopped.

    Intrigued, I looked toward the mysterious side lane and saw a black column of smoke rising from a chimney hidden behind the tall trees. I got up and, as I cautiously walked toward it, the outline of a huge stone building came into view. The horses and carts had been left unattended in the front yard. Loud, angry voices coming out of the side windows of the building made me shy away. I had never before experienced crowds. The thought of so many people in one place was upsetting to me. My curiosity, however, got the better of me. I had to see what it was like inside. As I approached the half-open front door, the voices seemed to grow louder. I leaned against the door as a strong, offensive smell of wine made me feel nauseated, forcing me to hold my nose. At that moment, someone came out suddenly and bumped into me. I lost my balance and fell to the ground. I must have fainted, because the next thing I remember is finding myself in a heap on the cold cobblestones of a round threshing floor. In front of me stood the man who had inadvertently made me fall. He was dressed in a fine long, dark coat. As he bent over me, I saw his thick gray-streaked beard. "Who are you? Where do you come from?" he kept asking. I knew he was really concerned about me, but I felt too weak to answer. "Are you hungry? You look so ... so thin," he said. Then he straightened up and called to a boy who was coming out of the house carrying some jugs. "Gerosimo, ask

Maddalena to give you a bowl of soup and some bread for this girl," he ordered in a strong voice.

Confused and embarrassed, I tried to get up, but the boy soon arrived carrying the bowl of soup and a very large wooden spoon, which seemed to be as big as my head. The gentleman went back inside, and the boy sat on the low stone wall, chuckling as he watched met. I struggled with the spoon for a while as I tried to sip my soup. Then, to distract him from my clumsiness, I asked, "What is this place?"

"Don't you know? This is the hill of Anchiano and this is the Anchiano Tavern, where men come to drink wine and eat Big Madd's minestrone," he replied, still chuckling.

"Why do you call her Big Madd?"

"You'll find out soon enough!" He laughed, rushing back inside.

The gentleman returned and stood there waiting for me to finish eating. I stopped shyly and set the bowl down on the wall next to me. "Do you feel better now?" he asked. I nodded. Taking me by the hand, he said, "Come with me!" and led me to the tavern. Once again, I had to cover my nose at the door. It was crowded inside. I was taken aback by the sight of so many slovenly men sitting at long tables, avidly gulping wine from heavy metal tankards, shouting and gesturing wildly at each other.

A huge, stout woman wearing an apron heavily soiled with wine stains came before us and scowled at me. I would have jumped out of my skin were it not for a reassuring squeeze from the gentleman's hand.

"Maddalena, will you put up this girl for the night?" he asked. "She seems to be lost," he added compassionately. She brought her apron to her nose and blew loudly into it, giving me another start. "Please, Maddalena, help her! She may turn out to be useful to you." I trembled at the thought of working for her. She gave me the same suspicious look as the woman in the garden and then grimaced, suddenly drawing attention to the hair on her upper lip. And before I could overcome my repulsion, she snatched my hand from the gentleman and dragged me outside. I looked back at him imploringly. He followed only as far as the doorway, watching us go to a small house just by the threshing floor. Before entering, she swung around to face him and grunted, "Don't worry, Ser Antonio! I won't hurt her."

Though filled with trepidation, I was glad to note the gentleman's name, repeating it a few times in my mind so that I would not forget it, for I was certain that he had just become my first protector.

When we were inside and she lit the lamp, I was pleasantly surprised to see the brightly colored bedspread on the big bed against the wall and a tablecloth in exactly the same fabric on the table in the center of the room. "This is my home!" she announced haughtily. "As you can see, I have only one bed, but I can prepare something for you." She went to a closet and took out a sack full of straw, which she laid out on a long trunk in a corner. I gazed at her enormous hands as she slapped the sack violently to smooth out the lumps of straw. Reaching again into the closet, she produced both a sheet and a blanket in a single grasp, threw them on the trunk, and headed for the door. Before I could say anything to thank her, she raised her finger and, glaring at me, shouted, "Don't you dare leave this room!" And without a backward glance, she left, locking the door behind her.

I couldn't wait to try out my new straw pallet, barely having the strength to climb up onto it. In a moment, I was lulled into a deep, soothing sleep by the pungent smell of the dry straw.

2
THE MOST BEAUTIFUL CORNER OF THE WORLD

Something prodding my shoulder woke me up. I opened my eyes and saw Big Madd's huge finger about to thump me again. I sat up and cringed before her gigantic frame towering over me. "What's your name?" she began abruptly in her booming voice.

"Ca-Caterina," I answered, holding up my blanket as a shield.

She tied a large white apron around her shapeless mass and said, "I left some bread and milk on the table." Then, hurrying to the door, she pointed her menacing finger at me again and bellowed, "When you've finished, come and show me if you can really help me!"

Over breakfast, my thoughts on Big Madd's unreasonable harshness were soon blotted out by a sudden flutter of birds chirping outside. Gulping my last bite, I rushed out to the threshing floor, where I was dazzled by a marvelous display of birds circling in the bright blue sky above. They were black with a white spot on their breasts, just like the ones that used to fly over my home. After a few rounds, in single file, they dived into the valley behind the house. "They're swallows!" I cried, remembering why those pretty black-and-white creatures never stopped on our land.

"They're swallows," Father used to say, "migratory birds. They only stop where there's plenty of water. They scoop it up with their beaks in flight. They'd never drink from puddles like our simple sparrows do!"

Now, seeing them fly so close, I couldn't believe my eyes. It seemed like a miracle! I ran to the back of the house to find out if there really was water nearby, but I could see only the deep, narrow valley into which the swallows had flown and a very steep cliff, thickly covered with tall, green vegetation on the other side. Soon my ears tingled at the sound of running water, and without hesitation, I took the slippery path downhill to the bank of a most beautiful stream. Now, with my own eyes, I saw that the swallows in flight were indeed grazing the water with their beaks! I danced around, enraptured by this sight. Then I bent down, scooped up some water in my hands and drank it. "I love this place!" I shouted to the sky.

Filled with great wonder, I went to explore the springs flowing from the rocks under the trees. Thrills of joy shook me as I held my hands under the jets. Then, running along the bank, I jumped and sang, splashing water in the air and crying with delight, "Oh, how beautiful! I've never seen anything like this! This is paradise! Paradise on earth! I want to stay here and live here forever!" Then I got down on my knees and prayed, "Oh, please, dear God! I want to stay here for the rest of my life!"

Alas! The enchantment was soon broken by a loud echo resounding in the valley. It was Big Madd's angry call. I had disobeyed her. I scrambled back, grasping the shrubs along the slope to pull myself up. As I reached the edge of the courtyard, I caught sight of her impatient glare. Still exhilarated and out of breath, I approached her boldly and curtsied with a smile; a courteous greeting my mother had taught me. "Good morning, Monna Maddalena! I just discovered a nice place to wash your aprons."

"Oh, yes?" she said, frowning. "And where is it?"

"Down there ... in that beautiful clean water!" I said enthusiastically.

Her grimace turned into a smile. "Ah, down by the *ruscello*," she said in a softer voice. "Why, do you know how to wash clothes? Well, we'll see." Then, in her usual way, she added, "Now, come and help me with the chores in the tavern. We have to fill up the wine jugs for the drunkards tonight."

As she turned to go, I burst into laughter, which I quickly smothered with my hand. Then I daringly asked, "Why do they drink so much, if they end up like ... like that?"

"Because men are stupid!" Then she peered at me and said, "I think you ask too many questions for a child who supposedly got lost! Who are you?"

I didn't answer, for I had no intention of telling her my life story.

She walked on, and I, still feeling elated by the discovery of my new beautiful corner of the world, followed her, swinging my arms and humming to myself a little tune: *"Ru-scel-lo! My beau-ti- ful ru-scel-lo!"*

The tavern was filled with fumes coming from the fireplace. Big Madd's minestrone was in full boil in a big pot hanging from a hook inside the fireplace. She resumed her vegetable cleaning, throwing them one by one into the pot, thereby splashing the boiling contents all over the fire and creating the most disgusting odors, which made the air in the room almost impossible to breathe.

I got busy cleaning the dirty tables as she had told me. Then I started filling the metal tankards with wine from the terra-cotta jugs she had brought up from the little cellar underneath the tavern. Luckily, I had gotten used to the smell of the wine, which was less offensive than the fumes. However, when the heavy jugs were too full, I couldn't help spilling some of the wine on the tables. Unfortunately, these accidents never escaped Big Madd's attention, prompting her each time to whack me on the shoulder with her wooden spoon, which I found very humiliating.

Later, when Gerosimo came in and saw me, he shook his

head resentfully and got busy sweeping the floor. He was a little older than I with dark bushy hair and bright black eyes. After a while, he came up to me and whispered, "So, she gave you the job, eh? She wouldn't take my sister, though, saying she wouldn't allow any girls in here."

"Yes, she did take me," I said, looking sadly at the wine stains on my dress. "How old is your sister?" I asked.

"She's about your age, but she's more delicate. She cries all day long since our poor mother died. Now she lives in my aunt's house, but they're poor, too. I really worry about her."

"I've lost both my parents, too. But she's luckier than I am. She has a brother who cares about her."

"Enough chatting, you two. Work or get out!" roared Big Madd.

Gerosimo promptly got back to his sweeping, darting glances at me that were a little more benevolent.

As the first customers started to come in, Big Madd took a small metal pail, filled it with her minestrone, and, grabbing a piece of bread and some fruit, motioned to me to follow her. I obeyed her, bewildered. When we entered her room, she put the food on the table and explained, "I don't want you to be there at night—it's too dangerous." Then, turning harsh again, she added, "Now, are you able to light a fire?" I just nodded, I was much too tired to speak. "Well, there's some wood next to the fireplace. Make sure that the room's warm when I come back tonight!" Pointing at a pile of dirty washing, she continued, "See those dirty aprons? Tomorrow morning you'll wash them in the *ruscello*." And before I knew it, she was gone.

It was cold, so I started the fire and had my supper, all the time trying to understand the strange woman. I finally came to the conclusion that she was afraid to be pleasant with people, using her harshness as a protective shield. She seemed unable to realize, though, that a child like me could not be a threat to her, and I felt a little sorry for her.

Though sleepy, I was terrified at the thought of the fire being out on her return. So I just sat staring at the flames and soon found myself reminiscing about my not-too-distant past.

I thought of my loving parents lying all alone in their graves. I saw the great elm tree, and I was glad it was there watching over them. I remembered my goat, my sweet Jasmine, too, and before I realized it, I was crying my heart out. As I calmed down, the meaning of the prophet's words crystallized in my mind, convincing me that what he had said about my being protected was true. I already had proof in Ser Antonio's kindness, and I even believed that Big Madd was somehow being prevented from treating me much worse than she was.

Having overcome my feelings of loneliness, my thoughts went to my lovely *ruscello,* which I would be seeing again in the morning. Then I whispered a little song: "My *ru-scel-lo!* My beau-ti-ful *ru-scel-lo*! How I love you, I'll be there to tell you!" Suddenly I heard Big Madd at the door and quickly jumped up on the soft straw mattress, hiding under my blanket.

The next morning, the moment Big Madd left the room, I opened the window wide. The sun was rising into a clear sky and the air was fragrant with sweet-smelling herbs. Even the swallows were there, cheerful as ever!

Carrying the heavy basket on my head, I struggled down the slope with a heart full of expectation. When I reached the bank, I gave out a sigh of satisfaction. I eagerly touched the water, but it was still cold from the night air, so I decided to wait for the sun to hit the stream. I wandered over to see the springs again. As I stood listening to their fascinating sound, I discovered a new, more powerful spring gushing out from behind a large rock. It smelled of wet soil and ancient rocks. The friendly sound of water pouring over clean rock blended with the softer sounds of the other smaller springs. To this jovial harmony I contributed the humble whistle of my little flute.

But soon my sense of duty called me back to the dirty aprons. I tried to soak them, but the rush of the water carried them away, so with stones I constructed a kind of pool that became my washing basin.

Alas! Those wonderful mornings came to an end. The

days had turned much colder, and the vivacious swallows had departed. Wind and rain overpowered the countryside. The tavern was closed through the winter months and I had no choice but to stay in Big Madd's room all day long. She never talked to me, except to order me around. She slept a lot, sometimes the whole day, but even in her sleep, she was unpleasant, constantly snoring like a growling animal. So whenever there was a little sunshine, I slipped outside. One day, I found a broken spinning wheel in the cellar and a sack full of cotton. I repaired it and stood it near the fireplace. So, with cotton stuffed in my ears, I was able to pass the time, spinning yarn.

The long-awaited spring returned at last to warm the earth, inviting the primroses to sprout all over the fields and the lovely swallows to come back to us! I resumed my washing trips at the brook, where I also played my flute to the sound of the springs, watching them run swiftly to unknown, far-away lands I would probably never see.

Before the tavern reopened, the masons came to build another cellar. There were plans to reactivate the olive-pressing mill, which had stood abandoned behind the tavern for many years. So they dug deep into the rock to make the new cellar cool and big enough to store the oil jars, as well as the wine barrels.

"Now that the old cellar won't be used anymore," said Gerosimo as we watched the masons at work, "maybe you could move in there with my sister. Would you like that?"

"Not really. It has very small windows. Besides, it smells too much of wine," I answered with indifference.

"I'll help you clean it up if you let my sister stay with you. I'll also put in a good word with Ser Antonio, who authorized these changes," he said, giving himself importance.

"I could talk to him myself, but he hasn't shown up lately."

"He's been sick, but I saw him a few days ago. In fact, he asked me if Big Madd was treating you well." I felt my heart leap, knowing that my protector had not forgotten me.

So, within a month, there we were, cleaning and scrubbing the small cellar room, which was to become the most memorable home of my life. Ser Antonio had sent two beds with regular mattresses and blankets, and soon Gerosimo's sister, Beniamina, arrived. She was shy, sensitive, and looked as delicate as a flower, with her silky blond hair, blue eyes, and pale cheeks. I put my arm around her shoulders and asked her to come in. She soon felt at home with me, and I did my best to make her feel welcome and not miss her parents so much. We became friends, and I taught her how to do little chores around the place so Big Madd would not scold her. It was not long before the color came back to her pretty cheeks.

One morning while we were sweeping the courtyard, Gerosimo appeared carrying a fine gold chain bracelet, which he put on his sister's wrist. "A gift for your birthday!" he said. He told Beniamina that he had bought it with the money he earned as a delivery boy at the town market, but he confessed to me that he had really found it on the grounds there. Waving her wrist, Beniamina was overjoyed. The three of us did a little dance, until Big Madd appeared on the doorstep, roaring, and we froze like statues. Later, I whispered to them that, as soon as she left for the village that afternoon, we would go to the brook, pick some fruit on the way there, and dance to the music of my flute.

"Caterina, I'll never forget you for taking such good care of my little sister!" said Gerosimo with genuine appreciation.

"You're my family now. I've never been so happy in my life!" I beamed. We were finally able to enjoy our party at the brook together that day, but unfortunately it was to be our last time together.

A few days passed and Gerosimo didn't show up. Beniamina started to cry again and got on Big Madd's nerves. Life became very difficult because Big Madd blamed me for taking her in, and I didn't know what to do. I covered up for the girl by doing her chores, but that didn't help. Beniamina spent the whole day crouched on her bed, crying over and over again, "Where's my brother? I want to see him. Has he died, too? Tell me the truth, Caterina!"

I assured her that he had not died because he was young and strong. He had probably found a new job and would soon be coming back with another present for her. But nothing would pacify her.

One day, I was able to take her outside, and we sat on the low wall, where she stayed staring into space. I heard a light carriage entering the yard. It was Ser Antonio's gig, and Gerosimo was at his side. Ser Antonio got off first and helped the boy down. I knew that something was wrong with him and I looked to make sure that Beniamina wasn't behind me. Ser Antonio held Gerosimo by the arm. I was stunned by his appearance. His eyes were swollen shut. His left eye had a reddish scar, and his mouth was misshapen. He gazed at me, but didn't seem to recognize me.

"What happened to him, Ser Antonio?" I asked, keeping my voice down.

"A woman found him lying unconscious on the street with a head wound and took him to the local infirmary. I went there as soon as I heard and learned that his brain had been damaged, maybe forever," he said, deeply concerned. "It's a pity, because he was a very intelligent boy."

"Who did it to him? And why?" I asked angrily.

"It seems that he stole a gold bracelet, and the guards beat him up and left him bleeding."

"But he told me he had found it."

Gerosimo had a brief flash of memory, recognized me, and forced himself to speak. "Yes, Caterina, I found it ... I found it," he said, uttering those words from the side of his mouth.

"He may have found it, but it was on the grounds of the goldsmith's market. Their guards are like animals," Ser Antonio said indignantly. "The only thing to do now is to take him to a home where they'll take care of him," he added, looking sadly at the boy.

I heard Beniamina's voice calling me. "Please, Ser Antonio, she mustn't hear this terrible story! Tell her that it was just an accident," I said hastily.

"Gerosimo, Gerosimo!" called Beniamina, rushing to hug her brother. He stood quite still, not recognizing her. She looked at his face and started to scream. I quickly put my arms around her.

"He had an accident, Beniamina! An accident! I'll take him to the hospice. He'll be all right," comforted Ser Antonio. He came up to me and patted my head. "I'll see what I can do for the poor girl," he whispered. Gerosimo just stared blankly as Ser Antonio helped him get back on his gig.

For the next few days, Beniamina refused to eat. She became so thin and weak that I was really worried. Big Madd kept saying that she couldn't stand sick people around her and that the girl would have to go back to her aunt. I told Beniamina that if she wanted to stay with me, she had to eat and regain some strength. So, finally, one day we sat outside behind some shrubs where Big Madd couldn't see us, and Beniamina ate a little food.

I heard the sound of a carriage coming into the courtyard, but I stayed hidden because I knew Big Madd was there. Peeping through the shrubs, I saw a well-dressed couple getting out of a fine-looking carriage. They approached her, and I overheard the gentleman say, "We're friends of Ser Antonio. My wife and I have come for little Beniamina. We want to take her in as our own daughter."

"As a daughter?" she snorted. "But she's a sick girl, and stupid, too! Do you really want her?"

I motioned to Beniamina to wait for me and went up to them. "That's not true—she's not stupid! She's just weak, because she doesn't eat and she cries a lot over her poor brother," I explained, infuriated.

Big Madd raised her hand to hit me, but restrained herself. Then, shrugging her shoulders, she turned away and went into the tavern.

"Good girl! May I see Beniamina?" asked the lady courteously. I went to fetch the girl. When I brought her over to them, the lady smiled and gently stroked her soft blond hair. "We want to take you to our home. Would you like to come with us in our coach? We need a daughter just like you!" I watched the lady as she was talking and was struck by her resemblance to Beniamina. They both had golden hair, blue eyes, and even a slight similarity in their features.

But the girl's slender arms clung to me. "I want to stay with Caterina! I want to wait here for Gerosimo...."

"The lady looks like she could be your mother. See!" I whispered in her ear. Beniamina stared at the lady, whose eyes shone in expectation.

"We'll love you as if you were our own. You'll be happy, you'll see!" the lady pleaded.

Her husband patted her on the arm. "We're friends of Ser Antonio. We'll help your brother, too. As soon as he's better, we'll take you to see him," he said reassuringly. Beniamina looked at them, still undecided.

"Go, Beniamina, go! They'll take good care of you. They'll bring you to visit me sometime, won't you?" I added, turning to the couple. They agreed with a warm smile. Beniamina slowly held out her frail hand to the lady, who gracefully took it and cuddled it. I shook my head in amazement. I had never seen such a sweet encounter. In no time, Beniamina was inside the carriage with them, waving goodbye, on her way to a bright new future.

Overcome by mixed feelings, I gazed sadly at the empty courtyard. Then I ran inside to gather Beniamina's few belongings on her bed and just sat there staring at them. Big Madd's heavy footsteps above reminded me that she was waiting for me, but I couldn't face her ill-tempered outbursts just yet. Instead, I rushed down to the edge of my *ruscello*, where I wept my heart out for having lost my dear little sister, my new family, so abruptly. The sound of the water soon soothed my spirit and assuaged my loneliness.

A terrible winter came down upon our hills, during which I was again compelled to sleep in Big Madd's room, because in my room there was no fireplace. And since she had found out that she could sell the yarn I spun on my old spinning wheel, she made me work hard at it. The pleasant tool became an instrument of torture, which, added to her animal-like snoring, made my life even more unbearable. So, whenever I could, I rushed outside and ran about crazily in the wind and snow until my hands and feet couldn't stand the cold anymore.

This is the way I spent the first three years in my new home, gradually learning how to endure the distasteful facets of this new life. I had grown into a tall girl, and though I wasn't as huge as Big Madd, she didn't dare hit me anymore. Whenever she got angry at me, I kept her away with menacing looks. Nevertheless, as I entered adulthood, I found I was not ready to deal with certain new situations. Judging from the way men of all ages kept looking at me, I became aware that I had grown into an attractive woman. I knew my long, thick hair was a rich dark brown and my skin was very soft, yet I didn't know what kind of features I had or what color my eyes were. The only available glass in which I could see my reflection was Big Madd's coarse, dark-green windowpane, and, since nobody was allowed to go near it, I could see myself only from afar. She had often boasted that it was a rare gift from a special friend who used to work in a glass factory. In fact, it was the only object on which she lavished any tenderness whenever she polished it.

That spring brought other changes, too. The old tables and chairs in the tavern had been taken away to be replaced. One morning as I was sweeping the threshing floor, the young man who usually brought in the groceries entered the yard with a cartload of new chairs. He jumped down and strutted toward me. "Hello, beautiful! I hear Ser Antonio's decided to turn the tavern into a hunting lodge. With the new chairs and all it's going to be popular with the gentlefolk! Eh?" he said, ogling me.

"So what?" I retorted. I could never stand his rude ways.

"So watch out! They like to hunt healthy young country girls, too...."

"What do you mean?" I snapped, already regretting my question.

"I mean, they like to hunt them," he growled, smacking his lips, "just to play with...." I picked up a stick and threw it at him. He ran away laughing, and I went back to my work, slightly disturbed.

"I think it's time you gave me a hand serving the wine," Big Madd said while we were arranging the new tables. "Your manners are better than mine for waiting on the gentlefolk. But don't expect them to be easier than the countryfolk. In fact, I'm not really looking forward to it much."

"What do you mean? They couldn't be any rougher!"

"No, but they can be worse in other ways," she mumbled.

The new customers, we found, were mostly middle-aged men who dropped in mainly at weekends during their hunting trips. They wore smart hunter's outfits and endlessly bragged about their hunting exploits. But after gulping their first tankards of wine, they appeared and sounded as stupid as the old customers. One day, I tried to eavesdrop on their conversation.

"You should have seen the way that lark was gliding, when, boom! It spread its wings wide and fell right into my dog's mouth!" rambled the fat one, his large belly swaying as he cried, "What a shot!"

"Once I shot a falcon! Just like that!" said the bald one, snapping his fingers. "And you know how tough it is to spy a falcon! Yet what I really enjoy most is frightening the birds out of their nests. Ha! Ha! Ha!" He laughed, drooling wine. At first I laughed, too, mainly at their ungainly expressions, but their talk upset me, so I moved away. I couldn't stand the thought of these pompous oafs feeling so proud about killing such beautiful creatures, who only gave joy to humanity. When I came back and overheard them telling another one of those tiresome shooting stories, I purposely let a large tankard fall in the middle of the table, splashing wine all over them.

"What's the matter with you, girl? Can't you see what you're doing?" one man shouted as they all jumped back.

"I was getting carried away with your stories. Sorry, I made you jump like the birds out of their nests ... and you don't even have wings with which to fly away," I said derisively and flounced off.

"Who d'you think you are, behaving like that?" demanded the one with the biggest belly.

"I think that girl needs a man," said the one who hadn't taken his eyes off me. They all laughed. Then the whole group got up and staggered out, some of them bumping into Big Madd as she entered.

"What made them leave so soon?" she inquired as I cleared the tables.

"I don't know. Maybe the old men couldn't wait to go and shoot some more birds. Why on earth do they want to do that?" I asked, not expecting an answer from her.

But she turned to me and shouted, "Because birds can't shoot back at them, that's why!" As she went about her chores, she announced, "By the way, Ser Antonio said that later in the summer their sons will be coming here, too. I know they'll cause trouble."

"Why? Do they drink more than their fa—?" I stopped as I remembered what the cartman had said.

"No, but they ... Are you stupid or just pretending to be?"

"Then I refuse to wait on them. I'd rather wash tons of clothes."

"I know you like to be by the water. But I give the orders around here, and you'd better do what you're told, if you want to go on working here." She started to choke on a piece of raw celery she had tossed in her mouth, but clearing her throat noisily, she went on, "Besides, you're big enough now to defend yourself from their advances. If you know how to keep your place, they won't bother you." I glared at her and went outside.

It wasn't long before the tavern resounded with the young hunters' boisterous voices. They were, in fact, much more arrogant than the older men. They sported short hunting jackets over fitted pants and brandished shining new rifles. One day, while Big Madd had stepped outside, they seemed to be having fun, whispering among themselves and then bursting into uncontrollable laughter. At first, I thought it was strange, but then I noticed that they kept glancing in my direction while whispering.

"Where do you come from?" asked one of them as I

looked down my nose at them. "Do you know you're very beautiful?" he said, winking at his companions.

"Where I come from and how I look are no concern of yours. If you have to giggle like girls, you can keep your silly conversation to yourselves," I said, enraged.

"Oh, our pure little country girl has some pride, eh?" laughed another.

"Don't worry, it won't last," said the more arrogant one. A young man who had been sitting quietly raised his hand, admonishing them, and they were suddenly silent.

I didn't know what to make of the incident, but after that experience, I pleaded with Big Madd not to leave me alone in the tavern with the young men, but to give me some other job to do, no matter how heavy. She didn't answer, but from that day on, she somehow kept a protective eye on me, and for that I was very grateful. I did not know then that I was just as vulnerable as any other young girl.

I was hanging clothes one morning when the young man— the quiet one in the group—came up the path and across the threshing floor. He was in his twenties, of medium height, with curly chestnut hair. I observed that he was hiding a flower behind his back, but I pretended not to see.

"Would you mind if I asked you a favor?" he began shyly.

"No, what is it?" I answered.

He showed me the rose he had been hiding. "I would like you to wear it in your lovely hair," he said, holding the rose carefully with both hands.

I hesitated awhile, then, laughing, I said, "All right, give it to me." I was impressed by the gentle way in which he handed it to me. As I took it and felt the touch of his hand against mine, a warm shiver ran right through me. I had never been approached with such gentleness. Recovering, I laughed again as I pushed the stem casually through my hair.

"No, not that way. This way," he murmured and, moving closer, adjusted it next to my ear. His touch made me blush and move back, embarrassed. "Thank you," he whispered, his eyes brightening. "It looks lovely with your brown hair and your beautiful blue-green eyes!" I was still taken aback by his respectful manner when with a dreamy smile he stepped back and waved good-bye. As soon as he was out of sight, I rushed to Big Madd's windowpane and daringly, but keeping some distance, I looked at my reflection, curious to see how I really looked to the charming young man. The red rose was striking against my dark hair, and somehow the pink shawl I had tied around my small waist emphasized my well-shaped figure. A warm shiver ran through my body again as I continued to gaze at my reflection.

The following days, I couldn't help glancing at the same path, hoping to see again the attractive man whose charm had awakened that pleasant new feeling in me. But the days went by, and he did not come to see me or show up at the tavern with the other young men.

One day, though, while the tavern was closed, he reappeared from behind the same slope, greeting me with a more daring smile and saying, "You are more beautiful than the sun and the moon put together!" I was so overcome by his words that I turned aside. "Where do you come from?" he asked rather suddenly. "You have the manners of a lady. Who are your parents?" He sounded so friendly that I regained my confidence.

"I come from the lower hills on the other side of Mont'Albano. Both my parents died."

"I am sorry," he said tenderly.

"They were very old. My father, before dying, revealed to me that they weren't my real parents, but it didn't matter to me, because they had loved me very much." I stopped, as I couldn't understand why I was telling him about my private feelings.

"How did you come to work here?" he asked, gazing into my eyes.

"I was afraid to live by myself. The house was falling to pieces and ..." I stopped to look at him and abruptly asked, "And what about you?"

"I live in Vinci. My father wants me to be a notary like his father and his grandfather before him to resume the family tradition."

"And what does a notary do?"

"He writes figures all day," he said sadly.

"What would you like to do instead?"

"I don't know what else I could do. I only know that I'd like to live in Florence," he said, touching my hand.

"Is Florence very far from here?"

"Yes, very far from here. What's your name?"

"Caterina ... just Caterina. What's yours?" I blushed as he brought my hand to his lips, kissing it and holding it against his breast with so much tenderness that I felt my heart leap to my throat.

"Piero, just Piero," he said, smiling so seductively that I was quite overwhelmed. Then his smile faded, and he let go of my hand, backing away slowly. He mounted his horse and rode off. I stood spellbound, gazing at him as he galloped away, both disturbed by his loving gesture and puzzled by the sadness that had overcome him so suddenly.

It was a glorious summer morning when I woke up to the unfamiliar sweet song of a bird. I jumped out of bed and went to look for it. There was a multicolored bird perched in a milk-white cage hanging next to my stone windowsill. I got dressed and ran outside. I held up the cage and started to talk to the singing bird. Attached to the cage was a note with a few words written next to a picture of a funny smiling face. Unfortunately, I couldn't read the words, but I knew it was a gift from my new friend.

Yet many more days were to go by before I saw Piero again. In the meantime, my cheerful canary received all the loving care and attention I would have liked to lavish on him.

It was a warm afternoon. I had taken the canary down to the cool brook and placed the cage on the wet slope. Gathering the sparkling water in my hand, I splashed it around the cage and tried to imitate the bird's constant melodious chirping. Laughing as my bare feet slid into the water, I lay on my back on the grassy bank. Then I noticed Piero standing on the slope, watching me with amusement, and I quickly composed myself.

With a broad smile, he climbed down toward me. "How are you, lovely girl?" he teased as he sat down next to me.

"Why didn't you come before?" I said much too anxiously.

"I had a lot of studying to do."

"Look! What a beautiful canary I found on my windowsill!"

"That's not a canary—it's a nightingale! Didn't you find the note?"

"Yes, but I couldn't read it. I knew it was yours, though!"

"How is it you speak like someone who can read?"

"My parents came from good families, and I learned to speak like them."

"Would you like me to teach you how to read?"

"Yes, but how? If Big Madd finds out about us meeting, she'll beat me."

"Don't worry about her! Next time, I'll bring some books with pictures drawn by the priest who was my first tutor. You'll find them very amusing and easy to study by yourself," he said, taking my hands in his. I trembled with emotion as he kissed them. Then he put his lips on mine, holding me tightly to his breast. I tried to free myself, but the warmth of his body weakened me, and I yielded. Entwined in each other's arms, we slid into the water. We both looked at his wet shoes and laughed. He took them off and, holding me tight again, he kissed me tenderly on the cheeks.

As he released me, I saw his eyes glistening. He got up, picked up his shoes, and silently walked away. Puzzled again by his sudden change of mood, I turned away, but he had dropped his shoes and was running back to me. He pulled me to my feet, wrapped his arms around me, and kissed me more passionately than before. "I love you so much!" he whispered in my ear. Then, moving away from me again, he said, "I'll be back, my love, I promise you! Next time, I'll be back sooner." As he spoke these words, instead of joyful anticipation, I sensed a cold determination in his voice. Yet, somehow I felt closer to him than I had ever felt to anybody before, and I wished with all my heart I could release him from his sadness, his strange melancholy. It seemed that his enigmatic behavior, besides arousing an intense attraction to him, had also stirred my compassion; two different feelings taking hold of me as one: a deep affection. My singular naïveté prevented me from calling it love.

I was in the same confused state of mind when the heat drove me out of my room a few nights later. I sat against the wall under my window, finding relief in the light breeze ruffling my short-sleeved cotton nightdress. As the stars, one by one, lit up the dark sky, the warm glow of a shooting star reminded me of the tiny star that had risen above the old well to comfort me on that eventful night so long ago. I thought of the marble slab with its mysterious symbols and the faraway childhood home that I had forsaken, and wondered if I would ever see it again.

A rustling of leaves behind the house startled me as a dark figure of a man sprang out from the shadows. Afraid of being out there alone, I was somewhat relieved to see that it was Piero, holding out his hand for me to get up. I was embarrassed to be seen by him in a thin nightgown and drew back, crouched against the wall, but he pulled me up and held me tight.

"I love you dearly, Caterina," he murmured against my neck. "I can't resist your beauty any longer." Feeling very weak in his arms, I suggested that we should sit down. "Why don't we go inside?" he whispered in my ear, pulling me gently to the steps leading to my room. I wanted to tell him that it was much too hot inside, but his sudden nearness confused me, rendering me quite helpless. He put his hands under my knees, picked me up, and carried me inside.

My room was lit by a votive lamp like the one we had had at home. In the dim light, he found my bed and violently threw me on it. I cried as he grabbed my nightgown and pulled it quickly off my body. I shut my eyes, feeling faint, yet relieved that he had taken his hands off me. But I soon realized that his body was naked, too, and was shaking against mine. I sat up and pushed him away. He fell with his back against the bedpost. Then he stood up and threw himself over me, as if meaning to crush me under his weight. Gasping for breath, I tried to free myself. But then I felt something penetrating my body, hurting me badly. I cried out in pain and fainted.

When I regained consciousness, slowly looking around, I was shocked to see Piero asleep beside me. I realized that what had happened hadn't been just a nightmare. I started to wake him, but an excruciating pain in my abdomen held me back. I put my hand on it, hoping to ease the pain. Then, closing my eyes, I must have dozed off again.

The nightingale was singing as the dim light of dawn filtered through my tiny window. I opened my eyes, sat up, and looked around the room. Through the open door, a light breeze blew on my nightgown hanging over a chair. I felt tears rolling down my cheeks onto my naked breast. I pulled up the sheet in shame and stared at the open door, the door that had witnessed my lover's escape; the door that had seen him fleeing from me, perhaps forever. A gust of wind opened it a little more. "If it wasn't a bad dream, what was it?" I shouted, falling back on my pillow. My head began to ache, and I cried myself to sleep.

Waking up to an intrusive early-morning beam of light slanting through my window, I was finally able to grasp fully what had really happened. So wrapping a cloth around my body, I quickly got up, rolled the bedsheets into a bundle under my arm, and on my way out, threw on a dress.

Barefooted and fearful of being seen, I rushed wildly down to the brook, stepping blindly on spiky bushes. Through my mind flashed thoughts of what happened to girls from the hills, who like me had been intimate with men of higher standing. I recalled hearing how they had been treated and then thrown out of their homes into complete perdition.

Still in pain, I hid behind the thick foliage in the shallow part of the brook, fiercely scrubbing off all traces of my shameful part in the unholy union with the man for whom I had felt compassion ... the man I was learning to love ... the man from whom I had expected only a little tenderness.

3
THE GIFT

It was a scorching summer afternoon. I sat under my window in the cool shade of the building, where even on a hot day the refreshing wind from Mont'Albano never failed to reach my sheltered corner. I was hoping that the fresh air would also cool the thoughts burning in my mind and quiet my tormented soul. Weeks had passed since that terrible, unforgettable night when my lover had fled from my room like a thief, leaving me there in pain. Yet, I still asked myself so many questions. Why had he behaved that way with me? Why had he been so violent with me after declaring his love for me? Was lovemaking really like that? Was he an evil man? If so, why couldn't I have perceived that? Most of all, why hadn't I been protected as the prophet had promised? I wanted so much to believe in that promise. Perhaps Piero would come back one day and hold me in his arms again with the same respect he had shown me at the brook, apologize to me, give me back my self-esteem, enable me to regain my peace of mind.

I started as exuberant voices reached my ear. I peeped through the leaves; it was a group of young men passing by on the path leading up the mountain. I held my breath when I saw that Piero was with them. I saw he was lagging behind the others and thought he was coming to see me. I was enraged at first, but then I hurriedly tried to fix my hair and adjust my skirt gracefully around me. I waited with my heart in my throat, looking forward to hearing him say he was sorry for what he had done to me.

A long time elapsed, but, alas! Piero did not stop by, after all. My bitter disappointment soon turned into fear as I heard Big Madd's heavy footsteps shuffling along the cobblestones of the courtyard. I knew her siesta was over and that I hadn't done my chores. "Caterina, where are you? Come to work right away, you lazy girl!" she thundered as she entered the tavern.

More days went by. I had almost succeeded in accepting the fact that I would never see Piero again, when he suddenly appeared from behind the same slope, carrying a package. I stood with a broom in my hand, glaring at him and trying to decide what to say. But he looked at me kindly and softly whispered, "Will you come down to the brook?" I did not answer. He started down the path, and knowing that nobody was around, I quickly followed him.

He stood on the bank with arms open wide, and I fell into his tender embrace. He kissed me on the mouth. "I'm sorry, my love. I couldn't come because I had to work for my father." Then, gazing longingly at me, he said, "You look more beautiful than ever!"

"But brokenhearted! I thought you despised me after that night," I said naïvely.

"On the contrary, I love you more than ever! But since that night, I've been feeling guilty for having been so violent with you. Forgive me, my darling! You didn't deserve it. On my way here the other day, I wanted to see you so much, but I decided to punish myself, instead, by not seeing you anymore. Today, I couldn't resist any longer. I had to see you and talk with you. So here I am!" he said reassuringly, squeezing me tightly. Then he bent down to pick up the package he had put on the grass. When he stood up, I saw tears in his eyes. "I've brought you the books I promised. These will help you learn to read."

"What's the matter with you? You look so sad. Is there something troubling you?" I asked with tender concern.

He turned pale and motioned me to sit down. "Yes, rather." He sighed. Then, forcing a lighter mood, he added, "I have to go to Florence to finish my studies."

"For how long? I'll die if I don't see you," I whispered.

"It'll be hard for me, too, my love!" He said, putting his arms around me again. I pulled back, for I suddenly remembered with disgust his rough behavior that night and wondered who he really was. He looked into my eyes as if reading my thoughts. Then, drawing my attention to the books, he started unwrapping them and said, "I'm sorry I can't teach you how to read them, my love, but you'll enjoy looking through them."

I got up, feeling my hurt again. Yet he just sat staring coldly at my long face. Then he got up, too, and started slowly up the hill. Suddenly, he rushed back and forced another hug on me. I didn't move. I felt as if I were made of stone. Somehow, it no longer mattered that he was leaving me forever. Nor did I care about his sadness. Then, seeming somewhat relieved, he proceeded up the slope, saying, "Good luck, my dear little friend. I'll never forget you, I promise." I turned my back to him, never wanting to see him again. A feeling of having become disentangled made me want to run along the bank and recapture my childish simplicity. Later, I took the books to my room and put them out of sight, hoping to forget him forever.

Little did I know that a more significant memento would prevent me from ever forgetting this meaningless love affair. The strange pains in my abdomen had come back. I often felt nauseated and could not bear to work in the kitchen when food was being prepared. At these times, I had to run outside, clutching my stomach, only to face Big Madd's sinister stare on my return. One day, she purposely threw more vegetables than usual into the bubbling pot, causing the fumes to smell worse. "You there!" she shouted. "Don't get sick again! If you do, don't come back in here—go find work somewhere else! You know I can't stand sick people around me!"

"It must have been something I ate last night," I said, running outside again as she bellowed from her cooking corner.

But soon these unpleasant symptoms stopped, and I was glad, because I had been afraid they were due to some incurable disease. One night, though, as I was undressing, I saw that my belly had swelled. To my horror, I realized that a baby was growing inside me. My first concern was how to disguise it from Big Madd. In the beginning, I managed to do that by covering my body with more clothes and aprons. But the approaching winter made my situation harder to handle, because my room was much too cold, and I would have to stay in her room. On the first chilly night, I went down on my knees and prayed for help.

Those days, I used to bring some soup to the elderly man who had come to repair the old olive-pressing mill. He was thin, but full of nervous energy. He often chatted at his tools. This time he chatted to his hammer. "How do they expect this ancient mill to work, if it hasn't been used since the Romans left?" he complained, throwing the hammer down in disdain. Seeing me, he smiled, deep wrinkles creasing around his piercing eyes. He asked me to sit down and keep him company while he ate his meal. Making conversation, I talked about the winter coming upon us. "I often wondered how a fine girl like you can work for that old hag," he suddenly remarked.

I laughed. "It hasn't been so bad since I got my own room, but soon I'll have to move back in with her, because I don't have a fireplace," I said worriedly. "In winter, she sleeps day and night like a bear. So I have to put up with her loud and perpetual snoring," I added just to amuse him.

He laughed heartily, displaying the few teeth left in his mouth. "I have an idea!" he exclaimed, his eyes shining like bright steel. "There's an old brazier in the back there with a hole in it, but I'll repair it for you and even teach you how to light it with the hot cinders from the oven. There now! Your problem's solved!" I got up and kissed his cheek. "You're such a gentle, well-bred girl, you must have grown up in a noble household, not on this damned hill!"

"Don't say that! This is a beautiful place!" I cried.

The brazier the kind old man repaired for me was a godsend that cheered me when I thought of the dreary months ahead.

A chilly morning breeze blew hard on my face as I brought the washing up to the threshing floor to hang. I started to feel the strain of my daily work, but tried to be cheerful, remembering the joy I had felt the night before, when for the first time my baby had moved inside me. It had seemed like a miracle, making me the happiest girl on earth. But now a sinister wind swirling around me forced me to see the cruel reality of life and realize how little I had to offer that child of mine. As the wind grew fiercer I put my hand on my abdomen, fearing my baby would feel the cold, too. The baby moved again, and I knew that its gentle kick was assuring me not to worry, that everything would be all right for us!

That ghastly wind, though, had yet another, more painful message in store for me. A loud burst of ringing bells came up from the town below, piercing my ears and disrupting the peacefulness of our hills.

Big Madd appeared on her doorstep, combing her hair. "Why are the bells ringing so festively?" she bellowed to the cartman coming into the courtyard with a load of manure.

"Why, don't you know? It's Ser Antonio's son's wedding!"

"Which son?"

"Ser Piero, the younger notary. You should see the church decorations! Flowers everywhere! Everyone's dressing up to see the bride. They say she's fair and comes from a rich family!" he shouted at the top of his voice.

"Well, Ser Antonio's a rich man, too! I'll go and see the bride myself. Will you take me?" she asked excitedly, now fussing with her hair.

Shocked, I retreated behind a tall bush where they couldn't see me and held on to the washing line. The smell of the manure made me feel sick and my legs began to shake. To keep my balance, I followed the line all the way to the post, which I clutched for a moment, wishing that I could die. Everything grew dark, and I suddenly crumpled to the ground, unconscious.

When I recovered, all was silence. Getting up slowly, I made my way back to my room and collapsed on my bed. It was already getting dark when I woke up, so I forced myself to go outside. I was thankful to see that the tavern was still closed. Apparently, everybody had gone to town to see the bride and take part in the festivities. Taking advantage of this privacy, I set out for the brook, but decided, instead, to sit on a large rock on the edge of the slope.

Although it was half-hidden by shrubs, from there I could still watch the sunset and think. I felt the baby move inside me again and crossed my hands on my abdomen to protect it. "Don't be afraid, my little baby!" I cried softly, "You're all mine now ... only mine!" Then, as if by magic, a golden ray of sun filtered through the branches, warming my rock, and the prophet's words rang again in my ears. I knew then that my mission in life was my child! I stood up as a burst of energy overpowered me. I raised my arms and shouted at the top of my voice, "Yes, you are my mission! I promise you, my child, I'll take care of you! And I'll give you all the love I can summon from the bottom of my heart!" I felt so elated as I spoke those words; tall as the sky above my head, strong as the earth under my feet! From that day on, I became healthier and more confident.

As time went by, though, the size of my growing abdomen did not escape Big Madd's eyes, which kept darting suspicious glances at me. I thought of confiding in her, but I could never bring myself to do so.

One day, she stood on the doorstep, staring at me as I was carrying a heavy bucket of water, when suddenly she roared, "Hey! What have you got there in your belly? You're pregnant, aren't you? This is a respectable tavern! This isn't a place for the likes of you. It's a respectable tavern!" I dropped the bucket on the ground and covered my stomach with both hands to protect my baby. "Tomorrow I'll tell Ser Antonio what you've done. He'll throw you out of here himself, you dirty bitch—you and that bastard you're carrying!" she blustered. I covered my ears so my baby wouldn't hear her and ran straight to my room. Locking my door for fear she would follow me, I fell on my bed, sobbing like a child.

By the middle of the night, I had decided that it was time I left the tavern. Putting my few belongings together, I tied them into a bundle and waited for the first glimmer of light. Afraid to be seen, however, I tiptoed out into the cold night while it was still dark, wrapped in a thick blanket, and carrying the covered birdcage with one hand and my bundle with the other. As I hurried toward the main road, I heard the rumbling of carts on their way to the fields, so I took a path leading to the lower hills, determined to find my parents' old house again.

"Don't be afraid, my baby! This time, I'll find my way, you'll see! I'll fix up the house and I'm sure you'll like it," I kept saying with my heart pounding. "We'll go back to the *ruscello* one day, and I'll show you the springs I discovered, and the swallows, and we'll play there together!" My voice weakened from the strain, and I had to rest under a tree.

Seeing the sun rising, I uncovered the birdcage. "Why don't you sing for us, my nightingale? Don't be sad! We'll go back one day, I promise. Now, please sing for us. Look! The sun's coming out!" The bird began with a very faint whistle, giving me sufficient courage to resume my journey.

We had made a little progress, but by the time the sun was high in the sky, I was weak and hungry. With frost on the ground, a search for fruit would have been in vain, so, spotting a comfortable tree trunk, I sat down again. As I leaned back against it, I started feeling like a helpless child, but soothed by the bird's dulcet chirping, I soon dozed off.

"What are you doing here, my girl? Are you alone?" I heard a voice ask.

I opened my eyes and saw a middle-aged woman looking at me. "Yes, I am, except for my ..." I answered, touching my abdomen.

"Are you expecting a baby?" she asked softly.

"Yes, and I already know it's a boy!"

"Where do you come from?"

"I was working in the tavern in Anchiano, but I left because I didn't want my baby to hear their insults."

"Where are you going?"

"I'm looking for my parents' house, but I haven't found it yet. I can't walk too fast, because of the baby."

She smiled. "What a beautiful canary you have!"

"It's not a canary—it's a nightingale! When he's happy, he sings beautifully!" I said, taking the hand she was holding out to me.

"What's your name?"

"My name is Caterina," I said, looking at the halo of thick, silvery hair framing her amiable, chubby face.

"Mine is Margarita. Would you like to come to my house? I live alone. It would please me to have your company." Then, patting my stomach, she added, "And your son's company, too!" In her gentle, motherly way, she guided me up toward the higher hills, holding my hand and carrying the cage for me. Though she was rather plump, she seemed agile and sturdy.

We took a shortcut through thick foliage that led to the yard of a delightful little house built on a rocky cliff. The veranda was richly decorated with ornamental vases containing a glorious rainbow of flowers, a kind I had never seen before.

"The seeds of these plants came from faraway places. The vases were given to me by my masters, who were renovating the terraces of their villa when I retired from service," she explained, noticing my interest. "Come inside and rest. I'll prepare something hot for you."

I was touched by the tone of her voice, which somehow reminded me of my dear mother. Pretending not to notice my emotion, she helped me sit on a comfortable chair in front of a fireplace shielded by a shiny golden fireguard. Then she busied herself at her small iron stove.

I looked around, impressed by her quaint, yet attractive, furniture and the decorative glass and porcelain jars gracefully arranged on the sideboard. I had never seen anything so lovely in my life—objects displayed for the sole purpose of pleasing the eye. I observed admiringly as she handled her kitchenware with swift dexterity. As her soup simmered on the stove, she proudly set the table, covering it with a white tablecloth embroidered with tiny red buds. Somehow I knew that she had sewn it herself, for her fingers were nimble, just like my mother's.

She served the soup in two bowls, white on the inside, painted on the outside. "You can't imagine, my dear child, how much it pleases me to have you here! Usually I sit at the table by myself." She smiled, encouraging me to help myself. "After we eat, would you like to rest a little? You may stretch out on the extra bed in the room next to mine. It's always ready."

"No, thank you, Donna Margarita, not yet. I'd like to sit here with you for a while," I said, enjoying her company.

"Very well, but just call me Rita," she said, patting my hand. "Would you like to tell me a little about your parents?"

"That part of my life is really over," I said despondently.

"Don't worry, my dear. You and your baby are safe now. That's what counts," she said, clearing the table.

But I felt a sudden urge to open up to her, relating all the events that led up to my employment at the tavern and my meeting with Piero. "I really don't know how it happened," I sighed, wiping away my tears. "Maybe it was my fault, too. I believed that he loved me, and he took advantage of me one night when I was all alone."

"Is he from around here?"

"No, he's from Vinci, and has just married a rich girl."

"The scoundrel! Does he know about the child?"

"No. He was in Florence when I found out. It doesn't matter anymore. The baby's going to be all mine now." She stroked my head. "Rita, you speak with such a beautiful accent, do you come from Florence?" I asked. I knew of no other city name.

"No, my dear, I have a Spanish accent. I grew up in a Spanish gypsy camp." I nodded, for I had heard people talking about those camps. "One day, I discovered I was a foundling and not one of them, so I ran away." Her body shook with laughter.

"What's a foundling?" I asked.

"A foundling is a baby who's been abandoned by its real parents. Then it's found and raised by complete strangers."

"Then I'm a foundling, too!" I exclaimed. "The elderly couple who brought me up as their own daughter found me when I was just a baby!"

"You poor girl! How did you find out?"

"My father told me before he died. It really upset me at first. I always had a strange feeling about those fine linens my mother kept carefully stored in a trunk."

"What linens, my dear?" she asked, raising her eyebrows.

"The ones in the wicker basket in which I was abandoned on their doorstep that stormy night." I saw her face flush.

"Do you have any of the linens with you?"

"Yes, a few on which my father used to draw my face every year."

"May I see them?"

"I really don't recognize myself in the drawings, but I kept—"

"Anything you have with you ..." she interrupted.

"Rita, is something wrong? You don't look well."

"I'm all right. Can you show me one of them?" she urged.

Although it was a strain on my aching back, I reached for my bundle, rummaged through it, and pulled out the embroidered handkerchief.

When she saw it, she jumped up from her chair, exclaiming, "Oh, my God! You're Lisa, my little Lisa!"

"No, my name is Caterina," I corrected her.

She flung her arms up to the heavens, her face aglow with perspiration. "Fernando! Nando, *mío*, you were right! You were right when you said a miracle could happen. This is a miracle!"

Too tired to follow her rambling, I peeped into the next room, simply longing for a bed. A thought suddenly struck me, and I turned back only to see her still in deep conversation with the invisible Nando. "Rita!" I exclaimed. "Are you ... are you my real mother?"

"No, my dear, but I knew your mother ... I'm sorry I got a little carried away. Fernando was my husband. Before he died, he told me that one day I'd find you." She paused to take a breath, then went on. "We searched these hills for the little house where we left you that unforgettable night, but we couldn't find it again," she said breathlessly. "That's why I retired up here after he died, hoping to find you one day ... and here you are! Now, come here, my dear Lisa. Let me look at you! I can't believe my eyes. Now I must tell you everything about that tragic night."

I fell back on my chair, exhausted. Her words seemed to come from a distance as in a nightmare. She held my shaking hands as I tried to free myself, refusing to learn about my mother or to listen to the story I had wanted to hear for so long. I was baffled by my own confused feelings.

Rita offered me another hot aromatic drink, but I couldn't hold it, because my hands were shaking so badly. "*Dios mío! Dios mío!* You're still upset ...," she murmured.

I recalled my father telling me about the woman's cries. "Was it you crying '*Vaya ... con ... Dios!*' outside the door?" I queried.

"Yes, my dear, it was me," she said, drawing her chair nearer. "We were ordered to do it. I'll tell you everything that happened. You must know the truth, my child, you must!" she insisted.

"Your mother, Principessina Alicia, gave birth to you," she began, "the same night her father had arranged to have her taken to a convent. He wanted her baby to be delivered there in great secrecy."

"Why delivered in ... great secrecy?" I heard myself ask.

"Because she wasn't married, and he wouldn't let her marry the man she was in love with," she continued, shaking her head. I sighed, as I was reminded of my old parents' similar situation.

In a soothing voice, she related the entire story, ending with my poor mother's horrifying death.

"What was wrong with the man my mother loved?" I asked. "Who was he?"

"He was ... Your father, Ser Leonardo, was the most handsome young man I have ever seen. He was tall and had dark hair; in fact, your features remind me of him. He was a fine gentleman with the talent of an artisan, for he painted and engraved beautiful things on silver. But her father wanted her to marry a great warrior, as powerful a man as himself."

"What do you mean, a warrior?"

"A great fighter of wars. Her father was a French captain of fortune, who had become a general in the pope's army because of his bravery. He married a Roman princess who died very young. He was very ambitious, soon appointing himself as *condottiere* of his own army. He wanted a strong son-in-law to help him make his army more powerful and win battles. So, he arranged for his daughter to marry a great *gonfaloniere*."

"What happened to ... my father? Do you know about his family?"

"No, I saw Leonardo only once long before the tragedy. The *condottiere* perished in the fire, too, and the villa was abandoned. Nando and I got married and went to work somewhere else. But we've prayed and searched for you all these years, my dear Lisa! And, look, God brought you back to me and here you are, my Lisa! My Lisa! This is a true miracle!"

"Please, Rita, don't call me Lisa anymore. I know that every time you mention that name, I'll see my poor mother and feel her pain."

She got up and stroked my hair again, placing a kiss on my forehead. "I understand, my child. Whatever you say. Now go and rest in the room I've always kept for you, and dream of happier times with your baby!"

She kept her promise and never talked about my family again.

The following day, a bright blue sky welcomed us as if spring had returned, and I went outside to explore the grounds around the house. Tall pine treetops peeping over the edge of the cliff filled the air with their fragrance. From that height, I had a full view of the hills sloping toward the flatlands spotted with green woods and scattered groups of slender cypress trees. I admired the perfection with which Mother

Nature had planned our wonderful Tuscan countryside as I searched in vain for a trace of my *ruscello*. Instead, I discerned a calm river flowing from under the mountain, winding around the lowlands and through the old towns. With my eager eye I traced it back to its starting point and realized that it originated at the bottom of our cliff. I guessed then that the back of the cliff with the pine trees faced the hills of Anchiano. Next I discovered that on the lower hill opposite us stood the buildings of the tavern, assuring me that under that cliff was my beloved *ruscello!*

I felt my baby kick inside me and I knew that in some magic way he was seeing those wonders through my eyes. "Oh, my Leonardo, see how wonderful the world is! See how far the water of our *ruscello* goes!" I exclaimed, my voice echoing over the hills. I found my tiny window half-hidden by a tree, and suddenly felt homesick. Tears ran down my cheeks. Then my heart froze as I caught sight of Big Madd striding across the cobblestoned courtyard.

Rita had followed me. "Do you miss that place, my dear? Don't you like it here?" she asked, gently putting a hand on my shoulder.

In my embarrassment, I tried to hide my tears from her, but I couldn't lie to her. "Yes, I miss it very much, Rita, though I'm so lucky to have found you. You saved me from utter destitution."

"What makes you so sad then, my child?" she asked with concern.

"My dream—a dream that now will never come true."

"Tell me about your dream, and I'll make it happen!"

"I used to be comforted by the thought that my child would be born in the same place in which he ... he was conceived," I explained, blushing.

"Be born in that squalid little room?" she said, dismayed.

"Well, yes, mainly because I dreamed of taking him down to the *ruscello* and playing with him in that most beautiful corner of the world!"

"But you said you were so unhappy there," she protested.

"Yes, but I loved being by the *ruscello*. It made up for

everything. Now I feel that my baby wants to be there, too," I added with assurance.

She patted my back, comforting me. "Let me see what I can do, Lis—Caterina," she said, shaking her head in bewilderment.

During the days that followed, Rita seemed to enjoy pampering me, never leaving my side, except to go shopping in Vinci in a neighbor's cart. One day she returned, all excited. By chance she had met a mason, working at the tavern, who informed her that it was going to be closed down.

"Why?" I asked.

"It seems that the real owners of the estate are monks, and they refuse to sell it to Ser Antonio unless he promises to use it solely as a farm. If not, he would forfeit the money he has already advanced. What choice does he have? Therefore, my dear, now is the right time to tell him the truth about your condition, if you really want to go back to that place."

"But he's the last person I would want to tell."

"Well, there's no other way. Besides, he should know, in case one day I shouldn't be here to protect you."

"Why shouldn't you be here? Please, Rita, don't say such things!"

"Unfortunately, my dear, my health isn't quite what it should be. So ..."

"What do you mean? You're young and strong. You'll see my son grow up into a young man!"

"I hope that is God's will, my dear," she sighed, pressing her hand against her chest.

I had an uncomfortable feeling, but did not dare ask any more questions.

Some days later, I was sitting near the fireplace sewing a baby shoe from a piece of red cloth Rita had given me before leaving for Vinci. My eyes turned to the door after every stitch as it grew dark, but there was still no sign of her. Her uncommon tardiness conjured up visions of her taking sick on the road. I suddenly felt guilty for having expressed my dream of having the baby in Anchiano and sorely regretted not having told her to forget about it. How silly to think that a baby would care where he was born! The moment I heard the cart, I leaped to the door, but Rita's radiant smile barred my way. She said it was too cold for me and sat down with cheeks pink from excitement as I hurriedly poured her a hot tisane.

"My dear, I have some wonderful news. I've finally been able to talk to Ser Antonio. When I told him about your situation, he was speechless." She stopped, surprised to see I was upset, and reached for my hand. "My dear, he's a good man and very understanding. Don't be afraid! When I told him about your wish to return there, he said"—she paused to clear her throat so that she could imitate his voice— "'It's the least I can do for the poor girl! Tell her that as soon as the place is fixed up, she can go and live there the whole summer, if she wants. Maddalena has already left, and there won't be anybody living there for quite a while.'" We both laughed at her good rendition. "Are you happy now?" she asked, getting up again.

I hugged her. "Yes, dear Rita, even my baby is happy—feel how he's jumping!" She bent down and put her ear on my stomach, but quickly stood up, looked for the nearest chair, and fell into it. "What happened, Rita? You've turned pale. Don't you feel well?"

"I'm all right, my child. Just a little too much excitement!"

The long winter passed, and warm spring air filled the trees with new buds. The first purple anemones covered the fields around the house and the friendly swallows came back to the valley. Every day I stood on the cliff and followed the renovation of the tavern, looking forward to the time when I could see my *ruscello* again. At long last, a messenger from Ser Antonio came to announce that the place was ready for me.

Rita and I made a grand entrance into the courtyard on a mule-drawn cart, the one that always took her to Vinci. Giuseppe, the driver, was a polite, middle-aged man with a weather-beaten face, a short beard, and a cap with a long point, which he always wore slung over his shoulder.

They both had to help me down, since I was already in my

last month of pregnancy and very heavy. Carrying my nightingale's cage, I waddled merrily toward my little room under the tavern while Rita went to look around the rest of the house.

The room seemed much smaller than before, but I was pleased to see that the stone floor had been repaired and the walls whitewashed.

Rita came in and sat on one of the beds, which had new covers. "Ser Antonio has really done his best to make you feel welcome! Even the mattresses are good," she said, patting the bed. "I'll spend the nights here until the baby is born, after which we'll go back home just as you promised," she said, looking into my eyes. "You can always take walks down here later."

"But the baby may not come for another month."

"Don't worry. Time goes more quickly than you think."

"Thank you, Rita, for your patience. Now, I'd like to take the nightingale outside," I said, picking up the cage on the way out.

"By the way, there's a beautiful rosebush under your window. Did you plant it?" she asked, following me out. I nodded as I hurried myself to where it stood. Overtaken by mixed emotions, I gasped when I saw it covered with pink buds, realizing that it had grown from a shoot I'd cut from the same rosebush from which Piero had plucked my red rose.

"You have green fingers, Caterina!" cried Rita to cheer me up.

We heard the wheels of a gig entering the yard and Giuseppe's voice repeating, "Donna Rita, Ser Antonio's here!" Rita rushed over to meet him, while I stayed behind, embarrassed to be seen by him in my condition.

Ser Antonio solemnly alighted from the gig and came toward me. "I'm very sorry for the trouble my son has caused you. I promise you, my dear," he said, taking my hand, "that I will provide for you and your son—or daughter."

"I know it will be a boy. I feel it!" I exclaimed, easing the tension.

"In a way, my girl, you are lucky. My daughter-in-law, unfortunately, cannot conceive." Lowering my eyes, I folded my arms over my stomach. He went on, "Donna Rita told me that you prefer the room downstairs, Caterina. But you can have a larger room upstairs as soon as it's ready. The whole house will be empty through the summer. I'll send you a supply of food every week."

"Ser Antonio," interrupted Rita, "I already told you that after the baby's born, we'll be returning to my house, and I'll take care of Caterina and the baby," she declared, looking straight at me.

"Yes, Ser Antonio, the small room is enough for me," I confirmed. He looked at me, shaking his head perplexedly, reminding me of the priest whose hospitality I had refused at my father's burial. "But, Ser Antonio," I added firmly, looking squarely into his eyes, "I want you to know that I am staying here only on one condition. You must promise me that your son will never know about this." He nodded, looking completely baffled, and turned to survey the repaired walls. Then, in deep thought, he returned to his gig.

Rita took my hand and winked approvingly while Giuseppe quickly began to carry my bundles into the room.

"Caterina, we'll be back later with the rest of the things we'll need. You take a little rest now," said Rita, getting back on the cart, after we had put everything away.

I had to wait until the cart had left before I could take the path leading down to my *ruscello*. Moving carefully, I held on to every shrub I could so as not to fall or tear the new cotton dress Rita had helped me sew. At last, I reached my favorite spot. I sat on the grass, adjusting my skirt around me, and took out my little flute I had hidden inside my skirt pocket. Then, to the refreshing sound of the bubbling water, I serenaded my baby to my heart's content.

Although Rita would spend several hours a day with me, tending to my needs, it still left me plenty of time to be by myself and stroll around the estate. One day, I noticed that an old shed on the slope had tumbled down and that it had sheltered the remains of a dried-up well, which consisted of an elaborate stone arch supported by two handsome ivy-covered columns. The board covering the mouth of the well was also overgrown with creepers. With care, I stripped away the rotting remains of the wooden shelter, exposing the ornate structure of the well to the fresh air. In a few days, wild buds started blossoming around it and the ivy grew thicker and greener around the columns. Early each morning, I sat on its top step, which was steeper than the others, and, as I waited for the sun to rise, I chatted to my baby. "You see, my son, it's still dawn. Very soon a beautiful golden ball will appear from behind the mountain, and our world will have light." Then I went on describing to him the birds in flight and let him listen to their singing. I told him about the flowers and the fruit growing on the lovely trees, and promised him that he would be happy to be born in our beautiful countryside.

Tidying my room one day, I found in an old basket the books Piero had given me. Though they reminded me of those unhappy days, I was somehow prompted to look at them. I took the package to the brook, where I untied it. Each book consisted of several sheets bound or sewed together, on which were drawn amusing figures pointing at tiny objects. Near their mouths were large, hand-printed words, which I assumed were the names of the objects drawn. As my ability improved, I started recognizing those words and reading them aloud, placing my hand on my stomach to make sure that my baby was listening. I knew he was blessed with the "gift of God"—the same gift that was making it possible for me to learn how to recognize those simple written words.

One morning while I was sitting at the old well having my usual conversation with my baby, I caught sight of an old woman peering at me from a distance and encouraged her to come near. Her face was very wrinkled, but her toothless mouth curled into a warm, friendly smile.

"How long until the birth of your son?" she asked sweetly, her eyes shining brightly like those of a young girl.

"How do you know it's going to be a boy?" I smiled back.

"I've seen too many pregnant women in my long, long life not to know!" she answered complacently.

"Where do you live, good woman? Why haven't I seen you before?"

"Call me Nonnetta! I live in a little house behind the olive grove over there and only come up here if the weather's good," she said in one breath. "I never go near the tavern, though," she went on drolly, "not since the day I asked the old dragon for work and she chased me away with a broom!" I couldn't stop giggling as she entertained me with her comical gossip, ending with a hilarious description of her large family.

"Would you be offended if I asked you to share some of my food?" I entreated when she paused for breath. "I just can't eat it all by myself."

"Oh, no, not at all, my dear girl!" she said eagerly.

From that day on, Nonnetta became my daily companion, always keeping my spirits high with her tireless chitchat. She told me the most fantastic fairy tales I had ever heard while waiting for Rita to come for the night.

One evening when Rita was delayed, it was warmer than usual, and I felt very tired. So Nonnetta let me lay my head on her lap and sang me a sweet lullaby. Suddenly, a long shadow stretching from behind the house startled me. I hid my face, fearing Piero had come back. She hugged me and laughed, showing me it was only Rita carrying something on her head. Putting a large cloth bundle down in front of me, Rita unwrapped a small wooden cradle and lifted it up for me to see. Through the flower-shaped carvings on its headboard, I could see the blue twilight of the sky.

"It's a cradle! Oh, my sweet Rita!" I exclaimed.

"I had it made specially for you," Rita declared proudly.

"It's the most beautiful cradle in the world!" I cried out with joy, getting up to hug her, but a sharp pain in my back made me keel over.

"The labor pains, the labor pains!" Nonnetta announced.

"Let's take her inside," said Rita nervously.

"No, please don't take me in there. If the baby's coming, I prefer him to be born out here," I whined, clutching my belly.

"But didn't you want the baby to be born in your room?"

"It doesn't matter. It's too hot inside, anyway," I heard Nonnetta say. "Nobody will bother us out here. So, calm down, Rita! Besides, the baby won't be born before daylight."

"How do you know about these things?" Rita asked almost defiantly.

"I know, I know. Now let's go get a mattress for her to lie on."

As they rushed indoors, I patted my stomach. "See how excited they are? Please make things easy for them, won't you, my darling?" I said as I tried in vain to hear what the two women were arguing about inside. They came out dragging a mattress and helped me to stretch out on it. The moment I felt the soft surface under my body, I fell soundly asleep.

I don't know how long I slept, but I woke up when the contractions became painful again. I remember clearly, though, that the baby was born without much suffering.

As my baby's first cry echoed in the valley, there were brilliant shafts of rose-colored light radiating across the pale blue sky behind the mountain. It was against that golden dawn that I saw my little son for the first time!

"Caterina, it's a boy! It's a boy!" I heard Rita cry excitedly as she held up his tiny body.

I raised my arms and whispered, "Hello, my Leonardo! See how beautiful the earth is! She welcomes you and the divine gift God has bestowed upon you!"

PART TWO

MATERNAL LOVE

4
THE WONDERS OF CREATION

The sweet sounds of spring reached invitingly to my room. In the semidarkness I could discern my son's angelic little face with his pouting cheeks and his tiny mouth making sucking motions in his sleep. Knowing that Rita had gone to town and wouldn't be back for a while, I impulsively decided to fulfill a desire I had nurtured for months. I got up and dressed, then I bundled Leonardo in the same pink blanket I had had as a baby and raced outside with him in my arms.

The air was mild and fragrant as I ventured down the valley toward the brook. My body was still weak, so, all the while, I had to rely more on my will and determination than on my free hand to maintain my balance.

Giddy and breathless, I fell on my knees by the water and, still clutching my baby to my bosom, I made myself comfortable on the grass. As soon as the warmth of the sun started filtering through the trees, I took my baby out of the blanket and held him up proudly to the wonderful world around us. Under the clear blue sky, his bright eyes seemed even bluer. I dipped my Leonardo's little hand in the water, and a smile appeared on his lips. He shook with joy as I wet his other hand, too, making his first encounter with the wonders of nature a very happy one. Filled with contentment, I lifted him high in the air and cried, "Thank you, God, for this beautiful gift!" Then we quietly listened to the joyous gurgle of the sparkling water.

Realizing we might be missed, I clambered arduously back up the slope. Rita was already back, rushing toward me in a state of alarm. "Where have you been?" she fretted, taking the baby from me. "Don't tell me you took the baby down to the *ruscello?* And without his swaddling clothes? Besides, Caterina, you should be resting, my dear!" she admonished.

"Rita, I couldn't resist it. The air was so inviting." She saw the wet hem of my skirt and shook her head. "You have an obsession with that *ruscello* and you want your baby to be obsessed, too." Then, with a smile, she handed me a set of keys. "These are for the rooms upstairs. You like it here so much I thought you should accept Ser Antonio's offer and live in a more decent place. It will make it easier for me, too, since I can't stay away from the baby." I hugged her and ran upstairs to open the door of the newly restored building.

So, with the help of Rita and Nonnetta, I transformed what was once a smelly, noisy tavern into a permanent home for the first years of my son's infancy; a sanctuary of peace, disturbed only by his sweet laughter.

In comparison, Big Madd's old dwelling by the threshing floor, with its broken roof tiles and peeling whitewashed walls—ravaged by the winter storms—stood in ruin. A wooden board across the window had replaced her precious windowpane, the thick green glass in which I had seen my pleasing womanly reflection for the first time. "Long-forgotten feelings!" I said to myself, reminiscing. I knew now that vain desires would never trap me again, for love for my baby had completely filled my heart.

The inhabitants of Anchiano, who could be counted on the fingers of two hands, looked with pride at the majestic sanctuary standing on a higher hill called Paterno. The church had been built some centuries before in honor of the miraculous patron saint, Santa Lucia, whose noble origin went back to the early Christian era. The legend of her martyrdom never failed to fascinate the worshipers from our hills.

A month after the birth of my son, we took him up there in Giuseppe's cart to have him baptized. Rita and I had made a white christening gown lavishly trimmed with bits of lace she had saved when she still sewed for her mistresses. She had also picked the finest flowers that had blossomed on our hill that morning, arranging them in the basket she now carefully balanced on her lap.

Nonnetta sat quietly, clutching her stomach until, seeing my concern, she raised her hand reassuringly and chirped, "I'm fasting for my Communion." Showing me a piece of bread she kept hidden in her pocket, she added in a whisper, "It's for later." Then, tucking her wispy hair under her black shawl, she confessed, "I'd never have been able to get up the hill if I had to rely on my old legs!"

I cuddled my little Leonardo. His blue eyes twinkled under his white lace cap. "My darling, this is your first journey. I pray it will be the first of many happy ones!" I said to him as the cart took the last turn into the square. It was a privilege for me to visit this church, because Big Madd had never allowed me enough time to walk up here.

On that Sunday, a new young priest was serving the church temporarily. I sat on a bench as Rita and Nonnetta helped him create a makeshift font by putting a large bowl of holy water on a table that Rita had covered with her flowers. Donning a special robe, the priest performed the ceremony as Rita cradled Leonardo in her arms, and Nonnetta held on to the hem of the baby's gown. My son looked like a prince! When the priest was ready to pour the water on Leonardo's head, I removed his lace cap and shut my eyes.

"Leonardo, son of Caterina d'Anchiano and of an unknown father, I baptize you in the name of the Father, the Son, and the Holy Spirit!" The priest's mellow voice resounded richly in the sanctuary.

I opened my eyes in surprise. The water hadn't made the baby cry! Rejoicing, I looked up at the statue of Santa Lucia. A golden ray of sun from a high window was reflecting on her face, creating a pink aura of light around her head. Enraptured by her beauty, I prayed for her light to shine on my son, so that he could always be able to distinguish good from evil, always take the right path—the path of divine wisdom! I held my breath as I perceived a hint of a smile on the saint's lips.

Our happy outing was to end on a sour note, however, due to the unexpected presence of Ser Antonio in the middle of the courtyard on our return. Undaunted by his stern look, I triumphantly alighted from the cart with the baby in my arms and warmly invited him to take part in the christening celebration.

"Christening? And where did this event take place?" he asked.

"Up on Paterno in the Church of Santa Lucia," I replied, perplexed.

"But they have no baptismal font there, so the christening is not valid," he said rather smugly.

"We helped the new priest make one," Rita interjected. "After all, in God's house holy water is enough, don't you think, Ser Antonio?" she affirmed, forcing an open smile, but he turned away without answering. I peered at him, disappointed that he didn't even look at my beautiful baby.

"Did you see his eyes? They were green with envy!" sneered Nonnetta, breaking the silence. "I wonder what thoughts were going through his mind." Before I could consider her remarks, she rushed over to help Rita set up the table outside, and on a pretty white tablecloth, they arranged all the tasty cakes they had baked for the occasion.

In the months that followed, I struggled against Rita's insistence that my baby Leo's body should be confined in swaddling clothes as was the custom with all infants up to the age of one. I could not bear the thought of imposing such a cruel restriction on my fast-growing son, particularly during the summer months. Finally, she let me have my way, and I was delighted to see him growing healthy and strong.

*   *   *

One day, while I was sitting on the grass by the brook sewing, Leo, who was then only two years old, toddled over to me and, standing quite erect, stuttered, "Mama, where does ... this water ... come from?"

My eyes widened in astonishment as he had never stood up so straight or pronounced words so clearly before. I hesitated, not knowing what to say, but he still waited for an answer. "My little Leo, I really don't know," I said. "It comes from far away."

"What's that?" he asked, pointing to the sky.

"The sky, the blue sky. Do you like it?" I said, still confused.

"Blue, blue ... sky!" He bent and touched the water. "Wa ... ter, blue water!" He pointed to the grass. "Gra ... ss, gre ... en gra ... ss!" Then he stood on his toes and pointed to a tree. "Tree, gre ... en tree!"

I suddenly realized he stressed his words in the same way I used to recite the ones from my picture books during my pregnancy. Even his gestures seemed to mimic those of the figures sketched in the books. I recalled, too, the times when, tired of the tedious repetitions, I dozed off, soon to be reawakened by my baby's feet kicking inside me. "So, you were listening ... and learning with me! No, I was learning with you!" I cried. "You were helping me then! You were my teacher, weren't you?"

"Yes, Mama, yes," he said, laughing. Then he ran along the bank, repeating those words. I chased after him with my arms wide open, ready to catch him in case he fell, but I soon realized he was not toddling anymore. His walk was well balanced and steady.

Nevertheless, that moment of joy also marked the beginning of my son's detatchment. He did not play as a child anymore. Every day, he wandered about with a worried expression on his pretty face, his curly golden hair dirty and damp, as he explored caves on the opposite side of the brook, seeking out the most hidden springs. Then he would spend hours lying next to an anthill in the field, watching with amazing intensity the insects crawling in and out of the holes. My concern grew when I saw that these pursuits invariably left him dissatisfied and irritable.

One day after he had stretched himself out on a low branch of a tree, watching a flower bud since morning, I approached him slowly and asked, "Leo, darling, our evening meal is ready. Aren't you hungry? You've been up there for hours and it's getting dark."

"No, Mama, I'm not hungry yet. I'm waiting for this bud to open first. I have to see how it happens."

"Darling, it may not open until morning. Please come and have something to eat, Leo. You haven't eaten all day."

He did not answer, and I sat on the grass and waited helplessly, fearful that something was really wrong with my little son's mind, for in just a few months, he had become alarmingly thin, yet much too tall for a child under three years old. My fear turned into resentment toward nature for robbing him of a normal childhood, for denying him the desire for and the thrill of playing as I thought a child should. Then an idea came to me, and before he finally fell into my arms half-asleep, I said, "Why don't I wake you before sunrise and we'll both watch the bud open?" He smiled at me, and I helped him climb down. So for the next few days, we studied the miracle of nature together, getting up before daybreak.

Then he turned his attention to the ever-changing sky. For days, he would lie on his back on the grass, sometimes squinting, watching the sky grow dark, again refusing to answer my calls until, exhausted, he fell asleep on the ground, and I would take him in my arms and carry him to bed. One evening, while he was still lying on the grass, I approached him with tears in my eyes "Darling, I'm hungry and I'm very lonely, too. I would like to eat with you and play with you, as before. Tell me! What am I to do?"

He got up and came to me with concern. "I'm sorry, Mama, but I have to wait for more stars to light up so I can find out how it happens."

"We can eat out here if you like, and while you look, I'll tell you beautiful stories about the stars and the moon."

He beamed at me. "All right, Mama, and I'll help you

bring the food out." We found a nice patch of grass in an open space on the hill, and I set out food on a white cloth.

Later, I told him some of Nonnetta's stories about the stars and the moon, embellishing them in order to make them more mysterious. Though I couldn't answer all his questions, he listened patiently for a few days. But, one evening, he just got up and walked away. "What's wrong, Leo?" I called after him, dismayed. "Don't you like my stories?"

He stopped and looking sideways at me, he answered, "Yes, I do. they're very pretty, but I don't believe it when you say that it gets dark at night because the sun goes to sleep behind the hills. It doesn't go to sleep. I still see some light up there in the sky at night, though it turns into a darker blue."

To my surprise, I realized that he was right, but I kept silent.

"And about the stars: I don't believe they're dancers dressed in silver. They must be made of something like the pebbles in the brook, which reflect the sunlight. The stars, though, are so high up that they can still see and reflect the sun after it has gone down. Oh, I wish I knew what really happens!"

"But the sun at night isn't there anymore. And if the stars were made like the pebbles, they would fall on our heads."

"Maybe they don't fall because they're much too far away. There must be a way to find out!" he cried, restlessly pacing in a circle around me.

"My dear, I'm sure that one day you'll find out about it and the many secrets of our beautiful heavens. But for now, since you're still a child, you should play more. You know, darling"—I sighed—"I really miss playing with you as we used to." He gave me a long, pensive look and turned away again. "I have a good idea, Leo. Tomorrow I'll bake some cakes and we'll eat them at the brook. I'll teach you a lovely song to sing while I play my flute. How would you like that?"

"Oh, yes, Mama!" he exclaimed, bursting into laughter and jumping up and down. My heart swelled with so much happiness from the reassurance that I could still appeal to the child in him.

Next day at the brook, an unexpected summer shower interrupted our merrymaking. I gathered up my things and urged Leo to follow me home, but he stood there with one foot planted in the brook, while holding out his upturned palms, one above the water, the other above the grass. "Wait, Mama! See? I'm measuring the rainwater. You know, it feels so much heavier when it falls on the brook than on the grass. Why is that?" I shrugged my shoulders. "Tell me, Mama, what makes the rain fall out of the sky? How does it get up there?" Then he shook the water from his hands and cried, "If only somebody would explain these things to me!" Heavy rain kept pouring on our heads. I just stood motionless, amazed by his eagerness to understand things that I had never heard other people question and, even more, by the way he expressed himself. We lived a rather isolated life, and nobody else on the hill ever made such observations, not even Rita, who had worked for educated people.

Finally, the rain stopped. I beckoned Leo to sit by me and, hugging him, said, "You know, Leo, when I was about your age I got impatient, too, because there was nobody to answer my questions. My parents were very busy working the nearby fields, and I was always left to play by myself. Being old, they were too tired to answer my questions when they came home at night. And I was curious about things, like you. Anyway, one day I became very impatient and stamped my feet. I was furious." Leo laughed. "Then, out of the blue, a tiny little man appeared before me. 'Why are you making so much noise?' he asked with a grown-up but soft voice. 'Can't you see you're disturbing those little people working around the plants?' 'No, I can't see anyone,' I said. 'You don't see them because you're always upset. If you keep quiet, you'll see them and hear them singing, too.' I looked around and saw no one. When I turned to tell him, he was gone, never to be seen again. But from then on, I learned how to quiet myself whenever I got upset, and I was finally able to hear the little people through the silence. They even answered some of my questions sometimes. Of course, my questions were not as complicated as yours," I concluded, looking into his eyes.

"Mama, did you ever see the little people?"

"Sometimes when the air was clear, I caught glimpses of them, always in groups, busy working around the plants. They became my friends."

"How big were they?" he asked, wide-eyed.

"They were different sizes. Some were as small as your little finger," I said, taking hold of his hand. His eyes twinkled. "Some had gossamer wings and often flew around me. But I was able to hear them only when I became still and listened."

"Oh, Mama, I wish I had such friends!"

"I'm sure they're everywhere, especially around the *ruscello*. They like the sound of running water. I remember when I watered the flowers in the garden I heard them giggling."

"Do you still see or hear them, Mama?"

"No, darling. They only show themselves to children, for they are children of Mother Earth. But I heard their singing up to the time I learned to play my flute. It's how I got the idea for some of my tunes."

"Oh, Mama, it must have been wonderful! Do you think I will ever see them?"

"Why not? Learn how to listen carefully to the sounds in the wind!" He hugged me and helped me pick up my things. Then he went on ahead of me, looking around. I followed, amazed at myself for having revived a childhood memory I had hitherto forgotten.

In the following months, though, Leo developed a new interest. He had started constructing little huts out of small stones he had picked up, straw from the fields, and clay from the brook. In a few weeks he had filled the corner of the threshing floor with strange little huts for the little people. The roofs were linked to one another by paths in midair, making it easy for them to communicate with one another. Leo had created his own tiny village.

These physical activities had stimulated his appetite, making him more robust and turning me into the happiest woman in the world, for I knew now that my son was, after all, a normal, healthy, God-gifted child.

* * *

One day, the ground began to shake under our feet. I was terrified, as I had never experienced such a phenomenon before, but Leo quickly stretched out with his ear on the threshing floor, attentively listening.

"Leo, what are you doing there? Get up, please. You're getting all red in the face." He didn't move. "Do you hear something?" I asked, my voice still trembling.

He got up and walked away, saying, "I hear a fire burning under the ground. It sounds like the wood burning in the oven."

"What are you saying, my dear? The hill is made of rock. It cannot burn like wood."

He stopped in the nearby field and, lying down again, put his ear to the grass. "Come and listen. You can hear it better here."

I got down on the ground, but couldn't hear anything. "Well, I hear it just a little" I said, humoring him.

"Don't be afraid, Mama! The burning is very deep down underneath the hill. It won't reach up here. The little people told me so," he assured.

"Did you see them?" I asked curiously, as he had not mentioned them for some time.

"No, I only heard them. I think I should get some clay from the *ruscello* and make some dolls like them, before I grow up, and they stop showing themselves to me, too."

"That's nice. I'll come to help you."

One summer morning, I saw Nonnetta standing at the edge of the olive grove, holding a boy by the hand. "How nice to see you back again, Nonnetta! I was worried when I didn't see you last spring," I said, going to meet her.

"It's indeed nice to be back here!" chirped Nonneta. "Because of my shortness of breath lately, they wouldn't let me come without Tommaso, my great-grandson."

From under his bushy dark hair, the boy kept peering at Leo, who was playing with his constructions. "I thought it would be nice for Maso to play with your son sometimes," she suggested tentatively.

"Of course, Leo will like the company of another boy. Come, Maso, let's surprise Leo!" I said. The boy followed me, taking awkward strides, as his boots were much too big for him. "Leo! Nonnetta brought her great-grandchild, Maso, to play with you."

Leo looked him up and down first and then said, "All right, but please don't step on my huts." Maso sprawled himself on the low wall, and I returned to Nonnetta, who had stayed back.

"Maso is more than seven years old, three years older than your boy, but, with Leo being so bright," she explained, "I thought he could get along well with an older boy." I looked at Maso, who was standing now next to Leo, and noticed that they were the same height.

Nonnetta left, and I got busy in my garden, where I could keep an eye on the boys.

"What did you say these things are?" I heard a disinterested Maso ask.

"They're huts. Can't you see? I like building them. Do you want me to show you how to make them?"

"What for? They're too small for people to live in."

"They're for the little people," explained Leo.

"What little people? You're a strange one."

"Well, I'm practicing, really, so when I grow up I can build them in real size."

"You don't need that," contested Maso, blowing the hair off his eyes. "My father's a mason. He learned his trade without having to do that."

"But this way, I can experiment, making new shapes," Leo explained.

"Well, I think it's a waste of time," the other boy scoffed.

"So what would you like to do instead?" Leo asked, facing him squarely.

"I like hunting out nests! Would you like to come? But you have to be a good climber," he said, giving Leo a challenging look.

"Do you mean birds' nests? What for?"

"To get the eggs!" Maso said gleefully.

"Why do that just when the chicks need their mother's care most in order to come out of the eggs safely?"

"How would you know? 'Mother's care,' indeed! Don't make me laugh!"

"I've spent a lot of time lying on branches, watching them."

"Without stealing the eggs?" Leo ignored him. "Birds make too much noise anyway," Maso went on, stamping around the threshing floor.

"Not as much as your big boots!"

"They're a gift from my uncle, who's a soldier, you know," he boasted.

"What does a soldier do?" Leo asked.

"He fights, and for that he gets a brand-new suit, new boots, and a rifle!"

"A rifle? What for? To kill birds?"

"No, people! And gets paid for it, too! I want to be a soldier, too, when I grow up," said Maso proudly.

"So you can kill people?"

"Maybe. What about you? Are you going to live with your mama for the rest of your life? Where's your father, by the way?"

"I don't have a father and I don't need one."

"Why? Are you like the chicks, growing up with your 'mother's care'?"

Leo swung around and punched him in the mouth. There was blood running from Maso's nose. By the time I got near the boys, Maso had smashed a group of huts, trampling them with his boot, and Leo had given him a hard push, making him fall over the wall. The boy got up and ran away.

"Leo, why did you do that?" I asked reproachfully. "You shouldn't treat your playmate like that. He was visiting with you."

"I didn't like the way he talked. He doesn't understand what I'm doing. He even made fun of my huts."

"My dear, you must be patient with the other children. Not everyone is able to do the things you do. That's why they don't understand. In any case, tomorrow you will apologize to him." He nodded sulkily.

Fortunately, the next day Maso had gone back to his parents' home. "I'm better off by myself, Caterina," said Nonnetta with a smirk, standing on her doorstep. "And you, Leo, won't have to apologize to anybody after all!" she declared, ruffling his curls.

When Leo was about five years old and taller than a boy of eight, I noticed that, while playing with his constructions, he stopped every now and then to whistle at a beautiful golden pheasant perched on a tall olive tree nearby. I was watching from my window one day when I heard a gunshot and saw the bird drop to the ground. I ran out of the house as the hunter was picking up his prey and Leo was running after him, yelling, "Why? Why did you kill him? He didn't do anything wrong! He was a nice pheasant! He was my friend!" Short, burly, and coarse, the hunter seemed taken aback by the boy's excessive reaction. I put my arms around Leo, who was still shaking.

"Please go away. This place is not a hunting ground. You could have hurt my little boy."

"Little boy? Huh! He's almost bigger than you! Hasn't he ever seen a bird shot before?" he snorted.

"The boy is only five, and you frightened him."

"Five? Maybe his brain is a five-year-old's! Have him hoe the soil so he'll grow up a little," he said, sneering. I picked up a shovel and went after him. He backed off, shouting, "This farm belongs to my friend, Ser Antonio. He'll have you and your stupid son thrown out of here!" he howled, stamping off like a wild animal.

"He … was my friend. He kept me company. He was … so nice," Leo kept saying between heavy sobs. My child, who never cried, who never complained, was really upset.

"Yes, my dear, I know. I'm sure another pheasant will come to keep you company—maybe his brother," I said, holding him tightly in my arms. During the following days, I watched him waiting quietly under that tree, while from a distance I prayed for another similar pheasant to come and perch on it. One morning, I rejoiced to see Leo go back to his construction to start a new hut, and after that, I never asked him again if another pheasant ever perched on that tree.

One day, while I was helping Giuseppe unload the food supplies that Rita sent us every week, he said that she had asked him to tell me she would come to see us in a couple of days.

"Why? Isn't she well?"

"No, she's all right now. She just felt a little poorly lately, but she was anxious to know how your little boy was doing these days."

"He's fine, thank you. Let me call him," I said, scanning the threshing floor. "Well, he was playing over there awhile."

"That's all right," said Giuseppe, getting ready to leave. "As long as I can tell her you are both well."

The moment he left, I nervously started searching for Leo, who was nowhere to be seen. When I saw the basket he used to carry clay from the brook for his figurines was missing, I guessed that he had gone there to fill it. I became worried that the slope was much too slippery for him due to the previous night's downpour, so I hurried down there as quickly as I could.

The waters had risen and were flowing fast. There was no sign of Leo, except his small basket floating near the bank. I called him several times, but the noise of the rushing water seemed to drown my voice. Thinking he could have been drawn to explore the foot of the cliff on the opposite side, I scrambled upstream along the bank. I was terrified to see him looking down from a high rock across the brook.

"Leo, what are you doing up there?" I screamed.

He gleefully pointed to the spring gushing out from the rock and cascading all the way down into the brook. "Mama, I found the place where the beautiful waterfall comes from!" he yelled in the same cheerful way he did every time he discovered something new.

"But, my dear, how are you going to get down from there? It's much too steep and slippery," I shouted, my heart pounding.

"Don't worry, Mama. I can make it, you'll see," he said,

edging along the wet ridge. His foot slipped, and he grabbed hold of a shrub. I watched in horror as his little body swung out high up over the torrent. "It's all right, Mama. I'm holding on."

I gathered up my skirt, tucking the hem inside my apron, and awkwardly waded across the overflowing brook. Once I was on the other side, I realized that I couldn't ask Leo to fall into my arms, as he was much higher than the roof of a house. So I looked for a way to get up the cliff, clutching at any twigs or branches within reach. As I got closer to my son I could see his hands were turning blue. "Mama, don't hurt yourself! I can hold on." As his voice rang out, it became obvious that the only way to get hold of him was from above. But the higher I reached, the stronger the wind blew. Step by step, grasping every crevice, I managed to crawl up to what appeared to be the most strategic spot. By now my hands were bleeding, but the sight of my son, still hanging in midair, was the only thought going through my mind.

In order to secure myself, I had to lie on my stomach and reach down over the shrub to get a grip on Leo's arms. The moment he clung to me, I felt as if I held heaven in my hands, and only God knows how I found the strength to hoist him up into my aching arms.

I hugged him and rubbed his little fingers, which were now red.

"Mama, your hands are all scratched! You hurt yourself because of me," he said, starting to sob.

"It's nothing, darling, as long as you're safe." I made him sit on my lap and, fully convinced there was no turning back, I looked around to see if there was another way to get home from there. But the face of the sloping cliff, impressive backdrop to our sweetly undulating valley, seen close up was just a rough and scrubby crag, topped with tall pine trees.

Leo had stopped sobbing, and, in order to cheer him up, I playfully said, "I wonder if by climbing over this cliff we might find our way home before it gets dark. You must be starved!"

Laughing, he jumped up, picked up two thick sticks and

gave one to me. "With these we can clear a path for ourselves," he declared, leading the way. Forcing our way through the shrubs and bushes to higher ground, we could not help stopping to catch an unusual view of our lovely valley. For the first time, we could actually look directly down into the brook. I started to get dizzy. Then, pulling me away, Leo said, "Look, Mama! What's that on the mountain over there?"

"Oh, how wonderful! It's the bell tower of Santa Lucia's Sanctuary! That's where you were baptized, Leo."

"What do you mean, baptized?" And so, for the rest of the way home, I satisfied his curiosity by explaining the meaning of this sacrament and describing what happened during his christening.

We were so exhausted when we entered the yard that we both dropped on the cobblestones. "I promise you, Mama, I'll never be as naughty as I was today. Never again," he said, embracing me. I got up on my knees and held him in my arms, trying to quell the shiver that ran through me as I remembered those frightful moments. Then, looking over his shoulder, I saw Rita's baskets of food still lying where I had left them, and I let out a nervous laugh for no reason at all. Leo glanced at me, a little puzzled. Later, while helping me carry the baskets inside the house, he suddenly said, imitating my voice, "We must make some nice cakes and bring them to Aunt Rita, don't you think?" He knows she can always find the right words to calm my anxieties, I thought. But he didn't know that through all those years, I had never shared with her my apprehensions about his strange precociousness, for I had felt it was my duty as his mother to deal with them by myself and maybe gain a better understanding of him.

During those years, I went through the strangest phase of my entire life. I watched my cooing, babbling baby Leo as he grew, becoming always more curious, keener, bent on understanding things about nature that had taken my attention, too —beauty that we had noticed together. He went ahead to find out the deeper reasons for why things looked and moved as they did when we noticed them together as we played and sat outside. It was like a dream we lived together, seeing things in ways I never did before. Leo seemed to become inspired by everything around us, and so was I, following him from one activity to the next, mainly because I was always concerned for his safety. I took part in his pursuits, encouraging him, not only to help him, but also because my feelings about nature, the things I had noticed and shown him, were part of me. I could not teach him whys and hows, but we excitedly shared his discoveries, and this helped me put aside my fears about his health and well-being.

5
SHATTERED ILLUSIONS

This lulling of my fears was upset by a worse fear, when after several years of absence, Ser Antonio appeared. He stood on the slope behind the threshing floor for a while, observing my son. I saw him from my window and slipped outside. I hid behind Big Madd's house to keep an eye on him.

"Leonardo, what are you doing?" he asked, approaching him.

"I'm building a hut with a new shape," he replied, hardly turning.

"What for?" he asked with interest.

"For the ants, so they won't have to sleep underground anymore."

"But they like to sleep underground," said Ser Antonio, amused.

"Maybe. But I want to see what they do with all the things they take with them." It was obvious that Leo didn't want to be distracted.

"Do you know who I am?" he asked, patting Leo's head.

"No. Why? Should I know who you are?" retorted Leo, ducking.

"I thought your mother had told you."

"No, she didn't," Leo said, scarcely interrupting his building to look up. Ser Antonio smiled to himself and headed toward the olive grove.

I leaned against the wall, and froze as, for a fleeting moment, I heard the remark Nonnetta had made the day of my baby's christening. "Did you see his eyes? They were green with envy." Then I rushed up to Leo and hugged him protectively.

"Mama, why are you scared? You're crying!"

"No, darling, the wind made my eyes tear. Let's go inside!"

"But, Mama, there's no wind, don't you see?"

"You're right! Well, my eyes don't hurt anymore now. You go on building your little huts, then," I said, trying to compose myself.

"Mama, do you know who that man was?"

"Yes, I know him. He's Ser Antonio, the owner of this place."

"Did *he* scare you? Is he very bad?"

"No, he's a very nice gentleman. I just didn't want him to disturb you while you were playing with your construction."

"I see. I'll finish the hut for the ants. Then I'll try to think of a way to make them go inside it," he said, stroking his chin like an adult. I giggled, and he laughed. Then, as he went back to play, I suggested we ought to go visit Aunt Rita the next day. He turned to give me a smile of approval. I knew he enjoyed walking up the narrow path between the tall shrubs that led to her house, stopping under the wild cherry trees, now in season, to admire the boughs laden with shiny red fruit.

To avoid another encounter with Ser Antonio the following day, we started early. Leo stayed on Rita's veranda to examine a butterfly and I, seeing her front door open, hastened to her bedroom. "What's happened to you, dear Rita? I've never seen you sitting in bed like this."

She promptly tried to distract me with a piece of embroidery she was working on, but noticing my concern, she said, "Oh, it's nothing. I just listened to my heart for a change. Lately, it's been begging me for a little rest. Maybe it feels the burden of my years! Where's my little wonder boy?" she asked eagerly.

"He's outside watching a butterfly. He'll be in soon. In the meantime, I must tell you about something that happened yesterday." She dropped her embroidery and grasped my cold hands. "I may be imagining things," I began, "but I shudder at the thought of what it may lead to." Then I told her about Ser Antonio's visit after such a long absence and about the preceding incident with the hunter.

"That idiot hunter must have told him what happened and aroused his curiosity regarding his forgotten grandson. He hasn't been well lately. Did you know? But don't worry. He wouldn't take the boy away from you like that. He's much too clever. So calm down, my dear."

"I've been hoping that his daughter-in-law would give him lots of grandchildren."

"She can't, unfortunately. I heard that the poor woman is not very strong and that a pregnancy would be fatal."

At that moment, Leo came in with a large butterfly on the back of his hand. "Look, Mama! Aunt Rita!" he exclaimed, ecstatic. "Look at this butterfly! See the beautiful colors of its wings?" It seemed odd that the delicate creature remained on his hand. "Even though its body is so tiny, it can still balance those huge wings. See how his legs cling? I'd better put it back on its flower now. It might get frightened of the dark. Butterflies love sunshine," he whispered, tiptoeing out of the room.

"So, do you really think you can keep such an intelligent boy tied to your apron strings forever?"

"My son will always stay with me. Always!" I cried.

"You can't let him grow up on this hill, cut off from the rest of the world. You'd better be prepared, my dear, because in one way or another, he'll have to leave you someday. The sooner you resign yourself to the fact, the easier it will be when the time comes. Remember," she said, squeezing my hand again, "your son will always be your son!"

Rita's words were not enough to subdue my persistent fears, however. Like a watchdog, I constantly kept an eye on Leo, terrified that Ser Antonio would suddenly reappear. Also, my heart pounded whenever Leo's attention was drawn to the slope or the entrance of the yard.

"Mama, will you help me?" he said one day, trying to build a tent under a tree with an old sheet I had given him. As I held a corner of the sheet for him, he asked, "Mama, why do you look so worried these days?" Not knowing what to say, I shrugged my shoulders. "All right, I think we both feel a little tired, so we'd better stop for today," he said, unconsciously imitating my voice.

"Good. I'll pack some nice food for a picnic, and we'll have it down by the *ruscello*. Would you like that?" I asked, trying to appear calm.

"Very much! You'll play and I'll sing!"

So I quickly got ready, and we set out. Holding my hand, Leo pulled me along as he hopped and sang:

"'Trit-trot, little horse, trit-trot! To new lands far away
Trit-trot, little horse, trit-trot! And never tire or stray
Trit-trot, little horse, trit-trot! As heroes every day
We'll run and play, we'll lose our way,
and then come home to stay!
Trit-trot! Trit-trot! Trit-trot, little horse, trit-trot!'"

"Oh, how nicely you sang my song! You learned it so fast! I'm proud of you! When you grow up, I'm going to get you a beautiful horse."

At the brook, I sat on a patch of grass and, overcome with gloom, I started setting out our picnic. Then, looking up, I saw Leo, arms raised, striking a comical dance pose. "Please, Mama, I'm waiting for your music!" I quickly took out my little flute and started to play his favorite tune. He danced and sang, making funny faces, which made me burst out laughing. All of a sudden, he stopped, came up to me and put his little finger under my chin. "You see, Mama! I made you laugh. You look so pretty that way!"

I recalled the numerous times when I had distracted him from his all too serious pursuits in the same playful way, so in a little girl's voice, I said, "Yes, and I feel so much better, too!"

*   *   *

It wasn't more than a few days, however, before I again felt something was stalking us. Leo had just finished fixing his tent when, from a short distance, I saw Ser Antonio sidle up to him. "Good day, Leonardo!" He greeted him with a familiar attitude. "What are you building today?"

"Good day, Ser Antonio," Leo replied, looking back to see if I was aware of the visitor's presence. "It's a tent for me to sleep in when it gets too hot."

Ser Antonio made no comment, as he had already seen that I was approaching them. "Good morning, Caterina! How are you? I have to talk to you," he said matter-of-factly.

I gathered all my strength. "What about, Ser Antonio?" I asked, trying to keep calm for Leo's sake. Ser Antonio walked toward the yard, and I followed him, noticing from the corner of my eye that Leo was watching us.

"I'm a little concerned about the boy," said Ser Antonio abruptly, as we reached the yard. "He should be going to some kind of school. He'll never have the opportunity for an education up here, don't you agree?"

"Why should you worry? He's *my* son and I'll take care of his education when I feel the time is right," I said, suppressing my anger.

"Yes, but he's also my grandson!" he hastened to add, his face reddening suddenly.

"I'd appreciate it if you didn't think so. Leo belongs to me, and I'll do what I have to do without your help."

He withdrew a little. "I thought I could take him to school myself. I could pick him up in the morning and bring him back to you at night." I gave him an angry look, and he put his hands out to pacify me. "Next to the Church of the Holy Spirit, there's a small school run by religious sisters who teach the Holy Scriptures and basic reading and writing to a select group of children."

"Why should I let you do that? He's *my* responsibility. I'm his mother. I'll find a way," I raved, heading back to the house.

"Caterina, wait! He's my flesh and blood, too. This is a reality you have to accept. Please, Caterina, let me take him to school. I promise I'll be good to him." He said, touching my arm to hold my attention.

I shook him off. "Never! I don't want anybody meddling in my life. I want to be left alone with my son. Besides, you seem to have forgotten about our agreement not to tell your son about Leonardo!"

"I can assure you, he knows nothing about him. He's in Florence now. I haven't told him, even though I know how much he misses having children."

"How do you expect him not to find out, if you take my son to school every day? Do you think I'm stupid? I may be a simple woman, but I'm certainly not stupid. And, now, please go! Go!" I cried.

Leo ran up to us. "Mama, why are you upset?" He turned to Ser Antonio. "Why do you upset my mother every time you come? I won't talk to you anymore!" Ser Antonio looked at me pleadingly.

"No, my darling, it's not him. It's me. I don't feel well. Let's go inside the house now," I said, taking him by the hand. Ser Antonio waited for a few moments and then left.

Feeling drained, I sat on the doorstep with Leo next to me.

"Mama, why did you shout at him? Did he say something bad?" he asked, looking into my eyes.

"No, he didn't. He wants to take you away from me, that's all."

"But I wouldn't go with him. I'd never leave you by yourself." He took my hand. "Mama, you're shaking. Are you really afraid I'll leave you? I'd never do that. Besides, I would never leave this place ... or our *ruscello!*"

"No, my dear, I must be sick. I feel feverish."

"What's feverish?"

"You feel pains all over your body, like the time you were sick."

"Then you should go to bed, and I'll put my hand on your forehead like you did to make me go to sleep and tomorrow you'll feel better! And we'll go and visit Aunt Rita. I know she loves you the same way you love me!"

I hugged him tightly, reflecting upon the maturity of his

remark, and went inside to lie down. He came to my bedside and placed his little hand on my forehead. Then he laid his head on my pillow and soon fell asleep. I got up to put him to bed, and as I sat next to him, the events of the last few days—Ser Antonio's proposal and Rita's words—ran wildly through my mind. I knew then that sooner or later I would have to give in to a painful change in our life. I spent that night crying and remembering the anguish I had felt the night Piero had abandoned me. He stole my love then and now he could steal my son's love, too, my only source of affection, and destroy my entire existence.

In the morning, with my eyes still swollen from crying and my spirits low, I prepared the dough for a cake and went to light the oven in the bakehouse. As always, Leo, his pretty face flushed with excitement, stood on a stool next to me, watching the flames in the oven.

"Look at those bright blues mingling with the orange reds. A pity that they only last a few moments, like all beautiful things in life," I whispered slightly resentfully. Leo clutched my shoulder and looked at me. "Look at the cakes I made for Aunt Rita. I made that small one to look like you, see?" I said to distract him. He giggled, but his attention was again captivated by the beauty of the fire. As soon as the flames died down, I closed the oven door and we waited for the charred wood to turn into embers, when the oven would be ready for baking. "As soon as I put the cakes in, you go and play," I said, hugging him. "I'll call you when they're ready and we can leave for Aunt Rita's."

Later, as I returned to the bakehouse and looked around for Leo my heart sank. From behind the same slope he had climbed when he first approached me, Piero emerged. Shock blurred my vision. I rubbed my eyes in disbelief, hoping it was somebody else; he looked different from the way I remembered him. He had lost the youthful looks and slender body that had served him well in my seduction. Overwhelming rage overtook my disbelief in seeing him spying on Leo from a distance. Sneaking up behind him, I took him by surprise. "What are you doing here?" I whispered harshly. "Your father didn't waste any time in breaking his promise, did he? Go away! I won't even allow you to look at my child."

He glowered at me and in a furious whisper snarled, "You had no right to hide my son from me. I could have you punished, and have the boy taken from you by force."

"With what authority? That of a rapist?" I railed, keeping my voice down. He was about to slap my face, but seeing Leo rush to my side, he hastily lowered his hand.

"Mama, who is he?"

"Nobody. He's a stranger, and I don't want him to bother you."

"But he wasn't bothering me. He stood there very quietly. Don't worry, Mama. You don't have to stay with us."

Humiliated, I glared at Piero, but he smiled arrogantly and, ignoring me, followed the boy as Leo returned to his constructions. "What are you doing, Leonardo?" I heard him ask the boy.

"I'm building an overpass—a smaller version of the one I'll make when I grow up. That one will be big and strong and will reach the other side of the valley, so it'll be easier for us to visit Aunt Rita."

"Ah, you mean a bridge. How are you going to build it?"

"With very thick, strong pieces of iron."

"That's a good idea! But in order to do that, you have to go to school first," he said, turning to me, "to learn how to read and write and also how to draw."

"But I already know how to draw. I drew Mama's face on a cloth, like my grandfather used to do." I was hearing about this for the first time.

"Which grandfather?" Piero asked.

"The one who had a little house on a hill far away. He died a long time ago, but when I grow up, we'll find it again and rebuild it," Leo replied resolutely.

"Would you like to have another grandfather?" Piero continued.

"Yes, but I don't have another one."

"Do you know Ser Antonio?"

"Yes, I know him," Leo said peevishly.

"He would like very much to be your grandfather!"

"Really? Why doesn't he ask me? Maybe he's afraid Mama will shout at him," Leo said with a chuckle.

"Do you know why she shouts at him?" Piero asked sedately.

"I don't know exactly, but I think it's because he wants to make me go away with him."

"Would you like to go with him?" probed Piero audaciously.

"No, not without Mama. I love her. Besides, he made her come down with a fever."

At this point, I couldn't listen anymore. I came forward and took Leo by the hand. "Come, Leo, it's mealtime." He hugged me and followed me without a backward glance, leaving Piero speechless as he watched us momentarily before making his retreat.

"Mama, that man told me that Ser Antonio wants to be my grandfather," Leo said, a little puzzled.

"And what did you say?" I asked, pretending not to have heard them.

"I said he should be the one to ask me. By the way, who is that man? Do you know him?"

"He's Ser Antonio's son."

"But he's much too old to be his son."

He's right, I thought. Ser Antonio was taller and sturdier, a man who never seemed to age. "By the way, Leo, why haven't you shown me the drawing you did of me?"

"It's not right yet. I'll show it to you when I can make you look as good as you really are," he said, darting ahead of me. "Oh, what a nice smell! I'm hungry! Are the cakes ready for Aunt Rita?"

"Yes, and we must hurry if we want to take them to her while they're still hot!" I said, trying to raise my fallen spirits.

It was a pleasant, sunny day. The air was fragrant with the scent of pine from the trees around the house. When I found Rita's door locked, I thought she had gone to town and wondered why she hadn't stopped by as usual to ask me if I needed anything. I decided that we would wait for her and opened the door with my key. Hearing a cry, I rushed to the bedroom where Rita was lying in bed, unable to speak, her hands pressed on her chest. "What happened, Rita, what happened?"

"I don't know. Maybe I took too much of that ... medicine," she whispered, relaxing her hands.

"I'll go and call somebody—a doctor ... Oh, Rita, it's all my fault! I've been worrying about my stupid problems, and here you were all alone."

"Please don't blame yourself," she said, breathing normally again. "I think it's my heart giving up, and if it's God's will, there's nothing you can do, my dear."

Leo pulled my skirt. "Mama, what's God's will?" he asked.

"I'll tell you later, darling. Go and play outside now. I have to look for Giuseppe," I said, guiding him to the door.

"No, my dear, don't leave me. If my time has come, I want you near me. You know there's no help here in these hills. We're all in the hands of the Lord." She looked into my eyes and smiled. "I'm glad you've become more mature and don't need my moral support anymore."

"That's not true, Rita! I need your advice more than ever! If only you knew what's been happening," I said, trying to control my agitation.

"My dear, I'm sure you'll make the right decision. In that drawer are the papers for this house. It will be yours, so you'll have a place of your own. It's a beautiful house, don't you think?" Her eyes shone and her face flushed, making her look much better.

"Look at you, Rita! You're getting better already," I said, straightening the bedcovers. "Calm yourself now! Later I may be able to tell you what happened today, so you can advise me."

"Oh, I think I know what's bothering you. Remember, my dear, your son will never forget you, no matter where he is, but you can't stop his future." She flung up her arms. "Oh, look! There's Fernando!" She pressed her hand on her heart and fell back on her pillow, the color fading fast from her cheeks.

"Rita, my dear, don't strain yourself," I said, touching her gently. But she was quite still. I shook her arm to bring her back to life, then realizing she had left me forever, I hugged her close to me. I felt utterly helpless and began to cry. Leo ran in, frightened, and I made him sit on my lap. "Listen, darling. Our Aunt Rita is dead."

"What do you mean, she's dead? I thought only old people died."

"Yes, but she has died and won't be with us anymore," I said, walking to the door with him. "Now, stay out here, darling. I have to get help."

"No, Mama, I'll stay with Aunt Rita in case she needs something."

"No, my dear, she doesn't need ... anything, anymore. Sit outside on the bench and wait for me. I'll be back soon." He obeyed without another word, and I ran down to the open road. I saw Giuseppe's cart coming up the hill and called out to him at the top of my voice.

He whipped his mule to a faster trot. "What's happened?" he asked. When I told him about Rita's death, he turned the cart around, saying, "Go back! Don't leave the boy alone in the house. By the way, Ser Antonio said he's coming to see you tomorrow."

"Tell him I don't want to see him anymore," I shouted, returning to the house. "Oh, my Rita, why did you have to leave me, too? Don't you see how hopeless I feel? Yet you left me ... just like my other mothers!"

I remembered how much more courage I had had when, still a child, I lost my parents. How sure I was of myself when I ventured out into the world. "So we don't become stronger as we grow up," I cried. "My body may be stronger, but my spirit is frail."

Not seeing Leo on the porch, I hurried into Rita's bedroom, where I was startled to see that he was sitting on her bed, gently trying to open her eyes. "Mama, why don't her eyes move anymore?" he asked after I pulled him away.

"Because poor Aunt Rita is dead."

"You haven't told me what dead really means and why people die."

"I have told you. It means that a person doesn't live anymore, doesn't talk or do anything anymore." He seemed to be waiting for a better explanation. "I don't know, darling, why people have to die. Now, please go outside. I have to tidy up Aunt Rita's bedclothes—get her ready for the priest."

Once I was alone I couldn't bring myself to do anything. So I sat and gazed at Rita's motionless body. She lay seemingly oblivious to the world she had left behind. As I glanced at her peaceful face, I ached, knowing that with her passing, my last protector had gone, and that now I, alone, was responsible for my precarious future, and that of my son.

"Mama, I hear a cart with a bell coming!" cried Leo, and I was overcome with embarrassment for neglecting to tidy up the room. Giuseppe came in and put his hand on my shoulder.

"Come outside, Caterina! The priest wants to talk with you," he said.

"You are dear Donna Rita's protégée, aren't you?" the priest asked as the sexton and his wife carried baskets of thick candles inside.

"Yes, she was like a mother to me," I said, holding in my sobs.

"Stay out here! They'll take care of everything. You see, Donna Rita left a donation to the Church of Santa Lucia for her funeral. Did you see the lovely candles we brought?"

"Then she knew she was dying?"

"Well, she didn't know when, but she wanted to be ready. She asked to be buried in the church cemetery. It's very small, so we can't have many burials there now, but she especially asked for this privilege."

At dawn, I got up from my chair and went to open the windows to let in the soft scent of the pines Rita loved so much and to dispel the sweet, waxy smell of the candles. Then I stepped out on the porch where Leo had been sleeping, bundled up in a blanket on the wooden bench. "Mama, did Aunt Rita wake up?" he asked, still drowsy. I held him tightly in my arms. Not even a child could accept her premature death.

Sitting on Giuseppe's cart, we followed the sexton's cart, which served as a hearse. One of Rita's best blankets covered her coffin, around which we placed some flowers from the vases on her veranda. On top of the blanket was the small bunch of wildflowers Leo had gathered in the fields. On the way up to the cemetery, sitting on my knees, Leo kept turning his observant glance from me to the hearse and back to me. From time to time, I felt his cool little hand gently drying my tears.

I spent the following days withdrawn into myself. Leo, too, seemed to be far away in his thoughts, taking long walks around the grounds, not going near his constructions. One morning, though, I decided to visit Nonnetta, whose chirpy vitality, I knew, would cheer me up.

Having crossed the olive grove in childlike anticipation, I was sadly disappointed to see her door still closed and the flowering plants around the walls of her cottage completely overtaken by weeds. As I stripped the flower beds of the unsightly weeds, doing my best to revive her plants with water I got from the well, I gradually felt more sadness come over me, for I knew in my heart that her long absence meant only bad news.

I went back home, utterly dejected, and sat down to rest on the low wall of the threshing floor. A shiver ran through me as I looked over my shoulder and saw Leo, expectantly watching the same slope from which the da Vincis had each appeared. Although I was thankful that neither of them had called on us, I knew that Ser Antonio, at least, was only giving me a little time to recover from the loss of Rita before resuming his line of attack.

When Leo came over and straddled the low wall next to me, I leaned over to give him a hug, not daring to ask him what he had been looking at. Instead, I suggested he should think of a game for us to play, and his eyes lit up. My plan to distract him was just beginning to lift my spirits, too, when alas! I was about to be subjected again to Ser Antonio's art of persuasion.

This time he had entered the courtyard, driving a bright new gig, dressed in what might have been his official attire. My eyes nearly popped out of my head as he pompously alighted, showing off the folds of his sleeveless dark-silk *lucco* worn over an embossed brocade doublet, the sleeves of which sparkled as they caught the sunlight. After carefully examining his outfit, my eyes were all but hypnotized by his tall, shiny hat, which seemed much too frivolous for someone like him, and I smothered a giggle with my hand. But, suspecting the old man's motive, I asked myself if he showed up dressed that way in order to assert his social position, or to impress Leo.

"How are you, Caterina?" he asked, strutting toward me with hands outstretched. I just stared at him coldly. He quickly turned his attention to Leo, who rushed to my side like a faithful watchdog.

My heart froze, though, when Leo said brightly, "Ser Antonio, why didn't you come back?"

Ser Antonio smiled. "I've been very busy. How are you, Leonardo?"

"Fine, thank you, sir. Is it true you want to be my grandfather?"

"Why? Would you like that?" he asked him, his eyes glinting at me.

"Yes, I would. But only if you promise not to upset Mama anymore." I felt as if I were falling into an abyss.

"I promise. But if I become your grandfather, you'll have to go to school." Then, completely ignoring my presence, he continued, "You can learn many things in school: how to read and write, and also how to draw. You'll be with other children, and you'll live in my house next to the school during the week."

"Oh, I'd like that!" Leo said, looking at me. "But I don't want to leave my mother alone. Can she come and stay in your house, too?"

I took his hand. "No, darling, there wouldn't be enough room, and I'm too busy here." But before I knew it, I heard myself say, "Leo, if you promise to come back home to me every afternoon, I'll let you go to school, but only to school," I added, glaring at Ser Antonio, whose eyes gleamed in triumph.

"Yes, Mama, I promise. I'll only go to school."

"Now, darling, go and cover your constructions. It's going to rain soon. I have to talk to Ser Antonio," I said, trying to appear calm. Leo walked away slowly, turning a few times to look back at us. I swung around, already regretting what I had said. "This is a trick to take my child away from me, isn't it?" I snapped at Ser Antonio.

"No, I promise you I'll bring him back every week."

"So, from every day, it's become every week, has it? You've betrayed me already by informing your son. How can I trust you now? I know that little by little you and your insolent son will take him away from me."

"I assure you we'll treat him well, better than you think."

"I prefer to wait. I'll find a way. I'll move to the village and take him to school myself."

"But to put him in a school, he must have a family name, a father who is recognized in the town hall. If you take him, he will be treated no better than a foundling."

"A foundling?" I cried, shocked by the implication. "A foundling? How dare you say that! I may have been a foundling, because I was taken from my real parents, but he has his real mother who cares for him, who loves him with all her heart, who would give her life for him. Doesn't that count for anything?" Ser Antonio just stared at me, aghast. I felt a sudden pain in my head. "Please go. Tomorrow we'll move to Rita's house, where you can't bother us anymore. Now, please go. Go!" I shouted.

Leo came running back and took my shaking hand. I pulled him toward the house while he kept scowling at Ser Antonio. We went inside, and I slammed the door. "Let's wait here until he leaves," I said.

6
THE SEPARATION

Next morning, under a blue sky, we silently climbed down the path leading to the brook. I laid out the usual picnic on the tablecloth and sliced a fresh loaf of bread. Leo knew that we were moving to Rita's house. Having taken off his shoes and turned up the cuffs of his pants, he started crossing the brook toward the springs flowing from the rocks. I didn't dare call him, as I realized he was saying good-bye to our haven. There wasn't the usual thrill in his expression while passing his hands under the gushing water, and I felt guilty for not trying to compromise with Ser Antonio. But how could I trust them? The da Vincis were much too conniving for me. I knew that they could easily trick me into letting them take my son away from me forever! Then the words I had spoken to Ser Antonio rang in my ears. Could I have been lying when I said I would give my life for my son, if I couldn't even accept being separated from him while he went to school?

Examining my situation, I came to the conclusion that I must have been out of my mind to imagine I could afford Leo an adequate education. Not only did I lack any social status, but also the financial means for even the bare necessities of life. As long as Rita was alive, she provided us with flour, olive oil, and dairy foods. Now we were left with only the produce of my kitchen garden and the preserves I made from the few fruit-bearing trees of our valley.

I hid my face in shame, realizing that I was forcing my son to live in poverty with me and waste his God-given gifts in these hills. As tears filled my eyes, I felt Leo's hand touching my forehead. "Mama, do you feel sick again?"

"No, my dear, I'm all right, just tired," I said, straightening up.

"Mama, why didn't you believe me when I said I'd come back?" I was unable to speak. "You see, Mama, I could never leave you or our lovely *ruscello* forever. I belong here, too. This is our home!" He said, looking into my glistening eyes. "Oh, Mama, don't cry! Look, I brought your flute." He took it out of his pocket and gave it to me. "Please play it! I'll sing and dance and make you laugh again!" he exclaimed, clownishly poised.

Suddenly won over by his heartwarming smile, I cleared my throat and resolutely said, "All right, then. I promise you, Leo, that we'll never leave this place. Yes, you're right. This is our home! And here I'll stay and wait for you forever!"

"'Trit-trot, little horse …,'" he sang, "Please, Mama, play!"

And our musical *momento* began.

Next morning, Leo seemed very restless as he came running whenever there was a sound of wheels from the road. This time, the awaited visitor had provided himself with a reinforcement, for he made his appearance in the company of a woman. Leo ran to meet them, but seeing me come outside, he drew back and, holding a pleat in my skirt, stood by my side.

We both stared at the lady sitting on the gig next to Ser Antonio and waited for them to get off. She advanced slowly in her fine, yet somber, outfit, followed by Ser Antonio. Her lined face was bordered by a dark, draped veil. "Good morning, Caterina," she said, forcing a meek smile. "I'm Donna Lucia, Ser Antonio's consort."

I only nodded. Ser Antonio came forward and stood next to her.

"The reason I came to visit you," she said, glancing at Leo, "is to see the little boy. They told me how tall and beautiful he was, but I see that he's much more than that...." She hesitated, perhaps intimidated by my silence. Ser Antonio touched her shoulder encouragingly. "I ... I want you to know that we all want to give the boy a good education, my husband, myself and ... and my ... son." After having said that last word, she sighed with relief. "My dear Caterina," she went on, "you're a fortunate woman to have been blessed with the gift of such a wonderful child. God has willed that my daughter-in-law is to be a barren woman. She cries all day!"

"And now she wants my son, eh?" I burst out.

She started. "No, it's not true. She doesn't know about the boy yet. About .... *your* boy! We're here to help you—in any way we can—to give your son the education he needs. I promise that my husband will bring him back here to you at the end of every week and whenever the school is closed. I promise!" she said, before taking a deep breath.

"Only once a week?" I cried in anguish, knowing that there was no escape from that predicament.

Leo pulled my skirt, and I looked down at him. "Mama, I promise you I'll be back every day! Ser Antonio will bring me back every day. You will, won't you?" He said, turning to him.

"Oh, how beautifully he speaks! What a pretty voice!" Donna Lucia exclaimed, diverting attention from her triumph.

"All right, then," I murmured faintly. Before I knew it, Leo had dashed to our visitors, who bent over to kiss him on the head.

"We'll take him with us now—just to see the house," she tested.

"I'll bring him back tomorrow," added Ser Antonio, reassuringly, "and he can tell you if he wants to sleep there sometimes."

"What? Right now? And spend the night there?" I shouted, alarmed.

"Yes, Mama, let me go! I want to see their house. I want to ride in that lovely coach!" he cried, running toward it. He put his hand on the horse's leg. The horse shook his mane wildly, and I jumped with fear for the boy's safety, but Leo shrieked with joy, and the others laughed.

Then Donna Lucia surprised me by putting her hand on my arm and whispering in my ear, "Don't worry, Caterina, he'll never leave you. The mother ... is always ... the mother!" As she spoke I saw sincere compassion in her eyes, and I was touched.

So I went inside and took the small cape Rita had made for Leo, put it around his shoulders, and hugged him tightly. So great was his excitement and impatience to jump on the gig that he forgot to hug me back! They placed him between them, and with false smiles, they waved good-bye. Unable to move, I watched the noisy gig disappear into the main road, taking my most valuable possession farther and farther out of my reach. I stood unmoving for what seemed an eternity, feeling as if my body had become part of the cobblestones under my feet, until all was silent.

That night, I spent hours sitting by my little son's bed. In my eternal memory, I still hear myself singing his favorite lullaby, a heartbreaking lament from my very soul, striving to reach a distant place where it mingled with children's silvery voices until it finally met with my little Leo's bursts of laughter in my dreams.

The gentle whistle of my nightingale made me realize that it was daybreak. I stood up and ran outside to Leo's unfinished constructions, which I had forgotten to cover for the night. The little huts were still moist from the night dew, so I dried them one by one with a piece of cloth.

It was almost nightfall when, with fear in my heart, I stood on the slope, watching the sun set on the town below and listening for the sound of Ser Antonio's gig, but the silence was deafening on the deserted roads. Even the countryfolk were all safely in their homes as the sky behind Mont'Albano grew darker and darker. Dreading the idea of spending another night like the previous one, I wandered to the back of the tavern from where I could see any approaching vehicles and lay down on the grass.

Soon the dampness permeating my tired body became unbearable. It was strangely like the pain in my heart, deep and relentless. In my extreme despair, I raised my arms and implored the Almighty Father to quiet my torment and to give me the strength I needed to face this unhappy plight. Suddenly, a gleam reached up from the pink embers of the sunset below, pouring forth warmth on my being. It lasted only an instant, but it was enough to replenish my lost energy. A few drops of rain fell on my face. I got up, ran to Leo's constructions, and lovingly spread a heavy sheet over them. Then I dragged myself to my room, fell on my bed, and slept until dawn.

That new day became a day of jubilation, for my son came home! He came into sight from around the corner, wearing a brand-new, cherry-red velvet suit, and threw himself into my arms. As I held him, I thought that this moment was worth all the pain I had suffered.

"Mama! Mama! I'm back!" I heard his voice ringing in my ears. "The school is nice. I like the children. We're learning how to write words, too," he added with excitement.

"I hope you don't get into fights," I said, looking sternly at him.

He laughed. "No, Mama. They're nicer than Maso. But when they can't learn something, I feel like hitting them on the head, too." I gave him a disapproving look. "But I have to be patient, I know," he said, smiling.

"Did you like your grandfather's house?" I asked much too anxiously.

"Yes, and I like Donna Albiera, too. She's a nice lady and—"

"Who's Donna Albiera?" I interrupted, without thinking.

"She's the wife of the other gentleman who came to see me, remember?"

I tried hard to keep my expression unperturbed as I glanced around to see who had brought him. I relaxed when I saw no one else except Ser Antonio, who was already taking his horse to the nearest field. Meanwhile, Leo slipped away from my arms and ran to his huts. I gazed at him, enthralled by his straight little figure in the magnificent suit. Yet my thought went back to the other woman who was having the pleasure of taking care of my son, and my heart ached.

Ser Antonio's voice behind me broke my train of thought abruptly, as he said, "I'm sorry, Caterina. I had to keep the boy at the school for a couple of days to see how he liked it. As you can see, he is very enthusiastic."

"Well, I'm not surprised," I retorted, "with his intelligence and his eagerness to know more about things. But you could have sent me a message of some kind," I added reproachfully as he looked away. "How long can I keep him? You can see that Leo is still attached to his home."

"Until tomorrow night. On Monday, he has to be back at the parish school, at which time I must give them his family name ... in order to have him fully accepted there," he said in a firm but mellow tone.

"Give him mine!" I said absently.

"Which one? Of which father, I should say!" he corrected sarcastically.

I wanted to rail at him, but realized that, in fact, I had never known either of their names. My stepfather had never used his real name since the elopement, and I could hardly avail myself of the nickname, Venturiano, which he had obviously made up. I felt so humiliated by the tenuous position in which the da Vincis had placed me that I burst out, saying, "I suppose your son is part of this plan. Why doesn't he ask me these things himself? He uses you, because he doesn't have the courage to face me himself!"

"Exactly. He's afraid that you will throw him out."

"I know, I know. I'd rather not see him. Seeing him makes me angrier."

"Besides," he continued, "he's unhappy enough about the situation."

"Is he? What about me? Am I happy?" I exploded.

"You're right, Caterina! But, stay calm! ... For Leo's sake. We have to talk about his future—your little boy's future. I'm sure that it's in your interest, too."

"All right, we'll talk about it ... tomorrow," I said, realizing not only that what he was saying made sense, but also that, after all, he, too, loved my child. Somewhat relieved, he went over to Leo, who was bending over his constructions. Yet, as I watched him stroke Leo's blond curls and overheard him talk about the school, I felt hopelessly cut out; more so later, when I noticed Leo fondly waving good-bye to him.

Once we were alone, I led Leo by the hand to the low wall, and put him on my lap. "Leo," I said, steeling myself, "I know you like the school, the children, and your grandfather, but do you really want to live with ... those people?" He peered at me, trying to guess what was upsetting me.

"Yes, I do, Mama, mainly because they let me go to school. But if it makes you sad, I'll stay here with you. I don't want you to cry for me."

"No, my darling, I promise I won't cry," I said shamefacedly. Then, changing the subject, I said, "Now, let's go down to the brook and there you can tell me all about the school and the children!" He smiled and skipped alongside me as he had done so many times before.

On that fall afternoon, the low, golden rays of the sun sparkled brightly on the bronze leaves as the breeze blew them gently onto the crystalline water. We joyfully watched them float on the ripples, and running along the bank, we followed their course, shouting and laughing.

The sun shone again the following morning, but as the afternoon drew on, the sky turned gray, matching the sadness in my heart. A chilly gust of wind blew on us as we waited for Ser Antonio. I sat on the doorstep with Leo on my knees wrapped in his velvet cape, cuddling and kissing him so he would always remember my great love for him.

At the rattle of wheels, I started. Leo jumped up and ran to meet Ser Antonio, who turned his gig around, without getting off, and waited for him. Leo kept saying, "Don't cry, Mama. I promise you I'll be back!"

All the time, while he helped the boy get on, Ser Antonio stared at me questioningly. I was much too devastated to think clearly and didn't understand what he was waiting for me to say. "Caterina, have you decided?" he finally asked. On seeing my confusion, he cried, "About the name, Caterina, the name! I must know now! It's important for the school." I really hadn't given it another thought and suddenly felt like screaming, but I just nodded yes to him, for I felt Leo's attentive eyes on me.

"Good for you, Caterina," he said, cracking his whip. "Next week I'll have the papers ready." And beaming with satisfaction, he drove away with my son.

"What papers ... ?" I cried, but the gig had turned down the road.

At that moment, Nonnetta's prophetic words came back into my mind once more. Thinking of her and how wonderful it would be to have her shoulder to cry on, I went to her house again, but with little hope. Maso was there, violently uprooting the plants around the dilapidated walls. "Where's Nonnetta?" I asked in dismay.

"She's gone to heaven," he said, without looking up. "We're going to live here now." Then, leaning on his rake, he asked brightly, "Is Leo around? I'm lighting a bonfire tonight!"

"No, he's away ... at school," I replied, sadly moving away.

"At school? You must miss him," he said unexpectedly.

"Yes, I do, and I will miss Nonnetta, too. She was a good friend. Oh, God! I can't believe I've lost her, too!" I said, covering my face. He shrugged his shoulders and went back to work.

As I could not face my solitary room that night, I sat on my doorstep with my head on my knees and cried myself to sleep.

The smell of something burning roused me from my torpor. The light of the few visible stars had been blurred by clouds of smoke rising into the sky from Maso's bonfire. "Oh, my dear Nonnetta," I cried out, "those are your plants burning! May their flames burn in honor of your soul, my friend!" Nonnetta's family, I found out later, never came to live up there, and so her house began to fall apart.

My thoughts went to my dear Rita's house, which I had neglected, even forgetting about her plants needing water. Making up my mind to devote the next day to working in her house gave me the resolve to go straight to bed and, therefore, to get a good night's rest.

The high hills were still under a veil of fog as I made my sad ascent toward the lonely abode of my dear friend, who lavished her generosity upon me even from her grave. I opened the door and went straight to the windows to open them wide and let the mountain air dispel the lingering scent of the funeral candles. The sun had caused the mists to evaporate, so I stripped the bed linens, took the mattress outside, and laid everything out on the field. I trimmed and watered the withered plants with cool water from the well, praying out loud for them to grow back, at least for the new season.

Then, after scrubbing and polishing the furniture and all of Rita's pretty ornaments, I finally sat outside on the porch bench in the mild afternoon air and reminisced.

As dear Rita's image appeared in my mind, I was prompted to converse with her, telling her everything about my hopeless situation. I envisaged her sitting in bed during my last hour with her and suddenly remembered her pointing to the chest of drawers. I rushed inside her bedroom and looked at the pretty chest I had just polished. I touched its golden handles, but I didn't have the heart to open it. Finally, I timidly pulled open the top drawer and saw a card with the words "For My Lisa" placed on a gold-painted, carved wooden box. I stepped back, recognizing my real name. Then, opening the box, I saw a roll of papers on top, neatly tied with a delicate ribbon. I knew those were the papers for the house Rita had mentioned, but since I couldn't read them, I put them aside. On a package underneath lay another card saying, "For My Leo." As I carefully opened its pretty cloth wrapping, I marveled at the sight of the most beautiful tiny colored porcelain dolls and figurines of strange animals I had ever seen. I thought how thrilled Leo would be to have them, particularly as lately he had been making clay dolls to populate his village of huts. At the back of the wooden box, Rita had hidden a small leather purse. As I emptied its contents, my hand was filled with small, shiny gold coins stamped with a pretty lily. I had no idea of their value, but slipping them back into the bag, I knew they would be of great help to me. My eyes were then attracted to a purple silk bag on which lay another note saying, "For Lisa from her father." My heart leaped to my throat. Inside the bag, wrapped in a fine handkerchief similar to the one in my baby linens, was a very small painting of a slender figure of a lady standing next to a round fountain with the statue of an angel pouring water into it. She had one hand resting on the tip of the grand basin while with the other she gracefully held a large white hat, her lovely blond hair, swept gently around her face, enhancing her delicate features. In the corner of the painting, there was a name written, part of which seemed to have been scorched by fire. I gazed at the lovely figure for a long time, certain that it was the image of my mother, my unfortunate mother! Through my tear-filled eyes, I saw a silver medal that had fallen out from the same wrapping. On one side was engraved the beautiful profile I recognized as my mother's, and on the other side a heart on which lay a delicate flower. I had no doubt that both those works of art had been made by my father. I stared at them, trying to imagine how my parents might have felt being so much in love with each other. I knew that theirs had been true love! Abandoning myself to my emotional reverie, I was suddenly swept up in the sensuality of their passion, vicariously savoring the thrill of it.

Still glowing from what seemed to be more than just a daydream of my parents' love, I strode lightheartedly down the lane with Rita's precious box of gifts tucked under my cape. The cool breeze blew on my face, sweeping back my hair I had let fall loose on my shoulders the way my mother had in her picture. Realizing that Leo was also part of my parents' love, I cried out into the wind, "Oh, Father, my beloved Father! Please be part of this world so I may find you, so you may rescue our Leo from the clutches of those strangers, for Leo belongs only to us! Yes, only to us!"

I stopped as I heard the rumbling of a cart, mingled with

Giuseppe's familiar grumbling at his mule. He smiled when he saw me. "Caterina, you look very happy! Your cheeks are as red as an apple! The mountain air must be good for you!"

"I've been cleaning dear Rita's house."

"You should go and live in her beautiful house, instead of that old building. By the way, I left some food for you from Ser Antonio."

"Why, after all this time? Tomorrow take it back and tell him I don't need his charity anymore. There's still plenty of food in Rita's pantry I'd like you to bring me when you have time." An idea suddenly crossed my mind. "Giuseppe, do you ever go to Florence?" I asked.

"Are you joking?" he scoffed. "With my old mule? Why do you ask?"

"I'd like to go there sometime."

"Well, the chestnut vendor from Santa Lucia goes there often. If you like, I can mention it to him."

"Oh, thank you, Giuseppe. I wouldn't mind traveling with chestnuts."

"I'll take care of it. It's getting late now. Go home, before anyone sees you looking so ... so *good!*" I laughed and rushed home in high spirits.

So one chilly dawn, wrapped in a heavy blanket, with one of Rita's gold coins in my pocket, I ventured off to Florence on the chestnut cart. My hands clutched a hot terra-cotta bottle wrapped in woolen rags.

I held my breath as we went through the sleeping town of Vinci. My eyes searched eagerly among the buildings, wondering which one could be the house where my son lived, as I visualized the bedroom in which he slept. But soon we were out in the flat, open countryside. I gazed in wonder at the well-kept fields covered with rich crops. The result of dedicated labor, I thought. The country workers, carrying their hoes, started to gather in the fields. I noticed, though, that the group consisted only of old people, women, and children.

We passed by a wide brook, and I wondered if its deep waters came from the tireless springs in my valley.

"Caterina!" called the old cartman. "Are you all right back there?"

I looked over my shoulder and, seeing only his crumpled wide-brimmed hat, cried, "I'm fine, good man. The chestnuts smell nice!"

"My name is Nicola," he said assertively. "We have to stop soon. I have to deliver a sack of chestnuts in the next village."

When we reached the village square, the cart stopped near some horses drinking from the fountain. Nicola got off and came around to the back of the cart. His body was straight and sturdy, and only his wrinkled face under his old hat gave evidence of his age. "Make sure nobody sees you," he warned. "Hide behind those sacks. The village is full of young men just escaped from the *condotta*. Because of them, women here have to stay shut indoors—" His voice stopped as he pulled a heavy sack on his back. Though taking him lightly at first, I immediately dropped out of sight as some street roughs ambled by toward a notice that a youth was attaching to a nearby wall. He read it aloud in a monotone, pointing at each word, but before he finished, his public lost interest and drifted away, leaving him gaping over his shoulder with his finger still hovering on the placard.

From my hiding place, I saw Nicola on his way back exchanging words with the youth and asked him about the notice. "It's nothing—just a call from a *gonfaloniere* looking for soldiers. But men are tired of wars. They want to be left in peace to till the soil and take care of their families," he grumbled.

"What's the name of that *gonfaloniere*?"

"I didn't pay any attention. Who cares, anyway? They're all the same." He went on, still grumbling. "They want peasants to fight their battles, that's all. They say we have to protect our land. Bastards! Protect it, yes, but from *them!*" He cracked his whip in the air, and we jerked forward.

Back on the road, I settled down to enjoy the steady rhythm of the horse's trot. The afternoon sun had warmed the chestnuts, releasing their pungent fragrance. I stood up for a moment to see where we were and was confronted by the splendid view of a city on the distant horizon, its golden domes glimmering in the sun like a vision from a fairy tale.

"Nicola, what's that beautiful place?"

"That's 'la bella Fiorenza'—the largest city in the world!" he announced proudly. "But be patient! I have to make another delivery first," he added. We were, in fact, entering a nearby valley, and soon the lovely view disappeared behind the tall trees of the woodlands. I was just recovering from my disappointment when, through the trees on our right, I glimpsed a black tower and the ruins of a castle.

"Nicola, does anyone live there?" I asked, intrigued by its macabre appearance.

"I don't know—nobody, I think. They say it's haunted by the people who died there in a raging fire. They all died—masters and servants!"

We skirted the old walls of the estate, and as we reached the iron gate, I saw a dim light in the tower window and stood up. "Nicola, could I get off here? I want to take a look."

"Are you crazy? There's nobody there, except maybe ghosts!"

"But there's a light in the tower."

"They must have lit it," he said, flustered, but then he slowed down.

I jumped off. "Look! It's an oil lamp. I think this is the place where Donna Rita used to work. I must look inside," I insisted.

"Well, all right, then," he said, wearily. "Mind you, if you're not out here when I return, I'm not coming after you! I'll go to Florence without you and leave you to the ghosts!"

I just nodded, without even taking my eyes off the tower window. Yet I hesitated in front of the gate, held ajar by a heavy stone, its rusty bars overgrown with twining creepers. As I plucked up my courage and slipped through the narrow opening I was alerted by the steady barking of a dog. Black as coal, it leaped out from behind a bush, slowly advancing toward me. I was afraid to move, but to my amazement, the large creature stopped in front of me and wagged its tail. Thinking it would be a good idea to show my appreciation, I daringly touched its back. Flattered, it lay down at my feet, gazing up at me with sad eyes. "Who lives here?" I asked just to hear the sound of my own voice. As if it had understood my question, the dog got up and walked ahead of me down the wide alley leading to the entrance of the tall, dark tower. The rest of the building seemed like a pile of debris overgrown with unsightly forest shrubs and thick, contorted trees.

Half-hidden by wild bushes was the old fountain I had seen in my mother's miniature painting. The graceful jets of water had gone, though, and ugly, greenish-black streaks defaced the round marble basin and the dainty statue standing in the middle of it. I paused to admire it for a moment, trying to imagine the way it had been when my mother had posed next to it for my dear father, and hoped that the same fate that had brought me here today would also lead me to him.

The dog stopped and invitingly turned its head toward me. I followed it to a large door patched up with boards and hesitated while the dog kept brushing against me as if egging me on. I knocked gingerly.

"Who's there?" came the question in a deep voice, followed by the clatter of heavy footsteps coming from the upper floor. "Wait! Wait! I'm coming!" the hoarse voice kept shouting.

I waited quietly until I heard the latch being lifted. "I'm passing by—I need shelter," I said in a shaky voice.

A hunchback opened the door. Disheveled white hair and a long white beard covered his face except for his large hooked nose and piercing eyes. He held the door open with both hands as if holding it up and, staring at me suspiciously, asked, "Where are you from? And what are you doing here?"

"*Messere,* can I wait inside until morning?" I began, almost stammering. "I was going to Florence, but the cartman had to go somewhere else first, so he left me here. He may be returning later, though to ... look for me," I added to cover myself.

"Well, make up your mind about what you want to do. I

live here alone. If you aren't afraid of me, you can come in," he said, opening the door wider. I bravely stepped inside. He closed the door behind me and, in an overly chivalrous way, ushered me through a dark hallway. On seeing that he had a bad limp, I backed up, frightened, as Rita's vivid description of the mysterious man crouching next to my dying mother flashed through my mind. But my burning curiosity eclipsed any mounting fears, quickening my step as he showed me into a big, shabby kitchen at the back of the building.

The fireplace was almost as wide as the wall before us. He motioned me to sit on a long bench at the table and limped over to the fireplace. Somehow his manners compensated for his awkward gait and terrifying countenance. Although his silk *lucco* was badly soiled and the gold-embroidered sleeves of his doublet had long lost their glitter, they still lent a certain dignity to his appearance.

"I'll warm up some milk for you. I have two goats, you know," he said, hanging a milk churn in the fireplace. "I see you're trembling with cold." I was trembling all right, but only with apprehension of what I might find out from him. "Up there in the tower," he went on as he lit the fire, "there's a spare bed in the chambermaid's room next to the old mistress's room where I sleep. You can sleep there if you like."

"No, thank you. I'll just rest my head on the table ... in case ... the cartman comes for me," I explained, peeved at having to miss the opportunity of seeing the rooms.

He suddenly turned and stared at me suspiciously again. "Where do you come from? And why were you going to Florence?"

"I just wanted to see the great city. I come from the hills of Anchiano, on Mount'Albano," I answered, trying to justify myself.

He went over to the sideboard, took some buns out of a large glass jar, and put them on a porcelain plate, which bore the same pattern I had seen on some of Rita's dishes. "These are sweet buns—you'll like them. I made them myself," he said, setting the plate before me. A hint of a smile twisted his misshapen lips as he poured the hot milk into a white china cup and served it to me. I drank it slowly and nibbled on a bun, showing approval.

He limped to the opposite bench, sat down, his hand pulling his bad leg under the table, and gave me a stern look. "Now, my girl, tell me the truth! You're looking for your lover, aren't you? Did you expect to find him here? Don't you know that all the young men in this county have been recruited by the damned *condotta?*"

"No, I'm not looking for anyone. I'm married and I have a little boy!" I said proudly. "Why do you live all alone in this dilapidated place?" I asked, changing the subject. "Is this your house?"

"No, it's not my house. I left my home and came to live here to ... to atone myself, to expiate a sin." I looked at him questioningly. "To ... punish myself for ... for something awful I did ... for a crime!" he said, his eyes flashing.

"A crime? What crime? What sin?" I persisted.

"Why are you so inquisitive?" he said, giving me a sidelong glance. "I was just talking to myself."

"But if you speak about sin and crime, you have to explain more about it. Don't you think so, sir?" I rebutted, daring to reason with him.

Then, reaching across the table, he picked up a black leather-bound notebook and held it in front of him with both hands like a screen. After a long pause, he spoke again. "Yes, I chose to live in this godforsaken place to wait for the end."

"What end? And who were the owners of this house?"

"Who are you, anyway? You speak so well. Why are you questioning me? You remind me of someone I used to know," he said, scanning my face.

"I'm no one important. It's just that I find your story so interesting!"

"I don't remember the owners' name. I've forgotten it. Maybe I wanted to forget it after what happened. What was the use? They all perished in the fire!" he said, with an odd laugh. "The fire that I caused myself!" he cried, showing the white around his blazing pupils.

"Why did you do that? What made you do it?" I asked,

unable to stop the tremble in my voice as I pictured Rita's account of the fire.

He stared at me more intensely. So to distract him, I reached for another bun. "But you haven't really told me who you are. There's something familiar about you. You don't behave like those people in the hills. You look too ... too intelligent."

"Thank you, *messere*. I believe intelligence isn't something we can acquire. We're born with it. It's a gift of God!" I said, thinking of Leo.

"You're right, my girl. What I meant ... was ..." He stopped and covered his face with both hands. "Oh, the anguish! The despair!" he went on as if to himself. "I wanted to help her. Instead, I caused her death. What a fool I was to let such a mighty passion take hold of me!" He raised his long, thin fingers, then closed them tightly as if trying to take back the wrong he had committed and erase it. Then, glancing into space as if searching for a reason to justify or diminish his deed, he said in a softer voice, "How thrilling it was to just immerse myself in my all-consuming desire for her. She was so beautiful! So angelic! Yet so far out of my reach ...! I wrote poems for her, which she returned to me. And I passionately kissed the paper she had held in her hand. I often waited for her on her father's grounds, hiding behind a tree so I could watch her taking her morning ride. One day, I had brought her a special bunch of flowers selected lovingly from my conservatory. As she appeared, my heart missed a beat. Her windswept hair seemed spun of gold as it shone under the morning sunlight. No artist ever painted a face of such beauty! I went forward and offered her the flowers. Pulling up her horse, she gently took them from me, brought them to her lips, and smiled at me. I was in heaven!" he sighed ecstatically. But his expression grew bitter as he continued, "Then, she caught sight of someone in the distance and, in a flash, she rode off. My flowers fell to the ground, one by one, from her grasp. I looked up and saw a handsome young man on a horse waiting for her at the edge of the thick wood. As she drew near him, he snatched her effortlessly from her horse, and placed her on his. I watched in anguish as, wrapped in each other's arms, they disappeared into the thickest part of the wood. The bastard! He had stolen my angel!" he cried. "Oh, how I wanted to kill him! Devastated and enraged with jealousy, I gave vent to my anger, crying out and cursing my deformities. Then, sobbing like a child, I followed her trail to pick up the flowers my beloved had touched and then tossed on the ground!"

At this point, still clasping his black book to his chest, he rose to his feet, staggered toward the chair by the fire and slumped into it, exhausted. I was amazed to see how intensely passion could keep its hold on someone even after such a long time, and wondered if it would finally loosen its grip with death. I jumped as his voice resounded in the room again.

"From that moment, I became as bad as a demon! I couldn't distinguish good from evil anymore." He fell back in silence, his face drained, his body almost lifeless.

"And then? And then what happened?" I cried, fearing he was dead.

He opened his eyes wide and sighed as if relieved to be back in the present. He brushed back his disheveled hair, revealing a large forehead that seemed out of proportion to the rest of his face. "Then what?" he echoed, staring blankly. "What do you care?"

"But if she was in love with somebody else ..." I began again.

"Yes, but I lost my reason. My deformities tormented me more viciously than before. The thought of her in the arms of that, that man ... so .... *handsome* drove me insane."

"Who was that man?" I asked abruptly.

He sat up and peered at me suspiciously again, but I waited calmly for his answer. "I never knew his name. I wasn't interested," he said with a slight shrug.

"Who was his family? Please try to remember!" I pleaded.

Though he seemed perplexed by my question, I could see he was making an effort to remember. "His family?" He shook his head. Then, suddenly lighting up, he said, "Ah, I believe ... his father was a *gonfaloniere* of some army or other."

"A *gonfaloniere?* What is that?"

"He brandishes his army's banner and protects the soldiers' rights," he scoffed. "I wonder if the idealistic *gonfaloniere* ever found out that his son favored the artisans' workshops over his battlefields! Ha! Ha!" He laughed maliciously. "I know that *her* father was enraged when he found out! The French bastard! The *condottiere,* as he liked to be called. Huh!"

"Who told you these things?"

"The same person who found out for me that the *condottiere* was going to lock up his daughter in a cloister for the rest of her life. The news made me lose my mind, for I couldn't bear the thought of not seeing her anymore, not even from afar!" I saw tears rolling down his face and onto his beard. Suddenly his eyes flashed as he shouted, "Revenge! Revenge had become my obsession! So that night, when I saw the coach leave with my beloved, I decided to turn this place into an inferno for that powerful man who had no love or pity, not even for his own daughter." He hunched over and stared at his shaking hands. I was horrified as the shaking seemed to become worse. I took a mugful of water and handed it to him. Unsteadily, he took it from me with both hands and gulped it as if trying to drown an unquenchable thirst. Sighing heavily, he sat back, and I waited for him to speak. "No one has ever heard this before," he murmured. "For years, I have felt smothered by my secret and the dead silence of this house. No one, not even these walls, has heard this before."

"What happened to the lady?" I asked innocently.

"Ah, my dear, if I'm so tormented, it's because instead of saving her, I killed her! Yes, I killed her and her child I didn't know about until that last moment. Yes, I did it with these hands. Caused her death ... with these hands," he cried, collapsing again in his chair. "And here I am condemned to eternal damnation ... for I was never forgiven by her."

"I'm sure she forgave you—she had a kind heart! I'm sure she—" I stopped, frightened by his look of astonishment.

"How ... how do you know that?" he asked. "Who told you that?"

I looked at him defiantly. "Because I am Lisa, the daughter she was looking for ... asking for ... before she died." His twisted mouth trembled as he stared back at me, unable to speak. "Her maid saved me by leaving me on somebody's doorstep—an old couple. She found me again when I was already an adult," I said in one breath and waited for his reaction. But his stare remained fixed on me. "I stopped here hoping to find out something about my father," I continued. "You see, I have a little son to whom I'd like to give my father's name."

"Lisa!" he exclaimed finally. "So you're her little Lisa she was asking for. That's the resemblance! Though your eyes are darker and your hair is brown. Your fine features do remind me of her." He raised his bony hands again. "Oh, my child, how I wish I could help you and atone a little for my foolishness." His book slipped to the floor. I saw that it was filled with loose pages covered with dense writing. As I bent to gather them, he touched my head, and I jumped away from him. "Don't be afraid, my child. I only wanted to ask your forgiveness."

"I think you've suffered enough in your life," I said, suddenly feeling sorry for him. "Forgiveness will come from God! You'll see," I reassured, setting the book, which was so precious to him, down on the table.

Finally, he managed to get up and, taking me by the hand, he said, "Come, my dear. I'll show you to your room." I hesitated at first, but the desire to see my mother's room induced me to follow him. He guided me up the narrow, winding staircase, lighting the way with a thick candle in one hand and holding the banister firmly with the other. The steps creaked badly under his tottering legs, while the dim light of the candle was enough to show the filthy state of peeling walls.

When we finally reached the landing, he took me into a little room opposite a large bedroom. There he lit a small candle in a candleholder, placed on a tiny round table under the window. He pointed to a bunch of faded clothing piled on a small bed. "Those belonged to your mother," he said in a detached way, as if he had already been freed from the compelling memory of her. "I found them in an iron trunk. That's why they weren't ruined by the fire." Then, limping worse than before, he dragged himself into the large bedroom.

I picked up the candleholder and went to look at the clothing. I stood there for a while, trying to imagine my mother wearing those soft pastel-colored clothes. Suddenly feeling my head spin, I went to sit down on the chair by the window. There was a frayed, but comfortable, damask cushion on it. Unable to think anymore, I gazed at the pale stars through the charred shutters until I fell asleep.

It was early dawn when I woke up and quickly jumped to my feet. I looked again at the pile of long-abandoned clothes, feeling the delicate fabrics. A soft, diaphanous cloth got caught on my finger and, giving in to an impulse, I pulled it out and hid it in my bundle as a keepsake.

I tiptoed out of my room, wanting to leave before the man woke up. His door was wide open. From the window opposite the landing, a rude light came through the torn and faded green curtains, giving the room a ghostly appearance. I could also see part of the tattered draperies of the canopy bed, which seemed to be empty. I regretted not having been the first to get up. Then, overtaken by curiosity, I slowly entered the room.

I screamed! The man was lying motionless on the floor next to the bed. After making sure his hand was stone-cold, I flew down the old staircase, through the kitchen and the hallway. I pulled open the door, which crashed to the floor. Stepping over it, I ran outside, almost bumping into the black dog, who was waiting for me, happily wagging his tail. "Your master is dead," I cried, running to the gate in the hope of seeing Nicola. The dog followed me and stood next to me. "Loneliness is sad, isn't it?" I said, stroking him. "I wonder how much you've witnessed in this place. Were you here during the fire?" He looked at me with his tired eyes, his tongue hanging out.

The sky was grim and dark, the air was damp, and I felt homesick and frightened. "Oh, my God—the dead man! What am I going to do?" I cried, feeling guilty. "If Nicola stops by, I'll have to go," I told the dog.

He sauntered to the main road and barked. I followed him, hoping that he had heard Nicola's cart. But I heard, instead, the faint tinkle of a bell and saw the white figure of a priest followed by a boy with a bell in his hand. As they crossed the main road, I called to them, "Padre! Padre, there's a dead man ... in the tower!"

"Who? The man with the limp?" inquired the priest, ceremoniously holding a covered chalice.

"Oh, that's the ogre!" cried the boy.

"He's not an ogre! He was a very unhappy man who deserves burial rites like anyone else. Isn't that so, Padre?" I said, still shaken.

"What were you doing in that woeful place?" the priest asked.

"Well ... I brought him something ... and found him dead."

"All right, let's go. We have plenty of holy water, anyway," said he.

"Padre, I'm afraid to go in there," the boy protested.

"Afraid? We have the Holy Sacrament! Where is your faith? Come on, boy! I'll just bless him and then we'll call the gravedigger."

I followed them to the door, but quickly rushed back outside, feeling cold and lonely. Soon, though, the rattling of Nicola's cart warmed me.

"Ah, I'm glad you're here!" he exclaimed. "Last night, when I didn't see you, I was really worried." He looked at me with concern and asked, "Have you eaten?" Shaking my head, I jumped up on the cart and settled down on the empty chestnut bags. "Here, take this! There's some bread and fruit in it," he said, handing me a white linen bag. "Did you see dear Rita's friends, then?"

"Yes, just one, but ... he didn't remember her."

When we reached the bend of the road at Anchiano, he said, "I'll be going back to Florence again in a couple of weeks. But you must promise not to stop halfway. I know you have a son, and I feel responsible for you." I nodded and smiled at him. His words had touched me deeply.

In the days that followed, two things were firm in my mind: to find my father and to begin my search in Florence. But I knew that I would soon be gripped in Ser Antonio's invisible vise. In fact, the joy of seeing my Leo get out of the gig and fall into my arms at the end of that week was soon clouded by the determined expression on Ser Antonio's face. I waited for Leo to go and play before asking him how long I could keep the boy.

"Until tomorrow afternoon," he said coldly, "but then we'll have to settle the matter of the name. I hope you understand the importance of this." Then, softening, he handed me a basket. "Here are some specialties the boy likes."

"I told you that I don't need anything from you."

"Please accept it, Caterina. It's a present from my wife."

"Well," I said, taking it reluctantly, "thank Donna Lucia for me, and tell her that Leo still likes the simple food he's eaten all his life."

"I'll see you tomorrow, then," he said, turning the gig around.

I went to Leo, who was bending over his huts, and took off his velvet cap. His hair had been cut shorter. I was hurt and started to ask Leo who had done it, but I changed my mind. "Leo, do you still like living there ... at your ...."

"Yes, Mama, but I like going to school and playing with the other children more. Do you know I have a father, too?" he said, looking up at me. "It's Ser Piero. He asked me, and I agreed, so now he's very pleased about it," he explained, waiting for my reaction.

"And what about you—are you pleased?"

"I suppose so. We talk about what I should study. But what I really want to do is ... make my mechanical constructions move by themselves," he said, daydreaming. "Anyhow, he wants me to follow in his footsteps, from which he says I would profit greatly. But having seen what he does all day, I know I would find it very boring, because he just writes figures all the time." He paused to reflect. "I suppose I could do that, too, if I had to." Noticing my concern, he added, "But, in any case, I'll be learning how to read and write well, and then I'll teach you like you taught me when I was still in your tummy, remember?" We both giggled.

"And I'll be a good pupil, you'll see!" I vowed, amazed that he could remember the day when he started to speak. "Now let's pack some food and take it down to the *ruscello!*"

"I'd love to, Mama. I miss playing down there with you!"

The autumn sun had warmed the air, affording us a wonderful time together. Yet I couldn't put Ser Antonio's pressing request out of my mind.

When my moment of trial finally came, it was worse than I expected. He had brought help. And that help was Piero! I was stunned when I saw him sitting solemnly in the gig next to his father. I couldn't believe my eyes. "Why did you come so early? Leo isn't ready yet," I snapped.

"That's all right," Piero said, brandishing a roll of papers like a threatening dagger. "We have to talk to you first."

"What's that?" I cried, shrinking back.

"They're the papers for you to sign to let Piero give his name to Leonardo," Ser Antonio explained casually as he climbed down.

"We have to baptize the boy, you know," said Piero, without moving.

"I had Leo baptized in the Church of Santa Lucia," I protested.

"Yes, but it wasn't valid, because the priest in charge then died without signing the papers," he said, still in the gig, as if he could control the situation better from that vantage point. "Besides, they state, 'Leonardo, son of Caterina d'Anchiano and of an unknown father,' which is not true," declared Piero, resentful.

"But my son was born in Anchiano and not in Vinci."

"Yes, but da Vinci has been our family name for generations," intervened Ser Antonio. "We are part of that community, and Leo's future would benefit greatly from it, too."

"So, once I sign that thing, it will mean that, besides giving him your name, you become his owners, too," I remarked. "And what about me? Should I then disappear from the face of the earth just to make everything more convenient for you?

Never! That will never happen!" I cried. "Besides, I'm not ready yet. I need more time to think it over."

Piero was about to oppose my demand, but acquiesced to Ser Antonio's admonishing glance instead, just as Leo rushed to my side. "All right, next week then," he said sheepishly.

"What happened? Why did you upset my mother again?" shouted Leo, getting in front of me. "I'm not going back with you!" He was vehement.

"Caterina, please explain things to him. Leo, listen! Your friends will be very disappointed not to see you tomorrow," reasoned Ser Antonio. "You'll be back to see your mother in a few days, and I promise we won't upset her anymore," he went on, trying to placate Leo.

"It's all right, my dear. Go with them! Don't worry about me. I'll be here waiting for you," I said, holding him in my arms. As I turned to the chair near the door for his little velvet cape, from the corner of my eye, I saw Ser Antonio whisper something to Leo, who promptly ran back to hug me again. I wrapped his cape around him and cuddled him for a moment while the two men waited patiently in the gig.

After they left, I considered Piero's behavior, and it became clear to me that his seductive melancholy, which had moved me years ago, was just a form of cowardice. I sighed deeply in appreciation to our Creator for having shaped my son's character completely overlooking any of his father's traits.

7
LA BELLA FIORENZA

Determined to find my father, I sat on the chestnut sacks once more on my way to the grand city of Florence under a clear sky. I was wrapped in a thick blanket again, not only to keep me warm that chilly dawn, but also to protect my deep-red woolen *cioppa,* a kind of capelike dress with ample sleeves and old-rose flannel lining. Since Rita had given it to me, I was too self-conscious to ever wear it in the hills. That day, though, it gave me the confidence I needed in the new world to carry out my important plan. "The most important plan of my life!" I kept saying as I touched my mother's profile on the silver medal my father had made. For safety, I had threaded it with the pretty ribbon that had served all these years to tie up my bundle of baby clothes.

"Caterina, are you warm enough?" asked the concerned cartman.

"Thank you, Nicola, I'm very comfortable," I replied, warming my hands on the hot tisane bottle in my lap.

"This time, there won't be any stops along the way, for I'm taking the whole load to Florence," he said. "This is the last trip of the season for me. My old bones can't take the cold weather."

I brought the medal close to my lips, saying, "Oh, Father,

dear, let me find you this time! I must find you!" Then, still in prayer, I called upon my mother's spirit to guide me. Confident in having been heard by both my parents, I closed my eyes, letting myself be cradled by the steady rocking of the cart.

When I woke the sun was in the middle of the sky, and outlined on the horizon was "la bella Fiorenza," its towers and domes growing larger and taller before my eyes. I held my breath at the beautiful sight, which reminded me of the paradise I had seen in my childhood dreams.

When we finally entered the walls of the city, I gazed increduously at the tall, massive buildings, surprised by the great number of people hustling around the limited space between them.

Two young men on horseback, wearing brightly colored jackets with caps to match, suddenly charged down the street, cracking their whips loudly. People on vehicles, intimidated pedestrians, one and all, were forced to stop and back up against the buildings. A grandiose but noisy carriage pulled by four white horses appeared from around the corner, carrying an overdressed couple wearing a great deal of jewelry and tall feathered hats. They paraded and pompously looked down at the crowd of frightened people.

"Nicola, who are they?" I asked, overwhelmed by this spectacle.

"To me, they're nobody, but to the Florentines, they're the owners of the city. They're feared like gods," he sneered. "They just turn my stomach! But don't worry! We're going to a place where all men are equal, because they work for their living. I call them 'the humans.'"

When we reached Nicola's world of humans in the large square, called *mercato grande,* I was able to get a good look at these working people from whose mouths came the most disgusting language I had ever heard. The ill-tempered vendors, who set up their stalls and hung smelly skinned animals on poles, were the most foul-mouthed of all. The women, who were greater in number, flattered the menfolk, but fought fiercely with one another. Two squabbling women landed in a mud puddle in the middle of the square as scornful men jeered at them. Unable to watch anymore, I covered my eyes until the clamor had died down.

"Caterina, do you see that place there? That's where my sister works," Nicola announced as we pulled up in front of a tavern after leaving the market behind us. "I'm going to take you to meet her," he said as we got down. He insisted on holding my hand firmly when we pushed our way across the crowded room. Some of the men at the tables waved their tankards and snickered at us as we went by. I shielded myself with the blanket I had brought with me. "Quickly now, before they eat you alive!" muttered Nicola, practically dragging me into the kitchen.

A tall, florid woman in her middle years, absorbed completely in her cooking chores, suddenly stopped in midstream to stare at me. Then placing her hands on her full hips, she asked abruptly, "And who is this?"

"Nobody," replied Nicola, slightly intimidated. "Her name is Caterina. She's a poor girl from Anchiano who has come to ... see some relatives. Would you put her up for the night, Francesca?"

She looked at me from head to toe. "Come with me, then," she said sharply, strutting down the hallway. Then, noticing I hadn't moved, she glared at me impatiently. Nicola motioned me to hurry after her, and I promptly marched behind her into a long, narrow room.

"You can sleep here, but lock yourself in for the night! You're too good-looking for those devils out there." She delayed to observe me as I timidly slipped by her. "I'll bring you some food later," she then said in a softer tone of voice, returning to the kitchen.

I went straight to the small bed in the corner and sat down on it. It was hard as stone, but very welcoming to my weary body after all those hours of bouncing around on the cart, so I stretched out on it, grateful for having found a peaceful refuge in the noise and confusion of the city. But I soon jumped to my feet again as Francesca came back in with an appetizing bowl of soup and fresh bread, saying briskly, "My brother is going back home tomorrow. So, what are you going to do?"

"Oh, my good woman, it's too late in the day to start looking for my relatives, especially since I don't even know where they live." She glanced at me in surprise. "But I'm sure I'll find him ... them," I added, quickly correcting myself. "It's just that I have no other way of returning home."

"Well, we'll see what happens tomorrow, my dear," she said, placing the food on a tiny table wedged between the bed and the wall. "Now eat and get a good night's sleep! And by the way, call me Francesca!" she added before closing the door behind her.

There was so little space in the room that I had to sit back on my bed to enjoy the tasty meal, with bread still hot from the oven. In the quiet of the room, under the faint light of the lamp, I started to plan the next day. As I really had no idea where to start, just to amuse myself, I began to visualize a story and, since I expected fantastic results, my story became a fairy tale in which the main character was, of course, my father!

At the end, I saw him arriving in Anchiano on a prancing white steed to rescue Leo and me. So the three of us rode off to his splendid home in a castle on the banks of a large brook, where we happily spent the rest of our lives! With this wonderful image in mind, I drifted into deep sleep.

A fine ray of sunshine bursting through the tiny window high above my bed brightly illuminated the opposite wall and brought me back from the land of dreams. Once on my feet, I found a pitcher full of warm water in a basin on the table. I knew then that Francesca was now my new friend.

Soon I was standing at the kitchen door, ready to set out. Francesca, who was taking some loaves of bread out of a small oven, saw me and greeted me with a smile. "Come in! Don't stand there. There's nobody else in here yet, so have some hot milk." She pointed to the full jug on the table. "You know, I was thinking you should go to the *catasto*. That's the building where they have large registers with the names and addresses of all the families in Florence. I hope those relatives of yours will appreciate the trouble you're going to," she said with motherly concern.

"I'm not doing it for myself, but for my little son. I want him to know the family he comes from."

"So, you have a son! And so young!"

"I'm not so young. My son is already over five years old, but he has the intelligence of a grown-up," I said proudly.

"What about your husband?" she asked. I lowered my eyes sadly. "Oh, what a tragedy that must have been for you! Wait, I'll get you some food to take with you." I watched her plump fingers fill some hot buns with cheese and drop them into a bag similar to the one Nicola had given me the morning I returned from the villa. Her face radiated kindness as she handed the bag to me, wishing me luck.

"Thank you, Francesca. You remind me of a dear friend I've just lost. Her name was Rita. Now I must be on my way," I said, tucking the bag in my skirt pocket. The main door slammed open and a group of men, grumbling and yawning, came in, the lines of sleep still etched on their faces. With a rapid glance, she indicated the backdoor, and I slipped out.

I stopped a moment to memorize the location of the tavern and then took the first street ahead. I quickened my pace when I saw that it led to a tall church and soon found myself climbing the steps to its large portal. Powerful bells resounded inside the square. I stopped to marvel at the resplendent setting for the genteel couples entering the church in all their finery. I stood back wonderstruck, not only by the ladies and gentlemen in their tasteful clothes and hats, but also by their graceful movements and refined way of exchanging glances with each other and whispering discreetly among themselves. They seemed to be part of a design to enhance the grandeur of the square.

I entered the great church and looked around, awed by its scale. The main altar seemed to be far away, and the churchgoers, scattering in the spacious aisles, looked like dolls in relation to the dome's magnitude.

I saw a young priest standing near the main door. "Padre, could you tell me where the building of the *catasto* is? How far is it from here?" I asked, approaching him.

"Not too far. Why, my child ... sister," he said, correcting himself shyly, "are you looking for someone?"

"Yes, for my father. I've ... lost him." I regretted my lie.

"Do you know his name?" he asked politely, straightening his slightly curved back.

"No, I don't. I really ... I've never seen him," I faltered.

"It won't be easy, my chil ... sister," he said, a little embarrassed. "What's your name?" he then asked awkwardly.

"Caterina," I answered and paused as he seemed to want to ask another question, but he restrained himself. Then, with a twinkle in his eyes, he declared, "My name is Filippo. If I can help in any way, Caterina ..."

"I don't know, Don Filippo. Perhaps you would pray for me?"

"That I will certainly do. And remember: this is the Duomo—the greatest house of God in Florence. It is always open to anyone in need of a miracle!" he said earnestly.

"Thank you, Padre," I said, crossing myself, and left.

Outside, a kindly woman directed me to the *catasto* building, which was, in fact, not far from the square. When I entered the large doorway, I found myself between two wide staircases. Instinctively, I took the one on the left. At the top, I entered a vast hall suffused with a pale pinkish light filtering through its long, narrow windows and encountered the solemn faces of a row of gentlemen writing at tall, pulpitlike desks. An elderly man behind the nearest desk looked up at me and asked indifferently, "What are you looking for, young girl?"

I must look really young, I thought, disappointed. "I came to ask you to find my father," I answered boldly.

"What's your father's name?" he asked flatly.

I hesitated a little, as his voice reminded me somehow of Ser Antonio's. "I don't know. I really know only part of it."

"Part of it? Tell me *your* name, then."

"My name is Caterina. My father's name was ... no, *is* Leonardo Battis—. Maybe it's Battistero." I had heard that name mentioned in the square.

"Battistero, indeed! Why do you know only half of it?"

"The other half was burned. I mean, his signature on the painting that was found after the fire," I said, thinking that I was confusing him even more with my scanty information.

"What fire?" he shouted as he scowled at me over the tiny, round glasses he wore hooked on his nose. All the other clerks turned their faces in our direction. "What about *his* father's name? Maybe we have a record of *him*."

"I ... I only know he was a *gonfaloniere* of an army."

"A *gonfaloniere*? Are you sure? Which army?"

"I don't know. It all happened before I was born," I whispered, getting closer to his desk. "You see, my father wanted to marry the daughter of a *condottiere*, but her father didn't want her to marry him because he was only an artisan." I saw that the man's patience was running out, so in a single breath I blurted, "But the villa burned down and my mother died in the fire!"

He shook his head and brushed back thin strands of gray hair falling limply on his face. "My dear girl, in Florence everybody is an artisan! And as for *gonfalonieri* and *condottieri*—the world would be a far better place without either of them." Seeing my long face, he added, "All right, then! Come back in a couple of days. I'll see what I can find out."

"But I can't wait. I have to go back home tomorrow. I live on the hills of Anchiano, under Mont'Albano."

"How on earth did you get here?" he asked, twitching his eyebrows in surprise. "And where are you staying?"

"I came on the chestnut-seller's cart," I replied casually. "I'm staying at Francesca's Tavern at the market."

"Oh, my Lord, things go from bad to worse! Come back tomorrow, then."

I thanked him with a hint of a curtsy, and turned to leave, but stopped as I heard him murmur to himself, "This world is becoming more and more corrupt, and what comes out of it? A bunch of foundlings!" Seeing my injured expression, he lowered his eyes awkwardly.

Out on the landing, I lingered in front of a painting on the wall, trying to read the distorted signature. "Do you know who Andrea del Ver ... roc ... chio is?" I asked a guard as he approached.

"Yes, indeed. He has the most famous art studio in Florence, in Via dell'Acqua, not far from here. He's also an eminent sculptor and engraver," he added, taking pride. Thanking him, I left the building.

Before planning my next step, I decided to return to the Duomo square, where a tall, bright-looking young man, probably in his teens, dressed in a red overall and matching cap, walked briskly by me, a large drawing of a building under his arm. He stopped on the other side of the square to gaze at the Duomo's façade. I went over to where he stood, and looking up too, I commented to him, "It's hard to believe it was built by mortal man."

"It is, indeed!" he agreed, still transfixed. "That's why I never get tired of admiring it."

"You're an artist, aren't you?" I asked, looking at his drawing.

"Yes. Well, I'm trying to become one."

"Then you must know Verrocchio's studio."

"Yes, I'm one of his pupils. I'm going there now, if you want me to show you the way. It's a beautiful part of Florence. The Arno runs near it. Follow me, and I'll show you!" I nodded, and we set off. He took such long strides that I had to run to keep up with him.

We passed by a large stretch of water. "What's that?" I asked, gasping for breath.

"That's our River Arno. It runs through the whole city."

"Where does the water come from?"

"It gathers here from the nearby mountains, and then it flows toward the sea, beyond the town of Pisa. It's marvellous, isn't it?"

I nodded approvingly. "You know," I said, "in our valley there's a small river we call the *ruscello,* which has many springs. They come out from the rocks of our magnificent Mont'Albano!"

"Then that water must end up in the Arno, too!" he exclaimed with conviction before drawing my attention away. "And over there you see Verrocchio's *bottega*!" Lifting his red cap, he waved good-bye and hurried into the building.

Built slightly below street level, at first the old house appeared austere, but as I stepped down into the small front garden, colorful flower beds and delicate white statues, no taller than my little boy, gave a friendly welcome. So I pushed open the door and entered.

Unfinished, abandoned works of art covered with dust were propped up on each side of the wide hallway, from which one could see as far as the back garden. Out there, young men were busy painting, but inside, everything was quiet. My guide came through one of the side doors along the hallway and whispered, "Oh, did you want to see somebody here?"

"Yes, the *maestro*."

"Does he know you? Maestro Andrea's a very busy person."

"No, I've never met him, but I must talk to him."

"Follow me," he said, taking me to a very large doorway. "There he is, sitting at the table over there. I'm sorry, but I have to go now."

"Thank you, *messere*," I said. He turned and smiled, perhaps flattered by the way I had addressed him, and I smiled back at him.

I peeped inside at the man, who was seated at a wide table. Bright sunlight poured through the skylight above his head, making the metal objects of art in front of him shine like gold. Both his elbows rested firmly on a large sheet of pink paper.

Slightly intimidated by the nervous way he kept running his fingers through his dark, frizzy hair, I stepped back a little, but by now he had become aware of my presence. His plump, clean-shaven face grew tense as he fixed his fiery eyes on me in such a way that I dared not take another step. "I don't take women apprentices. This is a studio for men only," he announced, examining the tip of his pencil.

"Excuse me, *maestro*," I said, clearing my throat. "That's not why I'm here."

"Oh, what is it, then?" he asked, a little intrigued. He put his pencil down. "Where do you come from? You're not a Florentine, are you?"

"No, I come from very far away, *maestro*. It's very important for me to talk to you," I said solemnly.

"Come in and speak up, then. I'm listening." He crossed his arms and sat back, his mood softening.

"I'm looking for a person," I said, stepping nearer, "who may have been one of your pupils. He painted very small pictures and engraved medals. I know that he came from a good family."

"All my pupils come from good families. Art is a very noble profession. What's the name of this young man?"

"I don't know exactly, and he's not a young man anymore—he's my father." I took the silver medal from my neck and handed it to him.

He examined it carefully with a special glass. "But this is the type of work that used to be taught by my master, Giuliano dei Verrocchi! What's your father's name?"

"Leonardo, but I'm not sure of his family name. If I had known it, I would have found him by now."

"Why did you wait all this time?"

"I didn't know much about him. Now that I have a little son … But my story is too long."

"I understand. Wait, I'll call Giovanni, the sculptor. He was here at that time." He turned to an older man across the room, who was vigorously polishing a bronze bust of a thin-faced man with short hair. "Giovanni, come here. Take a look at this." Without a word, the sculptor came over to the table, cleaning his hands with a rag and staring at me intensely. "Ask him! Describe this person to him," encouraged the *maestro*.

"I am looking for the man who made this medal, but, as I told the *maestro*, I have never seen him. All I know is that he was dark and very handsome and that he was in love with the daughter of a *condottiere*, who died in a fire at her father's villa."

Giovanni took the medal from the *maestro's* hand and studied it. "I think I remember this apprentice.… A very private young man … mysterious. He never revealed his origin. One day, he disappeared. A pity, because he was a good engraver!" he said, still contemplating the medal.

"Can you remember anything else about him? Please try!"

"Well, the last time he was here, he seemed distraught. I recall his friend telling me that the day before he left he had confided to him a terrible tragedy: the woman he loved had just perished in a fire."

"Then you must have known his name," I pleaded anxiously.

"No, because in those times, most of the apprentices used only a nickname. Maybe, like many others, he had a father who forbade him to become an artisan." He narrowed his eyes in an attempt to remember. "Yes, I know! They called him Cireno, because of his patrician Roman features!" Turning to the *maestro*, he asked, "Who is this woman?"

"She's a relative," the maestro answered, winking at me.

"From her features," he retorted, returning to his work, "I would've said more precisely a daughter."

The *maestro* shrugged his shoulders. "Well, he knows too much about faces. His expert eye is never wrong. Anyway, I'm sorry I couldn't be of more assistance, my dear." I wasn't listening. My eyes were still on the sculptor, who knew more than I about my dear father. I wanted to ply him with questions, but the *maestro* had gotten up and was handing me back the medal. "I hope you find your father soon," he said sincerely.

"Thank you, Maestro Andrea, I'm sure I'll ..." He kindly led me to the front door, surprising two apprentices who happened to be passing by. Overwhelmed and confused, I headed to the riverside and leaned over the wall. Gazing at the water, which seemed to run much too slowly compared to our brook, I thought of my father when, young and bold, he must have wondered along this spot! A shiver ran through me as I felt his grief for the loss he had suffered.

I decided to go back to Francesca's, but having lost my bearings along the busy streets, I suddenly found myself in a large square where crowds of protesters were shouting in unison outside a very tall building topped with a high tower, the highest I had ever seen! Curious to see what was going on, I went to take a closer look. They were all country people, mainly women, like the peasants I had seen working the fields, brandishing hoes and sickles. I looked in consternation as they pounded their fists fiercely on the large door of the palace, which nobody bothered to open; a scene so different from the one I had witnessed earlier in front of the Duomo. Engrossed as they were in their protests, the women still had to tend to their sobbing children, who stood on one side.

The crowd formed a circle. They swayed and chanted as one: "Pater Patriae, Cosimo de' Medici, stop the wars! Stop the cruel wars once and for all! We want our men back in the country with their families in their own homes. Condemn the cursed *condotta!* Condemn it! You can do it! Pater Patriae, help the poor Tuscans!"

The strip of sky above us had turned darker and the air chillier. An ailing little boy who had been left behind sat on the ground shivering with cold, his dirty face streaked with tears. I dried his face and gave him the bag of food that Francesca had given me.

"Cosimo de' Medici, Pater Patriae, speak to us!" the rioting crowd went on. I covered my ears as the screaming and lamenting became more intense. The moment the boy's mother came for him I fled from the square, not knowing where my feet were taking me. I kept running until I reached the market, finding relief in the vendors' raucous voices, which by comparison sounded almost cheerful!

I crept into the tavern through the kitchen door. "Oh, my dear, I was getting worried about you," cried Francesca. "What happened? Why are you frightened?" But I had to sit down, as I was still out of breath.

The market stalls were being dismantled, and the tavern was filling up with people wanting to eat before returning home. I stood up and started to help her, but she flatly refused.

"But, Francesca, I did this kind of work in Anchiano," I protested.

"My dear, this is not Anchiano. Fill this bowl with soup, take some of that bread, and go to your room," she said firmly. "I'll see you later."

Not feeling hungry, though, I went straight to bed to think about the little bit of information I had gathered concerning my father. Instead, a pleasant dream came to soothe my troubled spirit and alleviate my exhaustion and disappointment. I was strolling across a field dotted with yellow primroses and suddenly saw my beautiful mother sitting on the grass, adjusting her wide skirt around her. She placed her hat next to her and from her gown pulled a panel of the same diaphanous silk I had taken from the tower. Smiling sweetly, she held it up, letting the wind whisk it up into the sky. Then she pointed to a place in the distance, and I saw that the fluttering piece of silk had turned into a translucent bird gliding soundlessly toward a hill. Surveying the hill intently, I found it was just a desolate wasteland. I turned to ask my mother what that place was, but she had already disappeared.

A knock at the door startled me. Francesca squeezed herself through the narrow passage, carrying my meal, and sat on the edge of my bed, anxiously waiting to hear my news. I shook my head, wondering where to start. "Francesca, I just had a fantastic dream!"

"Tell me about it tomorrow! You look very tired. I have a feeling that you haven't found any of your relatives yet, have you?"

I tried to remember some of the events, but after the dream, they seemed too far away. Then I said, "I went to the *catasto* first, then I went to see Maestro Andrea del Verrocchio. Do you know of him? There I found out something about my father, but not enough, unfortunately."

"Of course, I know the *maestro!* The greatest sculptor in Florence! He comes here sometimes."

"He was very kind to me. Anyhow, tomorrow I have to go back to the *catasto,* hoping they've found out something for me."

"Don't worry, my dear. I'll convince my brother to stay a couple of days longer, since he won't be back for months. Now eat and rest."

The next morning, I rushed to the Duomo first, to pray a little, but on the way, my attention was caught by a tousled man polishing the bronze doors of the building opposite the Duomo. Seeing me admire them, he took pleasure in pointing out the workmanship. "These doors lead to the largest baptismal font in the world. We call it the Battistero! Did you know the artisans worked on them for twenty-seven years? They were finished only five years ago."

"Oh, the same year my son was born! One day, I'll bring him here to see this wonder. You know, my son has the same gift of God as the artisans who did this work. I'm sure he'll do great things, too!" I said confidently, to which the polisher gave me a disconcerting glance and returned to his work. Feeling that I needed more than ever to reinforce my vacillating faith under the sacred roof, I hastened up the steps of the Duomo and, kneeling inside, fervently prayed for help. I jumped as the voice of the young priest rang in my ear. "Did you find him, Caterina?"

"Not yet, Don Filippo," I said without turning, a little annoyed with him for interrupting my invocation. "But I have to go back to the *catasto*."

"If they don't find him, what will you do?" he asked.

"Keep looking for him," I answered, getting up to go.

"God be with you, my sister," he said softly.

"Thank you, Padre." I started to leave.

"I prayed for you," he said shyly. "I know how you feel because I never knew my parents either. Now, of course, I have the Lord as my father!"

Touched by his openness, I regretted my abruptness. He looked deeply concerned about me. I held out my hand, which he squeezed warmly with both of his. "I'll keep praying for you, Caterina."

As I walked down the marble steps, I still felt the warmth of his slender hands and, for the first time in my life, I felt the comfort one could derive from brotherly love.

When I entered the hall of the *catasto,* I approached my gentleman's desk, but he pretended not to see me. I coughed. "Oh, it's you, Caterina. It's much too soon. I haven't found anything yet."

"But I know now that he was a pupil of Giuliano dei

Verrocchi. Do you think, *messere*, that after my mother's tragedy, he may have decided out of despair to join his father's army?"

"My dear girl, if he had decided that, he wouldn't have come to tell us about it. Besides, the volunteers are all crazy anyway. Go now! If by some miracle we should find something out, I'll inform your friend at the tavern. Go back to your peaceful country and pray!"

"By the way, who is Cosimo de' Medici?"

"He's the governor of the city. Why do you ask? Do you want to go to *him* now?" he said with a cynical smile.

"No, but yesterday I saw people crying outside a very tall building, his palace, I think. They kept calling him Pater Patriae, why?"

"Ah, the Palazzo della Signoria! Well, he's like the father of our land, but he's getting old, too, so he can't please all his subjects," he explained, falling back in his chair as if identifying himself with the Pater Patriae. "Who were those people who were crying?" he asked.

"Peasants from that 'peaceful country' you just mentioned!" He straightened up, suddenly indignant.

Later, as I entered Francesca's kitchen, she greeted me with open arms. "Oh, my dear, I'm glad you're here. My brother has decided to go back home today because he felt sick all night. Are you ready to go back, too?"

"Yes, Francesca, I am. The clerk from the *catasto* will let you know when he has news for me."

"So, nothing yet, eh? Leave it in the hands of God! I'll look forward to seeing you next year, my dear."

Staring blankly, I nodded. But remembering the gold coin, I reached in my pocket and gave it to her.

"What are you doing, my dear? This is a gold florin!" she exclaimed.

"That's all I have. I don't even know what it's worth. My friend Rita left it to me."

"Wait, then. I'll change it into smaller coins for you." She went to her counter and opened a drawer with one of the keys hanging from her apron. She filled a small bag with other coins and swung it from left to right, feeling the weight. "There, this change corresponds to the value of your florin, so you can use it more easily."

"But there's too much!" I protested, taking a handful out of the bag and handing it back to her.

"My dear, I don't need it. Look how much I'm blessed with! Keep it for your little boy," she said, hugging me. "Now go, and God bless you! Hurry! Nicola's waiting for you."

I sat on the empty sacks, feeling very helpless and tense, but as we moved through the fresh country air, I began to breathe more easily. I stretched out and gazed at the white clouds floating across the sky, thinking that after all we are like those drifting clouds, swept by the winds of fate to places unknown.

Nicola had coughed a few times, which worried me, but I knew we would get home before evening. After a while, however, I realized that the trotting had slowed down and that Nicola hadn't been hurling any insults at his horse. I sat up, concerned that the sky was getting darker and that there were no familiar landmarks in sight. In fact, I didn't know where we were at all. I stood up and saw that his head was tilted to one side. "Nicola, I think we're on the wrong road!"

"Ah, you're right," he said, waking up. "This is the shortcut to Pisa. Well, when we get to the next turning, we'll go back."

"But we'll never get home before night," I said to myself, as we bumped along the narrow, dusty road. Wilderness was all around us when we finally reached a turning at the bottom of a steep slope. It reminded me so much of the barren wasteland the translucent bird had flown over in my dream that I couldn't take my eyes off it. Though a veil of mist obscured my view, I could still see a horse not far from us sniffing the ground as if searching for something, its broken saddle hanging loosely to one side. Suddenly, the mist cleared and I saw that there were bodies scattered all over the ground. Dead bodies! I clapped a hand over my eyes and screamed.

"Caterina, what happened? Did you hurt youself?"

"Nicola, Nicola! Where are we? What place is this?" I cried.

"Oh, my God! I forgot all about it. We shouldn't be here. This is the godforsaken battlefield!"

"Why do you call it that?" I asked.

"Because it's cursed!" he cried. I peeked out through my fingers, but the horrible sight had disappeared.

"A terrible battle took place right on that spot there," he explained with fear in his voice. "During the last skirmish, all the soldiers were killed. They were taken by surprise in their sleep!" He forced the horse to make a quick turn. "Let's get out of here before it gets any darker! They say that at night their ghosts come back in search of their bodies." He crossed himself and cracked his whip fiercely. The horse broke into a mad gallop off the road and down a rocky slope, barely missing the trees on each side. Nicola started to cough violently and lost control of the reins, falling back on his seat.

I moved quickly to the front of the cart, grabbed the reins, and tried to hold the horse back. "Nicola, what'll I do now? Help!" But the horse had gone wild, and in the struggle, I could hardly follow Nicola's vague instructions, a series of waving gestures of the hand while he continued to cough and choke.

"Trit-trot, my good horse," I chanted, fearing for our lives, "and take us home safely, please, as I really don't know how to handle you!" We shot through some more deserted woodland until, finally slowing down, we came out on the main road leading up to our hills. The horse snorted, trying to get back its breath, and Nicola's cough seemed to have subsided. I gave a sigh of relief when I saw the towers of Vinci come into view, after which I began to enjoy driving the cart. In fact, it was quite exhilarating to communicate with the horse's intelligence, so much so that for a while, I forgot the strange apparition I had witnessed.

It was nightfall when we reached the bend in the road by the tavern. I woke Nicola up, putting the reins back in his hands. "Oh, here we are!" he said. "Now I can go to sleep—my horse will take me home." I got down, and he shook the reins. "Go on, my good horse! Santa Lucia will guide us!"

Still amused by his remark, I slowly headed toward the nightingale, who welcomed me with its song. I glanced around as I took its cage off the hook. "This must be what the old clerk was talking about!" I said to myself, taking in a deep breath of mountain air.

I went indoors, certain that I would not be able to sleep that night with the events of the last two days going through my mind, but, instead, no thoughts disturbed my rest.

During the days that followed, however, I found myself doing heavy work in my kitchen garden and the most tiring chores around the house in order to avoid thinking about my disappointing journey. Though the awesome vision on the wasteland had confirmed my fears concerning my father, I convinced myself that it was just an hallucination caused by the dream. Yet every time I remembered it, the ensuing depression drained me both physically and spiritually.

It was unfortunate, therefore, that I was in one of these depleted states when my son's predators made their next appearance.

8
THE FORCED SURRENDER

Though I rejoiced in having my little boy in my arms again, my blood boiled at the sight of the two men high up in their gig, especially Piero, who, without uttering a word, still firmly clutched his scroll.

"Leo, why don't you go and play with your constructions?" said Ser Antonio, getting down. "We have to talk with your mother. We won't upset her, I promise." Leo looked at him sulkily. Then he took my hand and kissed it. It was the first time he had done that, and it couldn't have been at a more appropriate time. I stroked his head and he reluctantly edged away. "Caterina, I'm happy to say that your son, Leonardo, is the best student in the whole school!" stated Ser Antonio, coming toward me.

"I knew that," I said, glaring at Piero as he got out of the gig.

"He's very good at drawing, too," Ser Antonio added brightly.

"He takes after his grandfather!" I commented casually.

"Which grandfather?" interjected Piero.

Startled by the offensive tone of his voice, I retorted, "My real father, who else?"

"Ah, that one!" he said offhandedly.

I felt obliged to control my temper as Leo had started edging back.

"Mama, it's true. I'm learning to draw. Grandfather ... Ser Antonio bought pencils and charcoal for me. When I grow up, I'll draw your face, you'll see. I promise, it'll be the most beautiful portrait in the world!" I placed a kiss on his forehead and encouraged him to go back and play.

"You're here for the name, aren't you?" I snapped. Leo, however, had quietly moved closer to Ser Antonio.

"Well, we had to proceed with the registration of his name ... for the school, you know," he said, stroking Leo's head.

"Yes, Mama, now I'm called Leonardo da Vinci, like my grandfather and my ... and Ser Piero."

"So, you went ahead without my permission, eh?"

"We told you we couldn't wait, but it doesn't make any difference. He's still your son," remarked Ser Antonio. Seeing that the conversation was proceeding calmly, Leo finally went off to play.

"If it doesn't make any difference, why did you come back with those ... those stupid papers?" I was incensed at them, but kept my voice down for Leo's sake. There was no response.

Then Ser Antonio came closer. "But, Caterina, you cannot hinder your son's future. You cannot keep him forever in these forgotten hills."

Suddenly recalling Rita's words, I looked over at Leo and my eyes filled with tears. "I understand what you are saying, Ser Antonio," I said hoarsely. "I'll agree to it, but on one condition."

"What condition?" interrupted Piero's irritating voice.

"That you bring my son back to me every week," I said firmly.

Piero was about to object, but Ser Antonio raised his hand to silence him. "All right, Caterina, we'll do as you like," he said and then pointed to Piero's scroll. "Look, you only have to put your name on it," he said casually. Piero was livid, but kept quiet.

"What have you written on it? My death sentence? You

know that I can't read well enough to understand it. Nobody ever taught me," I said, giving Piero a reproachful look. His face turned pale.

Ser Antonio looked at us inquiringly. Then centering on me, he went on, "Signing it is only a formality, Caterina, but it will mean a great deal to Leonardo's future. You understand that, I'm sure," he said meekly.

"I must know, Ser Antonio," I insisted, dabbing my eyes. "Don't you see?"

"This is just a document enabling Leo to be registered in the *catasto* files as a member of my family, too. There's no harm in that."

"Ah, the *catasto!*"

"I see you know what that means," said Ser Antonio, raising his eyebrows. "So you know also how important it is! Now, my dear, we only need a table." I was not following him anymore, as the disappointing and shocking events of the trip to Florence had invaded my mind again, reviving the devastating feeling of utter helplessness they had given me then. I wrapped my arms around my shoulders to shield myself from the cold, sinister world that had suddenly appeared before me.

"We need a table, Caterina," resounded Ser Antonio's request again. I just indicated the door and followed them as if in a trance, no longer able to fight or protest.

Inside, I couldn't see clearly what was going on, for tears clouded my eyes and pain filled my heart. It was like another bad dream! In the dimness of the room, though, I realized that Piero had taken out a bottle of black liquid and a quill pen from his bag. He dipped the pen in the bottle and handed it to me. The forced wide smile on his face was the only visible feature to me. My eyes moved to the scroll on the table held open by Ser Antonio, who was gently urging me to take the pen from Piero's hand and sign it. Why was my name on this paper so important to them? I asked myself. Was it just to make me feel committed? But before I could reflect upon it, the pen was in my hand, scribbling my name next to Ser Antonio's finger. Without letting me look over the scroll, he suddenly let it roll up and handed it to

Piero, who, in turn, put it away in his bag together with the pen and ink.

"Thank you, Caterina," said Piero, breaking the silence. "You must realize that now Leonardo is officially *my* son."

"What do you mean?" I asked. The two somber figures just bowed and left the room without any explanation. "What have I done?" I cried.

Then, rushing after them, I shouted, "Wait! Wait!" But they were already sitting stiffly in their gig. "Wait!" I cried again. "At least promise me that you'll let my boy study what he likes!" But they pretended not to hear me and, with an instant's sly, sidelong glance, they pulled their cloaks tightly around them. I jumped as their whip cracked through the air. The gig jerked forward and the two black, sinister shadows were soon out of sight.

I called Leo, but there was no reply. Alarmed, I rushed to his play corner, but he was not there. "Leo! Leo, my child, where are you?" I cried, panic-stricken. "They've stolen my child!" I was sure they had hidden him under their cloaks when they left. I fell to the ground, sobbing bitterly.

Leo's little laugh reached my ear. I looked around uncertainly and saw that he was sitting up in a tree at the edge of the olive grove. I ran to him. "Mama! Come here! See what I found!" he said, showing me a cluster of tiny green olives. "There were no flowers in the fields to draw so I climbed up here to get an olive branch. Look how beautiful it is!"

"Why did you hide up there all this time, darling?" I snapped.

"I was waiting for you to come by—to see you from up here."

"All right, come down now! I want to talk to you." I reached up to help him get down, but he jumped off by himself. "Listen, my darling," I said, regaining my composure as we sat on the ground, "I promise I'll grow a wonderful garden—the best that's ever been seen around here—so you'll have flowers to draw all year round! But you must promise to come back to me always!" He nodded, and I kissed his blushing cheeks.

"I will, Mama, I will! I promise you!" he said, hugging me.

The following day, a four-wheeled cart drove up to the building. "I'm Gian Pietro, Ser Antonio's gardener," said the driver, as he got down. "He's very busy today, so he sent me to get the boy," he said, glancing around inquisitively. He was a short, dark southerner with graying hair.

Leo came to my side and took my hand. "Good day, Gian Pietro. Thank you for coming. I'm ready. This is my mother, Donna Caterina!" Gian Pietro eyed me guardedly, then bowed his head slightly. "Don't worry, Mama, he's a good man," said Leo in a whisper.

Yet, I stood there, still unsure of what to think about him and his masters, who no longer seemed to be interested in coming here. I couldn't help taking it as a bad sign, but I tried not to dwell upon it, attributing my negative thoughts to the dashed hopes of ever finding my father and to my extreme sensitivity to all that had passed and might yet come to pass. As it turned out, though, my foreboding was justified, for weeks went by without my seeing Leo again.

I was working in my vegetable garden when Giuseppe came to see me one day looking very concerned. "Caterina, I must talk to you. I heard that Ser Antonio is sending some people to harvest the olives."

"What's wrong with that? Why are you so worried?"

"Because he's hired a group of soldiers, deserters from the *condotta*. They're not from these parts and, since they can't go home for fear of being caught again, they take any kind of work they can find. So I advise you to shut yourself indoors while they're here. If they find out that you live alone ...."

"Oh, Giuseppe, you're exaggerating."

"No, I'm not. They're tough men, hungry for women." He paused a moment, then proceeded, "Listen, Caterina! We hill people know your story and we respect you. But they're mercenaries—unscrupulous men."

"I think you worry too much. But thank you, anyway. I'll watch out."

* * *

On the morning I saw the rowdy harvesters climbing up the slope, I was at the well, hiding behind some bushes. I ran inside and locked my door. From the small opening in my window, I could count about ten men wearing worn-out soldiers' uniforms. The rest were women, about five of them, carrying empty wicker baskets on their heads. As they reached the olive grove, the men started to climb the trees in order to shake the olives off the branches, while the women stretched cloths out on the ground below. The men were so rough, though, that the branches broke off, falling on the backs of the poor women gathering the olives. The more the women shouted at them to stop, the more the men persisted, laughing convulsively.

In the afternoon, the whole group came toward the courtyard. I barricaded my door, placed a beam across the shutters, and stood with bated breath, peeping through the small hole again. I saw the women carrying the heavy baskets full of olives, while the men staggered behind, swigging wine from terra-cotta bottles. When they reached the threshing floor they sat down and ate what looked like bread and cheese from the women's bundles. Without waiting for the men to finish, the women gathered at the entrance of the courtyard, looking out for the cart to arrive. The soldiers, who were already feeling the effect of the wine, followed and started molesting them. The women yelled as they fought them off. But the struggling stopped as a heavy cart rumbled into the courtyard. The women then hastily loaded up the baskets and jumped into the cart, crying to the cartman, "Save us! Take us home to our families! You're from our hills. You must help us!" The drunken soldiers jeered and swore at the shrieking women. The cart driver cracked his whip and turned the cart around back onto the road, taking the women and their olives to safety. The soldiers chased after the cart, hurling insults.

The silence that followed made me think that they had all gone. But I went down on my knees in prayer as footsteps approached my door.

"Why don't we break down that door? We can spend the night in here," said one of them.

"Maybe somebody's hiding inside," said another, snickering.

"I'll look for something to ram it down with," a third voice said. A loud ram against the door toppled me from my knees to the floor. A louder one followed, and I knew then that the end was near. I crossed myself and asked God to forgive my warring forefathers for their part in turning good peasants into such terrifying beings. I thought of Vincenzo and how he had reformed and found a way to stay with his family. Yet that was of little comfort at this point, since my life was in serious danger. Another terrific blow almost unhinged the door, and I knew that sooner or later the old door would give and fall to pieces, bringing me a fate worse than death! Finally, one of the boards cracked under the force of the blows, and I screamed.

"There's a woman inside!" one soldier exclaimed lasciviously. "Let's get this door open fast and have some fun!"

"Stop it! Leave her alone!" shouted another in a commanding tone. "Let's go to the town! It's downhill all the way." As the sound of their boots gradually faded away, I knew that a miracle had taken place!

When next morning I opened the window, a veil of fog had enveloped the whole countryside. I went outside cautiously, still upset from the nightmarish experience, and started to sweep up the mess left by the soldiers when Ser Antonio appeared in hunting clothes and greeted me. Seeing he was alone, I scowled at him. "You have a nerve showing up after all these weeks without my child!" I shouted, paralyzed with anger.

"I was hunting nearby with some friends and thought I'd stop to see how you were and how the olive harvest went."

"How can I be? I've a broken heart, because I haven't seen my son for weeks—the son you took away from me with your false promises!"

"Caterina, be patient! You must know that when you signed that paper you acknowledged that Piero is Leo's father. Therefore, by law, the boy has to live with him," he said coldly. "And if we let him stay with you sometimes, you should consider it as an expression of our good will."

"So you did trick me, you wicked men! You and that scoundrel son of yours waited for me to bring up the boy in order to see if he was bright or not, before plotting to steal him from me," I said in one breath. "And, now, what do you tell him when he asks about me?"

"Frankly, he's so excited about school that he never asks to be brought up here anymore."

"I don't believe you!" I cried furiously.

"My dear, you're still so young. You could have all the children you want, if you would only think of getting married."

"Never! I would never do that. God gave me a son, and he will be my only son, and nobody—but nobody—will take him away from me forever!"

"Look how many young men are returning from the wars ...."

In that terrible moment, I realized why he had hired the soldiers, why he had shown me such contempt. "Now I know why you sent that band of drunkards here," I cried accusingly.

"What drunkards? They're just harmless young men, happy to be coming home at last and working in the fields!"

"Oh, yes? They destroyed your olive grove, molested the poor women you dared send to help them, and nearly broke down my door, trying to attack me!"

"You don't think *I* instructed them to behave that way, do you?" he said, looking at me incredulously. "But, in any case, you must accept the fact that it is up to us whether you ever see your son again or not."

"How dare you! How dare you say such wicked words! You vile people, you and your son! Get out of here and never come back without my son," I cried, threatening him with my broom. He backed away with arms raised, trying to mumble calming words to me, but I brandished my weapon high until he was completely out of sight.

I wandered aimlessly for hours around the grounds, trying to overcome my grief, until I started to feel the night frost. So I took some wood indoors, lit a fire and, for a while, sat gazing at Leo's bed. Then I went and fluffed up his pillow, as I did every night, and sat on his bed. Soon I heard myself softly humming his lullaby, hoping it would reach my little boy in his dreams so he would not forget me. "Oh, my Leo, how can I see you?" I kept asking in my anguish. In a sudden flash of inspiration, I knew what I had to do. "I'm going to see you tomorrow, my son! Yes, tomorrow!"

Drawing my cape tightly against the morning chill, I set out for the town of Vinci. The bitter wind on my face blew hard, but the anticipation in my heart kept me warm and my stride swift. When I reached the center of the town, I approached a nicely dressed woman with a little boy, carrying a leather satchel. "Good woman, could you tell me where the special school is for little boys like yours?" I asked her eagerly.

"We're just going there. It's next to the Church of Santo Spirito, you see!" she said, pointing at a church surrounded by tall trees.

I followed them for a while, until the school door was in view. Seeing Leo arrive, holding a young woman by the hand, I quickly hid behind the corner of the church. Leo saw me as I put my finger on my lips, and only waited for the instant the young woman had kissed him on the forehead and turned to leave before racing toward me in delight. He threw himself in my arms, mindless of his heavy satchel falling and spilling on the ground. "Mama! Mama! I'm so happy to see you!" he cried.

I held him tightly, as tears of joy filled my eyes. "Why, darling, why didn't you want to come to see me?" I asked.

"I did! I did! But Ser Piero kept saying that you had gone to Florence."

"Why did he say that?" I asked, shocked. "I waited for you all the time. At the end of the week, I didn't even go down to the brook for fear of missing you!"

He was very upset. "Why should he lie to me? I don't like that."

"I don't know, my dear. Maybe because he loves you and wants you with him all the time," I replied, wondering if Piero really knew about my trip to Florence. It was obvious that Leo didn't believe the story about his father's great love for him. "I have an idea," I said excitedly. "Don't tell anybody about seeing me today, so I can come to see you here again."

"But I like to go up in the hills. How is the nightingale?"

"He's fine. I'll tell him I saw you and your lovely school, too."

"I'm so glad he didn't fly away last time when I opened the cage!"

"But he likes to stay in his cage—maybe he feels safer in there. I'll tell him you inquired about him," I said, while deciding whether to ask the next question, but I went on anyway. "Who was that nice lady who brought you here?"

"She's Donna Albiera, my fath—, Ser Piero's wife. She's like a mother to me while I'm living here. I pretend to be her son because she's very good to me," he explained, looking into my eyes.

"Oh, yes? Well, I suppose it's all right as long as you always remember I'm your real mother!"

"I know, Mama. You'll always be my real mother!" he said earnestly.

Hardly able to contain my emotion, I helped him gather up his things, kissed him good-bye and hurried him inside, gazing longingly at him.

The climb back home was arduous, for the wind had turned fiercer and dark clouds threatened to bring the first snowfall of the season, yet my heart was filled with happiness for having found the perfect way to see my son whenever I wanted.

The next day, though, the grounds, the trees, and the hills were all covered in white, making it impossible for me to return to Vinci. Defeated again, I hopelessly faced the loneliest winter of my life, not knowing how I would survive it either physically or mentally. The food from Rita's pantry had almost run out, and so distraught had I been in the last weeks that I had not even thought of providing a food reserve for the winter. Furthermore, I had nothing left from the change Francesca had given me in Florence, and the snow prevented Giuseppe from going to town.

Once I had asked him if he would change another florin for me, but he had refused, saying, "I'm sorry, Caterina. If anybody sees me carrying it around, they'll think I stole it—that's a lot of money for us countrypeople." As an afterthought, he added, "Too bad you didn't learn from Donna Rita how to do it. She knew how to handle her affairs!"

"Yes, too bad," I said, ending our financial discussion.

The following day, he showed up with a sack of flour. "Take this!" he said firmly. "You can pay me when you've found a way to change that 'thing,'" he added in a conspiratorial whisper. Thanks to him, I didn't starve during that long winter.

But I had to keep my mind healthy, too, so one day I started to take out of the trunk the dresses Rita had given me, not having worn them since she was young. She had also provided me with many pieces of braid she had kept from the time she was in service to noble ladies. I had found a wonderful pastime! What fun it was to fit and alter those dresses made of the finest fabrics and then to trim the necklines with those lavish braids! But I was soon to be faced with a greater challenge.

One evening, sitting by the fire, I decided to take out all the special gifts I had found in Rita's precious box. What I had previously mistaken for the lining of the box turned out to be a sheet of pink paper, folded in two, on which Rita had written a note to me. I was filled with excitement as I recognized the first three words, "My dear Lisa," and her signature. Unfortunately, I couldn't read the content.

Admiring Rita's neat handwriting, I recalled her telling me that her first job had been as a companion to a rich girl, who wouldn't take lessons unless she sat next to her. "I often learned more than she did," Rita had said, laughing. Anxious to read her message, I took out Piero's books and studied them with great determination.

So, between my sewing and the study of Rita's letter, my

lonely winter turned into a most productive one. By the end of it, I was finally able to decipher every word she had written, giving me a better understanding of my parents' plight.

> My dear Lisa, I salvaged these objects from the burning villa for you, because I always believed I would find you one day and make you proud of your parents. Your father never knew about the baby your mother was expecting. They had arranged to elope after he finished his secret apprenticeship in the *bottega* in Florence, and your mother planned to surprise him with you in her arms. But, as you know, your grandfather returned before her dream came true and everything went wrong. Forgive me for not talking to you about your parents, but I respected your wish. I'll be praying that you find your father. I know that by then you'll understand their circumstances better. I embrace you and love you eternally, Rita.

"Oh, my dear Rita, why didn't I let you tell me more about them?" I kept repeating every time I read it.

The snow melted at last, and I started strolling around the grounds already scattered with the first primroses and planning the flower garden I had promised my little boy.

"Caterina, I have good news for you," said Giuseppe one day. "Ser Antonio asked me to let you know he's sending Leo to spend the whole Easter week with you."

"Easter! When *is* Easter?" I asked, overwhelmed with joy.

"I really don't know. I'll ask my wife. She'll know, though she never goes to church herself," he said dryly.

"Why doesn't she go? Doesn't she believe in God?"

"She does, but she's afraid to leave the house," he said, shaking his head. "By the way, do you still have any of that flour left?"

"Not much, but now I have some vegetables growing in the garden."

"What about that gold …. 'thing'?" he asked below his breath, making sure no one was around. "You know, I spoke to someone I can trust who'll change it for me. But wrap it in an old piece of rag!"

"Thank you, dear Giuseppe. You're the only friend left in my life!" I did as he asked and told him to bring some food, too.

Wrapped in my lighter shawl, I climbed the road leading to the Church of Santa Lucia. On the way, I stopped briefly to admire the soft purple colors of the crocuses growing under the chestnut trees along the edge of the slope and wondered if they could survive being moved to my garden.

At the church, I went over to the old priest, who was busy adding new rows of benches. "Padre," I asked him shyly, "how soon will it be Easter?"

He looked at me in shock. "My daughter, don't you know when Easter is? If you came to church more frequently, like a good Christian, you would certainly know," he scolded, resuming his work.

I approached him again and fell contritely on my knees. "Padre, for God's sake, forgive me, but it's important that I know. You see, they're bringing back my little son at Easter. I haven't seen him for months!"

"Please get up, my dear. I didn't know." He pointed to the marble altar a boy was polishing. "Doesn't the bare altar tell you anything? Today is the anniversary of our Lord's death, so Easter is only two days away," he explained, helping me to my feet. "You'll hear my bells ring. Why don't you bring your son on Sunday?"

"Thank you, Padre, but he's still too small to walk up here."

He slipped his hand into his pocket and gave me a small card. It was a pastel drawing of Christ Arisen. "Give this to him," he began, but stopped in surprise when he heard me read the title under the picture.

"The Redeemer! Thank you, Padre! It's beautiful!" I exclaimed.

"I drew it myself. On the back, I wrote a short prayer. You may not be able to read it, but it will help you just the same."

I turned the card over and slowly read the prayer aloud. He listened carefully, then he exclaimed, "So you *can* read! How did you learn?"

"By myself, from some books I had."

"That's wonderful! You must be the only woman in our hills able to do that. Go home now. I see you're anxious to see your son again."

Yes, I was. I almost ran down the hill, stopping by the crocuses again, but on second thought deciding to leave them in their little meadow. Then, from the corner of my eye, I glimpsed some tiny snow-white flowers growing in the hollow of a tree trunk at the edge of a cliff. "How marvelous! White violets!" I cried. They were the rare mystical white violets of Mont'Albano! I recalled that, according to legend, delicate white violets always grew well out of reach on sheer cliffs, places where nobody could touch them.

With Leo, my little artist, in mind, I leaned forward, trying to uproot the whole plant with a long twig, but suddenly the rock I stood on fell away. Losing my balance, I grabbed the trunk with both hands, holding my breath as I heard the rock rolling all the way down into the deep valley, hitting the bottom with a distant thud. I gasped, realizing that it could have been me. With my heart still pounding, I climbed up to look at the violets, wondering if I had really trespassed on nature, but when I saw the plant lying uprooted, I decided that I should take it anyway and take care of it. I gathered it up in its own soil, and holding it in my cupped hands, I raced home in triumph.

I planted the white violets in the pretty terra-cotta vase on my windowsill and stood back to admire it from my artist son's point of view, smiling as my heart filled with great satisfaction.

After cleaning the house and baking bread and sweet buns for my Leo, I thought I should wear a new dress. Since the air was warm enough, I took out the sky-blue cotton dress I had fixed during the winter months. I had taken it in at the waist like the dresses worn by the ladies I had seen on the steps of the Duomo in Florence. But, to give it a final touch, I trimmed the neckline with thick white lace flowers, making a nice contrast with the blue of the dress and my dark hair.

When I heard the gig come into the yard, I rushed outside. "Leo, my darling, at last!" I cried. But my enthusiasm was crushed at the sight of Piero holding the reins. I frowned at him as he daringly smiled back.

Leo, looking taller, jumped off by himself and came to hug me. Then, joining hands, we danced in a circle around the yard.

"Mama! Mama! I'm so happy to be here! You look beautiful in your new blue dress!" he cried. But noticing that Piero's presence had upset me, he tried to ease the situation. "Mama, do you know that my father, Ser Piero, is letting me stay with you for a whole week?" he exclaimed. I said nothing. "Mama, you didn't even greet him!" he said with dismay, following me to the door.

"I really prefer to be alone with you, Leo!" But seeing that he was really upset, I motioned him to go inside, and I went back to Piero, who was slowly tying his horse to a tree. He glanced at me in his old seductive way, his eyes shining.

"What are you waiting for? The boy is going to stay with me for the week, isn't he?" I demanded. There was no response and I walked away.

"Caterina, wait! Let me look at you. You're so beautiful! You've blossomed during the last few years. You're ... more attractive than ever. With that blue dress, you're like a vision!" he said passionately.

I stopped and turned, but avoided looking him in the eye. "So, what of it? You didn't answer my question. I want you to know that the only reason I didn't show anger at you for keeping my boy away for so many months was to avoid upsetting him. Now, please go." He didn't speak. I stood with my back turned, waiting to hear him get back in the gig and leave. Then I rushed back to Leo, who met me on the doorstep. "He can't stay, my dear. He has to go home," I mumbled. Leo was not convinced, but followed me inside without a word.

We spent a delightful week together, which filled my heart

with joy and compensated for the solitude endured throughout the long winter.

On the last day, Gian Pietro reappeared with his cart, and as Leo went to get his things, he looked gravely at me, saying, "Did you know that Ser Antonio is still very sick?"

"No, I'm sorry. When did he get sick?" I asked, a little aloof.

"Quite a while ago. Poor man, I hope God'll let him stay with us," he said sadly. "Without him in that house, things will be quite different, if you know what I mean, Caterina." He looked at me to see my response.

I didn't know if he was trying to be friendly or to frighten me. "No, I don't know what you mean. Why? Is he that ill?"

"Yes, I'm afraid so. He's a good man, and without him ... I mean ..."

Leo arrived with a box full of small plants, tips of branches, all kinds of rocks, and dead insects. When he went back for his jacket, Gian Pietro peered into the box and asked, "What's he got in there?"

"Things he collected to draw from life, as he puts it."

He shook his head. "Oh, my God. The more the father wants him to become a notary, the more the boy wants to be an artisan! The fact that the boy's so bright doesn't make any difference to him."

I knew by now that he wanted to be recognized as a good judge of his masters' character, and touching his arm, I whispered to him, "Gian Pietro, don't tell Ser Piero about these things. Otherwise, he won't let my son come back." He nodded, happy to have become my confidant, and I turned to Leo, who was saying good-bye to the nightingale. "Leo, why didn't you tell me Ser Antonio was sick?"

"I didn't want to upset you. I know that you're fond of him. He's getting better, though," he replied, trying to cheer me up.

The next day at dawn, I decided to go back and sit under the shapely arch of my old well in order to resume my meditation, hoping to find guidance for my uncertain future. As I sat on its step waiting for the sun to rise, I was startled by the shimmer of a silver sun ray striking, like an arrow, the roof of Rita's solitary house on the edge of the green cliff. "You must be as lonesome as I am!" I said to the house, feeling a sudden urge to go there again.

The next morning I was crossing Rita's yard, feeling light and happy. As I opened the door and fond memories of Rita were going through my mind, the presence of an approaching stranger alarmed me. "Sorry, young woman. I didn't mean to frighten you," he said politely. "I was wondering if this house was for sale." Although he was dressed like a hunter, the elegant, middle-aged man did not seem comfortable in his brand-new hunting jacket, which fitted a little too tightly around his fat stomach. He carried a hunting bag but oddly enough, no rifle.

"No, it's not," I answered flatly, annoyed by the intrusion. "Why do you ask, *messere?*"

"My name is Ser Giuliano Giacomotti," he said, a wide smile across his chubby face. "I'd like to buy it. Who is the owner?"

"The owner is no longer with us. The house is mine now, but I don't wish to sell it. It holds special memories for me." My glance fell on Rita's plants, which badly needed watering, so I casually picked up a pitcher and started for the well. He followed me.

"But I know you don't live here," he persisted. "I've been here often the past few days." He slowed down, hoping that I would, too.

"I'm sorry, *messere,* I have to get some water. I don't have time for conversation now," I said, walking briskly. Yet he still followed me.

"Are you thinking of living here?" he asked, out of breath.

"I don't know yet. For the time being, I have to stay where I am. It's important for me to live there—" I broke off, realizing I had no reason to confide in him. Then it occurred to me that I had few opportunities to communicate with nice people, so after filling the pitcher at the well, I finally stopped to listen to him.

He cleared his throat. "You know, dear woman, my consort badly needs the mountain air to restore her health." I noted the anguish in his voice. Then he added, "I can offer you a good price! Money helps, don't you think? I have an important position in Empoli and I could be of help to you in the future." I was silent. "You would still be able to come here, I assure you," he went on. "My consort is a very amiable person and she'll be happy to have your company. I will be away a great deal, you see."

"I'll have to think about it," I said at last. Yet I was touched by his earnestness.

"Thank you, Donna …"

"My name is Caterina. I live down there in Anchiano," I said, pointing across the valley as we went back to the house. I started to water the plants, and he stepped back to take another look at the house.

"This little house would be perfect for my wife!" he said, glowing with enthusiasm. "You see, it would take too long to build a new one." I nodded sympathetically. Then, appearing more confident, he said, "Donna Caterina, I'll be back next week at the same time." As he bowed to me, the blood rushed to his full face, and I was so amused by his manner that the pitcher almost slipped from my hand.

After cleaning all the rooms, I took a comfortable chair and sat out on the veranda, where the mild afternoon air and the monotonous chatter of the cicadas made me drowsy. I found myself drifting into a dream.

I was on a sandy shore, looking at a vast expanse of water shimmering into the horizon. Captivated, I walked barefoot on the golden sand, listening to the waves stealing in. I had never witnessed anything like it before, but it was just as Rita had described it. "This must be the sea!" I cried as Rita herself glided through the air toward me in a dress that revealed her dancing feet. She was young and svelte, merrily singing one of her Spanish gypsy songs. Then I felt the warmth of her presence, and she murmured, "Lisa, my Lisa! You see, I've found my happiness! So I don't need my house anymore.… Go ahead with your plans, my dear! *Vaya con Dios! Vaya con*

Dios!" Her last words echoed, mingling with the splash of the waves—a sound that persisted as I woke up.

There were joyous tears in my eyes as I thought of my dream all the way home. Was it wishful thinking? Or was it really possible that the souls of our dear ones are, in fact, aware of what troubles us?

Entering the courtyard, I was amazed to see Ser Antonio's gig standing there. He was sitting with Leo on the low wall. "Leo! Leo, my darling!" I cried. "What a lovely surprise!"

"Mama, we looked for you everywhere. Where have you been? This place looks so sad without you," he said as he hugged me. "Today school was closed, so Grandfather said, 'Let's go for a breath of fresh air!'" We all laughed together at Leo's imitation.

"Ser Antonio, I'm so glad you recovered," I said, feeling a change of heart toward him.

"I'm not completely recovered, but much better, thanks to the spring weather, which, among other things, renews the health of an old man like me." He stroked Leo's head. "I went to see the new olive grove. Caterina, do you remember when I had those trees planted?"

"Yes, Ser Antonio. It was the year Leo was born!" I remarked.

"Well, when this estate becomes mine," he said with a sweeping gesture of the hand, "I'm going to bequeath it to Leonardo."

I smiled at him. "I'm sorry I wasn't here when you arrived. I went to air Rita's house."

"You should go and live there, because ..." He looked at Leo.

"Leo, have you said hello to the nightingale yet? If you don't, he'll cry," I teased. He went over to the cage, looking at me poutingly, and I immediately regretted having said something so silly.

"Caterina, I'm afraid the friars have decided to reactivate the olive-pressing mill," whispered Ser Antonio, "and turn this place into a farm at all costs, so ..."

"Ser Antonio, would you let me repair Maddalena's old house? I could live there," I said on a sudden impulse.

"It's falling apart, don't you see? And where would you get the money to restore it?"

"I could sell Rita's house. It's for Leo. He adores this place."

"Do you really think this land makes a difference to him? He comes here just to see you, which shouldn't be encouraged, for it doesn't help his future." He paused, and I kept calm, not to upset him. "Besides, his father is planning to move to Florence, so what would be the purpose of having a new house here?"

"It would always be his childhood home. As for the future, who knows? Maybe we won't need this place anymore! But for the time being it would make a difference." He stared at me skeptically. "I'm only asking for a small piece of land that is already occupied by a ruin. Is that a great deal? I've given in to you so much." My throat tightened.

"All right, then, do it! But remember that I'm not the owner yet. If the friars throw you out, don't blame me! Caterina, Caterina, you're impossible!" He sighed, pretending to lose his patience. Then, mellowing a little, he said, "Still, I wouldn't mind having you as a daughter!"

He rose to his feet and walked to the end of the yard from which he could see Rita's house. "Are you sure somebody wants to buy that house up there in the wilderness? Who would that be?"

I did not answer, as I saw Leo coming back. "What a pity we couldn't go and play down by the *ruscello* this time, Mama! I'm going to miss it ... a lot!"

I glanced at Ser Antonio, who was not able to hide his annoyance. "Leonardo, we must go now. It's dinnertime!" he said nervously. "They must be wondering where we are." He looked as if he had aged and somehow I felt closer to him.

The following week, I arrived at Rita's house a little early and just as I was opening the door, the persistent gentleman drove up the road in his gig. "Good morning, Donna Caterina!" He saluted as he jumped down. Walking briskly, he came right up to me and asked, "Well, have you decided, Donna Caterina? I think you have, haven't you?"

"Well, not really, but you can come in and take a look, *messere*."

"I'll be happy to." He bowed stiffly, motioning me to lead the way.

Once in the room I paused, glancing around and mentally asking Rita's permission. Then, still a little hesitant, I let him enter.

He took a cursory look at the rooms. "It's just as I thought it would be. I'm sure my consort will like it very much."

"I have a feeling that it's much too small for a lady used to a big house and servants. Maybe she should see it first."

"Oh, she's very adaptable, even about having fewer servants," he said confidently. "All she needs now is pure fresh air. Her breathing disorder is not infectious, just the cause of all her discomfort."

"I see. But where will I put all these things? The house where I live is too small and rustic for this type of furniture."

"You can leave everything here. It's all very suitable for a house in the mountains. So, shall we negotiate?" he urged, taking out some papers from his hunting bag. "Here's a contract with the price I'm offering. If it's all right with you, we can settle it now."

"But, Ser Giuliano, I can't read that and I have no idea of the value of the house. Besides, I prefer not to sell it. But please bring your lady wife! She can stay here. I'd like to meet her."

"I could not take advantage of your generosity." He paused. "Please tell me if there's anything you want. I'm sure there's something I could do," he said, almost pleading.

"Yes, there is something I want and I could use your help, *messere*. I'd like to have a little house repaired, down there next to where I live. I wouldn't know how to go about it."

"I'll send my builder to take a look at it." Then he emptied a bag of gold florins on the table. "Take this, Donna Caterina. You can use it to start fixing up the house."

"Oh, no, Messer Giacomotti, I can't take it. I wouldn't know how to handle so much money. I'd rather you held on to it until I need it. I trust you, Ser Giuliano. In the meantime, please bring Donna ...?"

"Grazia is her name. I'm sure she'll be happy to meet you. I can't find words to thank you, Donna Caterina. I promise I'll make myself worthy of your trust!"

I smiled, finally feeling I could confide in him. "My reason for improving that house down there by the old tavern building is so my son can spend his visits from school in the most beautiful corner of the world for us!"

"Ah, you have a son! You're a fortunate woman."

"There's a heavenly brook down in that valley," I continued to explain, "where we love to spend all our time together. Sooner or later, I will have to vacate that building and the nearby house is almost in ruin."

"Donna Caterina, rest assured I will do everything in my power to help you. Now, as soon as my wife is ready to come, I'll send my stableman to let you know. Now I must hurry home and give my consort the good news."

On the day of their arrival, I resolved to be at Rita's house really early, but a big cart full of large wicker trunks was already outside. Two tall, sturdy women dressed all in white were unloading it. In the morning sunlight, their plain white cotton scarves, completely hiding their hair, contrasted sharply against their olive-skin faces.

"Did you bring a spare key, Donna Caterina?" asked the younger maid, with a strong southern accent. "The masters will be here soon."

"I'm sorry if I'm late, but I didn't expect you to be here so early."

"We left before dawn," explained the older woman, coming forward. "The masters' carriage travels slowly so as not to tire Donna Grazia."

"Where will you put all these things? The house is already full," I asked, turning the key. They shrugged their shoulders and smirked.

In the bedroom, I dragged an empty wicker trunk, which I had found under a cover, over to the chest of drawers. When I opened them and saw Rita's personal mementos, I had qualms about removing them. But hearing the carriage arrive, I knew there was no more time for regrets. So I hurriedly packed them, fixed my hair, and went to greet my new friend.

Donna Grazia was in her thirties, but looked very fragile as she was helped down from the elegant carriage by her husband. She wore a soft green dress with a matching veil, which fell over her wavy, light-brown hair. Her pretty face lit up with a warm smile. "Good morning, Caterina! Thank you for giving up this charming little house for me," she said, holding out her slim, silk-gloved hand. Then, turning to her husband, she remarked, "Oh, Giuliano, it's delightful up here! Do you hear the birds singing? I feel better already."

"The house is very small, Donna Grazia," I said, thinking how well the name suited her, "but it was built and cared for with great love."

"Yes, Caterina, I can see that," she asserted, looking through the house approvingly. "Remember, though, I'm counting on your company, too!" Then, with Ser Giuliano's help, she sank into the chair on the veranda, which the older maid had covered with soft cushions.

"Donna Caterina, you can use my cart to take some things home," said Ser Giuliano. "The maids will help you. As you can see, we haven't brought any furniture yet. When your house is ready, you can take the rest."

A few days later, a man in his late twenties introduced himself as Ser Giuliano's head mason. We stood in front of Big Madd's old dwelling. "Well, Donna Caterina, are there any changes to be made?" he asked.

"Yes. Come with me!" He followed me to the back of the house. "See the back wall? I want a large window there overlooking the brook below."

He looked around. "Brook? I can't see any brook."

"You can't see it from here, but you can hear it. It's down this slope at the bottom of that high cliff opposite."

He gazed at me as I spoke and, changing the subject, he asked not very subtly, "Do you live here alone?"

"What does that have to do with this work?" I remonstrated. "Yes, I do, but not all the time. That's why I need another room to be added on that side." Noticing that he hadn't taken his eyes off me for an instant, I snapped, "I can see that you're not paying attention to what I'm saying. Maybe you're not interested in doing the work."

Rather taken aback, he only managed to say, "Donna Caterina!"

"Well, it doesn't matter. Ser Giuliano will find somebody else for me."

"Please, Donna Caterina," he pleaded, suddenly becoming serious, "let me take another look around the house so I can prepare an estimate." As he went off, I wondered if I had been too brusque with him. "Donna Caterina, when do you need the house?" he asked, returning.

"I have to move out of the house where I'm living now before they harvest the olives."

"I'm sorry, but it's impossible to do the whole job this summer. It takes time to bring the materials up here. We'll try to speed up the work to please Ser Giuliano, but for the additional room, you'll have to wait until next year."

"All right, then. I'm sorry if I was a little short earlier." Seeing my guard down, he leered at me again. So I stonily added, "My husband is a soldier of the *condotta*. He's ... a very jealous man. So he likes to show up unexpectedly." It was amusing to see him turn pale and bid me a hasty farewell, and I was more than relieved to have found a way of keeping molesters at bay.

It was thrilling to see the first building materials being delivered: stones, bricks, sand, and roof beams. But the thought of my Leo missing the excitement of seeing the house being rebuilt made his absence even more unbearable.

Determined to do something about it, the next morning I waited behind the corner of the church to see my Leo again on his way to school. This time, he came with Donna Lucia, who looked very tired and depressed as Leo pulled her along by the hand. I stepped out, and my Leo threw himself into my arms.

"What are you doing here?" Donna Lucia gasped.

"Good morning, Donna Lucia. I had to come. I couldn't wait any longer. I was much too worried about my Leo," I said, keeping my voice down so as not to upset her.

"Thank God, he's all right. We have enough illness in my home. With my consort sick again and poor Albiera ill, too, there was nobody to—"

"Mama, school is going to close for the summer. I want to stay in the country with you," Leo interrupted.

"Caterina, please go! If anybody sees you here with us, there will be problems at home," she said, looking around nervously.

"I'm putting an end to this nonsense. I'll come in Giuseppe's cart and pick him up myself when the time comes."

Donna Lucia pulled Leo from my arms. "Leonardo, go inside!" Leo kissed me and went on his way.

"Donna Lucia, you have no right to treat me this way. I'm his mother, or have you forgotten?"

She could see I was losing control. So after some hesitation, she touched my arm and said, "I know, my dear, I know, but we have enough problems between my poor husband and my son...." Then, hurrying away, she hid her face under a shawl, which seemed too heavy for such a fine day.

As I headed home up the dusty main road, I was so enraged by this absurd situation that I could barely restrain myself from going back and snatching Leo from the school. "I must find a way to get him back. I must!.... At least for the summer," I kept repeating, climbing the slope in the scorching sun.

Exhausted and devastated, I reached the courtyard, wiping the perspiration off my face with my scarf. Giuseppe was sitting on my doorstep, waiting for me. "There you are, Caterina! Donna Grazia sent me. She would like to have you over for a meal."

"I can't. I'm too upset about my son! The thought of him living in a house full of sick people, when he could spend the summer with me, just kills me!"

"Don't worry, Caterina. Things will work out. Now go and get ready! I can wait—the lady pays me well for my time."

I washed at the sink behind Big Madd's house with rain water from a large barrel and slipped on my blue cotton, which seemed to be the only suitable dress for a visit to such an elegant and noble lady.

"Welcome, Caterina. How beautiful you look in your blue dress! You remind me of a painting by one of the great Florentine masters!" she said warmly as I entered the living room. I was pleased to see a healthy bloom in her cheeks. She was wearing a lilac-pink gown with an embroidered bodice, which came down into a point, emphasizing her tiny waist. Her light-chestnut hair was plaited and neatly swirled at the nape, the way I had seen the ladies in Florence wear theirs.

"You look wonderful, Donna Grazia. I'm happy to see your cheeks so rosy," I replied, proudly touching my thick hair, which I had softly gathered in one of Rita's silk nets.

"Good morning, Donna Caterina. Is the work on the house progressing well?" asked Ser Giuliano, appearing in another smart hunting jacket, which also seemed too tight for him.

"Well, they're bringing the materials. But, Ser Giuliano, please just call me Caterina, like Donna Grazia does."

"She's right. She's too young to be called 'Donna Caterina.' Perhaps 'Monna Caterina' would be more suitable."

"Not even 'monna' is necessary," I said modestly. "By the way, did the head mason tell you about the additional room?"

"Oh, yes! Even so, I trust you'll be pleased to hear that you'll have money left over for other things," he said, taking his wife's hand.

"Caterina, you've saved my life, giving me the opportunity to come and stay here at such short notice," she said, beaming. "See how much I've improved?"

"And, now, my dear ladies, I'll leave you alone to enjoy your meal. I'm going to take a long hike in the woods. I need the exercise," he said, patting his stomach. "Besides, I'll never convince anyone I'm a real hunter until my jacket acquires a worn look!" We laughed heartily at his amusing observation as he waved good-bye.

"Now, Caterina, I want you to tell me all about yourself. I know from Giuseppe that you have a son, a talented boy, who's away at school, and that you, yourself, are very gifted, having created your own, very wholesome vegetable garden!"

"Well, my son is very artistic. Since he loves to draw flowers, the last time I saw him, I promised him a flower garden with the most beautiful flowers ever seen in these hills all year round. I've decided to start it, while waiting for the new house to be finished."

"Ah, my dear, you're in luck, because when it comes to growing flowers, you have an expert here! I spent the best time of my young years in the splendid gardens and conservatories of my father's estate in Pisa. It had become fashionable for girls of well-to-do families to learn gardening, following an investigation to determine why girls who entered convents turned out to be healthier than those who enjoyed the comforts of home. It was discovered that nuns not only tended their vegetable gardens for their sustenance, but also flower gardens for the purpose of spiritual contemplation. It was decided then that all girls should be allowed this health-giving exercise, which refined the spirit, too, and flower gardens sprang up in all the wealthy homes."

"So gardening is not such a lowly occupation?" I asked.

"Oh, no! Why, even gardening dresses were designed, similar to nuns' pinafore smocks. So your idea is in keeping with the times! Now, unfortunately, my health doesn't allow me any such activity, but of advice?—I can assure you, I can give you plenty! Just let me know when the soil is ready and I'll have seeds and bulbs delivered to you. And now let's toast to it with a glass of strawberry wine," she said, pouring from a pretty bottle, "and after we eat, we'll sit on the veranda and talk more about flowers." Then she asked me to sit at the table the maid had just set for us. I had never tasted food so delicately prepared as this, and served in such dainty, gold-painted china dishes. Later, explaining my situation to her, I couldn't help relating the story of my life.

On my way home, I cherished the soothing effect of that meeting with the noblewoman who had so kindly offered me her friendship and her help, enlightening my spirit and giving me a new confidence in life.

9
THE LOVELY ABODE

On that pleasant Sunday morning, the north wind had swept away the sultriness of the preceding hot days. My hair was drying in the sun as I cleaned the birdcage and chatted with my nightingale, expressing to him my heartache for not having my little son with me.

Leo's voice reached my ear. "Mama! Mama! I'm here! See?"

I ran around the corner and saw him rushing into my arms. "You're alone! How did you get here?" I asked, joyfully surprised.

"No, I'm not. My ... Ser Piero brought me. He stayed in the gig at the bend of the road, but he said he wants to talk to you."

"Go inside, then. I'll be back soon." I reluctantly walked down the road. Piero was sitting up straight in his gig, looking woebegone. He had a short gray-streaked beard, which gave him an air of maturity. He stared at me, spellbound. "What's the matter? What do you have to tell me?" I asked abruptly.

He shook his head. "I'm letting the boy stay with you for the summer," he said, still staring at me strangely.

"Thank you! Thank you, Piero! I can't believe you allowed it. Anyway, thank you again, Piero!"

"Unfortunately, my wife is very sick, and I felt it wasn't fair for the boy to stay in a house full of sick people, so I decided—"

"Why, is Ser Antonio still sick?" I interrupted.

He seemed surprised that I knew about it. "Yes. In fact, my mother has to take care of him, too." When he mentioned his mother, I lowered my eyes and nodded, knowing that she had influenced his decision. "I'll send the boy's things with Gian Pietro." When I looked up to thank him again, I couldn't help noticing tears forming in his eyes. I was both puzzled and concerned that there might be some other tragedy. After clearing his throat, he began talking in a voice that reminded me of the times he courted me. "Caterina, oh, Caterina! No matter how hard I try, I still can't get you out of my mind. Just look at you! More beautiful than ever!" I quickly pushed back the hair I had let flow to my shoulders, feeling guilty for appearing provocative to him. I looked up again, embarrassed, but he turned away, suddenly enraged, cracking his whip so fiercely that his horse bolted off down the main road.

A twinge went through my heart, and I felt sorry for him. "Yes, Piero," I said, "I see now that you're still attracted to me. But my love for you died long ago, when you took advantage of me." I sighed, realizing that, after all, fate had not been so kind to him, either.

Among the things contained in the box, that Gian Pietro had brought for Leo were many pencils and sheets of pink drawing paper. I picked up one covered with drawings in order to look at it closely. "What pretty drawings!" I exclaimed, aproaching Leo, who was sitting in the shade of a tree, counting the blank ones left over. "Who gave you all this paper?"

"My grandfather gave it to me, and my teacher, Sister Giuseppina, taught me how to draw."

"Where did she learn?" I asked, knowing that women were not allowed in any artisan studios.

"She learned from her father. He was a great painter of church frescoes, like Giotto di Bondone."

"Who is Giotto di Bondone?"

"He was an even greater painter! He painted the stories of Jesus Christ and the saints on the walls of churches. He also designed the Duomo bell tower in Florence!" he said, eager to tell me what he had learned.

"Look how many interesting things I'm learning from you! You see? You're still my teacher!" I said, pinching his chin. He gave out one of his little cascading laughs that never ceased to delight me.

In a few days, he had used up half of his paper supply, as if he had already known what he wanted to draw. I was amazed at the variety of subjects he had sketched: trees, tiny flowers, the nightingale in its cage, ants swarming, butterflies, swallows gliding over the brook, springs gushing water; everything depicted in such astounding detail that I asked myself how a little boy could capture nature's complexity so effortlessly.

He seemed to prefer sketching early in the morning or at dusk, I noticed, which I found peculiar. So, one evening while he was lying on his back under a tree, drawing a large leaf on a sheet of paper attached to a board, I sat near him. "Darling, how can you draw when the sun has almost set behind the hills?" I asked.

"I know, Mother, but I'm trying to catch the twilight reflecting on that leaf. Come here, and I'll show you what I mean." I quickly shifted myself in order to look over his shoulder. "See how those low rays light up that leaf? That's what I'm trying to capture. But I have to work swiftly, because it doesn't last," he said, concerned.

"Darling, I know nothing about drawing, but I'll tell you something that may be of help to you. Before you were born, I used to sit by the old well to watch the miracle of dawn, which fascinated me over and over again. I found, though, that by fixing my eye on one particular spot and concentrating my attention, I was able to soak up all the magnificent changes of light until they were indelibly impressed in my mind. Maybe you could do the same when you want to catch that fleeting light on a leaf or a flower. Come out before the sun comes up and just stare at the thing you want to draw until it becomes part of you, and, just like magic, it will stay in your memory forever."

"That's wonderful, Mother! And nobody taught you how to do that."

"Well, I had learned how to listen to the sounds in the wind, just as the little beings had told me." Leo smiled and looked around himself expectantly.

After that, he no longer had that worried look on his face when he came home from his drawing excursions.

When he had filled up all his drawing paper, however, he suddenly shifted his attention to something completely different.

He had started stripping the bark of a birch tree. After shaping it into bowls, he fixed tiny sticks in them. To these, he fastened scraps of cloth, after which he tied long pieces of string to the bowls and took them down to the brook. Curious to see what he was going to do with them, I followed him, keeping my distance. To my amazement, he placed the bowls on the water, holding on to the other end of the strings. Soon the wind caused the cloths to unfurl, making the bowls glide swiftly with the current and pull on the strings in Leo's hand.

"Darling, what are those things?" I asked as I got near, fascinated.

"They're boats like the ones that sail on the sea." Seeing that I was still puzzled, he added, "The sea Aunt Rita talked about so much. Don't you remember?" I said nothing, while vividly remembering my dream. "Sailors travel across it in very large boats called caravels. These are just small copies. Let's follow them downstream to see which one is the fastest," he cried in excitement as he ran along the bank, holding the strings like reins.

I ran after him, asking, "But, darling, you've never seen the sea ... or any boats."

"Oh, yes, I have," he said, still running. "In a large painting in Sister Giuseppina's room. Her father painted it. Of course, *he* had seen the sea, but I'll see it too one day! In the meantime, I'll sail my boats here. Look, Mama!" he cried, pointing suddenly. "Do you see that one? It's the fastest. I'm going to call it *Caterina!* Are you pleased?"

"Of course, I am! Thank you, darling," I said, stopping for breath.

In the years that followed, I often remembered that little boat bearing my name, especially each time I found myself being swept away by the menacing currents of my destiny.

At last, the masons came to begin the restoration of the old house. Leo gave up all his pursuits to watch them at work, devoting his entire attention to the progress they made, and often offering to fetch and carry for them. Happy to see his involvement, I started working the soil on the stretch of land overlooking the valley of the brook where I wanted to create my wonderful garden. Finally, my new home was ready. I had only to wait for the walls to dry before moving in.

Sitting on the threshing floor wall, we admired our new small white house with its green door and green window shutters shining in the last golden rays of sun like a vision in a fairy tale. Entranced, we waited until it was bathed in an indigo glow the very moment the sun was eclipsed behind the lower hills. The nightingale, perched in its cage hanging on the spotless wall, contributed to the occasion by singing one of its sweetest melodies. That night under the stars, with Leo's head on my lap, I cheerfully serenaded my lovely new abode with my little flute. But, having attained this wish for a house, the end of summer was upon us, and it was almost time for my Leo to be taken away from me again.

A few days later, he was packing his drawings and other objects in his travel box as I watched him, trying to hide my sadness. "Mama, I thought I should be ready when Gian Pietro comes for me," he explained.

"Yes, I know, dear. But I think we should visit Donna Grazia first," I said, changing the subject. "We must thank Ser Giuliano for helping us with our new house." He agreed whole-heartedly.

Donna Grazia was on the veranda when we arrived. There were builders inside, enlarging the kitchen. She looked very happy and healthy. "Ah, here is our boy prodigy! How much taller you've gotten since I first met you!" she exclaimed, stroking his golden curls. "With your curly locks, you remind me of an angel!" Leo's face turned red with a boy's embarrassment.

I offered her the basket of fresh figs we had brought. "These come from our valley, Donna Grazia. They're the first figs of the season. We also came to thank Ser Giuliano for helping my dreams come true!"

"Oh, thank you! He's not home today, but said to tell you he'll have the rest of the things you wanted sent to you as soon as you're ready," she said, turning to Leo. "Leonardo, you must be looking forward to going back to school?"

"Yes, but I hope they don't make us go over the same old things again and again. I want to be taught new things, but—" he paused to look at me—"the other children are much too slow! It gets a little boring."

"I know what you mean." She giggled.

"Luckily, I can improve my drawing in the meantime," he added, and Donna Grazia threw me a knowing sidelong glance.

Gian Pietro arrived the next day. Although both his and Leo's timing had been perfect, I complained that he had come too soon.

"I'm not too early at all. His school opens tomorrow. But I can wait," he said, looking around. "Oh! Look at the new house! How nice!"

"That's my new home. Ser Antonio gave me permission to have the old house repaired."

"You have money, eh?" he commented slyly.

"I sold a house up there that my friend had left me, but for God's sake, don't breathe a word about it to Ser Piero!"

"Of course, I won't tell him, but sooner or later, he'll find out. You know that, don't you? To think he was hoping that one of these days you'd leave Anchiano for good!"

At his last remark, I froze.

"Ah, Gian Pietro, you're here!" Leo cried, coming from

the back of the house. "How is Donna Albiera?" he asked with genuine interest.

"And how is Ser Antonio?" I interjected.

"One at a time, please!" Gian Pietro commanded, raising his hands. With a considerable sense of his own importance, he turned to Leo first and said, "Before anything else, you should know that school starts tomorrow."

"I know."

"And about Donna Albiera, she has recovered a little. But," he said, turning to me, "I'm afraid Ser Antonio's condition is still serious."

This latest news left me speechless. I felt as if a heavy menacing cloud named Piero had just stopped right above my head. Leo looked at me, and I hoped he hadn't guessed what was going through my mind.

He broke the silence by saying, "Gian Pietro, my box is ready, but I think it's still too heavy for me. I can't wait to get bigger!" His last remark couldn't have been more appropriate, following closely what was in my mind!

Letting Leo lead the way, Gian Pietro stayed back to whisper to me, "Yes, he's still a boy, but his brain is bigger than three adults' brains put together. Yet instead of being glad, his father is always complaining that he doesn't take after him." I should have laughed at his derisive comment, but I felt much too unhappy to appreciate his sense of humor.

"My goodness, look how many things he's taking home this time!" he grumbled as he carried the box to the cart. "A good thing that Donna Albiera is giving him a larger room."

If this news was meant to comfort me, it did the exact opposite, and as I turned to look at Leo reappearing in the same pretty outfit in which he'd arrived, I felt completely left out of his new world. But as if he had read my mind, he promptly took my hand and pulled me aside, motioning Gian Pietro to wait.

"Mama, from now on, whenever I think of you, I'll imagine you happy and contented in that lovely little house!"

I kissed his forehead, then his sunburned cheeks. "And I'll be counting the days until you come back, darling!" I murmured.

"Another thing, Mama: I'm growing so fast that very soon I'll be able to walk up here by myself, you'll see!" Then, passing the birdcage, he called out, "Good-bye, my friend! I left the seeds you like. Take good care of my mother and keep singing to her!"

I stood in the courtyard, watching the cart turn at the bend of the road, tearing my heart away.

Fortunately, before long, Ser Giuliano's cartman arrived with Rita's furniture. Among other pieces, he brought the large bed and her small iron stove. So I turned my attention to setting up my new home, arranging the furniture and displaying Rita's sparkling glass and chinaware on the sideboard.

Every morning, as I opened the back window facing the valley of the *ruscello,* I listened to the soft sound of running water and even smelled its moist plants. I marveled at seeing the birds flying off my roof gutter or from the holes I had built into the walls especially for them, and followed their graceful descent toward the brook, ever-grateful for the bliss of those magical moments.

One fall morning, before the frost hardened the soil too much, I decided to start planting the bulbs Donna Grazia had sent me. It was so quiet after the swallows had left for warmer places that I was able to hear light footsteps in the courtyard. I wrapped myself tightly in my shawl and went to see who had arrived.

There was a strange man surveying the buildings with great interest. He was tall and thin, dressed all in black. He raised his broad-brimmed hat to me, revealing a long, colorless face and bald forehead.

"What do you want?" I asked, startled.

"I was sent by Messer da Vinci—Ser Antonio da Vinci," he answered in a nasal voice. "He told me that this estate is for sale, so I came to see it. I'm interested in buying it," he explained, smiling grimly. Then pointing to my house, he asked, "That house over there—I presume it's part of the estate, isn't it?"

"Yes, but that's my home. I had it rebuilt at my expense with Ser Antonio's permission," I said, presenting a bold front.

"Well, I'll buy that one, too. I'll offer a good price for it," he said, baring his yellow teeth with an avid smile.

"This is my house, and nobody—*nobody!*—will have it at *any* price!"

"Good woman, there's no point in getting angry. Since it's on the grounds of the estate, it will consequently become mine. Nobody can stop me from owning it," he stated, raising his extremely long-fingered hand.

"Owning it? You're out of your mind! I won't allow you, or anyone else, to step inside my house, or even into this courtyard, until I've spoken with Ser Antonio myself."

"But Ser Antonio is very sick."

"Then how could he authorize you to come here? The truth is that you haven't been sent by him at all, isn't that so?" I said in a demanding voice. "Now, go! Go away from here and don't ever come back!" I turned away to wipe the tears from my eyes. Recovering a little, I looked around to see if he had gone, confronting instead his evil, bloodshot eyes still peering at me. I decided to hold my ground, staring him down. Then, to my utmost relief, he quietly mounted his horse and rode off like a bat from hell, his long black cloak billowing in the wind.

Collecting my heavy cape, I locked my door and went up to see Donna Grazia. She insisted on offering me a soothing hot drink before I could tell her about the stranger's visit. Then, gently patting my hand, she said encouragingly, "Don't worry, my dear. My consort would never allow anybody to hurt you. He'll think of something, you'll see!"

Nevertheless, the next morning, braving an icy, blustery wind, I trudged down to Vinci, directly to Leo's school. It was early. The streets were deserted. I paced around impatiently and breathed on my freezing hands, sheltering myself from the wind at my usual corner of the church, until the children started arriving with their mothers.

I was relieved to see Donna Lucia accompanying Leo

again. Although he had seen me, he seemed to be waiting for Donna Lucia to leave, but I went straight over to them. "Mama, how wonderful! You're here!"

"Caterina, you shouldn't surprise me like this," she said, looking about her uneasily. "I told you it's not good for us to be seen together. Think of the consequences!"

"What consequences? Worse than having to hide in a corner to see my own son? Is there anything worse than not seeing one's own child for months?" She just dabbed her eyes with her handkerchief.

"Mama, Donna Lucia's upset, because grandfather is very sick."

"I'm sorry, Donna Lucia, forgive me for being ..." Then I kissed the boy and whispered, "Leo, dear, go inside. I want to talk with Donna Lucia." He promptly obeyed me and ran into school, leaving us alone.

"So, I was right to think that Ser Antonio had nothing to do with the stranger—that horrible man who came to my house, saying that Ser Antonio had offered to sell him the estate." Though I spoke quietly, I was steadfast in my purpose.

Still wiping her eyes, Donna Lucia looked at me in astonishment. "What stranger? What estate? I don't know what you're talking about. The man must have lied. My consort is dying!"

"Then your son must be behind all this."

"I don't know anything about it and I'm not interested. I only know that I'm losing my consort, and I'll soon be left all alone," she protested, sobbing. I suddenly felt sorry for the poor woman and did not detain her any longer. She hustled away, hiding her face.

More depressed than before, I started home, the freezing wind still ravaging my face as I thought of Donna Lucia's oppressive fear of being left alone without her consort's support; a fear that resembled my own, that of being driven out of my own house. Little did I know that my new guardian angel in Mont'Albano was busily working for me.

* * *

"Caterina! Caterina! Where are you? I have a message for you!" cried Giuseppe at my door a few days later. "Donna Grazia sent me with another invitation," he went on excitedly. "She said she has good news for you and wants you to go and have the midday meal with them on Sunday. I'll take you, if you like. Those gentlefolks up there must really like you very much."

To lift my spirits, I decided to wear for the occasion a deep-blue woolen dress of Rita's, which I had also altered, trimming the neck with an ivory silk braid in one of my favorite loop designs to match a golden silk hairnet I had saved for this dress. While getting ready, I kept thinking of how much Donna Grazia's flair for dressing had influenced me, and I was sure that she would appreciate the little details of my new composition, too. Over this sumptuous dress, I wore the dark-red cape lined with rose flannel, which completed the outfit to perfection.

Carrying a tasty cake I had baked specially that morning, I set out on my way, preferring to go on foot, as it was a beautiful sunny autumn day. Passing under boughs loaded with multishaded golden leaves, I tried to visualize how my Leo would have drawn them.

"Good morning, Caterina!" said Ser Giuliano, welcoming me at the door.

"Please come and sit by the fireplace," called out his consort.

"Thank you, Donna Grazia. I'm not cold," I said, taking off my cape.

"How stunning you look in that cobalt-blue gown! Caterina, you have such good taste in colors!" she remarked.

I unwrapped the cake and placed it on the beautifully set table. "It's an apple tart I baked this morning."

"Oh, what a delicious smell!" exclaimed Ser Giuliano, showing me to a high-backed chair opposite Donna Grazia. He then stood behind her with his hand on her shoulder, his favorite pose.

Having just laid the table, the two maids returned to the kitchen.

"So, it seems they won't let you enjoy the new house, eh?" began Ser Giuliano. "Well, don't worry, Caterina! Your enemies won't get far."

"My main concern is that if Ser Antonio should die, his son not only won't let me see my son anymore, but he'll also make it impossible for me to go on living there."

"Have you ever thought of getting married?" he said out of the blue.

Disconcerted, I brought my hands to my blushing cheeks. To break the awkward silence, I said rather resentfully, "Why should I marry? I already have a son."

"What about a make-believe marriage?" he asked with a wistful gaze. I couldn't believe my ears and thought the gentleman had gone out of his mind. I looked at Donna Grazia for support, but she just nodded agreeably, encouraging me to listen to him.

He started pacing the floor, unperturbed by my reaction. "The so-called prospective husband," he continued, as if describing something happening before his very eyes, "would first buy the estate and then announce that he is marrying you. Then ... he would put ... the house ... in your ... name," he proclaimed, emphasizing each word as in a recitation. "After that, the actual marriage could be delayed indefinitely," he concluded casually.

"But, Ser Giuliano, how could I ever trust a person who would stoop to such a deception? Marriage is a sacred state; one shouldn't make false plans! Besides, this man would have to be a complete stranger, because I don't know anyone who would be party to such trickery!"

"We must fight fire with fire, my dear girl! Anyway, he wouldn't have to be a stranger, for the person I have in mind is someone I trust implicitly. So much so that I'm prepared to put up the money to buy the estate, in his name. You would have to leave the house for a while to avoid suspicion. Once the sale goes through, and a little time goes by, you'd return as the new owner."

"Ser Giuliano, I thank you for everything," I said, trying to keep calm, "but this plan is much too complicated for me ... and risky, for if the truth ever came out, that would really be the end."

The loud noise of an approaching vehicle interrupted our conversation. Ser Giuliano smiled complacently and rushed outside, and Donna Grazia went into the kitchen to instruct the maids.

Still bewildered by the strange proposition, I shied from meeting other guests and got ready to leave. My curiosity, however, got the better of me, and I peered out the window to see who had arrived.

From a new four-wheeled carriage alighted a very handsome man in his thirties who greeted Ser Giuliano with familiarity. He wore a riding jacket fastened at the waist by a wide-buckled leather belt. His hair was grayish-blond and his skin suntanned. He was slender and taller than Ser Giuliano, who kept patting him on the back, suggesting to me that he had to be a relative of some kind. Nevertheless, the whole situation was embarrassing, so I picked up my cape and headed for the door.

At that moment, Donna Grazia returned from the kitchen and, with something not far from dismay, cried, "Caterina, what are you doing? The food is ready!"

"I see you have other guests. I prefer to return another time."

"But I want you to meet Giovanni. You mustn't run away! He's like family to us—he's the manager of our farm in Santa Croce," she urged.

As soon as the other guest entered, he bowed to Donna Grazia, kissed her hand, and turned to greet me. I was standing with my back to the window, unable to move, but he smiled politely. I felt so awkward that the blood rushed to my cheeks.

"Caterina, meet Giovanni Accattabriga di Piero del Vacca, my husband's most trusted friend!" Donna Grazia exclaimed with a hand flourish.

Although amused by the fancy name, I tried to stay cool, because I assumed that he might be the man in Ser Giuliano's scheme, a scheme I decidedly intended to forestall. Yet, unable to resist a furtive glance at this trusted friend, I raised my eyes nonchalantly. As our eyes met squarely, I found myself blushing again! So, to cover my confusion, I stepped forward as if about to say something, but unable to think of anything, I retreated again.

Fortunately, everyone's attention was diverted by the host inviting us to take our seats at the table, which was impressively set with fine linen, china dishes, silverware, and crystal glasses, all of which I had not seen on previous occasions. Although Rita had shown me how dinner tables were set in rich homes, I had never seen anything to match this magnificent display. I was a little sad, though, to see a pheasant on a silver platter decorated with its own feathers, knowing that I would have to risk offending Donna Grazia by refusing it. She, however, kept up her charming smile all through the meal. At one point, explaining to me that it was Giovanni's birthday, she made a toast, saying, "To a dear friend of the family!" As we held up our wineglasses, I turned to the guest of honor, who seemed a little shy, too, blushing slightly.

At the end of the meal, the maid brought in my apple tart, and Ser Giuliano poured a liqueur into small red glasses. "I call this the Elixir of Happiness! Let us drink a toast to the ladies!" he exclaimed. Then, raising his glass, he pompously recited: "With this magic nectar, favored by the gods above, soldiers we salute our lovely ladies, temples of eternal love!"

We all cheered and drank the aromatic elixir. As I got up from the table with the others, I felt dizzy and went to sit in a chair near the window. Ser Giuliano refilled the glasses, bringing mine over to me, but when I refused, he replaced it on the table and cleared his throat. "Now, Caterina," he began, serious again, "I'm sorry, but we must resume our discussion. This is a good opportunity for you to hear Giovanni's opinion, since he's the one who's willing to take part in the plan."

I totteringly rose out of my chair, picked up my cape, and started for the door. I stopped to cover my ears as I heard Rita's voice say, "Don't run away! Listen! They want to help!" I ruminated for a moment or two. Then, dropping the cape on the chair, I turned to face the others, who, motionless as statues, kept their eyes fixed on me.

"I'm sorry. I wasn't feeling myself. The elixir, I think."

As I uttered these words, they all seemed to come to life, smiling at me sympathetically. Then I heard Donna Grazia say, "I'll have a hot drink prepared for you, Caterina. It'll do you good."

I sat down again, curious to see the guest's reaction to my strange behavior. To my surprise, he hinted at a smile and winked at me.

Ser Giuliano paced the floor again. Then, stopping in the middle of the room where he was sure to get everybody's undivided attention, he spoke again. "Now, going back to what I was saying before.... If you want to attack the enemy successfully, how do you do it? You attack him in the way he least expects!" Donna Grazia, as usual, laughed heartily at his amusing remark. For the first time, Giovanni laughed, too, stretching out his long legs. I did not laugh, not even out of courtesy for my host, because I was doing all I could to hide my anger. Unable to contain myself any longer, I spoke up. "Ser Giuliano, please understand that I cannot ask Ser ... Giovanni to get involved in this. He may only accept just to do your bidding, and that wouldn't be right." I stopped as I saw Giovanni shaking his head disapprovingly.

"If I follow Ser Giuliano's orders, it's only because I respect his judgment," he asserted. "We're helping out a friend in danger of losing her home unjustly." He paused to observe me. "Anyway, I've already seen the man in question and told him that I've convinced you to sell your house to me. The next step, of course, is to show him the contract, which Ser Giuliano is preparing. At that point, it would be advisable for you to move out of the house."

"I can't leave my house," I protested. "If I do, they'll tell my son that I've gone, and he'll think I've abandoned him for good."

"It'll only be for a short time," intervened Ser Giuliano. "You could go and stay at our farm. I can assure you they wouldn't dare alarm the boy right away."

"That's true, Caterina. Listen to their advice! It'll be all right," said Donna Grazia reassuringly.

"About our fake marriage, which should follow, there would be no obstacles," continued Giovanni. "It will be quite plausible. I'm a free man, Monna Caterina. I have no other ties. Please know that we understand your situation and that we very much want to help."

His controlled voice gave me so much reassurance that I almost wept. Recovering a little from this sudden burst of mixed emotions, I said, "I would like, though, to have time to think about it before making my final decision." They all agreed, at which point Donna Grazia got up, asking to be excused. Giovanni and I thanked her for her hospitality, and her husband took her to her room.

I went out on the veranda and sat on the bench, gazing at Giovanni, who was harnessing his horse to his carriage. I was impressed by the caring way he stroked the horse's silky brown coat, which shone like gold in the soft afternoon sunlight.

He returned and politely asked me if I would like to be taken home. "I'll be passing through Anchiano, Monna Caterina," he insisted when I hesitated.

At that moment, Ser Giuliano appeared at the door. "I'll have to excuse myself, too," he said. "It has been a strenuous day for my wife." We said our farewells, and he went back inside.

Giovanni offered me his hand, and I shyly placed mine in his. Together, we walked to the carriage. The horse shook his mane and stamped his hoof so violently that I leaped backward.

Giovanni laughed. "Don't be afraid, Monna Caterina! That's his way of greeting people he likes." Then he held my hand firmly as I climbed up and sat on the high cushioned seat. During the drive, I glanced around, enthralled by the view from that height. I also noticed how the soft rolling of the wheels harmonized with the gentle hoofbeats of the horse. I wanted to share my observations with Giovanni, but unable to overcome my shyness, we continued the drive in complete silence. Yet, all the way, I felt as if we were communicating without words and was even a little disappointed when, entering the courtyard, the drive came to an end. He alighted, took my hand to help me down, and continued to hold it tightly in his. "I want to thank you, Ser Giovanni, for your kindness ... and for wanting to help me," I said finally, blushing.

"I'd have done it even if it involved a sacrifice. But now that I've met you, I see that you're ... worthy of much more!" he said, looking deep into my eyes. He kissed my hand, gently letting it go, and jumped back on his carriage. Before reaching the bend of the road, he turned to wave to me, and I waved back, feeling the same warmth I always felt when saying good-bye to Leo.

Slowly, I made my way back to the empty house, smiling as my nightingale greeted me. I went in and lay down on my bed. Still tasting the elixir on my lips, I felt like a child in the land of fables. I lay there, clinging to the feeling, savoring the magic of a fleeting happiness for which we yearn and perhaps never find.

Again, I heard the sweet chirping of the nightingale, and, opening my eyes, I saw that the only light in the room came from the oil lamp. Since I was wide-awake, I thought it was already time to go and watch the sunrise from my old well. I couldn't understand, though, why I was still dressed. I threw open the shutters and saw that it was still the middle of the night. I ran outside and nearly lost my balance, gazing at the many newly polished stars shining over my head. I sat on the low wall and tried to recapture those happy moments with my extraordinary new friend, but it all seemed so far away that I began to think it had been a dream.

The chilly night air brought back to mind Ser Giuliano's strange scheme, which seemed entirely marred by deceit. I still felt that the father of my son should be given another chance to reconsider carrying out his dreadful threats against me.

These disquieting thoughts had spurred me on to march down to the town of Vinci in the morning. Still undecided whether to go first to the school or to the da Vinci house, I found myself at the foot of the church steps in the castle square. Counting on God's guidance, I ascended the wide stone steps winding up to the main door of the imposing church, but before I could reach it, the congregation started pouring out. I suddenly saw Donna Lucia, looking forlorn and destitute in the crowd. Meekly, I stood in her path, hoping that her spiritual visit might have influenced her enough to be more indulgent with me this time.

"Good morning, Donna Lucia. How are you?" I whispered.

It made no difference, for she was just as easily startled as before. "Caterina, you must not stop me on the church steps like this! Don't you see I'm not strong?"

"Donna Lucia, please have patience for a moment! I'm heartbroken. I don't know what to do. I must see Piero to ask him, no, to implore him, to stop persecuting me." She frowned at me. "Please tell him to let me live in peace in my little house."

"Persecuting you? What do you mean? He isn't in Vinci any longer. He has moved to Florence."

"When did he go? And where is my son?"

"Piero left yesterday with his wife to look for a house there. He took Leonardo with him, too" She sighed. My mind started reeling. "The boy wanted to go," she hastily added. "My dear, you have to face the fact that Leonardo's future is no longer in your hands and that you cannot do anything about it." I was speechless. Then, adopting a sweeter tone, she went on, "My dear girl, why don't you find yourself a husband? Maybe someone who would take you far away from here ... very far, where you can start a family of your own in peace."

I was flabbergasted. As I was about to turn on her, though, I saw her hands beginning to shake. She seemed to be losing her balance, so I took her arm for fear she would fall down the many steps, and drawing a deep breath, I found myself asking, "How is Ser Antonio?"

"Alas! My poor husband...." she began, suddenly softening and raising a frail hand to my cheek. But then she suddenly turned away, making it clear that she wanted to be allowed to go on her way. I stood aside, shocked to see her bent over like a very old woman, taking one step at a time. I waited until she had reached the bottom and had gone out of sight. Then, forgetting why I had climbed those steps in the first place, I began my descent, feeling just as old and stooped as she was.

Back on the road leading up to Anchiano, I realized I could hardly control my legs. My feet shuffled along aimlessly like Donna Lucia's. Just as the previous time I had seen her, I had unconsciously absorbed her state of mind. "Why hurry? For what reason should I rush anymore? There's nothing left for me to do," I kept muttering to myself. "Perhaps my mission is over. Yes, it must be over!" I cried in anguish. "Because my son doesn't need me anymore!"

I grasped the old stone wall on my right overlooking the deep valley below and gazed far away at the distant fields as the words of the prophet went through my mind. "Oh, my dear prophet!" I moaned with outstretched arms. "Is my mission really over? Why, then, was I urged to build my new home, the home intended for my son, for my Leo?" Feeling my legs give way, I turned to sit on the wall, but instead narrowly missed it and slid to the ground, tearing the back of my dress on a thorny bush. Though aware that the slash had uncovered the skin, cutting the dress all the way down to the waist, I felt no pain and welcomed the seductive sensation of release as I began to lose consciousness.

Hoofbeats reverberating on the ground revived me slightly, enough to make me realize that a horse was trotting briskly up the road. I forced myself to stand up, turning my back to the road to avoid being recognized.

"Caterina! Monna Caterina, what are you doing here? What happened?" It was Giovanni! I covered my face, humiliated to the point of wishing with all my heart that the ground would open up and swallow me. I heard him jump off his horse and felt his hands on my shoulders. "Are you all right? Your dress is torn!" he said solicitously, but before I could respond, he swept me up in his arms and propped me up on his horse. I shrank back with fear. "Don't be frightened—he knows how to behave," he murmured in my ear. "Don't you,

Thunderbolt?" The horse nodded in all seriousness as Giovanni mounted next to me, took hold of the reins, and, cradling me in his arms, urged the horse up the road.

I leaned against Giovanni. His warmth soon revitalized me with a comfort I had never felt before.

When we arrived at the house, without a word, he carried me in his arms again and carefully set me down on the wooden bench by the front door. I looked up at him, hardly believing that this handsome and kind man was showing so much concern for me. "What were you doing in Vinci?" I asked casually, longing to feel his nearness again.

"A little bird told me that the lovely Caterina had lost her way and needed help!"

"That sounds like something I heard in one of Nonnetta's fairy tales. She was an old friend, who knew how to take my mind off my troubles," I answered, surprised to be laughing and feeling so much better.

"How did your dress get torn?"

"I don't know—maybe on the shrub at the wall I leaned against," I said, trying to shut those bitter moments out of my mind.

"And, now, Monna Caterina, may I ask what *you* were doing in Vinci?"

"I went to give that coward another chance, but he's gone to Florence, taking my son with him. It seems he's planning to keep him there forever!"

He examined the scratches on my back, then pulled my torn dress together to cover me and stroked my forehead. "You need some oil on your skin. Can you manage by yourself?" he asked, showing more concern for my health than my affairs.

"Yes, thank you!" I said, turning around to face him. "Giovanni, if you hadn't appeared at that moment, I really think I would have died of grief and saved everybody a lot of trouble. But then you came by, and here I am, still having to go on with my struggle."

"You've forgotten that you aren't alone anymore," he said, smoothing a lock of my hair. "Remember that I'm here now, my dear!" His eyes lit up as he gazed steadily into mine.

"You're so kind, Giovanni!" I said, giving him my hand. He held it in both of his and then kissed it reverently.

"Ser Giuliano's waiting for me," he said suddenly, "and I should like to tell him if you've decided to go along with his plan."

I thought for a moment, then I burst out, "Yes, I have! Tell him yes!" He kissed my hand, this time rejoicing. Dreamy-eyed, I watched him ride off, trying to convince myself that he was real.

I spent the next few days fixing my rock garden, arranging the stones I had collected during the summer around the spots where I had planted Donna Grazia's bulbs. My continued dedication helped me to keep up my faith in miracles. I had to go on believing that the flowers I would grow in my garden would bring my son back to me, even if only for occasional short visits.

My thoughts often turned to Giovanni, particularly to the way he expressed his caring for me, and each time, I stopped to bask in the warmth of his protective kindness.

"Monna Caterina, where are you? Are you here?" echoed Ser Giuliano's voice in the yard one afternoon. As I looked up, he handed me a roll of papers, which I took reluctantly, as it reminded me of the one with which Piero had tricked me.

"These papers will protect your house," he explained carefully. "One is a deed of sale to Giovanni and the other is a document assigning the property back to you. But this will only take place after recording the deed and your ostensibly having moved out of the house. So hide the other paper for the time being. Now, in order for this to be sufficiently convincing, we must get you away from here for a while." Seeing my lack of enthusiasm, he added, "As I told you, you can stay at our farm for a few weeks. That will give me enough time to settle things with the notary. I have to make sure that he does everything correctly. He may be a notary, but I'm an attorney, and he can't play games with me," he said, turning to leave. "Anyway, Caterina, I'll let you know when you have to go."

"Thank you for everything, Ser Giuliano. I'm sorry I was so stubborn. By the way, how is Donna Grazia? I was worried about her the other day."

"Don't worry. She's fine." He came back and, with an arch smile, whispered, "She left the room to give you a chance to get better acquainted with Giovanni." Seeing me blush, he added, "Didn't you guess?"

The stretch of mild October days was at an end. Dark clouds in the sky were heralding heavy rain the day I saw a bunch of soldiers coming up the hill into the olive grove again. This time, instead of women, there were youths carrying the empty baskets on their shoulders.

Panicked, I crept back to the house and locked myself in. I suspected that this time they had been hired by Piero. That suspicion was confirmed when I heard one of the soldiers say, "I think this is the house where she lives, but it looks as if she's not in. You, boy, you're from around here. Do you know who lives in that house?"

"I really ... don't know. Why?" replied the boy, faltering nervously.

"What do you mean, you don't know? You live around here, don't you? We want the keys for the rooms over there."

"Well, I think I saw a woman working in the garden a few days ago. She must have gone somewhere."

"Where do you think she went?"

"I don't know where. But since the door's closed ..." It was clear that the boy was greatly intimidated.

"Well, keep an eye on the house and let us know when she comes back."

I waited for them to go back to the olive grove. Then, boiling over with rage, I dragged furniture across the room and barricaded the door and windows, inveighing against whoever hadn't sent word to leave the doors of the old building open. It suddenly dawned on me that the whole thing had been planned to take me by surprise. "Ah, Piero, you're becoming a worse menace than I ever expected!"

A terrific peal of thunder shook the house and heavy rain

started to fall. I heard the soldiers running back, swearing and cursing at the bad weather. I curled up in a corner, petrified. Someone banged hard on my door and shouted, "Anybody there? We need the keys. Are you there?"

"Let's see if we can break down one of the old doors over there," said another voice. All the soldiers, except two, ran to the old building.

"What are we going to do?" one said to the other. "How are we going to scare her if she isn't in?"

"I think she's shut herself inside. Let's knock harder!"

"Hey! They've opened the door of the cellar. Let's go!" said the first voice, and they both ran for shelter.

"Oh, they broke the door of my little room, my baby's first home!" I whispered sadly.

As soon as the rain stopped, they came back out, mumbling and shuffling along like drunkards. They all headed back to the olive grove, except the two who had obviously been sent to scare me. One sat on my doorstep.

"What are you two doing there?" someone shouted from a distance. "Let's go and finish harvesting while there's no rain!"

"I don't feel like doing anything anymore," replied the one sitting on my doorstep.

"You shouldn't have drunk so much!"

"Go on. We'll follow you," said the accomplice still standing. I heard someone running by. "You, boy, come here! Why are you shaking like that? I won't hurt you if you do as I say. Take a handful of mud and throw it on that white wall!"

"Why should I?" the boy gasped. "I come from these hills. If they find out, they'll kill me."

"And if you don't do it, *we*'ll kill you. And when *we* say 'kill,' we mean it!" bullied the soldier.

"Why don't you do it yourself? It's your idea."

"Don't be smart! If *we* do it, they won't hire us anymore. Go on—there's nothing to it." I heard the boy run away, but he was soon caught and dragged back, screaming. "Look! This is what you do ... after we leave." There was a thud on the wall, followed by a laugh.

THE LOVELY ABODE

"Stop! Let the boy do it!" But other thuds followed in quick succession. Then I heard stones hitting the door, interspersed with the soldiers' malicious laughter, and I wept at the havoc they were wreaking on my house.

At that moment, a cart rumbled into the courtyard, and I recognized the cartman's voice yelling at the two soldiers. "Stop that, you bastards! I'll tell the notary what you've done, be sure of that!"

"He'll tell ... the *notary!* Did you hear that? Ha! Ha! He doesn't know ... that it was *his* idea!" laughed the drunken soldier, falling back on my doorstep. Noticing that the door had given a little, he got up and lunged at it with brute force, before falling on the step again.

His friend came to help him up. "We'd better join the others now," he urged. "They've stopped harvesting. Get up!"

"Hey, look! The door's moved. It's almost open," said the drunken one.

"Come on! Let's go! We've done enough. Look! The cart's turning around. We'd better catch it. Hey! Wait for us, you mangy old crow!" he yelled at the cartman. "You jackass, wait for us if you value your life!"

It started to pour again, and the other pickers scrambled on to the cart, too. When I realized that everybody had left in the cart, I gave out a sigh of relief and went to the door, but I stopped as I heard some local boys passing by.

"Hurry up! Let's run home!" said the boy with the familiar voice.

"Why did you do that?" asked another.

"Stupid! Didn't you see he was trying to strangle me?"

Except for the rumble of a worse storm brewing, quiet had at last returned, at least for a while, until a thunderbolt seemed to explode right on my roof, making the house shake under my feet. Torrential rain and powerful winds soon engulfed the hill. I saw water rising to my door, flooding my room. The dreadful storm lasted only minutes, but it seemed like the end of the world. I opened the window slightly and saw rivers everywhere rushing down the slopes. When, finally, the wind and the pelting rain stopped, I opened the door, and the water flowed out down the doorstep. I waited, as I could still hear the roar of the floodwater rushing through the valley. Then, picking up my skirt, I gingerly stepped outside, anxious to inspect the foundation of the house as well as the garden.

I covered my eyes in horror, for the garden had completely disappeared. Even the larger rocks seemed to be sliding rapidly down the muddy slope. I waded through the mud to look for the bulbs, and as I bent down, a torrent of floodwater struck me from behind. I fell and found myself sliding down the slope, too. Tangled in my skirt, I was tossed by the slimy waves, together with broken branches and rocks. My only hope was that once I reached the flat bank of the brook, I could find a way to save myself. The brook waters, though, had risen to the lower branches of the trees, flooding the banks completely. Before reaching the bottom of the slope, I grabbed an overhanging branch, breaking my fall, and clung to it for dear life as the mud continued to pull me down. But the branch broke off, and I fell right into the middle of the torrent, still clutching it. Swirling currents overwhelmed me and, realizing that I couldn't escape death, I screamed, "Leo, my Leo! Your mama won't see you any—." Swallowing huge amounts of dirty water, I choked, and everything was over.

Regaining consciousness, I was pleasantly surprised to find myself floating peacefully in space, enjoying the quiet, undisturbed atmosphere around me. I realized then that I was above the valley of the brook, looking down, and was shaken by the sight of a lifeless body still clinging to the broken branch, which had wedged itself between two rocks in the rushing waters. "That's me!" I cried. "But if that's me down there, what am I doing up here?" Then I tried to reason, "Maybe I died, and this is my soul up here, separated from my body down there. Or am I seeing a vision? But, then, which is real and which is the vision?" The sweet sound of voices singing rang through the air, drawing me toward them. "This is delightful!" I said as a breeze rocked me gently.

But my attention was drawn again to my motionless body,

still afloat in the brook. There was a man rushing down the muddy slope desperately calling, "Caterina! Where are you? Answer me, Caterina!" I tried to answer, but my voice had gone. Spotting my body, he plunged into the brook without hesitation and, fighting the currents, pulled it closer to the bank. "Why does he want to save me? I like it here," I cried. "Let me go! Let me go!" But he couldn't hear me. He carried the body to a rocky ledge on the slope where the water had subsided and set it down. Then he started shaking it violently by the shoulders. Kissing it several times on the mouth and getting no reaction, he shouted at the top of his voice, "Caterina, don't leave me! What will I tell Leo—your little son? Come back, darling! Please, come back!"

Who is Leo? I wondered. Then I got a glimpse of a little boy picking flowers in a green field. "Oh, my Leo! My Leo! I want to be with you! How could I have forgotten about you, darling?" But he didn't hear me. I longed so much to be near the boy, but he was too far from me. My desire to hold him became so strong that I was suddenly whirled around at a dizzying speed, spinning out of control until I fell down on my lifeless body. I sighed deeply as a stabbing pain hit my chest. Something was pounding me on my back, making me cry out, and I began to spit out muddy water. Once I stopped, the man next to me turned me over on my back and stroked my forehead. I opened my eyes. "Giovanni, it's you! What happened? I thought I was ... I had ..."

He just smiled at me, still breathing heavily from the strain of those last few frantic moments.

"I saw my little Leo playing in the field. He's all right, isn't he?" I asked, still remembering him only as a younger child.

"Yes, he's ... all right," he answered, caressing my cheek. Then he looked at me and burst into laughter—a loud, childlike laugh he couldn't stop. I watched him in amazement. "It's your hair," he said. "The sun has turned it to copper!" I touched it and felt the mud in my hair hardening under the sun.

We looked up, surprised to see that the sun was shining brightly in the middle of a clear blue sky, as if completely unaware of the disaster that had taken place on our hill during its absence.

"Look, your hair has turned to copper, too." I started to laugh, but I had to hold on tightly to him as I was sliding down toward the water.

"Oh, no. Once is enough for one day!" Giovanni exclaimed, catching me.

Grasping every piece of shrubbery left by the flood, we climbed up the slick slope back to the courtyard. Giovanni went straight over to the stone trough and dipped his head in. I rushed to get a cloth still hanging on the washing line and offered it to him.

"Caterina, I'll get some water from the well for you to wash in," he said, wiping his face and hair.

"No, thank you. I'm sure there's plenty of water in the rain barrel. That's the best water for washing hair. Look at your hair—it's turned to gold!" Then, reflecting on the coincidence of fate, I asked, "What were you doing in these hills again? How did you know I was down there?"

"I was in Vinci when the storm came, so the moment the rain stopped, I rushed up here to see how you were. When I saw your scarf on the slope, somehow I knew you were down there."

"Thank you, Giovanni, for saving my life again."

He smiled and said, "But you must promise me, Caterina, that you'll be more careful from now on. That little bird may get tired of warning me. Besides," he added, turning serious, "have you ever asked yourself what Leo and I would do without you?"

I went right up to him and he took me in his arms. Then I burst into laughter once more. "Your face is dirty again!" I cried.

"That's all right. The mud down there brought me luck – it gave me a chance to kiss you!" I began to wipe the spots off his face. When I met his eyes, I saw so much love and tenderness shine through them that my heart was overwhelmed. I let him hold me in his arms for a long while.

"Now, my dear, I have to go and see if everything's all

right at Donna Grazia's," he said, reluctantly breaking the spell. I took his hand, and together we went to the back of my house, from where we were relieved to see her home standing intact high above the pines.

After he left, I looked around the countryside, catching my breath at the sad sight of the olive grove. The trees were as bare as in wintertime. All the leaves had disappeared. Heading back to the house, I was even more shocked to see smears of mud dripping all over the front walls. I ran my fingers over one of the spots, feeling a great surge of anger, but then, checking myself, I shook off my mounting hatred. I refused to let it spoil the wonderful sensation created by Giovanni's revelation of love! A revelation that had not only filled my heart with happiness, but also given me a new reason for living and maybe some meaning to my solitary existence.

PART THREE

ETERNAL LOVE

10
SWEET EXILE

Over the next few days, while scraping the mud stains off the walls, I couldn't help thinking how wonderful it would be if I could efface my vulnerability the same way. I took heart, though, in the thought that Giovanni had just that power, having come to my rescue in so many ways.

Then I couldn't help reliving, over and over again, the terrifying moments to which I had been subjected at the brook, and I continued to ask myself if my soul had really detached itself from my body in that way or if I had imagined it. But, then, was it my mind reminiscing or was it my soul that saw my little Leo in the fields? Unable to find answers to these questions, I finally decided to discuss them with Leo at the first opportunity. I knew that with his inborn wisdom, he would be able to shed some light on the mystery.

When I finished cleaning the walls, I stepped back to admire the result of my efforts and thought I imagined Leo's silvery voice coming from the courtyard. "Mama. Mama! I'm here! Where are you? I'm back!"

In a spontaneous reflex, I playfully hid behind the corner, took the scarf off my head and held it out, waving it in full view. "Who's there? No, *messere*, I'm not expecting anybody," I called aloofly.

He peered around the corner. "Mama, don't you see that it's me? Look!"

"*Messere,* you're too tall! You couldn't be my son. He's still a little boy." He stood there puzzled for a moment. "But if you can assure me that you are my Leo, come and hug me." Then, laughing, he raced into my arms. As I held him, I glanced devoutly up into the sky to express my gratitude for the many miracles recently bestowed upon me. "How did you get here? On foot?" I asked, not seeing a carriage in the yard. He seemed to be smiling at someone standing behind me. I froze.

"Monna Caterina, good morning!" greeted Giovanni reassuringly. I relaxed, but took note of how quickly my little game had misfired.

"This is the gentleman who brought me. Wasn't he clever in convincing Donna Albiera to let me come with him?"

"Yes, indeed!" I said with relief, smiling at Giovanni. "Now, darling, go and see how I've arranged things in the new house. I'll be along presently."

Leo ran to the threshing floor, instead, and began galloping in a circle, singing, "'Trit-trot, little horse, trit-trot! ...'" I couldn't believe my eyes as I gazed at him, enthralled, until Giovanni coughed politely to catch my attention.

"I'm sorry, Giovanni. I couldn't help myself. How did you do it? What did you say to her? Anyhow, whatever way you did it, I thank you with all my heart!"

He took my hand, and once again, I felt his warmth radiating all through me. "It wasn't difficult. Ser Piero wasn't there. It was, therefore, the ideal time, and I must have said the right words to move her. However, she made me promise to take Leo back tomorrow afternoon before her husband returns. That's all!"

"Giovanni, I don't know what to say, I'm so touched."

"Say nothing—just enjoy these few hours together. I'll be back tomorrow." His eyes shone as I touched his cheek. I longed to hold his face in both hands, but my other hand seemed to hesitate shyly in midair. His smile as he turned to leave made the lucky hand tingle, and I quickly brought to my cheek trying to hold on to the warmth of his magic as long as I could.

Leo came back, still excited from his running, and I took him into the house, eager to show him the new door before anything else. "Do you see this door? Next summer, your own room will be through there!"

"That's nice, Mama, but I'm afraid that from now on, I won't be able to come up here so often. We're going to live in Florence."

"Not even for the summer?"

"I don't know for sure. I may have to wait until ... until I grow up, when I can come by myself," he said sadly.

"Oh, no, dear! It can't be!" Then, to cover my pain, I asked, "Do you like Florence?"

"Yes, it's a lovely city! There are a lot of interesting things to see, lots of wonderful works of art!" Noticing that I was quiet, he added, "But I like to spend time here with you, too. You know I love it here, so I'll never stay away from you or this countryside for too long."

"Look, my dear, I may have to go away, too—just for a few days. So if they bring you here and I'm not home, don't believe what they tell you! I'll be back for sure, waiting for you here for the rest of my life. Just remember that!" He watched me attentively, but I quickly distracted him by showing him his old construction projects, which I kept for him by the wall under a cover. "See, Leo? As soon as your room is ready, I'll put these in there for you to play with when you come back."

"That's nothing. I can make better things now. Please, Mama, I can't wait to go down to the *ruscello*," he said, eagerly taking my hand.

"My dear, I haven't been down there since the flood. I couldn't bear to see it all in ruin. Besides, the water is still muddy." Leo seemed puzzled. "Didn't you know? There was a terrible storm! It seemed like the end of the world. We'd never seen a storm like that in these hills before. I was really frightened." I forbore to tell him about the drowning.

"Oh, I wish I'd been here! I like storms! The more terrifying, the better! Do you know, Mama, that after a storm some people seem to change?" I looked at him, amazed, and he shrugged his shoulders, saying, "Maybe it's because most people are afraid of things they don't understand."

"Who tells you about such things, your teacher?"

"Oh, no. I can't talk to her about these things. Besides, every time there's a storm, she hides in the chapel behind the altar." He laughed. "I notice things just by looking at people." Then he pulled me by the hand toward the slope.

I stopped. "Do you think I've changed, too, since the storm?"

He observed me closely and urgently. "Yes, I think so. Quite a bit," he answered. Then he looked around excitedly, trying to determine what changes had taken place in the landscape. "If I'm here during the next storm, I'm going to draw it." He giggled mischievously. "It'll be so scary, that it'll strike terror into anyone who sets eyes on it!"

"How can you draw during a storm?"

"I can't. I just study it intensely and commit it to memory, just as you told me to, so I can draw it later," he chirped, letting my hand go as the drone of the rushing brook reached our ears. "Let's run now! I want to see the colors of the muddy water."

At first, I hesitated, remembering how I had barely survived the deluge, but then, not wanting to miss one moment of Leo's company, I mustered up my courage and chased after him down to the brook.

Thrilled with what he saw, Leo ran along the overflowing brook. Then, noticing my downcast expression, he came back to take me by the hand and said, "Don't worry, Mama! The flooded banks are just as interesting. I'm sure that by next spring, there'll be a new crop of water plants, and maybe fishes will swim upriver from the sea like they do in the Arno River in Florence."

"Fishes? Are they like water worms?"

"Oh, no. Fishes are much faster and more intelligent than worms. I'll draw one for you, so you'll recognize them." With a stick, he drew a shape on the wet soil as he went on to say,

"Our teacher also told us they were Jesus' friends. He could multiply them, just like that, in order to feed his followers," he explained emphatically.

I listened in amazement to this revelation as I realized just how isolated my upbringing had been with my poor old parents, who didn't even own a donkey to take us to church. "I never had a teacher and we have never seen fishes up here in our hills," I said, justifying my ignorance.

The following morning I got up early to bake Leo's favorite cakes, *taralli,* made with anise. After watching the flames build up in the oven, he turned to leave, saying, "Grandfather asked me to pick a nice branch from the olive grove, one with lots of olives on it."

"My dear, he obviously doesn't know that they've all been shaken off and washed away by the storm." I refrained from mentioning the soldiers.

"I'll get one anyway just to show him," he said as he walked away, disappointed.

On such a beautiful October day, it was a pleasure to still be able to breathe clean, mild air. In my eased state of mind, I went back to the small bakehouse to see if the cakes were ready. Pleased to see their golden crust, I started to take them out when I heard heavy footsteps approaching. I turned around and saw Piero standing before me with the face of a madman, his eyes popping out of his head. Never having seen him like this before, I was so disconcerted that I could hardly hold up the shovel with the cakes on it.

"Where's that bandit accomplice of yours?" he exploded. I didn't answer. "And where's my son?"

My hands shook so much, more with anger than with fear, that I could not balance the cakes anymore. I had to reach deep inside me to summon up the strength I needed to rebuff him. Straightening up, I said firmly, "*My* son has just gone to get an olive branch your father requested." Taking a deep breath, I went on, "My accomplice, as you call him, isn't here. He'll be back in time to return Leo to your wife as he promised. So there was no need for you to come up here like this. Anyway, I think you already know that 'my accomplice' is the new owner of this house from which you've tried several times to evict me."

"Huh! Your Accattabriga! He tried to buy this estate, but under false pretenses. He told you he bought the house, too—and that's a lie! Now he says he's going to marry you—that's also a lie!" He got more furious by the minute. "He perpetrated this swindle with one thing in mind—and that's to have you! To possess you! Isn't that so? And because of your evil deeds, I will see to it that you're both charged with fraud and thrown into a dungeon!"

"*You* talk about evil deeds? When it comes to diabolical tricks, you're second to none! Trying to frighten me out of here in so many ways, to get me away as far as possible from my son! Haven't you learned yet that Leo is more mine than yours? He will *never* leave me!" I shouted, glaring at his distorted face. "And now get out of here before I tell my son about the soldiers you sent to scare me and throw mud at my house. I want you to know that the only reason I haven't told Leonardo about it yet is because I was ashamed to let him know what his father is capable of. So, get out of here before he sees you with the face of a madman! He'll be returned to your wife at the time they agreed upon."

"I'm not leaving here without him."

"Then, I'll have to tell him everything in your presence."

"Mama, what's the matter? Why are you crying?" asked Leo, rushing up to us with the olive branch in his hand. Piero turned away to hide his flushed face from Leo. "Why did you upset Mama?" Leo shouted. "Why? Why are you here?" I had never before seen the boy so enraged. "When you told me you were my father, I agreed to stay in your house and respect you," he chided, "only if you left Mama in peace. Remember?"

Piero seemed to be at a loss for words, but Leo's eyes demanded an answer. Then, still covering his face, he said casually, "Well, I came for you ... maybe a little too early, so she got upset." I threw an angry sidelong glance at him, which didn't escape Leo.

"There was no need. Ser Giovanni is taking me back today. Didn't Donna Albiera tell you?"

"Yes, she did, but she shouldn't have allowed a stranger—"

"Ser Giovanni is not a stranger. He is a gentleman friend of my mother, and you should respect this the way my mother respects your ... family!"

"And you should realize that you're my responsibility!"

"All right, then. Since I've already found what Grandfather wanted, I can come back with you now, I suppose." He noticed the cakes that had fallen on the floor. "Oh, Mama, your cakes! I'll pick them up for you."

Tempering his voice, Piero said, "Take your time, Leonardo. I'll return a little later," and headed back to his gig.

I was so upset by the confrontation that I still couldn't move. Leo kept looking at me as he picked up the cakes from the floor. "Pay no attention to his bad moods. Ser Piero is like that with everybody, even with poor Donna Albiera. You see, he works very hard, so he doesn't have the patience to be nice to the members of his family. He upsets them all the time, but I usually take no notice of his moods. I think he's important to me only because he lets me study and learn things I need for my future," he reasoned with me, throwing his arms around me. "But you, Mama, are important to me because of your love, because you taught me to love everyone and everything in the wonderful universe around us!" Handing me the basket filled with the cakes, he said, "I can always count on you. You are as reliable as Mother Earth is in this magic countryside of ours!" His words seemed to reach deep into my soul like drops of healing balsam, and I never forgot them for the rest of my life!

Nevertheless, the moment Leo left, I fell back into the abyss of depression that Piero had reopened, making my world sad and lonely again. In an attempt to estrange myself from my torment, I strolled absently to my favorite spot, my open-air temple, where I knew my aching heart would find solace. I sat on the step of the ancient well and, resting my head against the column thickly covered with soft ivy, I closed my eyes and let myself slip into an imaginary world of my own.

I found myself in a wonderful garden full of exotic plants rich with colorful blooms and suddenly realized I was not alone. Giovanni was by my side. Hand in hand, we dreamily strolled through our magic garden. "Caterina! Monna Caterina! Leo! Where are you?" echoed Giovanni's voice. I opened my eyes and, still mesmerized by my sweet vision, I hazily saw him hurrying toward me. "Caterina, what are you doing here all alone? Where is Leo? You look so pale," he said, taking my hand.

I shrugged my shoulders. Then, suddenly remembering the awful scene, I said blankly, "Leo has gone. His father came for him. That's all."

He started to lift me up, but instead sat next to me and held me in a warm embrace. Recovering slightly, I began to tell him what had happened, but he put his finger on my lips, then slowly pointed to the sun shining above the distant horizon of sweeping plains. I wanted to tell him all about my vision, but my modesty prevailed. After we had silently watched the sun setting for a while, I heard him say, "Let's go, my dear. You need some food." We got up and slowly walked back toward the house.

"Giovanni, do you know what he said? He said that we'll end up in a dungeon because of our scheme."

"That can easily be avoided simply by getting married, don't you think?" He laughed. "I have an idea. Let's go find Thunderbolt. In his saddlebag, he's hiding a small bottle of the same elixir we drank at Donna Grazia's. Remember how nice it was?"

"I don't think that's wise."

"What, drinking the elixir? Not if you have an empty stomach, like you do, my lovely! But after eating some of those cakes I smell, it would be wise, indeed!"

"Are you always in such a good mood?"

"Not always. Only when I'm happy, and this is one of those times." He added jokingly, "Why? Hadn't you noticed? Oh, I'm very disappointed. Now I'm going to cry." Lifting my chin, he said, "Wait a minute. You've stolen my tear," and with his finger he dabbed a teardrop on my cheek.

We were at the table about to sip the red liqueur from small glasses, while the cakes I had made for Leo remained untouched on the platter.

"Caterina, I know what's going on in your mind, what's really worrying you." I looked at him, wondering what he was trying to say. Then I set the glass down and started to eat a cake so that the liqueur wouldn't upset my empty stomach and cloud my mind. While I nibbled at the cake I studied his face, the pleasant lines of his high forehead and his tousled hair. "You're afraid that by falling in love with me, you'd be neglecting your son, and he'd lose your undivided attention, your whole love! Isn't that so?" he asked, reaching for my hand.

"I hadn't really thought of it like that, but you may be right in a way. I've never loved anybody else as much as I love my child. We grew up together, because I was no more than a child when I had him. I feel that if I loved somebody else …" My thoughts went to the origin of this feeling of mine. "You see, taking care of my son is a mission for me. I'm sure that's why I was saved at birth."

"My dear, we all have a mission in life, even when we don't know what it is. Right now, I feel I have a very urgent mission, too, and that's to take care of you, my dear Caterina! I feel it so strongly that it surprises me." His eyes glistened as he added, "There's something I want to confide to you." He paused as if finding it difficult to begin. "A long time ago, God gave me the chance to understand certain things. Until about five years ago, I had a wife I loved with all my heart and soul, and a daughter I adored. Unfortunately, in a very short time, a deadly fever took both of them away from me. But before it was all over, while still wondering, grief-stricken, if one might survive, I knew that I loved both of them with equal intensity. Though my bond to one was very different from the other, neither one diminished the other. And as I look at you, I see a big heart, overflowing with love, strong enough to sustain fully many different devotions!"

"You say such beautiful things! What a tragedy you went through, my poor darling!" I murmured, caressing his face.

He stood up and, taking me in his arms, whispered in my ear, "I want you to know, my love, that since then I've never touched another woman. I, too, had my misgivings ... until I met you." He kissed my face.

"Giovanni, I'm not sure if I could fill the void in your life. I wouldn't know where to start."

"You don't have to start anything. You love me already. Don't you feel it? Let's get married, my love! It'll make your son happy, too, I'm sure."

His strong hand around my waist awoke new sensations in me. Cold and then warm shivers ran all through my body. It must have been the effect of the elixir, I thought at first. But I hadn't touched it yet!

They were the same sensations I felt the time he held me on his horse, the time he held me at the *ruscello,* and, indeed, every other time. He kissed my cheeks passionately, and I felt my lips tremble. By then, I could not follow my thoughts anymore. My head started to spin like a wheel. Then, still holding me, he paused as if waiting for me to relinquish all my doubts and fears.

I embraced him, and suddenly all my anxieties melted away. His warm breath met my breath, his lips touched mine, and my trembling lips trembled no more.

When I awoke, bright sunlight was peeping through the shutters left ajar. It was strange to be in bed so late, but even stranger to be greeted with a tender smile. Giovanni was sitting, already dressed, on the edge of the bed. I tried to speak, but he gently put the tip of his finger on my lips and said, "My love, I'll be back in a couple of days and we'll talk about our future." He placed a long kiss on my lips, as if trying to make up for the time that we would have to stay apart. "And, remember, my beautiful, that now we belong together!"

"Giovanni, I love you, too, more than I ever knew I could," I whispered. "Please don't ever leave me."

He tilted his head and smiled. "Never, my dear. I will love you ... forever." I knew then I would again, and again, remember the sound of his voice as he said those words.

* * *

I was taking a walk around the grounds, trying to come to the right decision regarding my future—the future that Giovanni had spoken about so optimistically—when Ser Giuliano called me from his gig at the bend of the road. "Caterina, I'm in a hurry. I'm on my way to Florence to see Piero da Vinci at his new office there. Take these! They're the keys to our house at the farm. As I said before, you should leave immediately."

"But, Ser Giuliano, Piero already knows the truth."

"Don't worry, I'll take care of everything. Just pack a few clothes and be ready when Giovanni comes for you. I've got to go now."

Clutching the bunch of keys and feeling swept along a little too fast, I headed back to the house. It seemed that my future had already been planned by others, the way my son's future had been, and I was simply to follow the tide. I was determined, however, to go to Vinci once more and inquire about Leo before I submitted totally.

The next morning, as I was standing in front of the school door, a pretty young woman with a scarf neatly tied on her head looked out to make sure that all the boys were in. "Excuse me, Sister. Is Donna Lucia da Vinci coming with her grandchild today?" I asked, trying to sound casual.

"I'm Sister Giuseppina. Unfortunately, our clever Leonardo is not my pupil anymore. I think he's going to stay in Florence with his father for good. Sorry, I must go in now, but I'm sure you'll find Donna Lucia at home."

As we parted, she put her hands together, smiled and bowed her head. I managed to smile back, though feeling crushed for having lost the only opportunity I ever had to talk freely with my son's first teacher, and continued to stare blankly at the closed school door. The streets suddenly seemed deserted, and there was nothing else for me to do but to go home, more devastated than before, promising myself, though, to keep calm and not to view things as tragically as I had in the past.

Nonetheless, once home, I couldn't help crouching next to

Leo's construction projects and the blank sheets of drawing paper he had left behind. "Will I really have to wait until he grows up to spend time with him again?" I kept asking myself. "And here I am, struggling to keep this humble home for him," I shouted, crying my heart out. Then I remembered Giovanni's words and I felt the sudden urge to be close to this man, who always showed me the lighter side of things. So, refusing to give up hope, I rushed outside and, in a frenzy, I started digging up the bulbs I had salvaged from the flood. I enclosed the patch with a row of rocks and tried to visualize multicolored flowers growing in it and attracting the most beautiful butterflies with their sweet smell. Then I pictured Leo sitting there drawing those wonders of nature. The soothing sound of my *ruscello* reaching my ear suddenly induced me to go to the water's edge. I sat down on a large stone I had not seen before. Most likely it had been washed down by the flood. Stroking it as if it were a living being, I murmured, "You were brought down here by the storm, just as I was by my destiny. But you will stay here forever, perhaps, while I ... Who knows?" I got up to look at the water more closely and saw that its reddish cloudiness had disappeared, leaving behind the sparkling clarity of before and revealing new weeds growing underneath. Two small creatures glittered in the sunlight, darting in and out of the weeds, and I remembered what Leo had said. "Fishes! Leo said there would be fishes. They're just as he drew them!" I cried excitedly as they dove under a rock. Maybe I had frightened them, but on the other hand, they had lifted me out of my depression, somehow giving me the confidence I needed to face my unknown future.

On my way back to the house, I began to wonder whether the place that had been chosen for my exile was to be of my liking. I knew, however, that it was much farther from Florence and from my son. "But I'll be with Giovanni!" I reassured myself, suddenly longing to be in his warm embrace and reliving the moments of delight we had shared.

Still in this dreamy state of mind, I decided to sit on the bench by my window and go over the sweet words he had whispered in my ear. My attention, though, was caught by something resembling a crack in my doorstep. The single step was an oblong stone, according to the masons, especially hewn at the quarry to fit my doorway. I leaned over to get a better look, only to find that it was an indentation, two fingers wide, running from the upper left corner to the lower right like a winding road. I could not get over how evenly it had been carved, and wondered who could have done such a thing during my brief absence. I sat down again as the marble slab of my childhood home inevitably came to mind with the carved symbols that had influenced me so. Why was I pursued by these signs? Would I have to face another strange occurrence? Troubled by these questions, I covered my eyes.

Suddenly, I felt a presence radiating warmth. Timidly looking up, I found myself staring at a man in soldier's uniform, whose handsome face seemed to pour deep devotion toward me, making me feel a comforting closeness to him. A poignant smile lit up his face as he spoke to me. "I'm your father, Leonardo, my dear Lisa!" For a moment, I was a helpless child in arms again, lovingly being lulled. He pointed to the doorstep and said, "Follow your new road and enjoy the happiness offered to you, dear child!" Afraid of breaking the spell, I didn't dare ask him about the doorstep. I tentatively reached out, trying to embrace him, but he had gone as quickly as he had appeared, leaving me stunned.

"What happened?" I cried earnestly. "Was I asleep? Did I dream up the whole thing?" Strangely, I still sensed the same warmth lingering around me, a warmth not unsimilar to Giovanni's. Casting my gaze down at the doorstep, I ran my finger along the mysterious notch just as I had done with the marble slab as a child. I desperately needed to know this was real. Then, still dazed, I went into the house and calmly gathered Leo's playthings, covering them with a sheet. I dragged Rita's wicker basket into the middle of the room and started packing my personal belongings.

When I opened the door the next morning, I noticed from the corner of my eye that all that was left of the carving on the doorstep was a pale shadow. Not wanting to let anything deter me from my plan, I didn't give it another thought and soon found myself climbing the road to Paterno, intent on paying a visit to our beautiful patron saint. Whenever I stopped to catch my breath, I couldn't help taking a last look at the lovely hills I was soon to leave.

It was Sunday, and I let the other churchgoers hurry past me, as I needed time alone to prepare myself for my communion with God. As usual, I wanted to pray for Leo and his future, but in particular, I needed God's forgiveness for having again been intimate with a man without the nuptial blessing.

As I turned into the churchyard, a man's hand grasped my shoulder. I started, but it was only Giovanni, who gave a boyish laugh.

"What are you doing here?" I asked.

Thunderbolt, who was following him, shook his mane.

"He's bored, because I made him go slowly so as not to pass you. I wanted to let you complete your pilgrimage undisturbed."

"So you were stalking me, eh?" I said complacently.

He smiled impishly as he tied his horse to a nearby tree.

"To think that I came up here to ask forgiveness ... and here you are right in front of the church. You spoiled my act of contrition."

"Don't let me stop you," he said, ignoring my reproof. "You go ahead—I'll wait for you out here. But first ..." He reached for my hand, and I slipped away nervously. "Wait!" he said. "I have an idea. Let's go in together! We can both be contrite, since I, too, have sinned, don't you think?"

"No, don't. I can't go in with you." He withdrew and I went in alone.

When Mass was over and most of the congregation had dispersed, I was curious to see if he had come in. He was standing at the back, and I beckoned him to come and sit by me.

He lovingly took my hand and whispered in my ear, "Let's ask the priest to marry us right now! I'm sure he doesn't need much preparation." Winking at me, he added, "At least you won't have to ask for forgiveness anymore." I looked into his eyes. "I'm serious, Caterina," he said firmly.

"No, I want my son to know first. We'll do it next Easter or, better still, on his birthday in April."

"Then come with me, my dear Caterina! Let's go and kneel in front of the altar. See! The others have gone now." I followed him, looking in admiration at the beautiful saint, whose kind eyes seemed to be on us. "Come pray with me: 'We are here together' ... Repeat after me: 'We are here together in Your presence, oh Celestial Father, to humbly ask You with all our heart and soul to lay Your divine hand upon us and join us in Holy Matrimony.'" He paused. "'Father, we are waiting for a sign from You to let us know that You bless this our union, that it is according to Your Will, forever and ever, amen!'" Like a child, I repeated after him, word for word. As we both remained still, waiting, I felt warmth radiating from his hand to mine, spreading all over my body. Then for an instant I saw a pink aura flickering around us, and Giovanni squeezed my hand. He had seen it, too, and we looked at each other in amazement. Then, Giovanni took off a ring from his little finger and placed it carefully on the finger of my other hand. As we touched, we knew that our union had been blessed.

Outside, the air had turned chilly and everyone had gone home. We decided to return to Anchiano on foot. My bridegroom kept his hand around my waist, while with the other he held the horse's reins. We walked in complete silence, only communicating through our thoughts.

As we neared the house, Giovanni pointed to some heavy gray clouds in the distance and said, "There's a snowstorm coming. Have you made up your mind yet, my love, about going to Ser Giuliano's farm? We'd have to leave immediately to avoid being trapped up here."

"Yes, darling, I have. In fact, I packed two days ago. I even have the keys to Ser Giuliano's house."

On hearing about the keys, he seemed slightly perturbed, but there was no more time for discussion as we made haste to leave.

Giovanni loaded my wicker trunk on the back of his carriage, and I put on my golden-brown pinafore dress over a long, warm flannel shirt and my dark-red cape. Carrying my birdcage, I went around making sure I had left everything in order. Then I stopped to kiss the white wall of my little home.

I insisted on dropping in on Donna Grazia, even though I knew that going up Mont'Albano would delay our journey. She was glad to see us and advised me to stay at the farm until the worst of the winter had passed.

"What will you do, Donna Grazia? Are you going to spend the winter in Empoli?" inquired Giovanni.

"I really don't know, Giovanni, but we are thinking about it. The mountain air may be better for my health, but the constant traveling in the cold will be too hard on my dear consort." Then she looked at me sorrowfully and said, "You don't know how much I'm going to miss you, Caterina. I'll have to pretend that you may knock on my door at any time. Take good care of her, Giovanni." We both blushed and, like a sister, she hugged us both.

As we passed Anchiano again, I glanced nostalgically at my little corner of the world I was leaving behind. Noticing my sadness, Giovanni offered me his arm, and I pressed myself tightly against him, receiving a loving smile in return.

After passing through the town of Empoli, we were on the road to Pisa, and soon the flat farmland in the county of Santa Croce came into view.

As we crossed a bridge over a wide river, I asked, "Is this the same river that goes through Florence?"

"Yes. Why do you ask? Have you been to Florence?" he inquired.

"Yes, I have. One day I'll tell you the reason I went."

"Barges float along this river to Florence and Pisa. Years ago, I used to travel on them. I enjoyed it then. Now I just travel in my carriage."

"Do you go to Florence often?"

"Only on business. We produce a lot of cheese at the farm, and most of it is sold in Florence." Then he looked at me curiously. "Why? Would you like to go there with me sometime?"

"Yes, darling, yes! They took Leo there. This time for good."

"I had a feeling that that was the reason. You see, Caterina, you can't keep any secrets from me." I laughed, still holding his arm tightly.

The farm we approached was as big as a village. In addition to the tall building at its center, surrounded by a wide esplanade, there were several huge barns, some for cattle and sheep, others for cheese-making. Scattered around farther out were the farm workers' rural cottages.

As we entered the esplanade, a man and two women welcomed us, "Good day, Donna Caterina. Welcome home!" I turned questioningly to Giovanni.

"As far as they're concerned, you're my wife." He chuckled.

I stiffened, however, for the welcoming committee was strangely entranced by us, as if they were seeing angels descending from heaven. Not knowing what else to do, I forced a smile. As soon as Giovanni helped me down, I took the keys out of my bag and handed them to the older woman.

"The keys to the master's house!" she exclaimed. "Is that where you're going to stay, Ser Giovanni?"

"Well, it seems that's Donna Grazia's wish," Giovanni answered, giving me a secret wink. Then he offered his arm in an affected gentlemanly way. Determined to overcome my lack of composure, I slipped my arm firmly through his. As the woman led us up the front steps of the tall stone building, Giovanni's attention was caught by a group of farmers who seemed anxious to greet him. He broke away, urging me to go ahead.

"I'm sorry if the place is stuffy," said the woman, ushering me into the house, "but it's been closed for a very long time."

"Where does Ser Giovanni live?" I asked uneasily, as we stepped into the spacious living room.

"His quarters are on this floor, too, but the entrance is at the back," she said as she rushed to open the window wide. Then, with an understanding smile, she added, "It would have been too small for the two of you, anyway." I nervously looked away to view the room.

Among other heavy pieces of furniture I saw a splendidly carved sofa covered with red velvet cushions in front of an imposing fireplace.

Two men came into the house carrying my wicker trunk, and I followed them into another spacious room dominated by an extremely wide bed with a thick white cotton cover. Scandalized, I scurried back to the living room, bumping into the younger maid, who had come in with the birdcage.

"What a beautiful canary, Donna Caterina! May I take care of it?"

"If you wish, but it's really a nightingale," I stuttered.

"Donna Caterina," interjected the older woman, "my name is Filomena. Would you like a hot bath prepared for you? You look chilled and you must be very tired." Too embarrassed to speak, I looked up at the portrait of a man with a chiding face! "I'll have young Girolamo bring some firewood. We're going to be snowed in soon," she added, leaving the room.

Being treated like Donna Grazia already made me uncomfortable, but pretending I was Giovanni's wife was putting an even greater strain on me—not only did I have to be on my guard constantly, but also the lie was seriously troubling my conscience. Things had gone too far, I thought, and it was time to have a talk with Giovanni. I stood at the window, waiting for him as he shook hands with each of the farmers in front of the house. As soon as he saw me beckoning to him, he left them and came upstairs.

"I'm at your service, Donna Caterina!"

"Why didn't you tell me you were going to let them think we're married?" I demanded.

"What's wrong with that? Are you ashamed of me?" he teased. "If you'd rather, I won't use these stairs anymore. Of course, there's a connecting door to my apartment, but then they'd probably get suspicious, wouldn't they?"

"Why can't you be serious!"

"Well, what about our secret marriage in the house of God?" he said sofly, putting his arms around me. "Didn't it mean anything to you?"

Once again, he had succeeded in allaying my anxieties. I

succumbed to his warm embrace as he kissed me on the lips over and over again.

Since I had everything I needed in the house, I hardly ever went out, only seeing Giovanni when he came in for a brief midday meal during the course of the day. Dinner on the farm was the most important meal, which Filomena insisted on preparing, despite several attempts on my part to convince her otherwise. "Donna Caterina, I wouldn't dare let you do that! It's my job. I've cooked for Ser Giovanni ever since he came here," she explained firmly. But at least she let me stay in the kitchen to learn some of her recipes.

"Filomena, I would like to do something," I said sweetly one day. "As you know, Ser Giovanni is out all day. With nothing to do, I get bored. Maybe some evening I could serve dinner, so you can retire a little earlier." Although she looked at me suspiciously at first, she finally agreed. Gradually, I managed to persuade her to let me cook and serve most of the evening meal myself and, in this way, my days became more interesting, my evenings more delightful with Giovanni, as we were free to talk and joke together. But, most of all, it left me less time to worry about my Leo.

"Caterina, I've been thinking," began Giovanni one evening at dinner. "What would you do if our union were blessed with a child?"

His question took me by surprise. "Well, I would take this as a sign that I was being relieved in some respect of my responsibilities toward Leo—that he really didn't need me anymore. I would then ask you to take me to the nearest church and have the priest make our union official."

"But if you had other children, wouldn't you still love Leo and care for him as you do now?"

"Yes, but in a different way, because I would be able to let go, knowing that my mission was over."

"As he gets older, though, your great sense of reponsibility should diminish anyway, shouldn't it?"

"I don't know, Giovanni. Maybe then I'll know. Maybe the ..."

Taking my hand, he gently pulled me to our red velvet love nest in front of the fire. Locked in each other's arms, we listened to my nightingale warble sweetly and made tender, passionate love.

When spring came back again I kept glancing from my windows at the vast grassland getting greener by the day. I was fascinated by the large number of grazing cows, followed closely by their little calves. At the cheese-making barns, the activity had increased, and I watched with wonder as the workers loaded the carts with crates of cheese. "Filomena, where are they taking all that cheese?" I asked her one day.

"They're taking it to the market in Florence."

"Is Ser Giovanni going too?"

"He usually does, Donna Caterina." She eyed me with concern. "Donna Caterina, you look worried. Are you afraid to be here alone? Why? You have us! We're all very fond of you, because you make Ser Giovanni very happy, and if I may say so, I love him like my own son!" I patted her arm in return for her kindness, but my thoughts were far, far away.

That night, anxious to speak with Giovanni in private, I tactfully dismissed Filomena, who had stayed until dinner was over. "Is it true, dear, you may be going to Florence soon?"

"Yes, I may go next week," he replied, looking at me from the corner of his eye. Then he placed his finger on my lips. "Don't say another word! I know why you asked, but there are no decent places to stay during market week. Besides, that area is much too rough."

"I told you I know a lovely woman there—Francesca. Remember?"

"All right, we'll see when the time comes. Now let's go and enjoy our favorite spot." We snuggled up to each other on our love seat again.

So, on a glorious spring day, I found myself on the spruced-up carriage next to my Giovanni on our way to Florence. All the familiar places we had passed before seemed more beautiful this time with the prospect of seeing my dear Leo again.

When we pulled up in front of Francesca's tavern, I jumped down by myself, while Giovanni went to talk to the men in the carts behind us. "Caterina, wait! I want to go in with you," cried Giovanni as I hurried to the door. I stopped and held out my hand to him. He called orders to his men and, putting his hand on my waist, escorted me inside.

We went directly to the kitchen, where Francesca was taking bread out of the oven. I went up behind her and covered her eyes. "Who is it?" she snapped, taking my hands away. "Ah, I know whose pretty hands these are. Caterina's!" she exclaimed. "What a wonderful surprise! How well you look! You've blossomed like a flower. Have you gotten married?" I pointed at Giovanni, who was at the door enjoying the whole scene. "Ah, he's the one, eh! Wait, I think I know him," she said, going over to greet him. "You're from Santa Croce, near Pisa, aren't you?" Giovanni nodded brightly. "Well, since you're in good hands, wait here while I see what's going on out there." She went to the dining room, but reappeared at the door soon, inviting us to sit at a corner table. "Sit down there! And I'll bring you something I'm sure your handsome husband will like," she chirped at me.

I noted, though, that her face was drawn and her cheeks had lost their color, so I followed her back to the kitchen. "Francesca, my dear, have you been sick?"

"A little. But seeing you with that good-looking man, I feel completely recovered. Now, tell me about your son. He must be big."

"Almost seven. He's in Florence now. He moved in with some relatives who send him to school. Unfortunately, I don't know their address yet."

"My dear, you're always looking for somebody! Anyhow, I'm glad you've found that nice man. You certainly deserve him. Now, come and taste my soup to see if it's good enough for him," she said, handing me her wooden spoon.

"Giovanni, I really should go to the *catasto* to see if they know Piero's address," I said when we finished eating dinner.

"Yes, but come back right away. Don't try to see him by yourself!"

"No, I won't. I promise you, darling! We'll go there together," I assured him, getting ready to leave.

We went our separate ways through the crowded streets, but they were still so familiar to me that I was able to get through quite swiftly.

When I entered the *catasto,* I saw the old clerk sitting at the same desk, looking over his papers as before. I coughed to get his attention. "Good day, *messere.* I'm Caterina. Do you remember me?" I asked with a friendly smile.

He looked up at me as if waking from a nap. "Ah, you're the young girl who was looking for her grandfather, the *condottiere,*" he answered rather superciliously.

"No, I was looking for my father," I answered dryly.

"Did you find him? You look much happier now."

"No, I didn't. I think, though, that he died on a battlefield. Anyway, now I'm looking for somebody else, a notary called Piero da Vinci. I know that he's alive and that he moved to Florence recently."

"Well, a notary who's alive should be much easier to find. Wait here! I'll be back soon." Moving slowly, he went into the next room, soon reappearing with a satisfied look. "You're lucky this time! The notary's residence is in the suburbs near Santa Maria in Monte, where he's now the procurator. But he also has an office here just around the corner." He handed me a piece of paper. "Here's the address! Everybody knows the place. Just show this to the street guard!"

I thanked him and hurried back down the wide staircase, planning to find the place right away. I was directed to a round, enclosed courtyard where various carriages were stationed. Intending only to reconnoiter, I went straight to the center door, which was decorated with stained glass. Finding it ajar, I was tempted to push it open. At a table facing the entrance sat a clerk busy scribbling. He looked up at me vacantly. When I asked if that was Ser Piero da Vinci's office, he simply pointed to the next room. I went toward it on impulse, realizing that I was failing to keep my promise to Giovanni. From the doorway I caught sight of Piero sitting at an enormous oak desk, working with some papers. Overcome by hostile feelings, I moved to the center of the room and planted my feet firmly on the floor. He looked up at me and jumped to his feet, clasping his forehead. "What are you doing here?" he growled, clenching his fists.

"You dare ask me!" He fell back into his chair. Silence followed. "Where is my son? I must see him."

"He's at school," he said, growing bolder. "Where else would he be? I brought him to Florence so he could get a better education." He nodded slowly, giving me a sidelong glance. "A good intention *you* couldn't appreciate."

"Not when the purpose is to keep him from me!"

"To prevent disrupting surprise visits like this one! He's very busy with two courses of studies, one for his regular education, the other for his drawing. Though I hardly find the latter useful," he added peevishly.

"You could have let me know you were moving here. But it seems I exist only as a target for your threats. Remember that I am still Leo's mother and I want to be respected as such! And I have every right at least to, know his whereabouts." I stopped to control my tears and regain my composure. He remained silent. "I must see him and talk to him. Tell me where his school is!" I insisted, facing him again.

"His school is near my house, which is far away from here, and at the studio, he cannot be disturbed."

"Then I'll go to your house," I retorted, just to intimidate him.

"No, no!" he shouted as he rose nervously from his chair. "My wife is sick," he said, lowering his voice. "She couldn't cope with this nonsense. She's a very delicate woman—not as strong and aggressive as you are!" He paused, and as he stared at me the hostility in his eyes seemed to slowly turn languid, giving way to an expression of lust. I moved away. "All right, then," he relented with a shaky voice. "I'll bring him here tomorrow. He has to go to drawing school near here."

"Good. I'll be back tomorrow, then."

"I hope one day you'll ... appreciate my generosity," he said impudently.

"What do you mean 'appreciate'? 'Generosity,' indeed!" And before he could say any more, I stormed out.

When I reentered Francesca's dining room through the backdoor, it must have been mealtime, for Giovanni was already sitting at the same corner table. When I breathlessly sat down next to him, he looked at me resentfully. "I'm sorry I took so long, my dear. Piero's office was near the *catasto,* so the moment I saw it, I just had to go in."

"You went in there alone?"

"Yes, I'm not afraid of him now. Anyway, I made him promise to bring Leo there tomorrow, when I'd really like you to be there with me."

"Do you think I'd let you go there by yourself again?"

Squeezing his arm to subdue him, I murmured, "Thank you, my love, for being so patient with me."

Francesca, who had been observing us from a distance, came and put her hand on Giovanni's shoulder. "Caterina, you have a fine man here. Now let me bring you something good to eat. Later you can sleep in my room. I'll take the room you had last time, remember?"

That night, however, I was not able to sleep. Though I was looking forward to seeing my son, I was much too concerned about Piero's behavior toward me. It was obvious that he still desired me, and I knew that seeing Giovanni would make him extremely jealous. I wasn't afraid of what Piero could say, but I did fear what he could do to me without my knowledge. Yet, at this point, how could I ask Giovanni not to come with me?

The lamplight flickered as I felt Giovanni's hand stroking my forehead. "Keep calm, my love. Remember that you're not alone anymore. I'm with you now ... all the time!" whispered his soothing voice.

Next morning, we marched into the circular courtyard toward the stained-glass door, which I gingerly pushed open. Giovanni held me back, while he peeped inside the room. "Go in now! I'll be out here," he said, winking encouragingly.

I sighed with joy! Behind the clerk's desk sat my Leo, drawing on pink paper. When he saw me, he rushed into my arms, still holding his drawing. He was much taller and very poised. I gazed at him speechlessly, then, clearing my throat, I said, "How are you, darling?"

"I'm fine, Mama!" he whispered, pointing to the papers. "You see? I'm getting ready to enter a very important studio of art."

"Really? Which one?" I asked in the same whisper.

"It's Verrocchio's *bottega*."

"Ah, I know it ... I've heard of it." We both turned to look at Piero, who appeared at the door. "Come outside! I want to talk to you alone," I said aloud. Leo looked at his father for approval. Piero just shrugged his shoulders and went back to his office. As Leo led me to the exit door, I whispered, "Leo, wait a moment! I want you to tell me if you're really happy living here in Florence."

Still poised, he continued in a whisper, "Yes, Mother, for the reasons I explained to you in Anchiano. This is where I want to live when I grow up, too." Putting his mouth near my ear, he added, "Then I'll be able to come to you whenever I want."

"Good. When I heard that you left Vinci, I—" I began.

"Mama, we may be coming to Vinci at Eastertime," he interrupted. "Oh, I can't wait to see the flowers in the fields!"

"And the new house, too. Remember? By the way, I saw two fishes in the brook exactly as you drew them!"

"How nice! Mama, I miss you so much. How did you get to Florence?"

"Giovanni brought me," I said, lowering my voice even more. "Remember him? He's outside. He wants to say hello to you."

"Wait, Mother! I want to show you this oil painting. Look! It's you!"

"Oh, how pretty!" I said, admiring the small wooden tablet he held up.

"I did it from memory," he said, tilting his head a little.

"Don't you think it makes me look too young?" He smiled as I hugged it to my breast. "All right, dear. Now let's go outside!"

"Leonardo, you look fine and so much taller!" said Giovanni, coming up to us as I slipped the tablet into my pocket.

"Good morning, Ser Giovanni! Yes, I'm fine, thank you, but I have to study hard. Here in Florence you have to be very good in order to be accepted in the best studios."

"And good you certainly are!"

Piero appeared at the door with a stony look on his face. "Leonardo, I think there's been enough conversation. It's time to go to the studio."

"Yes, Ser Piero, I'll get my instruments," Leo said as he went inside.

Piero looked at Giovanni scornfully, displaying his bad humor. "And you, Accattabriga, what are you doing here?" Giovanni said nothing. But, bristling, he threw Piero a long, hard look, which almost made me wince.

"Why are you always so rude, Piero?" I interjected.

Leo came out with his bag, and a disgruntled Piero went back inside. "Thank you for bringing my mother, Ser Giovanni," said Leo, offering his hand. Then he hugged me and went on his way, almost strutting like a grown man. Giovanni and I looked after him with admiration.

My joyous feelings were soon clouded, though, by the thought of Piero's attitude toward Giovanni, and again a great fear took hold of me.

As spring advanced, I became more attracted by the view from the back window of the farmhouse. From it, I could follow the growth of the vast fields of wheat, getting taller by the day. They looked like an enormous expanse of green water undulating even at the touch of the gentle breeze reaching all the way down from the distant hills. Yet, I searched longingly for my faraway hills, remembering the wild, spontaneous way things grew up there like whims of nature. And I often thought of Leo and the Eastertide, which I knew was imminent, but I didn't have the courage to mention it to Giovanni yet, as it would have meant our being apart.

Although our home was a comfortable love nest, with the good weather, I began to feel much too closed in and quite homesick for my outdoor life. So one morning, I decided to take a walk to a meadow at the edge of the wood beyond the cornfield, which had drawn my attention from my window for some time.

Wearing my blue cotton dress and carrying the birdcage, I ventured out by myself. Taking a path around the cornfield, I headed straight to the meadow near the wood and, having hung the cage on a low branch and given the bird some soft grass to peck, I settled myself under an oak tree surrounded by patches of wild purple anemones.

In the beauty of that oasis, my thoughts went to my Leo again, and then I remembered Giovanni's experience, which had taught him one could love two people in different ways, but still with the same intensity. I could see now how right he was, for the love I felt for him was just as strong as my love for Leo. Still reminiscing, my mind went back to my childhood and to my dear parents. I was grateful to them, too, for imparting the values by which they lived, revealing the true nobleness of their souls.

A flock of twittering birds had gathered around the tree, so I took out my flute, leaned my head against the tree trunk and played one of the sweet tunes I used to play as a child. Feeling at one with nature, I stopped and closed my eyes for a moment. I jumped as something tickled my lips. It was a long stem of wheat Giovanni was holding. He laughed heartily, then, studying my face, asked, "What were you dreaming about?"

"I wasn't dreaming. I was awake."

"Then, why didn't you hear me?"

"I don't know. Maybe my soul left my body," I said jokingly.

"Did your soul go to see Leo ... and talk about Easter again?"

"So you knew about it all along! And don't say your little bird told you! I've been worrying about how to tell you!"

"I couldn't help overhearing Leo tell you about it. You

were whispering so loudly! I know you'd like to return to Anchiano, but what shall I do without you? You know my life is here."

"I don't know what to say, my darling. I only know that thinking of Anchiano breaks my heart in two."

"Well, it means that I'll have to be away more often then, and I don't think Ser Giuliano will like that, but let's talk about something else," he said, touching my chin. "You never told me you play the flute in such a heavenly way!"

"I forgot I had it with me. Besides, it's the open countryside that usually inspires me to play. This time, though, I was inspired by this wonderful love of ours, too. I realized that I couldn't live without you any—" He took me in his arms and kissed me passionately on the lips. "Darling, darling! I've just thought I'd like to play for you by the brook on the very same spot of our first kiss!"

"Then we'd better leave tomorrow. Easter's only a week away, and you may want to get the place ready for Leo." This time I kissed him.

Next day, we were sitting on the carriage ready to leave when a tearful Filomena rushed out to us, holding a palm. "Take this, Donna Caterina! It was blessed in church this morning."

We were welcomed by the brisk air from the hills and by the returning swallows flying in and out of my roof gutters. I hung the birdcage on the wall as Giovanni brought in the wicker trunk. "I want to give the place a good spring cleaning," I said as soon as I opened the door. "Darling, you will stay with me for a few days, won't you?"

"Not if you'll be cleaning the house," he said, grim-faced.

"I promise I'll spend all my time with you, but tomorrow I want to light the oven."

"Why? We've brought all the fresh bread we need."

"I want to bake my special fruit tart to eat by the brook."

"Now, that's a project I'm in favor of!"

Those two days we spent alone together were the best I could remember. It was as if a magic spell had been cast over my corner of the world! Every moment was golden as we ate our picnic and played like children, chasing each other along the bank, frolicking in the grass, leaping in the sunlight, singing and dancing till our laughter rang merrily through the seemingly enchanted valley.

11
BROKEN ENCHANTMENTS

Easter Sunday morning promised to be a beautiful day. When the bells of Santa Lucia started ringing, joyfully announcing the Resurrection of Our Lord, I was proudly admiring my garden. All the bulbs I had planted in a circle around the rocks had sprung up and were in full bloom. The colors of the tulips, the hyacinths, and the narcissus were breathtaking.

The moment I heard a cart coming, I dashed to the courtyard. "Good morning, Caterina. How are you?" greeted Gian Pietro. My eyes were on Leo, who jumped off the cart, wearing a brightly colored jacket over his fitted pants and looking like a real young Florentine. He ran to me and hugged me with happiness shining in his eyes, but without his usual squeals of joy. "Caterina, have you noticed how big he is now? Very soon I'll have to call him Ser Leonardo."

"Indeed!" I answered gaily. Nevertheless, Gian Pietro seemed a little downcast and looked considerably older. So, to cheer him up, I said, "Gian Pietro, would you like a slice of my Easter egg tart? And maybe a glass of wine?"

"You ask me if I'd like it? Sure, I would! At home, nobody's preparing anything for the holidays. It's a sad Easter this year! It hurts to see poor Donna Lucia crying all day long over her consort's tragic condition."

"Why? What's happened to Ser Antonio?"

Leo, who had followed the conversation, put his hand on my arm. "Mother, I thought you knew. He's had a terrible stroke."

I blushed, feeling a little guilty. "It must have happened while I was away. I knew nothing about it."

"Poor Ser Antonio!" Gian Pietro interrupted. "He was visiting his daughter, Violante, at the time, and since then, they have not been able to move him. And poor Donna Lucia still isn't strong enough to travel."

I hid my face from Leo, who was watching me, hoping he couldn't read the fearful thoughts going through my mind, for now Piero would be even freer to hurt me. I shook my head to chase away the gloom and uttered the very words I should have said to myself, "Try not to think too much about the sad things in life, Gian Pietro! Now go sit at the table and help yourself, while I show Leo something."

"You know, Caterina, you seem to have grown up, too. If I may say, you look more sure of yourself," he said, heading for the house. "You're more ... like a lady," he added, almost muttering to himself as he went in the doorway. Laughing, I took Leo's hand and pulled him toward the garden.

"Mother, this is like heaven on earth! How did you manage to grow such lovely flowers?"

"Well, I was determined to keep the promise I made of having a garden full of flowers for you to draw on your visits here! Remember?" He hugged me with the same spontaneity he had as a small child.

Gian Pietro was already getting his cart ready to leave, when I walked up to him with a large bunch of long-stemmed flowers. "Gian Pietro, would you take these to Donna Lucia and Donna Albiera with my best wishes for Easter?"

"Where on earth did they come from? I've never seen such large blooms in my life—and I'm a gardener!" he said emphatically.

"From my garden at the back of the house."

"Mother, thank you for being kind to them!" whispered Leo.

"Well, after all, they take good care of you," I said. "Now let's take your box inside."

As soon as Gian Pietro left, we each took one end of the box and carried it to the house, swinging it gently. "Leo, why did you bring home so much work? You need a little rest, too," I said, feeling the weight of it.

"Mother, this isn't schoolwork!" I realized suddenly that he had been calling me "mother" consistently since he arrived, somehow making me feel a little detached. "You don't know how pleasant it can be to do something that hasn't been set by the tutor!" he said, stopping to greet the nightingale. "Mother, I think the nightingale is sick. Look! He's fallen off his perch. Did you keep giving him the dandelion leaves I told you about?"

"They were hard to find where I spent the winter months." We set the box down and rushed to the bird, which was leaning against the edge of the cage, its head hanging to the side. Leo opened the cage door, took the bird in his hand, and cradled it. I looked on, stunned by the sudden thought that my singing companion could one day become sick and die. Leo took off his velvet cap and laid the bird in it. Then I went inside and brought out a white linen cushion on which to rest it.

"Mother, you watch over him, while I look for some of that grass," he murmured before racing off across the field.

"My sweet nightingale, please don't leave me!" I sobbed. "What will I do without your singing? I'll die, too." But the poor bird lay quite still on its side. "Please get better, my friend," I whispered. But there was no reaction. I whistled softly, imitating its sound. The bird slowly opened one eye. Leo ran back with a bunch of herbs, which he put close to its tiny beak, encouraging it to sniff them. The bird stood up and raised its wings slightly. "Try! Try to fly a little bit, my friend!" cried Leo. "Look, you're not in the cage anymore. Go on, fly! See how beautiful it is to fly!" he kept repeating. At last, the bird opened its wings wider and gave a slight trill, which touched my heart. But soon its legs gave way and it rolled over on the cushion. I couldn't stop the tears from streaming down my face.

"Don't cry, Mother! He'll get better, you'll see." We held our breath as the bird gave a last faint trill, then it just lay there with its beak still open and its wings outstretched. Leo stroked its chest, hoping to revive it, but I knew that my faithful companion had left me forever. We gazed at it as it lay perfectly still. Then Leo said, "For a bird, he lived a long life, didn't he? How old was he?"

"I don't know exactly. Maybe a little older than you. I wish I'd noticed sooner he was sick," I said, drying my face.

"It's not your fault, Mother. Animals have short illnesses, perhaps to be spared too much pain. He's lived a full life span. His time had come."

"But I'll still miss his company," I said, trying to compose myself.

"I'll make a small box, and we'll find a nice spot to bury him. Maybe under the peach tree? He liked peaches!"

"Oh, Leo, what would I have done without you here?"

As a resting place, we chose the peach tree standing on the edge of the slope. It was the one all the birds loved to pick at, for it bore the sweetest and juiciest fruit. Leo marched solemnly in front of me holding the tiny box he made from the bark of a birch tree, and I followed him carrying a bunch of field flowers. Leo had dug a small hole and decorated the edges with tiny sprigs of flowers from the brook. He placed the box in the hole and covered it with soil as I watched, wondering if birds had souls, too.

A voice that seemed to come from inside me said "Yes!," allaying my anxiety. Then I arranged the flowers on the little mound of earth, and we sat next to the tiny grave.

After a long silence, Leo took out my flute from his pocket and handed it to me. "Please, Mother, play a nice tune for him." I couldn't react, as my eyes were blurred with tears. "He sang so much for us," he insisted.

I took it with a trembling hand and held it for a while, for I was too crushed to find the breath to blow into it. Then, picturing the soul of the nightingale fluttering in full fettle, I suddenly felt revived, and the most incredibly sublime sounds began to emerge from my modest little flute. I played until the last glow of ruby-gold sunset flickered over the hills and the first star blinked in the deep blue of the night sky.

I set the supper table with two bowls of hot drinks and a tray of biscuits. Leo drank his milk and I sipped a cinnamon flavored tisane, but neither one of us touched the biscuits as, without a word, we stared vacantly into the drab light of the oil lamp.

During the days that followed, Leo would take long walks, carrying a small book in which he wrote notes. Sometimes, he went so far from the house that I lost sight of him. He even climbed down to the brook without asking me to join him, as he used to do. At first, his desire to isolate himself bothered me, because it reminded me of the time when, as a tiny boy, he would go off by himself, striving to uncover the mysteries of nature. I reasoned with myself, remembering that, in the end, he had allowed me into his world and that his desire for solitude was not a sickness. Now that he was almost as tall as I, on his way to becoming an adult, I had to understand his new ways and learn how to deal with him, just as I had adjusted to Giovanni's ways. Yet I still resented the fact that my boy had never really had his share of a normal, carefree childhood.

One day, I saw him stripping the leaves from some thin branches he had cut. When I saw him heading to the brook, I filled my picnic basket and went there, too. I stopped at the usual flat patch by the water's edge, spread the tablecloth on the grass, and waited. From a distance, I watched Leo as he ran along the bank the way he did with his boats. This time, he followed his sticks, which were floating freely downstream. Intrigued, I started toward him. By the time I got nearer, he had removed the branches from the water and was jotting something in his notebook.

"Mother, you wouldn't believe how the speed of these sticks differs according to their size and shape!" he then said, putting his notebook back in his pocket. "If only people knew more about the force of water and how to harness it! So much could be gained from it! I think one day I'll have to invent a machine to prove it."

"My dear, I thought that drawing was your favorite work."

"Yes, but mechanics is what really interests me. The science of making objects move by themselves. Or, at least, with the forces that nature offers us, if we only knew how to harness its infinite energy," he said, gazing around.

"Mechanics? How can you find time to study that when you're so busy developing your talent for drawing?"

"Yes, I do have a talent for drawing, but I know that I also have the ability to invent new devices that will help mankind. You see, Mother, it's like a mission given me by some kind of divine power. Therefore, I feel bound to apply my mind to this study, too." There was nothing more for me to say as the words of my prophet came vividly back to me.

Noticing my preoccupation, Leo took my hand and, swinging it playfully, said, "Don't worry, Mother, I'm not going to do it today. Oh, you've brought some food. Let's hurry up before the ants have a feast with it." His sudden lightheartedness reminded me of Giovanni. At the end of the week, while he was packing his box, I looked over his magnificent lifelike drawings of my flowers, trying hard to hide my sadness at his departure.

"Mother, my father wants me to stay with him in Florence this summer," he began. "He wants me to study Latin so I'll be able to write out contracts for him. Though I welcome the opportunity of learning Latin, the prospect of working for him makes me shudder."

"Latin? That would be good," I said, recalling the inscription on the marble slab. "But then you can't oversee the construction of your room."

"I'm sure I can leave it to you, Mother. Besides, a roof over my head for the night is enough for me. I'm always outdoors, anyway."

"I'll wait for you just the same, my dear. Maybe things will change."

* * *

Not long after Leo left, the first load of building materials for his room arrived. Remembering Leo's words, I looked at the bricks and boards with apprehension. Their delivery indicated, too, that Ser Giuliano had settled matters regarding the ownership of the house, so as soon as the cart left, I picked some ripe apricots from the tree behind the house, put on my shawl, and went to see Donna Grazia.

She was sitting at a small table on the veranda, holding a quill pen. Delighted to see me, she got up and hugged me firmly. "How are you, Caterina? You look so lovely!" she exclaimed.

"I apologize for not coming sooner, but with my son's short visit and with the death of my nightingale ... the days went rather ..."

"I'm sorry, my dear, Giuseppe told me about the loss of your pet," she said, patting my hand.

"Today, two men brought the materials for the new room," I said, changing the subject, "so I assume Ser Giuliano has settled everything regarding the property."

"Yes, he has. I'll let him tell you about it. Now come and sit down and tell me everything about the last few months!" I felt embarrassed, not knowing where to start. "We went home for Christmas, you know, but I had to come back here right away," she went on, seeing my hesitation. "It looks as though I may have to spend the rest of my life up here. So, to fill the time," she said, pointing to the loose pages spread on the table, "I started writing!"

Then I showed her the basket of apricots. "Oh, how beautiful they are! It's almost a pity to eat them." She paused, looking closely at me, and added, "I see a lot of sadness in your eyes, Caterina. You miss Giovanni, don't you?" She had finally found the words to put me at ease.

"Yes, Donna Grazia. I do already miss Giovanni ... very much."

"This is a busy season for him. But I must say, my dear, that I don't understand why you kept your marriage secret."

"We only made our vows to one another," I said, stroking his ring. "I didn't want to become his wife officially, because if I had, I'd have had to abandon my house. Not that I disliked it at the farm—on the contrary!—but then I wouldn't be here when Leo comes home. So it seems I've created a real dilemma for myself." She shook her head disapprovingly, I thought on account of my having lived with Giovanni without the blessing of the Sacrament.

"But as soon as your son grows up, he'll have less and less time to spend with you," she reasoned. "My dear, you'd better hold on to Giovanni, if you don't want to spend the rest of your life alone."

"Do you know something, Donna Grazia? Giovanni took me to Florence to see Leo!" I said, relieved to be speaking openly about our time together.

"So, now you must tell me about the whole trip."

The second load of materials had been delivered when Ser Giuliano drove into the yard. I rushed out to greet him, but stopped short when I saw him pressing his hand on his chest as he climbed off his gig.

"Good morning, Ser Giuliano. How are you?"

He did not answer at first. Then he said bluntly, "Come here, Caterina! Listen carefully to what I have to say." He waited for a moment. "That scoundrel, Piero da Vinci, never bought this property from the friars, the Servants of Florence, because they didn't have permission to sell it. It had been donated to their convent on condition that they would not sell it for a certain number of years. So he has no power to evict you." He paused, pressing his chest again. It reminded me of poor Rita, and I wondered if he was suffering from the same ailment. "Anyhow, I went straight to the convent and asked the abbot to give you an annuity on the house."

"What's an annuity?"

"It's a contract giving you the right to live in this house until you die," he said, handing me the scroll. "So you don't need the fake marriage anymore, and everything can go back as it was, except maybe—"

"Thank you for all you've done, Ser Giuliano, but now I'm so ... tied to Giovanni. We're – "

"I know, I know. I had somehow taken it for granted, though, that you had gotten married. So now, Caterina, you have to make a decision," he said abruptly. "Giovanni is a very important man to me, and I wouldn't like him to be distracted from his work. So unless you're prepared to stay on the farm with him, you'll have to forget him."

"I'm sorry, Ser Giuliano. I know I had no right to fall in love with Giovanni or to stay with him—"

"Love, my dear, is never ruled by right or wrong, but it has no value at all without a complete dedication to the person one loves and, of course, the official rites." Then, pressing his hand still harder on his chest, he simply climbed into his gig and drove off without another word.

Astounded by what he had said, I walked back to the house, feeling very guilty. As I unrolled the scroll, I couldn't believe how small it was. I turned absently to the cage still hanging on the wall and said, "Don't you think this paper is rather small to represent the rest of my life?" I looked up. Alas! My friend wasn't there anymore. Shaking my head, I went to sit down on the low wall of the threshing floor to reflect on Ser Giuliano's severe comment on the value of love, unable to avoid comparing it with Donna Grazia's warm understanding. But then I started to wonder why Giovanni hadn't shown up as he had promised. Since there seemed to be no easy way to resolve my dilemma, to take my mind off it, I went back to working in my garden, which seemed to be the only consolation left in my solitary life. The more I gazed on its splendor, the more I became convinced that angels came during the night to sprinkle my plants with heavenly dew, because each morning, unfailingly, they surprised me with colorful new blossoms. Yet, without a loved one with whom to share this beauty, this was a meager consolation.

So, deciding to do something about it, Sunday morning I began a weekly routine, cutting a basketful of long-stemmed flowers and taking it to the crossroad where groups of churchgoers passed on their way to Paterno. Afraid to leave the house in case Giovanni came to see me, I asked a family to take the flowers to church for me, and they put the basket on their small cart next to an elderly woman. "Padre Baldo, our new parish priest, will be thrilled," she said with the same sparkle in her eyes Nonnetta had.

More weeks went by without news from anyone. So, one morning, I set out for Vinci with an armful of flowers, intent on finding out if there was any chance of seeing Leo that summer. Circling the castle and the tall church next to it, I couldn't help remembering my last meeting with Donna Lucia. Unpleasant though it had been, she was now the only one to whom I could turn for information about my son.

As I marched toward the street where I had been told the da Vinci house was located, a meticulously well-dressed woman stopped me.

"Good woman, are you selling those lovely flowers?" she demanded, taking me by surprise. I didn't want to stop, so I just shook my head and smiled, but she pursued me and breathlessly asked again, "Where did you get them? I've never seen such beauties! From whose garden are they?"

"From my garden in Anchiano. I can't stop now. I'm sorry."

"I'll pay you whatever you want," she persisted, but I hurried on my way down the street, refusing to be sidetracked from my purpose.

I stopped in front of an austere old house a woman had pointed out to me. The small door in the large portal suddenly flew open, and Gian Pietro stepped out. "Caterina, what are you doing here?" he asked, alarmed. "Where are you taking those flowers? Who died?"

"They're for Donna Lucia. I must see her. Is she alone?"

"She's alone, all right. Since she fell sick, no one in her family ever comes to stay with her. Those sons of hers treat her so shabbily!" Seeing my determination, he moved aside, and I slipped through the door into a coach yard. "Since Ser Antonio is still at his daughter's, we decided to move her bedroom to the ground floor at the back of the house. This way, I can hear her if she calls," he explained, barely keeping up with me.

Inside the main entrance of the house, I found myself in a

large, dim front room. He showed me to the slightly open door of the somber room where a very frail Donna Lucia was sitting up in bed, staring vacantly into space. She started as I went in, my face hidden behind the flowers. "What beautiful flowers! Who sent them?" she asked feebly.

"They're from me, Donna Lucia. Do you remember me?" I said, peeping around them.

"Caterina, my dear, how happy I am to see you!" she exclaimed, opening her arms wide. "I remember the time I came to Anchiano to see your little boy. My goodness, how quickly time goes by!" Realizing her memory wasn't what it once was, I put the flowers carefully into her wizened arms. "They're the most beautiful I've ever seen, Caterina!"

"Donna Lucia, can you give me any news about my Leonardo? I haven't seen him for such a long time," I implored.

"My dear, neither have I. They all went to that cursed Florence and left me alone with this idiot Gian Pietro."

I turned to see if he had followed me, but he was just entering the room with a big smile on his face, carrying a vase filled with water. "Donna Lucia, do you know if they're coming back for the summer?"

"I don't know anything, my dear. Nothing at all. Maybe they're waiting for me to die first."

"Don't you have a woman to take care of you?"

"Sometimes during the day. But during the night, I have only that mumbling sleepwalker."

"Sure, I sleepwalk when I can't sleep in my bed! Anyway, Caterina, to answer your question: Ser Piero sent a message saying that they may come for a brief visit in August for the Feast of the Assumption."

"Gian Pietro, will you bring Leo to Anchiano the moment they arrive? I'll prepare a good meal for you," I whispered.

"Sure, Caterina. I haven't had a decent meal for … I don't know how long," he said, gesticulating as he left the room.

"Caterina, come here. I have a gift for you," said Donna Lucia when we were alone. She reached into the drawer of her bedside table and took out a gold medal on a chain. "Take it!

Put it on! It has the image of the Virgin Mary. She will help you. You're so good to me! Put it on and let me see!" I reluctantly slipped it over my head. She smiled at me, then dozed off, saying, "Oh, how I would have loved a daughter-in-law like you! You are healthy and strong like ... like the girls in our hills."

As she closed her eyes, I slipped the chain off and carefully put it back into the drawer. Then, on tiptoe, I left the room.

The enclosed empty coach yard resounded with heavy monotonous blows as Gian Pietro sluggishly beat the flagstone floor with his large broom. Before he could see me, I covered my ears and fled into the street.

My head still ached when I passed by the wall where Giovanni had rescued me the first time. I remembered how warm and comforting it was to have him near and began to miss him even more. "Oh, Giovanni! Giovanni, my love, have you left me, too?" I cried helplessly.

With dragging feet, I entered my courtyard, passing a horse tied to a tree. It was Thunderbolt! At first, I was so out of breath that I couldn't speak. Then, forcing myself, I cried out hoarsely, "Giovanni, I'm here! Where are you?" He suddenly appeared from behind the house and stopped to look at me, then he ran toward me and took me in his arms. "Giovanni, my love, why did you leave me? I cannot live without you anymore!"

"I was here early. I thought you were at Donna Grazia's, so I waited here because I wanted to see you alone, to take you in my arms. I can't live away from you, either."

"Please stay with me for a while, Giovanni!"

"I can't, my love. I have to get back. Tomorrow we start harvesting the wheat. Unless you want to come with me." I was too confused to answer, but took his hand and pulled him toward the door. "Come inside. I'll get some fresh water from the well for you."

"No, I'll get it. You look tired. Did you go to Vinci?"

"Giovanni, let's get married. I know that I can't stay away from you any longer."

"And give up all you've created here? Your new home?

Your delightful garden?" he said, hinting a smile as he started to reach for the pitcher.

"Yes, everything! Everything! And as for my son, I'm sure together we'll find the way for me to see him." Leaving the pitcher, he held my face in both hands and kissed my lips over and over again.

While Giovanni went to the well, I walked to the wooden enclosure at the side of the house and poured water into the tub from the rain barrel next to it filled with aromatic herbs. I left my clean clothes hanging over the wooden screen, while I bathed in the tub. Hearing Giovanni coming back from the well, I called out to him, asking him to wait for me inside the house, but there was no answer. When I reached for my clothes, they weren't there anymore. With my wet hair falling to my shoulders, I wrapped myself in a large cloth. Then, as I saw Giovanni's feet beneath the enclosure, I cried, "What are you doing here?"

He stepped into view, clutching my clothes, and winked at me as he leaned against the wall.

"I told you to wait inside," I said, pointing to the house. Just as I did so the towel fell to the ground, and I screamed.

"What? And miss this beautiful vision?" he exclaimed dreamily. After a breathless moment, he stooped to pick up the towel and, drying me gently, began to kiss me passionately. Wrapping me snugly in the towel, he picked me up, carried me indoors, and set me on the bed like some precious bundle.

When we awakened, dusk was approaching. We dressed and went to sit on the step of the well. Silently, in each other's arms, we watched the iridescent glow of the setting sun over the low Arno Valley.

"Do you see that spot there—under that ray of sun?" he began, whispering in my ear. "Tomorrow I'll be there, surrounded by swinging sickles and scythes. But I'll be thinking of you, still feeling your beautiful, soft skin, seeing your dark eyes, and searching for that water-green light glistening deep inside your mysterious iris."

"And what shall I be doing?" I said jokingly.

"You'll see that small dot down there in the chaos of the harvest and know that it's me." He paused. "Then you'll blow me a kiss, which will, by magic, land right here on my cheek."

I kissed his cheek and said, "I still prefer it this way."

"I'll be back soon, my darling. Meanwhile, get ready for the wedding!"

As the builders were putting the final touches on the new room, I realized that another dream was also coming true without my having someone with whom to share it. But not to lose faith, I began setting up the room for Leo, placing the table with his drawing materials under the large window and lining up his small construction projects against the wall. Finally, I covered the bed I had slept on at Rita's during my pregnancy with a bright bedspread and arranged Rita's beautiful tiny porcelain dolls in a row on the mantelpiece. Then I stood back to see how everything looked, not allowing myself to think that it might be years before Leo could enjoy it. "Oh, God! Will I really have to wait until he grows up? Oh, no. I promise you, Leo, that I won't stop praying until the Heavenly Father performs a miracle for me!"

Nevertheless, summer was almost over and there had been no more visits or even news from Giovanni. One morning, I felt so restless that I had to go outside and walk about in an attempt to calm my anxiety, but the thought of Giovanni not coming back for me had become unbearable. I was sure by now the harvest was over. "Giovanni, have you changed your mind about me?" I asked in despair.

The air had turned chilly, and hugging myself to keep warm, I called out at the top of my voice, "Giovanni, my love, why is it taking you so long? Have you really forgotten me? It can't be!"

Unable to overcome my fearsome state of mind, I collected my shawl and hurried up the road to Donna Grazia's house.

The moment I reached the yard, I was startled to see her running to meet me. "Caterina! Oh, Caterina, I'm glad you're here!" she cried in a state of extreme agitation. "I was going to send Girolamo to get you, but he went to the woods first for Giuliano."

"Why? What's happened, Donna Grazia?" I inquired, out of breath.

"It's Giovanni, my dear. He's been shot!" I felt as if the blood had been drained from me. I must have paled, because she started rubbing my hand in hers, patting my cheek, and calling my name. I dimly saw Ser Giuliano running out from the nearby wood, followed by Girolamo, the young stableman, as she cried, "Thank God! Here's Giuliano! He'll take care of everything, you'll see, Caterina!"

Puffing and panting, Ser Giuliano went straight to a chair. "Now tell me what happened, dear!" he said, still gasping for breath. "I thought it was you. I nearly had a fit!"

"I'm sorry, Giuliano. It's Giovanni who's in grave danger. What? Didn't Girolamo tell you?"

"Grave danger! What do you mean?" Turning to the young man, he yelled, "You, come here and tell me what happened!"

The boy took his cap off tremulously and, gulping, said, "He's ... he's been shot in the back, Messer Giacomotti. He has a high fever and keeps calling for Donna Caterina." He looked at me uneasily. "He's very sick!"

"And you, Caterina, why aren't you with him?" he demanded.

"I ... I didn't know anything until now," I said, coming out of shock. Then in a frenzy I blurted, "I'll ride with Girolamo. I'll sit behind him on his horse. I want to be there with him. Please, take me there!"

"Is he really bad? Who shot him? Have you called my doctor? Giovanni's as strong as an ox. He'll be all right."

"We think it was a hunter. We went after him, but he ran like the devil and disappeared," answered Girolamo.

"Son of a bitch! When I find him, I'll have him hanged in the square! Quick! Get my gig ready. We'll leave right away."

I had not moved all this time, aware only of my skirt being blown by the chill wind. Donna Grazia came out of the house, carrying her black woolen cape, its lavish crimson lining shimmering in the sun. I started when she wrapped it around me, embracing me warmly. "Have courage, my dear! I'll be praying for you both."

I sat in the gig next to Ser Giuliano, the hood of the cape covering my head. He drove his horse at a full gallop as Girolamo kept up on horseback. When we had reached halfway, I broke the silence, feeling I should speak up. "Ser Giuliano, I want you to know that the last time I saw Giovanni, we decided to get married as soon as the harvest was over. I came to your house today because I was worried— I hadn't heard from him for a long time." He said nothing. "How could a hunter make such a dreadful mistake?" I cried, enraged.

"That's what I want to know," he said grimly. Then he fell silent again, probably searching in his mind for the culprit. I didn't even dare to guess. I only wanted to keep my hopes up and be there soon.

When we drove into the esplanade, a group of farmers was waiting for us. We got off and, followed by them, we went to the back of the house. I rushed up the steps ahead of the others, brushing past Filomena, who avoided my eyes, and found my own way to Giovanni's bedroom.

Giovanni's eyes were closed. The thick bandages around his chest were soaked with blood. I threw myself on his bed. "Giovanni, I'm here! Look at me.... It's Caterina." He opened his eyes, and a faint smile tightened his swollen lips. "What happened, my love? Speak to me! Why didn't you send for me sooner?" There was a man in black standing on the other side of the bed looking sternly at me. As Ser Giuliano came in, he looked at him questioningly.

"He was shot in the chest," said the man in black. "The bullet is still inside. We couldn't extract it. His fever's still too high."

"You mean that there's nothing you can do? You're out of your mind! He's a strong man, Doctor. Do something! Don't just stand there!" Ser Giuliano insisted furiously.

"Giovanni, my love, try, try to overcome your fever. You must get better, you must! ... We have to celebrate our marriage, remember? Be strong. Get through the fever so they can save you!" There was no response this time, so I turned to the man in black for reassurance. "Doctor, the fever will pass, won't it? So you'll be able to remove the bullet? Say it, Doctor. Please say it!" I cried. But the doctor remained silent. Giovanni moved his eyes and I put my ear next to his mouth.

"Caterina, my love," he said feebly, "I'll always love you ... no matter where I'll be. I promise you. Always! You'll never be alone." His lips burned my cheek as they had in our moments of passion.

I kissed his lips until I realized they were turning cold and lifeless. I looked up, crying, "Doctor, do something! He isn't breathing!" The man just touched my forehead gently and leaned over to close Giovanni's eyes, while I stared in shock, feeling as if the end of the world had come. I pressed my face into the palm of Giovanni's hand, wishing I could disappear into it.

I didn't move until Ser Giuliano and Filomena lifted me by force and carried me to a chair in the corner opposite the bed. When I looked up, I couldn't see Giovanni's face anymore: they had covered him with a sheet. I saw several people hovering around Giovanni's bed and covered my eyes, trying in vain to remember his last words. Through a haze of tears, I watched his body being carried to the next room. I started to get up, but fell back in the chair. Suddenly, I was left alone in the room as if forgotten. Then some sobbing women came to tidy up the room, ignoring me completely. Maybe I've become invisible! I thought and shut my eyes again.

Soon everything was quiet, and I realized that the activity had moved to the living room. I stood up and crept slowly to the door of that room where some women wailed and prayed as others laid out Giovanni's body. The sight of strangers touching my beloved made me feel even more helpless. I put my hand on my aching heart to ease the unbearable pain and headed to the outside landing, from which, across the harvested cornfield under a darkening sky, I glimpsed my favorite spot in the wood. Without taking my eyes off it, I descended the stone steps, clinging to the iron rail, and proceeded there as in a trance. The drab haystacks spread around the naked field seemed like mocking ghosts ready to start their macabre twilight dance.

When I finally reached my oak tree, I sat down as before, resting my head against its trunk. A gray mist was dulling the miracle of sunset.

"Giovanni, oh, Giovanni, why can't I remember your last words?" I cried with anguish. But my brain had dulled, too. The wood seemed sinister and desolate, and I couldn't imagine what had possessed me to come there.

I shut my eyes, and as I dozed off, a delicate sound similar to that of my flute wafted in the breeze from the northern hills, making the tall ears of wheat sway in the field, under the benevolent rays of the setting sun. I heard a voice calling softly, "Caterina ... come here to me." It was Giovanni across the field of tall green shafts of wheat! I leaped up and ran toward him, my feet hardly touching the ground in my exhilaration. Soon I felt Giovanni's hand holding mine, and together we ran through the green field that seemed to turn, as if by magic, into a magnificent crop of golden corn under our very eyes. Bright sunrays dazzled above our heads, while we sang and danced jubilantly through the scented field in the same way we had done by my *ruscello!*

I don't know how long those exquisite moments lasted or whether it was a vision or a dream, but when it was over, a cold dawn was breaking! I rubbed my eyes in the dim gray light. I brought my hand to my chest, as in the distance I saw a coffin being carried by four men in somber attire. They lifted it onto a black-painted cart and covered it with a purple cloth. Behind it, a large group of men, all wearing the same black mourning hats, started to form a train led by Ser Giuliano.

Brokenhearted, I watched the dreary flowerless cart receding up a deserted country road and wondered where they were taking my beloved. They stopped and formed a circle at the top of a bare hill. Behind them, a group of cypresses stood forlorn under a sunless sky. I felt a wrenching pain in my heart that was almost too much to bear, at which point

Giovanni's last words suddenly came back to me, clear and soothing. I repeated them aloud to myself several times, as an immeasurable ecstasy filled my heart. "*Amore mio,* thank you! Yes, my love, I know that I will see you again in our celestial garden. I know it," I cried, and this sweet thought restored me. I breathed deeply and closed my eyes.

The sound of the funeral train returning to the farmhouse brought me back to reality. I rose and shook myself, realizing that I could be left behind in that cold place with people who had looked upon me as an intruder, ignoring me, perhaps even blaming me for Giovanni's demise. Prompted by this gloomy thought, I wondered for the first time if the culprit who had fired the fatal shot was someone who resented our relationship. "No, it couldn't be! No, Giovanni, tell me it wasn't my fault! Please help me erase this poisonous idea from my mind, otherwise, my life without you will be even more unbearable!"

I saw young Girolamo crossing the field toward me and I sighed with relief. He looked extremely depressed, his eyes red from crying. Unable to get his words out, he cleared his throat and said hoarsely, "Donna Caterina, Messer Giacomotti wants to know if you'd like to go back with him." I nodded and quickly followed him as he turned back.

At the esplanade, Ser Giuliano was already on his gig, sitting bolt upright with his eyes lowered. I slowly climbed up next to him. The farmers, still wearing their black hats, stared at me in silence. There was coldness in Filomena's eyes, too. I sighed, remembering when she had offered me her blessed palm on that happy Palm Sunday, and I pulled my hood over my eyes to obliterate those unsympathetic stares. With a sharp jerk, the gig turned and left the esplanade.

We were silent for some time until I became aware that Ser Giuliano was occasionally pressing his hand to his chest. "Ser Giuliano, would you like me to hold the reins for a while?" I asked with concern, but he said nothing in reply. Is he ignoring me, too? I asked myself. However, I repeated the question.

This time, he turned and looked at me, almost surprised to see me, but handed me the reins and sat back.

"Of course, not having married … Gio …," he began after a while, as if to himself. "Not being married to him, a fact that you, Caterina, openly admitted," he went on haltingly, "causing more resentment than necessary, has denied you a wife's right to inherit from him."

"But Ser Giuliano, I don't care about that at all. I miss him—my dear Giovanni—and nothing else!" My grief overwhelmed me, and I found myself crying out, "Oh, God! What a cruel fate was in store for us!"

"Caterina, do you feel that the shot was fired intentionally? That it was premeditated?" he asked as I calmed down.

"I don't know, Ser Giuliano. The possibility has crossed my mind, but I soon discarded it. Who could have hated him that much?" He saw my hands tremble as a shiver ran through me.

Giving vent to his anger, he took the whip and cracked it in the air. Consequently, his horse, which was much bigger, stronger, and more difficult to control than Nicola's, broke into a wild gallop. Ser Giuliano just looked on as I wrestled with the reins until the horse slowed down to a brisk trot. "That was very good, Caterina. You seem quite experienced!"

"Not really. I once happened to help the chestnut cartman with his horse when it turned wild. It was hard, but I managed somehow."

"What was the cartman doing?"

"He got sick and was overcome by a coughing fit."

When we reached Vinci, I took the side street skirting the back of the castle so as not to be seen. Not another word was said until we came to the bend in the road. Then, as I gave Ser Giuliano the reins and climbed out of the gig, he looked at me with sincere compassion in his eyes and said, "Caterina, please try to visit my consort more often. I'm going to be away a lot. Besides, when it comes to comforting people, she's much better at it than I am. I only seem to know how to talk about business matters," he said regretfully. Then, observing me entering the deserted courtyard, he asked, "When is your son coming to visit you?"

"I have no idea, Ser Giuliano. I've been waiting in vain all summer—I don't think there's any chance of seeing him anymore."

After he left, I was seized, once again, by an excruciating pain throughout my body. I went to the birdcage, hoping to find comfort, but seeing it empty, I snatched it off the wall and smashed it into little pieces on the threshing floor. Instant remorse made me bend down to pick up the white sticks. But, instead, I fell on them exhausted, finally overtaken by a long-repressed attack of sobbing.

Dusk had already spread its dark shadows over the hills, and as I started to lift myself up, a melodious chirping reached my ear, soon filling the air. It was similar to that of my nightingale! I got up, glancing all around, but could not see a bird anywhere. Drying my eyes, I hurried to the back of the house, still following the sweet whistle. I expected to find the bird's nest in one of the gutters, but instead I realized that the sound was the same wherever I stood and gave up the search as the beautiful, mysterious singing gradually faded away, leaving behind a lingering romantic atmosphere. Invigorated from running, I stayed outside in that sudden state of exhilaration and lifted my face to a caressing breeze. Then I heard Giovanni's resonant voice softly serenading me, "Caterina, *amore mio* ...."

12
THE PORTRAIT

Among the clothes Rita left was a drab dark-red cherry woolen dress, which I chose to wear in mourning during those saddest days of my life. I had neither the energy nor the desire to tend to the plants, which needed special protection from the approaching frosty nights, for it all seemed meaningless now.

One day, as I strolled aimlessly around, staring into space, my heart leaped at the sight of Giovanni's carriage entering the courtyard, driven by young Girolamo. Tied to the back of it was another horse. Girolamo got off and came up to me, holding Thunderbolt by the bridle.

"Good morning, Donna Caterina. This carriage is now yours! The other horse is for me to ride back," he explained.

I looked at him uncomprehendingly, expecting further explanation. He hesitated a moment, then went on, "When Ser ... Giovanni asked me to come and get you, he ..." His voice broke, but he continued, "He whispered that if he should ... that if anything should happen ... I was to bring his horse and carriage to you."

"Does Ser Giuliano know about it?" I asked.

"Yes. When I told him, he said it was all right, because it was Ser Giovanni's property." I was so saddened to see these things that I said nothing. "And I brought his saddle for you, Donna Caterina ... as a keepsake of ... him." He lifted it off the seat and carefully put it in my arms.

"I thank you, Girolamo, but I don't know how to care for Thunderbolt—how to feed him, where to put him to sleep, or even how to bridle him."

"That's easy, Donna Caterina. I'll show you how. All he needs is some hay and forage, because he feeds himself in the fields. Look, I've brought you some reserve—it's in the back."

Still holding the saddle, I approached Thunderbolt. The horse that had always seemed sprightly now stared at me imploringly, with shining forlorn eyes. I patted his leg gingerly, but he stamped his hoof as if sensing my misgiving. "Don't be afraid, Donna Caterina!" said Girolamo, suddenly smiling. "That's his welcome to you. You're still his friend."

"I see that you know Thunderbolt very well," I said, recalling Giovanni's words.

He nodded, stroking the horse's back proudly. "Yes, I took care of him all the time." His voice broke again, forcing him to clear it, before continuing. "Now I'll show you how to harness and unharness him."

I watched him absently, still holding Giovanni's saddle tightly against my bosom, almost feeling the warmth of his body. After showing me what to do, Girolamo took Thunderbolt to the trough to let him drink, but there was no water. So I rushed indoors, deposited the saddle on my bed, and brought him a pail full of water. I emptied it into the trough, while the boy unloaded the forage.

After he left, the animal and I stood staring at each other. "Now, Thunderbolt, don't look at me like that! I know how you feel. What about me? I'm lost, too." The horse snorted. I untied him from the tree and led him to the olive grove, where there was still some green grass. On the way, I kept chatting to him. "Now, Thunderbolt, you have to understand that I need time to get used to you. And don't expect the same excitement you had at the farm. Here, there's only me. That's all." However, the moment he smelled the grass, he quietly moved away. I threw the long rope over his back, letting him go free to enjoy nibbling the green blades.

Heading back to the house, I kept turning to marvel at the cumbersome gift, which, with so many memories attached, only served to increase my torment. "Oh, Giovanni, Giovanni, what am I going to do?" I cried.

Confused and listless, I ignored my garden of withered plants. In my heart, though, I desperately longed for a way to lift my spirits and break out of my utter and useless grief. Then my thoughts went to my Leo, whom I hadn't seen or heard about for months, and I realized that, if he were to arrive unexpectedly, he would be quite shocked to see my home in such a sorry state, with Thunderbolt's forage strewn all over the yard. Most of all, I would have hated for him to see my neglected garden, the garden I had promised to keep always in flower for him.

Next morning, I went directly to tend the garden and discovered the new chrysanthemum plants were covered with buds. Those flowers thriving on my negligence sparked new hope in me, lifting my spirits at last. So I got busy cleaning the garden, storing the hay in the tavern, and repairing the old cracked manger next to the trough.

Thunderbolt, obviously fascinated with my activities, followed me around everywhere, dragging his long rope behind him, often getting on my nerves. "Thunderbolt, stop following me! You're not a dog—you're a big animal. Why don't you go and graze in the fields? I told you that life here was boring," I shouted at him one day while I was sweeping the yard. He then went to the abandoned carriage and rubbed his leg against it. "There's no use showing me that. You just make me feel worse," I told him.

The horse slowly backed up between the shafts of the carriage. "I'd never dare drive you by myself, you're much too big," I cried. But he kept stamping and snorting. I stroked his back, and he quieted down. "All right, if you're good, I'll let you pull it around the yard a couple of times," I said, feeling sorry for the poor creature. Harnessing him to the carriage, I led him by the bridle in a circle around the yard. He seemed to enjoy it as he pushed for another round, and after the third one, he neighed so loudly that he gave me a start. "All right, then. Let's go as far as the crossroads!" I said, climbing into the driver's seat. As I sat on the high seat, I thought of the happy times when I had ridden next to Giovanni. At the bend in the road, the horse shook his mane fiercely, and I lost control of the reins. Before I knew it, we were on the road to Vinci, and his swift trot broke into a slow, steady pace.

When we reached the square at the foot of the church steps, people stopped and stared. The sight of a woman driving such a grand vehicle with an elegant horse was quite rare. Soon Thunderbolt was making a show of himself to the small crowd by trotting like a dancer around the square. "Good for you, Thunderbolt! Let's show them how a fine horse like you does the bidding of a simple woman like me!" I said, pulling the reins as Thunderbolt made a spectacular turn, leaving the onlookers gaping.

"See? Rich women can get away with anything!" cried a peasant woman, waving her hand indignantly.

I laughed. "Now, Thunderbolt, that's enough! Let's go home!" I said firmly, and he sped homeward at a full gallop. "Bravo, Thunderbolt! Just think! She called me a rich woman," I cried as we took to the open road. "Ah, Giovanni, Giovanni, my love! You knew that after all I would enjoy your gift. Thank you, my dear!"

As the anniversary of All Saints and All Souls drew near, the fall flowers in my garden had reached full bloom. I harnessed Thunderbolt again, and we went on our first flower trip up to the church of Santa Lucia. In the churchyard cemetery, I placed a terra-cotta vase full of white chrysanthemums on Rita's grave. "Do you see, dear Rita? I picked all the white ones for you. Now I'll be able to visit you more often," I said, breaking down. "I ... I'm sure, dear Rita, you already know of the loss of my dear Giovanni, the only love of my life!" I had to leave to stop an aching wave of grief. I went back to the carriage, took the multicolored bunch of flowers, and entered the church.

"What perfectly beautiful chrysanthemums!" exclaimed Don Baldo. "Needless to say, they come from the same garden where the other flowers came from last summer!" His suave demeanor seemed hardly that of a simple country priest.

"Yes, Padre. Now I can bring them myself. I have my own carriage."

"You're an excellent florist," he said, looking for an empty vase. "If you keep up the good work, you'll be able to sell them in town."

As he spoke, I spied the pew I had shared with Giovanni and went over to it. I sat on the same spot to recall how we were that day. With my arms wrapped around myself and with an aching heart, I turned to the patron saint, begging her for comfort. I held my breath when I saw that my flowers had been placed at her feet in a lovely glass vase, which, in the flickering candlelight, matched the rose hue of her shimmering gown. A feeling of peace suddenly washed over me.

On our way back to the house, I told my friend, Thunderbolt, how the priest had been impressed by my flowers and thanked him for having taken me up the steep hill. When we reached the house, my spiritual bliss, however, was to be enhanced by an even greater joy. My Leo stood outside! "Leo! Leo! You're here at last! How wonderful!" I cried.

"Mother, how lovely you look sitting on that grand carriage!" he gasped. "Isn't this Ser Giovanni's horse?" he asked, helping me down and hugging me. I did not answer, not wanting to spoil my happy moment.

"You see, I kept my promise!" interjected Gian Pietro. "They finally came to Vinci for this holiday, so here we are!"

"Very good, Gian Pietro," I said, eagerly hugging my son. "Now you have to give me time to prepare something to eat."

"Don't worry. I'll go for a walk around the estate. It's such a nice day! Besides, I don't have to rush back. Donna Lucia has enough company now," he mumbled, tying his horse to a tree.

As soon as he was out of earshot, Leo, who had been staring at my dress, asked, "Why are you wearing such a somber dress, Mother?"

"Ah, my dear, you don't know ... Ser Giovanni ... he died."

He watched thoughtfully as I unharnessed Thunderbolt. "I'm sorry, Mother," he said. "I'm sure he'd be proud to see how well you handle his horse and carriage."

Considering his remark for a moment, I took him by the hand and walked with him to the house. "Tell me! Was the summer very hot in Florence? I've waited for you every day. I'd really lost any hope of seeing you again this year, and here you are!" I said as we gaily swung our arms.

"Unfortunately, I couldn't come by myself. Besides, I had to study a lot with my design teacher. Maybe in a year or so, I'll be one of Andrea del Verrocchio's pupils!"

"Oh, Leo, I'm so glad. His *bottega* is such a fascinating place!"

"Yes, it is. When did you see it?"

"A long time ago, when I was looking for my real father."

"The one who drew your face on those linen squares?"

"No, that was my other father. My *real* father died before that. It was at the *bottega* that I found out he had been a pupil of Maestro Giuliano dei Verrocchi. I'll tell you all about it one day, I promise. Now, come and see your new room!" I said excitedly.

He stopped to admire the addition to the house from the outside. "I can see that it's beautiful, but if you don't mind, Mother, I'd like to take a stroll down the valley first. I can only stay for three days."

I let go of his hand and watched him as he walked away, wrapped up in his thoughts, poised like an adult. He has changed so! I thought sadly. But then I decided I should not complain on a day as miraculous as this.

When Leo returned, I was busy in the kitchen, and Gian Pietro was enjoying his meal and his glass of wine. He came in carrying a large bunch of plants and smiling apologetically.

"Leonardo, look! I've brought your bag with the drawing tools," said Gian Pietro, pointing at a flat black canvas bag on a chair. "You were in such a hurry to hug your mother, you left it in the cart." He chuckled.

I picked up the bag and took Leo to his room. "What a cheerful room! So clean and neat!" he exclaimed with shining eyes. "Thank you, Mother, for thinking of me."

"But I always think of you! Now, my dear, what do you want to do with those plants?" I asked, intrigued by the vast variety.

"I'd really like to have a large cloth or a sheet to spread on the floor." I took out a sheet from my trunk and helped Leo stretch it out on the floor. He placed the small water plants on one side of the sheet, carefully spacing them apart. I had seen them growing by the *ruscello* after the flood. "These are a special type of fall water plant, new around here. See the deep shades around the petals and the leaves? You can almost hear the running water still vibrating around them!" he said, brimming with excitement. He picked up a jug full of water from the basin stand and gently sprinkled water on all the plants. Then he took some of my jars and spaced them between the plants, and folded the rest of the sheet over them. "I want them to stay fresh until I'm ready to draw them."

"Did you learn to do this at the studio?"

"No, I thought of it on the way here," he said, looking up. "Those china statuettes are delightful. Where are they from?"

"Aunt Rita left them for you. I waited for your room to be ready, so I could surprise you."

"Can I take some with me to Florence? Maybe I can study them and trace their origin." I nodded, overjoyed at his keen interest.

After the meal, Leo went back to his room, Gian Pietro got ready to leave, and I went into the garden to cut some late-thriving gladioli. "Gian Pietro, would you please give these to Donna Lucia for me?"

"Of course, she'll love them. You know, she still isn't strong enough to go and see her husband," he said, sighing. Then, admiring the flowers, he added, "Caterina, I'll say it again. I've never seen a more beautiful garden than yours. You're a fortunate woman in many ways, you know."

I looked at Giovanni's ring, sadly remembering my great loss and visualizing his distant and solitary resting place. "Not so fortunate, my friend," I murmured as he drove off. "Not so fortunate." I turned briskly to shake off my melancholy and headed back to the house.

Leo's window was wide open, so, creeping up close to the windowsill, I peered inside. He was sitting on the floor with his head bent over sheets of paper, already drawing his plants. Holding a pencil in each hand, he moved both hands with incredible speed. With one hand, he outlined, and with the other, he shaded. I held my breath as I watched him, spellbound.

When he finally left his room, it was almost dark. He sat at the table, looking exhausted while I served him dinner. "I'm sorry I stayed in there so long, Mother. I had to draw those plants while they were still alive." I smiled at him to cover my feelings of concern. After dinner, he excused himself and, looking pensive, went back to his room again.

In the morning, I knocked on his door, but there was no answer. When I looked inside, I found the room empty and the window wide open. He must have jumped out of the window so as not to disturb me while I still slept.

The brightest blue sky I had seen for weeks graced the day. On my way to the garden, I held my breath to see a dream come true—Leo, blond curls falling on his face, sitting on the ground drawing a budding chrysanthemum.

Later, when I was warming a jug of milk on the hot embers of the fireplace, he returned, carrying his drawing, obviously satisfied with himself. He kissed my cheek and said, "I'm sorry I climbed out of the window this morning, Mother. It was too early to wake you." Sitting down at the table, he added, "I had to capture the bud blooming while it was still dripping with night dew. You showed me how to do that, remember?"

"Yes, my dear, but you haven't stopped a moment since you arrived."

"It's true, but it's been so long since I was surrounded by nature! How would you like to take a walk with me around the valley today, before going down to the *ruscello?* You can help me find some rare aromatic herbs I need for my botanic study," he said brightly, "and while we walk, we can catch up on the news of the past several months."

I stroked his curly head, knowing he had said that to please me. Little did he know that just seeing him happy was enough to fill my heart with joy. "Yes, my dear, and I'll wear my nicest dress for you." So I took out the cobalt-blue dress with the intricate ivory braid around the neckline that I had worn when I met Giovanni for the first time.

As I got ready, Leo, dressed in fitted pants and a white shirt under a brown velvet vest, sat on the low wall, waiting for me. When he saw me, he took a tiny box from his vest pocket, opened it, and brought out a blue silk ribbon woven with fine golden threads. I bent a little as he placed it on my forehead and tied it into a bow at the back of my head. "The ladies in Florence call it a *lenza*. They wear it mainly to keep their veil firmly on their head, but you can use it just to adorn your hair. It's pretty on you, Mother." We set out with the same exaggerated stateliness of the dressed-up couples by the Duomo in Florence.

We strolled silently for a while, soaking up the sunshine of that warm autumn day. Leo stopped to pick a wild mint leaf.

"What's a bota ... nic study?" I asked, just to break the silence.

"Botany is a science based on the study of plant life. I'm most interested in studying herbs, especially the ones used up to now only by witches, magicians, and some wise doctors. But I think the value of herbs should be made known to all mankind."

"I already use them for hot drinks and certain dishes."

"Yes, I know, but you pick them at random according to their aroma or their taste. There are also herbs that may not have such a pleasant taste, but have the power, instead, to cure various sicknesses."

"But, my dear, how can you find time to study that ... that science, too? After your regular studies, drawing keeps you busy enough."

"Drawing is the basis of everything I do, because it gives me the chance to record things—plants and people, too. Once

I know form and shape, I find it easier to understand potential and value." He paused suddenly. "But I don't want to bore you with my projects. I want to hear *you* talk. I want to hear about what happened to Ser Giovanni, unless talking about it upsets you."

I wavered for a few moments, because I didn't want to revive my pain by going over the terrible tragedy. Brightening up, I said, "Listen, Leo, I have an idea. I'll start from the time I was born, because I feel this is the right time for you to find out everything about me and about our ancestors." He agreed. So, with my arm around his shoulders, we strolled through the field, while I recounted to him everything I have disclosed so far to the reader of this book. When I finished my story, we found ourselves at the place where I did my morning meditation. "You know, Leo, I was told that this ancient well was built by the Romans," I said, catching sight of a cluster of grapes hanging from it.

"Yes, the style of the arch is Romanesque."

I picked the cluster from the pergola clinging around the supporting columns. "Take it, Leo. These are the first grapes of this vine. They'll bring you luck!" Then, with my arms folded, I leaned against the column at the corner of the well, feeling quite relieved at having at long last been able to make my son privy to the strange events of my life.

He stopped eating the grapes, observed me for a while, then putting them down on the steps, he exclaimed, "Mother, don't move! Stay in that position! I'm going to get paper and pencil." He raced to the house and quickly reappeared, carrying a wooden board with a large sheet of paper attached. He sat on a rock and started drawing so swiftly that the pencils didn't seem to touch the paper. I saw that with one hand he drew my features and with the other he drew circles and triangles around the features, both hands moving equally fast. When he stopped his frenetic sketching, he showed it to me. I could not see my face for all the unusual shapes on it, but I recognized the familiar background of the hills and the winding brook. Seeing my puzzled expression, he explained, a little amused, "It's not finished yet. This is only an outline for the composition of the drawing. Those circles and lines around your face are geometric proportions to guide me when I develop the drawing. This is Piero della Francesca's method. He's a painter I respect very much, because he's also the best mathematician of our time. When I improve my painting skills, I'll use this sketch to paint the best portrait anyone has ever seen!" Picking up the cluster of grapes, he added casually, "As for your features and the expression in your eyes ... I'll remember them forever." I was quite overwhelmed by what he had said, but not puzzled anymore.

The third day, the last precious day of Leo's visit, I found him sitting on a rock drawing Thunderbolt, who was standing very still, as if he knew what Leo was doing. Wanting to spend as much time as I could near him, I approached him almost on tiptoe so as not to disturb him. "Isn't he beautiful?" said Leo, without turning his head. "His muscles are so perfect. Look at the golden highlights of his brown coat! He's magical!"

"Yes. Giovanni used to tease him, saying, 'Thunderbolt, your coat may match the color of a monk's habit,'" I recited, mimicking the modulation of Giovanni's voice, "'but you're far from being a monk!'"

Leo laughed. "Mother, do you think I could ride him?"

"I don't see why not. He's still a young horse. I'm sure he'd like you to ride him. Wait! I'll get Giovanni's saddle."

The saddle lay under a cloth next to my bed. I held it close to me for a few moments, before taking it outside. "Giovanni, I'm sure you don't mind. I know you were fond of my Leo."

After we secured the saddle on Thunderbolt's back, I helped Leo mount him. Leo held the reins like an expert horseman, and the laudable Thunderbolt, obviously mindful of the young rider, carried him steadily through the olive grove and over the nearby hill.

"Oh, my son, you look like a young prince!" I said as he rode away. "My father would have been proud of you."

Leo's delightful visit had come to an end, and I resumed my solitary existence, this time faced with the saddest and longest winter of my life.

* * *

I had just managed to make a couple of visits to Donna Grazia to plan the flowers for my spring garden, so she could have them sown in the nursery of her conservatory in Pisa when heavy snow started to fall on our hills.

The old tavern made a good stable for Thunderbolt. I set up his manger near the window, where all winter he could enjoy the view of the white-clothed countryside. Sometimes, I lit a fire in the old fireplace and, while I brushed his back, he listened quietly and patiently to my chatter about my dream-garden. When I reminisced about the blissful evenings with my dear Giovanni, his eyes seemed to glisten.

However, spring finally brought that long, dismal winter to an end, and very soon, the golden primroses and tiny white daisies graced the lonely fields once more. I busied myself getting the flower beds ready for the small plants and the new seeds arriving from Donna Grazia's nursery. As the sun warmed the earth, my plants grew taller. Soon they would bloom and turn my garden into a burst of color.

Groups of countrywomen and their children often came to admire the wonderful display, and I filled their arms with bright bouquets.

One day, Ser Giuliano dropped by and was quite astonished to see the women leaving with my flowers. "Caterina, you're not giving them away!" he protested. "Do you realize that you could make money from them?"

"Money for the flowers? They didn't cost me anything. You know that Donna Grazia provided me with the seeds and plants from her conservatory. I wanted to grow them for my Leo," I explained sadly, "but I have a feeling he's not coming this summer. So why let them wither on the plants? Flowers are a gift from God, and it has to be shared."

"My dear child, corn is also a gift from God, but we don't give it away! You've worked long hours in that garden, and you should be compensated for it. Think of your future! Think of when you'll have nothing left of your modest savings from the sale of the house! How are you going to survive without an income?"

"I can't charge the countrypeople. They're too poor—they don't even have enough to eat."

"There's a small market in town. Load up your carriage and go there on Fridays when the ladies want to decorate their houses for the weekend." His face grew red with excitement as he spoke of his idea, but, realizing he had gotten too carried away, he composed himself and turned his gig around. I didn't contradict him anymore, remembering Don Baldo's words.

Deep in thought, I walked over to Thunderbolt, who was peacefully grazing grass, and told him about the idea. The horse looked up at me with blades of grass still dangling from his mouth, then stamped his foot and shook his mane. "You approve, then? Very good! Do you know that tomorrow happens to be Friday? I think it's time to get out my blue cotton dress. But first I must sort out the flowers by color and then plan how to match them, don't you think? Oh, if only Leo were here! He'd know how to do that," I said, stroking my faithful friend.

At dawn the following morning, while my dress aired on the line, I was already in the garden, selecting the flowers with buds just beginning to open. I started to count them in groups by color and kind, and as I completed the bunches, I tied them with the stems of herbs. When they were ready, I put them in pails of water on the back of the carriage. Then, shifting my attention to my own appearance, I bathed and fixed my hair in a braid around my head, all the time feeling an exhilaration I had never felt before. As I slipped into my dress, I was so wrought up that I could hardly fasten it.

Thunderbolt seemed equally excited as I harnessed him to the carriage and sat up on its curved seat. "Let's go, Thunderbolt! Let's surprise the people at the small market," I shouted euphorically. But he needed no spurring, starting off at full gallop down the main road to Vinci.

13
FLOWERS AND REVELATIONS

I entered the market square from a quiet side street and saw that there was no space available for me to display my flowers. All the vendors' stands were set up against the buildings, leaving the center clear for customers entering the market on vehicles. So I stepped down, turned the back of my carriage toward the square, and pulled forward the flowers. Thunderbolt snorted, perhaps not liking his undignified position. "Be patient, Thunderbolt. This is the only way," I said, patting his neck.

I was surprised to see how quickly my flowers caught the eyes of the ladies, who, accompanied by their husbands or followed by servants, soon gathered around my beautiful bouquets.

"Good woman, are those flowers for sale?" a lady asked.

"Of course they are," I answered.

"How much do you want for that bunch of roses?" This last question startled me, as it made me realize I hadn't priced my flowers. "This is your first time here, isn't it? I wonder if you remember me." Her face was, in fact, vaguely familiar, but I was much too concerned about what to charge for my flowers to remember her. "I'm sorry if I was too aggressive with you that time. Were you taking the flowers to church?

You seemed upset. I hope you got what you wanted," she rambled on. But I still didn't answer her, for my eyes were on the other ladies standing behind her, impatiently waiting for her to move along. "Look! I'll pay you one *quattrino* for those roses."

I thought she was teasing, but I handed her the bunch, hoping to get rid of her. Instead, she promptly slipped the coin into my hand, and thanks to her, the other ladies got their coins ready, too.

Very soon, all my flowers were sold. I went back to Thunderbolt, clinking the coins in my pocket. "Thunderbolt, do you hear this sound? We've earned it together!" I felt a gentle touch on my shoulder.

"Good woman, my mistress wants to know your name and where you grow your flowers," said a young girl, pointing to an elegant young lady sitting in a handsome coach drawn by two white horses in the middle of the square. At that moment, a young gentleman got into the coach and sat next to her, offering her a bunch of my roses.

A strange feeling overcame me. It was as if I had met them before. I experienced an affinity to them that I could not explain. I saw that they were watching me, and I impulsively turned to the girl and said, "My name is Lisa. Yes. just Lisa!"

"Oh, Monna Lisa, where shall I tell my mistress your conservatory is? You see, we're not from around here—we just happen to be passing."

"My flowers don't grow in a conservatory. They're from my garden on the hill of Anchiano." She nodded and hurried back to the coach, gave her masters the information, and climbed up next to the driver. The couple, still glancing at me, tilted their heads and smiled. As the coach moved off, I smiled back at them, still quite perplexed.

Although I made these trips until the spring flower season ended, I never saw them there again, and I often regretted not having asked the maid for their names.

Alas! Easter week had come and gone, and summer was advancing rapidly, but there was no sign of my dear son.

Little did I know that many more Easters and summers were to pass before I could see my Leo again.

Just as Ser Giuliano had predicted, the modest income from the sale of my flowers and the produce from my kitchen garden had, in time, become my sole means of survival. Although this activity had given me a new interest in life, I found that it required my almost constant attention. As a result I had less time to wallow in self-pity over the loss of my dear Giovanni and the extended absence of my child. Needless to say, though, over the years I had often felt the urge to set out for Florence to visit Leo, but the thought of facing Piero again and stirring up my feelings of anger discouraged me each time. So I hoped and prayed for the day when Leo would grow big enough to come and see me on his own.

One morning, noticing dark storm clouds approaching our hills with thunder and lightning in their wake, I ran outside to spread some canvas covers over the more delicate plants. After a brief shower, though, the storm started receding into the distance again, and I decided to return to work. As I drew back the canvases, I thought I heard Leo's voice, but dismissed it as wishful thinking. But hearing footsteps in the courtyard, I looked up in astonishment and saw Leo racing toward me, taller and broader than I remembered him. "Leo! Leo!" I cried, running to him. "It *is* you! I thought I was imagining things! You're soaked! What happened? Did you walk up here in the rain?"

"Yes, Mother, I did," he said in a deep voice, hugging me so firmly that I could hardly breathe. "But I'm all right. I ran, because I wanted to get here in time to see the rainbow from up here. Look! Over there! It's starting to show," he cried ecstatically.

"You're right," I said, seeing the rainbow descending in a grand curve. "You made it in time, but you should change first."

"Mother, where are my drawing board and pencil? I must get them before it disappears!" I made him wait while I rushed to get them for him. As soon as I returned, he took me by the arm, and we dashed to the edge of the cliff. Then he took the board from me as if his life depended on it and immediately began to draw. The awesome rainbow hovered above the valley of the brook.

Overwhelmed and out of breath, I kept shifting my gaze from the rainbow to my son and back to the rainbow, over and over again. I couldn't believe my eyes, whichever way I looked! Not only had Leo grown physically, but there was a new vitality about him. He had more presence. Deep gratitude filled my heart as I watched him and we shared this wonderful moment.

Suddenly realizing I had no food prepared, I left him completely absorbed in his sketching and went to the house. After starting a meal on the fire, I couldn't resist taking another peek at the rainbow's progress from my back window. Each one of its soft colors seemed to vibrate its own musical note as part of a visual chord; the raindrops clinging to the leaves—iridescent jewels throwing off chromatic dancing lights. My corner of the world had become the setting for a magic fable!

As I humbly thanked that shimmering arc for bringing my son back to me, I felt my heart pound, for through its opalescent light I glimpsed Giovanni's smiling face and shining eyes! The vision lasted for only one breathless instant, but it was stamped indelibly in my mind forever.

Later, Leo sat at the table in the old robe he had outgrown, his keen eyes sparkling with satisfaction. "I'm so thrilled that I was able to capture that superb rainbow! To think that I nearly didn't come, because Gian Pietro refused to drive me up here in the approaching storm! Anyway, I'm sure I was faster than his cart!" he added with a sly chuckle.

"When did you arrive in Vinci?" I asked, admiring his almost adult features and stature.

"Last night. My father at last decided to close the house in Florence for the summer. So, here I am, and in time for this magnificent spectacle!" I went over to him and kissed his forehead. He took my hand and kissed it with reverence. "Mother, do you mind if I retire to my room now? I have to write some notes." I shook my head as he got up and walked to his room with the bearing of an adult.

I was astonished to see that his shoulders were almost as wide as Giovanni's. Even though I was aware of the length of time he had been away, I still thought he was growing much too quickly.

The following day, while Leo was helping me repair the damage caused by the passing storm, I told him about my trips to the market, where I sold my flowers under my new name.

"Lisa of the Flowers! Yes, that name suits you!" he exclaimed as Gian Pietro's cart rolled into the courtyard. Leo ran to help him unload his things.

"If only you knew, my boy, how furious your father was when he heard you had come up here without asking his permission!" Gian Pietro cried, raising his thick eyebrows. "He even forbade me to bring your clothes."

"Who needs clothes up here? My cotton robe is enough for me. These drawing materials, yes, these are important to me!" Leo remarked, carrying his box indoors by himself.

But Gian Pietro had more to say. "Then he turned against you, Caterina." Imitating Piero's voice, he went on, "'If only that woman would disappear from the face of the earth, maybe then I wouldn't have these aggravations anymore!'" I shrank with fear, knowing that Piero could have really meant that. "Then," he added dramatically, "Donna Albiera scolded him for being so hard. And only after that did he let me come up he—" I interrupted him to inquire about Donna Lucia's health as Leo came back. "She's a little better. She suffers from the heat, though, poor woman! Do you know, Caterina, that since your visit, she would ask about you whenever she remembered the flowers you brought her?"

Touching my arm gently, Leo whispered, "Oh, it was nice of you to go and see her, Mother."

In the days that followed, though the summer plants reached full bloom, I didn't dare go down to the market for fear of being seen by Piero, so I started sending flowers to the church again.

FLOWERS AND REVELATIONS

* * *

The north wind had cleared the sultry weather, and on a delightfully dry day, Leo chose to go for a stroll through the surrounding fields. I was working as usual in the garden when the loud rumble of heavy wheels echoed in the courtyard. Lately, some of my market customers had been sending their stablemen to get flowers for them, so I was surprised to see a stately coach driven by a uniformed coachman. Inside sat a lady and with her a man of the cloth, whose important hat and large golden cross hanging on his impeccable robe indicated to me that he was a high-ranking prelate. "Monna Lisa's garden here?" he thundered.

I hesitated, as I had just recognized the lady as Albiera, Piero's wife. "Yes, it is. What can I do for you ... Padre?" I replied rather hesitantly, not knowing what his title was.

"We're looking for calla lilies. They told us that you're the only one who has them."

"Yes, I happen to have a few. How many do you need?" I said, hoping to make the sale quickly, before Leo returned.

"Donna Albiera! Donna Albiera!" Leo cried blithely. I was crushed.

"Leo—Leonardo—what are you doing here?" she asked.

Leo took my hand and said proudly, "This is my house and this is my ... mother." She lowered her eyes, and her pale face suddenly turned pink. "Uncle Alessandro, I'm so happy to see you, too!" Leo said, approaching the prelate, who was stepping out of the coach.

To break the embarrassing silence that followed, I started for the garden, saying, "I'll go and get the callas."

"Caterina ... I'm sorry if we imposed upon you. I didn't know that you were 'Monna Lisa of the Flowers,'" said Albiera in a low voice.

"I chose to use that name when I started to take my flowers to market, to avoid ... to avoid gossip," I said casually.

Leo, who was talking to the prelate in a very familiar way, turned to me. "Mother, this is the canon of Fiesole, Alessandro Amadori, Donna Albiera's brother," he announced, cleverly handling the situation.

The canon offered me his hand, and I bent to kiss his ring, as was the custom. "Donna Caterina," began the canon, "I want you to know that Leo is my favorite nephew and will always be so!" He paused, and when I said nothing, he changed the subject. "Now, going back to the flowers ... Because of a dream my sister had, she made a vow to present a bouquet of calla lilies to Saint Anne, whose feast day happens to be tomorrow. So, looking for them, we ended up here."

Without making any comment, I took him to the lily patch. "Donna Caterina!" he burst out. "What a magnificent view! This is a garden fit for a king!" Then, looking into my eyes, he went on, "Caterina, you're a more remarkable woman than I ever imagined. I already knew you must have noble qualities, because of Leonardo's character, and I'm aware, also, of the sacrifice you made." He paused to give more weight to his words. "But I can assure you, my dear, that you'll never regret giving your son a chance to advance his education. And I guarantee, dear Caterina, that your Leonardo will be one of the greatest geniuses of our time," he pompously declared.

"Thank you, Don Alessandro, for those kind words, but at times ... I find his long absences very hard to bear," I said, holding back my tears.

"But see how God repays you!" he exclaimed, flinging open his arms.

I cleared my throat. "Tell me, canon, which calla lilies would you like me to cut for you?"

"Monna Lisa," he said, his eyes twinkling, "they're all beautiful!"

When we returned to the courtyard, Leo was sitting in the coach next to Albiera, talking so cheerfully that jealousy swept over me, but then he jumped down and came to hug me. "Thank you, Mother, for picking the best!" he cried, taking them from me. Albiera remained quite still, her eyes fixed on me, and I knew she was trying hard to conceal her own feelings of jealousy. Our eyes met as we shared the same thoughts, and I smiled at her.

When the coach left, Leo and I walked back to the house in silence. Suddenly, he took my hand, swung it laughingly, and said, "'Monna Lisa of the Flowers.' That name really suits you, Mother!" Then he stood in front of me and bowed "Madonna!"

"Leo, please stop! You're making me blush. Look, there's Thunderbolt!" I said, changing the subject as the horse approached us, his rope hanging from his neck. "I think he feels hurt because you didn't ride him today."

"I'm sorry, Thunderbolt. I went searching for some special herbs."

"Thunderbolt," I said as I stroked him, "let's take our callas to Saint Anne tomorrow! What do *you* think, Leo?" He gazed at me complacently. "I would like you to come, too, so you can meet the new priest." Thunderbolt stamped and neighed, and Leo laughed the way he used to laugh as a child, which pleased me as I realized that my meeting with Albiera had somehow fulfilled a long-standing desire of his.

The next morning, we cheerfully set out for the Sanctuary, whose festive bells seemed to welcome us as we arrived. The inside of the church had been decorated in reverence to the Virgin's mother. When the priest saw my flowers, he rejoiced. "Donna Caterina, what beautiful calla lilies!"

"Don Baldo, this is my son, Leonardo."

"Ah, he's already a young man! You go to school in Florence, don't you?" he asked, turning to Leo.

"Yes, Padre. I study art," he answered composedly.

"Well, maybe one day we'll have one of your paintings in our church!" Leo smiled. The priest gave the callas to a woman cleaning so she could place them at the feet of Saint Anne, next to which he had placed the statue of the Virgin Mary with the baby Jesus on her lap. The figures were rather plain compared with the ornate statue of the patron.

"What a wonderful composition!" said Leo, admiring the interesting way in which they were grouped. Then he moved back, the way he used to do whenever something caught his attention, and stood there mesmerized. I knew he was under the spell of an inspiration, so I left him by himself and went to sit in front of the altar, recalling my prayer to Santa Lucia on the day he was baptized. I looked at Leo with warmth in my heart and thanked the saint for having granted my wish.

As soon as Leo finished drawing something in the notebook he took with him everywhere, we returned to the carriage for the vase of small white roses I had brought to place on Rita's grave.

For a few moments, we stood silently at the foot of her grave, gazing at the delicate flowers. Then Leo spoke. "Mother, do you know that when I was looking at the statues in the church, I kept thinking of Aunt Rita all the time? Saint Anne's devotion to the Virgin Mary reminded me of the motherly love Aunt Rita lavished on you, which in turn you lavished on me, forming a circle of everlasting love."

"Thank you, my dear son. What joy your words will bring to her soul!" I said, putting my arms around him.

"One day," he said solemnly, "I'll do a painting that will pay just homage to those sentiments."

We were both deep in thought as we drove down the road. "Slow down, Thunderbolt! We like to enjoy the view, too, you know," I cried.

Leo laughed, but soon turned serious again. "Do you know, Mother, that this fall I might be entering Verrocchio's studio?"

"You don't seem very happy about it."

"Well, Maestro Andrea wants me to go and live with him to have me under his complete tutelage. It's really a great privilege afforded to only a few pupils." He paused, as if not knowing how to go on. "But my father doesn't want me to leave the house."

Well, now it's his turn, I thought.

"The truth is that he's worrying that Donna Albiera would feel too lonely." I looked away to hide my resentment. "He doesn't know, though, that she's as understanding as you are," he explained.

"What would *you* like to do?" I asked.

"Stay at Maestro Andrea's *bottega,* of course. That's what I've been dreaming of for a long time."

I looked into his eyes, then, shaking Thunderbolt's reins, I said, "Well, keep your dream alive and the rest will take care of itself."

On the morning we planned to visit Donna Grazia, I went to the lily patch to select a few of the finest lilies to adorn her living room. In order to protect them from the scorching sun, I had asked Leo to help me build a tent over the patch. Donna Grazia had warned me that because they had been planted outdoors, they would be late-blooming. As I stood there in my blue cotton dress dreamily contemplating those magnificent flowers, a tremendous din in the courtyard gave me quite a start. Rushing to see what was causing it, I was confronted by two colossal white horses rearing up on their hind legs, bringing a grand coach to an abrupt standstill, a difficult maneuver for the coachman because of the limited space. My jaw dropped as I recognized the coach I had seen the first time I went to the Vinci market, and the same young gentleman jumped nimbly to the ground without touching the carriage step.

"Good morning, Monna Lisa. I apologize for the disturbance caused by my horses," he said as he raised his small hat, revealing a head of neatly trimmed dark hair. He was well built and wore a crimson damask doublet and gray fitted pants. "I hope you can help me. I came here myself because I heard that you grow the most exquisite rare flowers. What I'm looking for is a very special flower."

"What kind of flower is it, Messer …?"

"Battistiani, Massimiliano Battistiani," he said with a sweeping bow. As I heard the name, my heart jumped to my throat. "What I'm looking for," he continued, "is a rare type of lily. I know it's late in the season, but the conservatory where it was being grown for me was recently struck by lightning." I was still unable to say a word. "The French call it *fleur-de-lis*. It has a slight tinge of red inside the petals."

"I … I still have some lilies—late bloomers—but not red ones," I said tremulously. But before he could turn away, I motioned him to come with me to the lily patch.

He bowed and followed me. "You see, Monna Lisa, I need to have it drawn on my family crest. I'm taking part in the next Siena Palio."

From the corner of my eye, I looked at his tall, slender figure, then at the shape of his head, and thought of my father. "What is the Palio?" I asked, not having the courage to ask him what was really on my mind.

"The Palio is a kind of horse race. The contenders have to wear colors matching their family banner. It's really meant to be a kind of sport, but since the family honor is at stake, it can get quite rough at times." I listened to him, as all kinds of questions sped through my mind.

"Here is my lily patch! As you can see, they're all white. Very rarely is there one with a touch of pink inside the petals," I said, inviting him to examine them.

Lowering his head to get under the tent, he carefully stepped around the rows of plants, peering into every blossom. "Yes!" he suddenly exclaimed. "I see one with just enough red inside!"

It was incredible! One lily did indeed have rose-tinted petals. But I held back. "*Messere,* I can't give it to you. Not if it's the only one. I want my son to see it first. He should be back soon, though. We have plans to visit a friend."

"For a lily like this, I'll wait the whole night, if necessary!"

"Messer Battistiani, I have a small picture by an artist who had a name similar to yours. He may have been related to you."

He shook his head. "No, no, impossible. Unfortunately, in our family, there is nobody with that kind of talent."

"I don't think he's still alive. His name was Leonardo. His father was a *gonfaloniere.*"

"I had an uncle who was the *gonfaloniere* of an army, but he was much older than my father, and I never met him." He paused an instant. "I do remember now. He did have a son called Leonardo who died on the battlefield with him, but he couldn't have been an artisan." He grinned. "My uncle would never have allowed it! To him, the only honorable life for a man was that of a soldier." He turned to look at Leo, who was approaching. "Of course, I only heard about it from my family, you know. It might even have happened before I was born."

"Here is my son, *messere*," I said, covering my deep emotion. "Leo, I want you to see a special lily the gentleman wants to buy. I thought you might want to draw it before he takes it away."

"Ah, your son is an artist!" he said, seeing Leo's drawing board.

Leo went straight into the lily patch and cried, "Let the gentleman have it, Mother! Here's another just like it!"

As I went to cut that special lily, which had been the means to an important revelation, there seemed to be a cold silence between Leo and the visitor, who finally broke the ice. "I need to have it copied for my family banner in time for the Palio," he explained. There was still no comment from Leo. Yet, as I handed the lily to the young man, Leo stared closely at the unusual bloom, perhaps to commit it to memory.

"Leo, where did you see the other lily?" I asked as soon as the young gentleman had left.

"There was no other lily like that one, but it really doesn't matter," he said, shrugging his shoulders. "What he was able to tell you was worth any lily!"

I hugged him tightly. "So you overheard our conversation and you still remember the story about my dream and the vision of the battlefield!"

"Of course, Mother. I remember everything. That's why I stayed out of sight long enough to give you time to ask him those questions. Once you knew the truth, you wouldn't have to search for your father anymore or wonder where he might be!"

I took his hand. "Now, my dear, come inside. I want to show you the only keepsakes I have of him. When you see those works of art you'll feel proud to be his grandson!"

It wasn't until the following June that I saw Leo again. He appeared unexpectedly, as usual, saying his father had decided to bring Albiera, who was expecting her first baby, to the house in Vinci to spare her the unbearable heat in Florence. They were to go back in a week, leaving her in the family house with the idea of returning in time for the birth of her child. Needless to say, the end of the week came much too quickly, and Leo was already busy gathering all his materials into his box. He had run a few times to the bend of the road to see if Gian Pietro was on his way. When I looked at him questioningly, he said, "Mother, I'm really worried. I don't know why Gian Pietro hasn't come yet. I promised Maestro Andrea I'd bring my new plant drawings to him by next week." He went to take another look. I didn't know what to say, for the thought of his imminent departure was already weighing heavily on my heart. "Something must have happened," he said anxiously as he came back to the courtyard. "I know my father has to keep appointments in Florence, too."

"My dear," I said to calm him, "I can take you there in my carriage. We can leave at dawn, so nobody will see us." He agreed.

It was very early when we pulled up around the corner from the da Vinci house. Leo jumped off, saying he would call Gian Pietro, but I insisted on helping him carry his box to the main entrance, which was wide open. Inside the courtyard was Gian Pietro, pacing the cobblestone floor, his eyes lowered. On seeing us, he came forward with open arms. "Oh, thank God you brought him, Caterina! I couldn't leave at a time like this. We have a tragedy here, a real tragedy!"

"Has something happened to Donna Lucia or Ser Antonio?" I asked.

"No, it's poor Donna Albiera. She has lost the child. It seems very bad. The doctor's been at her bedside all night." Leo let go of the handle on his end of the box and ran indoors.

"Leo!" I cried. "Leo, I'll wait for you at the market tomorrow. Please come! Don't forget." He answered with a nervous nod and disappeared.

Gian Pietro took the box from me. "To think that she had everything ready for the baby, poor woman! All night she kept asking for Leo!"

At this point, I couldn't bear to listen to one more word about what was going on in that house, and ran back to my carriage in the street.

The next morning I drove down to the market with my heart pounding. I had picked a few flowers at random just for an excuse to be there. When I reached my corner, I found that another woman selling fruit and some wilted flowers had taken my place. She blushed with embarrassment when she saw me, but I told her not to worry as I had brought very little to sell. I stayed next to her, standing on my toes, hoping to see Leo over the crowd. Happy to see me, my old customers gathered around me, smiling and chatting, and, very soon, I had no excuse to linger there anymore, for my flowers had all gone. And still no sign of Leo.

"Ah, Monna Lisa, no flowers left for me!" a woman whined.

"I'm sorry, I had only a few this time. Go to that woman over there! She has some," I said, wishing to be alone.

"Monna Lisa, they're ... they're not fresh!" she complained. I tried to persuade the fruit-seller to invite the lady to her stand, but she hid her face in shame. "Don't you understand? I need fresh flowers for my friend's funeral. Poor woman, she just died this morning!" said the lady, in distress.

"Who died? What was her name?"

"Donna Albiera, the notary's wife. Everybody knows her!" I nervously wrapped myself in my shawl and looked over the crowd again, wondering what to say to Leo, if he came. The lady burst into tears, and after some doing, I finally managed to calm her by telling her to go home and rest.

Thunderbolt was stamping impatiently, so I tied him to a pole and climbed onto the carriage to see over the crowd. "Thunderbolt, I'm not leaving until I see Leo. He must be feeling wretched. I must wait for him," I cried, refusing to leave without being able to comfort him. I might not be able to see him before the funeral, and I knew that they would return to Florence immediately afterward.

I gasped as I caught a glimpse of Leo making his way

through the crowd. "Leo! Leo! Over here!" We drove to a secluded corner of the street. "I'm so sorry, Leo! I just heard the terrible news. I know you'll miss her. She was good to you." He kept his head down to hide his eyes, swollen from crying or having stayed up all night, I thought. I didn't know what else to say to relieve his sorrow.

"I must go back. Her ... brother is coming. The canon, remember?"

"Yes, I do. And I'm grateful for having met her that day." There was a look of surprise in his red eyes. "Leo, I have an idea. As soon as the weather is good, I'll find a way to come and visit you in Florence, so we won't feel so far from each other again for such a long time." He just listened. "I know that you'll soon be big enough to come by yourself, maybe on a white horse!" I said, smiling. "But in the meantime, I can visit you." He smiled back. "Ah, I'm glad I was able to make you smile! At my age, I can't make funny faces and dance as you did for me, remember?" He smiled through his sorrow and embraced me.

He jumped off and patted the horse. "Thunderbolt, take care of my mother," he said, raising his hand in leave-taking as he raced back into the crowd.

When I reached my front door and searched for my key inside my pocket, I found a roll of drawing paper the size of my hand. I knew that Leo had slipped it there. I sat on my bench and unrolled a miniature of a lily stalk full of buds. One open bud had a touch of rose in its blossom, like the flower I had given to my father's relative.

A veil of fog, the first of the season, layered the air next morning. I strolled aimlessly around the stone threshing floor, overcome again by a devastating feeling of loneliness.

A sudden burst of church bells pervaded the hills, bringing with it a chill breeze. As I gazed down in the direction of Vinci, the ringing turned into a heartrending toll. I crossed my arms as if to shield myself from the cold shiver the striking bells sent through me, but the shiver hit my stomach instead, making me feel queasy. Overpowered by this sudden weakness, I reached for the clothesline pole. In a flash, I recalled the day when, in the nausea of my pregnancy, I had grasped the same pole and listened to the same bells ringing festively, while I wished I were dead.

I thought of my young son having to be part of that household in mourning for the death of a woman who, through no fault of her own, could have been the cause of my demise and that of my unborn child on that fateful day. But other bells soon joined in with insistence, suddenly filling my heart with compassion for the unhappy, innocent woman, whose frailty and bereavement had driven her to an early grave. As the bells continued tolling in memory of her, I thought of the love and solace she had given my little son to alleviate his moments of bewilderment. My hard heart softened, and tears of somber gratitude filled my eyes.

As the weather grew colder, I made sure to visit my friend on Mont'Albano more often, at the same time giving Thunderbolt the chance to exercise before the snow season came upon us. Donna Grazia seemed to have taken her writing more seriously, claiming it was spiritually inspired. Sometimes, we spent the entire day together, I sewing and she reading passages from her writings.

"Caterina, I think I have an answer to your questions on the fate of souls leaving this life," she announced one day. "It came to me with two extraordinary words: 'Spiritual elevation.' These words troubled me for days, until their meaning suddenly became so clear that it took me no time to write it down." I put down my sewing and listened. "Well, my dear, it seems that this spiritual elevation begins as soon as the soul leaves the body and reaches the other side, where it is shown the possibility of attaining higher states of being, all the way to the center of God's light, the highest state of divinity. The process of elevation, though, can only be brought about if the soul's yearning is strong enough. Then it can be shown what it still needs to become worthy of elevation and is returned to another body in order to achieve it."

"And who chooses the new body for that soul?" I asked, spellbound.

"Angels look for the appropriate conditions that will enable that soul to refine itself."

"So when the soul returns to another body, it knows exactly what is needed for its elevation!" I exclaimed.

"No, my dear. That would be too easy," she said, shaking her head, "because the returning soul would do only that. Therefore, its memory is obliterated. However, it may be provided with talents and a strong will to develop those talents through which it can acquire the qualities it needs for its elevation."

"But if one doesn't know what is needed for one's spiritual elevation, how can one choose?"

"Ah, that's the secret, my dear. That's where the whole mystery lies. For that purpose, it's necessary, every now and then, to pray with great devotion so as to avoid being led astray. Silence and meditation provide us with the divine energy that inspires and keeps us on the right path."

"Could that kind of inspiration be in a form that we call 'mission'?"

"I believe so," she said, looking into my eyes.

"And what happens when one is taken away before that mission has been accomplished?" I asked earnestly.

She patted my hand. "My dear, it is we who believe that we've been called before our time. If we've reached the end, there should be no question that our mission is over. Maybe then we wouldn't suffer so much over the loss of our dear ones," she concluded pensively. Then, gazing into my eyes again, she smiled warmly. "And now, enough with the study of the soul! Let's take care of our poor stomachs, maybe ... with a good hot drink and some nice cakes?" she asked as she disappeared into the kitchen, leaving me rapt in my thoughts.

"Oh, my dear Giovanni, I see now that your mission had been accomplished. You understood the power of love and you taught me to understand it, too, making me aware of the meaning of its many noble levels, while I was blindly clinging to one. Oh, Giovanni! It was your love that fulfilled me as a woman!" I sighed with relief, knowing that his help would continue until my own mission had been completed.

Telling the maids to go on doing their chores in the kitchen, Donna Grazia brought in a hot jug and a dish of small cakes, and I went to the sideboard to get the cups.

"Donna Grazia, has Don Baldo ever read any of your writings?" I asked, remembering how my old father had offered the mysterious Latin writings he had found in our house to the priest. "They could be of help to many people."

"Not yet," she answered casually. "I don't know him well enough. Besides, whatever women write is never taken seriously."

"But *I* do! In fact, right now I have a great yearning, too," I began, thinking of my mission. "As soon as the weather gets warmer I want to go to Florence." She stared at me, a little shocked. "I promised my son I would go and see him there," I explained. "I'm sure he's living in Andrea del Verrocchio's house now."

"You can't make that long trip on your own! Why don't you persuade a few women from the hills to go with you? You can show them the beautiful churches. It would be like a pilgrimage for them!" she said, smiling encouragingly.

"But Donna Grazia, I've only seen the entrance of the Duomo."

"Ah, but I've seen all the churches there. I can tell you where to go and how to find the great works of art," she said eagerly.

Her idea at first seemed too ambitious, but as winter drew on, a plan started to develop in my mind, gradually casting out all my doubts and, at the same time, helping those dreary months go by more quickly for me.

When spring returned, I invited some of the women from the surrounding hills to come and see my new flowers. They were simple women who had very little to look forward to besides a lifetime of hard work and restrictions, so they gladly welcomed a pleasant diversion from their humdrum routine. I gave each of them a pretty bouquet, and they sat around me on the curved wall of the threshing floor. I began by asking them if they had ever been to Florence. Reacting as if I had asked a foolish question, they shook their heads and said, "Are you joking?"

"Would you like to take a trip with me and visit all those huge churches and palatial buildings? Then you could tell your children all about those famous places."

"Donna Caterina, I'm a widow," said a young woman with bright blue eyes, "and I could never leave my children by themselves."

"I have a husband," said an older woman, "but if I mention it to him, he'll kill me!" We all laughed.

"Well, that's all right," I said. "Maybe another time. But I have to go there to see my young son. It's too far for him to come here, so I have to go to him." They commiserated with me. "But I'll go only if you promise to keep an eye on my house and my garden."

"That we can do for you, Donna Caterina," said the older woman as the others nodded in agreement. "We like you, Donna Caterina. And we'll look forward to hearing about your trip. I've never been farther than Vinci!"

"And I haven't even been to Vinci yet," added the younger one.

"My husband tells me that a woman should never leave home, except for working in the fields and going to the nearest church," said the older one, slightly embittered.

"Don't worry. One day we'll find a way to convince them. We'll call the trip a pilgrimage, so it'll have a religious sound to it. Don't you think?" They were amused by the idea and continued to discuss it as they hurried back to their domestic chores.

The following day, I went to tell Donna Grazia about the failure of my plan and found her having refreshments with Don Baldo.

"Caterina! Come in! I invited Don Baldo to help us plan the pilgrimage to Florence."

"I like the idea very much," he said. "I've been wanting to plan one for a long time, but I needed someone to help me encourage our simple women. Now, I suddenly have two allies!" I tried to interrupt, but he continued ebulliently.

"Groups from other counties go to Florence. Some women even take their children to see the great works of art! That's how new talents are discovered nowadays. We're entering a new era. Knowledge will be available to everybody, even women! Soon women will be able to travel freely, without being frowned upon."

"But Don Baldo, it's not so easy. I spoke to them, and they're afraid to leave their children or even to ask their husbands. Besides, I really wouldn't know how to show them around the city."

"That's all right. There are men of the cloth working as guides at each church. What I need is a brave woman who's seen Florence at least once before."

"And this exceptional woman we already have!" exclaimed Donna Grazia, enthusiastically pointing to me.

"Donna Caterina, do you know what a mission is?" asked Don Baldo, suddenly becoming serious. Hearing that word, I just stared blankly and held my breath. "This is your mission, now," declared the priest.

I looked at Donna Grazia for help, but she only smiled. Then I remembered the priest at my old father's funeral explaining that a mission was bound to be a religious task and I suddenly burst into laughter, fully realizing that what he meant was that a mission is only a mission if it's assigned by the clergy.

Somewhat inhibited by their looks of bewilderment, I hastened to point out that, though they had convinced me, they still faced the task of having to convince the local husbands.

So, on a glorious spring day, there I was, high up on my carriage, on the road to Florence, ready to take advantage of that new freedom for women Don Baldo had heralded. "Go on, Thunderbolt! This is our chance to explore the world again! Look, the highway's all ours!" I exclaimed ecstatically.

As we skirted the edge of the wood, I saw a well-dressed gray-haired man standing at the side of the road leaning on his cane. When he saw me, he waved his cane in a friendly way to encourage me to stop.

I asked him if he needed help. "Yes, indeed!" he promptly answered. "Especially if you happen to be going to Florence. I'd appreciate a ride just to the outskirts of the city. The man who should have brought my gig hasn't shown up, and my bad leg has suddenly started bothering me."

"Please join me, *messere!*" I said, making room for him. After a few minutes of silence, I realized he was in pain, so I started to make conversation, hoping to take his mind off it. "Would it be too indiscreet of me to ask what you were doing here all alone, Messer ... ?"

"Ricciardini, Ridolfo Ricciardini," he supplied with an affable smile. "I was doing some research in the wood. I'm a scholar, you know," he added proudly. "I specialize in the study of botany."

"Ah, botany? Isn't that a science—the study of plants?"

"That's right! Where did you learn that? Not many people recognize the word, not even the farmers, who are the closest to it, Donna ... "

"Caterina. I know, I learned it from my son. Although he attends the school of art, he's been studying herbs since he was very young."

"How old is your son? You're still a young woman yourself!"

"He's almost thirteen, but he has the knowledge of a grown-up."

"And where is this phenomenon of a boy studying?" he asked, sitting up.

"In Florence. He is the reason for my trip. I think he's working in Verrocchio's *bottega* now."

"Then he must be very talented. Andrea del Verrocchio doesn't waste his time with boys who don't guarantee him success. He's as good a businessman as he is a great artist." I listened with interest to what he had to say, confident that I could learn a great deal from him about life in Florence. "So, you're going straight there, I imagine," he went on.

"I don't know yet, Messer Ricciardini."

"Because if you're going there, I'd like to stay on with your permission so that I can meet your son," he said brightly.

"Well, I was thinking of leaving my carriage somewhere first. The streets there are too narrow. In fact, I'm going to stop at the tavern in the *mercato grande*."

"At Francesca's *locanda*? I know her. She's an exceptional woman! As soon as I've had a glass of her good wine, I'll be ready to follow you!"

When Francesca saw us, she didn't know whom to welcome first. Then she hugged me, whispering in my ear, "My dear, I heard about your Giovanni. I'm sorry. The news broke my heart, and every time I thought of you ..." She sighed. She showed us to a table and then asked me to follow her to the kitchen. "Is it true that he was shot intentionally?" she asked, holding her hand to her cheek in dismay. Seeing that I was startled, she hastily added, "But I didn't believe a word of that rumor, and neither should you, my dear!"

"Thank you, Francesca. I'm going to take Messer Ricciardini to meet my son. When I come back, we'll talk about it." I went back to the table, and without being asked, she brought us a plate of her special small fresh loaves, a mug of warm milk for me and a tall glass of white wine for my elderly traveling companion, who patted her shoulder.

On our way to the *bottega* I had to repress my anxiety by stopping several times to give the gentleman a chance to rest his painful leg. When we finally arrived, Messer Ricciardini motioned for me to go ahead.

"Is there a young man called Leo working here?" I asked the boy who was sweeping the entrance.

"Oh, you mean the one called Leonardo da Vinci. He's in the backyard mixing the colors for the *maestro,* but he doesn't like to be disturbed while he's doing it."

"Please go and tell him that his ... his father's servant has to talk to him." The boy dropped the broom and ran inside. The gentleman was standing a short distance away from the building, leaning on his cane.

Leo appeared, wearing a leather apron spattered with paint. He had grown even taller, but much thinner. It was obvious he was annoyed to see me. "Mother, what are you doing here?" he cried. Then, becoming angry, he snapped, "And why did you say you were Father's servant?"

"Because I wanted to avoid gossip. Do you see that gentleman over there? He's a scholar who specializes in botany, and he wants to meet you." I took his arm, trying to calm him, and as we approached Messer Ricciardini, I added, "I'm so glad you were able to get into this studio!"

"So this is the boy phenomenon!" said the old scholar. "Your mother tells me you study botany. I wanted to talk to you, because I'm a member of the Accademia Medicea, where I'm trying to develop this science."

"I'd be happy to, *messere,* but if my master finds out I'm interested in anything other than what *he* teaches, he'll throw me out of here in an instant!" Leo exclaimed a little nervously.

"I know, my boy, I know. But next summer, we could meet in the country," he said, turning to me for support. I smiled approvingly.

"It would be an honor, *messere,*" said Leo. "I think I may be able to go to Vinci in July, when the workshop closes. We'll be free to talk at my mother's house in Anchiano. Thank you for asking me, *messere.*"

Somebody from inside called him, so he placed a kiss on my forehead and, excusing himself, disappeared through the door. Lifting his hat, Messer Ricciardini thanked me, bade me a warm good-bye, and slowly started down a side street.

Realizing then, with deep disappointment, that my visit was over, I started pacing about. In my confusion, at first I considered visiting the Duomo, but instead I decided to head back to Francesca's to plan my return trip, counting on the comfort only she could give me to compensate for Leo's unexpected behavior.

That night she and I discussed many things—everything, in fact, but the rumors about Giovanni's death. Then I retired to the same little room where I had dreamed of my mother showing me where my father had died. It all seemed so remote now, for the pain of Giovanni's death had dimmed even that memory.

* * *

On my return to Anchiano, I learned that there would be no pilgrimages, after all, this year. So I devoted myself to my garden again, looking forward to that precious month of July.

But July had come and gone when Leo finally appeared at my front door. Though he looked pale and emaciated, I tried to hide my concern, letting him talk about his trip, which seemed to have been very exciting for him.

"I came to Vinci with my uncle, Francesco," he explained, "because my father has just been given another important position and wasn't sure if he could come. Uncle Francesco and I talked all the way. He is such an interesting person! But, unfortunately, I'm rarely able to see him now. Anyway, I walked up from Vinci. So, you see? I don't need Gian Pietro anymore! In this bag, I have everything I need," he said, holding up a satchel with paint smears all over it. I noticed, too, that his clothes were a little worn, giving him the look of an artisan, rather than that of a gentleman. He had, though, become freer and more spontaneous in his attitude, and that pleased me immensely.

"So you're happy working with Maestro Andrea," I said affirmatively as he sat at the table.

"Yes, because I have a chance to be among the best artisans in Florence. Up to now, though, I've only been mixing colors for them, but even that has been a good experience for me."

The following Friday, under the impression that Piero was still away, I decided to take some flowers to the market. Leo helped me load them on the carriage. I wore my blue cotton dress, which had become my uniform on market days. "Mother, why don't you wear my blue ribbon in your hair? It's the same color as your dress," he said, smiling persuasively. So I went to get it and let him tie it around my head. Then he bowed with a sweeping gesture of the hand and uttered solemnly, "Hail, Madonna Lisa with the shining halo!" I blushed and covered my face.

As I was getting ready to leave, he came over to show me

a drawing he had started. "Look, Mother! I drew you wearing the ribbon. Do you like it?" I was amazed how, with a few lines, he had been able to capture not only my features, but also an expression in my eyes that made the sketch come to life. "I just had an idea," he said pensively. "I'll call your portrait 'Monna Lisa.' Everyone who'll look at it will ask, 'Who is that mysterious woman?'" We laughed, and I climbed into my carriage.

At the market, I had just finished arranging my flower display when I heard someone clear his throat. I was shocked by the sight of Piero's face, red with hatred. "Where's Leonardo?" he asked angrily.

"At my house. Why?"

"Because he left Florence ... without waiting for me."

"But you told him you weren't sure if you could come to Vinci. You know that Maestro Andrea has given him a brief time to rest. And he needs rest. He works hard there. You should see how thin he's become."

"You encouraged him to choose that profession, letting him draw your silly flowers! Do you know he doesn't even show up at the house anymore? He's incorrigible!" he said, glowering at me. "You're to blame for this irresponsible behavior, for his ... lack of character."

Having recognized some customers coming toward me, l refused to let myself be drawn into a dispute with him. So, to his utter amazement, I hastily handed him a bunch of flowers and said, "Then take these 'silly flowers' to Donna Lucia! Maybe *she'll* appreciate them!" His hateful expression turned into one of embarrassment. Then, collecting himself, he reached out for my hand, surprising me with one of his seductive smiles. For the sake of appearance, I held out my hand. He seized it and squeezed it in both of his. Then, clearing his throat again, he whispered, "Oh, Caterina, you're still so beautiful! Like a Madonna! Oh, Caterina! Caterina! I wish I deserved your love, or at least your forgiveness!"

I quickly wrenched my hand from his grasp, and he stormed off, disgruntled. I couldn't take my eyes off him, my mind afire with sinister theories of what might have caused Giovanni's death. My hate welled up.

"Yes, it was he!" I said to myself. "Oh, my Giovanni, if it's true, help me blot it from my memory! Take away this burden of hatred!"

"Monna Lisa," whispered the first woman in line, "I think he's in love with you. He's a widower, you know." She glanced at Giovanni's ring. "Aren't you a widow, too?" Then I looked at the ring and pressed it tightly against my heart.

The prattling of the women became unbearable. I shook my head to clear my thoughts and started offering the flowers for less money, saying I had to leave right away. When they had all gone I beckoned to the fruit-seller whose flowers nobody wanted. She approached me apprehensively. "Good woman, would you like to sell my flowers here in the future?" She nodded eagerly, her face reddening a little. "Well, then come to Anchiano to pick them up," I said firmly, trying to cover up the tremble in my voice.

The woman took my hand and kissed it. "Thank you, thank you, Monna Lisa! My name is Veronica. Yes, I'd like to very much! I don't live far from you," she said, her dark eyes shining like stars in appreciation. I gave her a warm smile as she awkwardly backed away. Then, still upset, I left the market for the last time.

When I got back home, still unsettled from my encounter with Piero, I saw Leo coming up from the brook, holding a small white kitten. "Mother, what happened? You seem very upset. Did you lose the ribbon?"

"No, I took it off. Thunderbolt went crazy on the way up, and I could have lost it," I said casually. "What a pretty kitten! So white!"

"I found it walking along the brook. It must be a newborn, no more than a few days old." I went to get some milk, grateful for the distraction. "You know, Mother, until today, I didn't realize how gracefully a cat uses its muscles," he said, observing the cat as it lapped up the milk.

"Why are you so interested in the muscles of animals?" I asked, steadying my shaking knees as I sat on the bench.

"Because muscles are their means of expression. That's why a horse expresses itself by trotting; its muscles have been created for that particular movement. See how the cat stretches itself? Its muscles have that kind of elasticity." Then, looking far into the distance, he said, "Now I'm also studying birds."

"What about people? What makes *them* ... change their attitude so suddenly?" I demanded, but quickly excused myself, realizing it was not pertinent to what he was saying.

"Ah, people—or better still, 'the human animal,'" he began, carefully considering my question. "Well, from the moment he is born, man is provided with a mind and a soul ... and with an infinite number of unexpected and misleading feelings, which he has to learn to keep under control in order to be part of mankind."

I gazed at him, thinking how appropriate his answer was in regard to his father. As he cuddled the kitten, gently feeling its tiny muscles, I asked myself from whom Leo had inherited his wisdom. Had it come from one of my ancestors? But then I came to the same conclusion as before, namely, that his great knowledge was simply of divine origin.

14
HERBS, MECHANICS, AND ANGELS

In the days that followed, I realized that Leo was, in fact, observing the flight of birds. I watched him from a distance as he sat on a rock, drawing board and pencil in hand, communicating in his own unique way with the birds chirping on the ground around him. "Go on, show me how you open your wings. Slowly, now! Please...." And the birds, as if captivated by the sound of his voice, paraded in front of him and then slowly flew into the air, showing off the magic of their wings in motion.

One morning, he took out the small tools he had brought with him from Florence and sat down in his corner on the threshing floor. After consulting his notes and drawings of birds, he started constructing a strange device, using some flexible branches and pieces of sheer multicolored fabric.

I was working in my garden when an enormous winged creature rising from behind a slope suddenly caught my eye. As it fluttered, it looked so ethereal, reminding me of the translucent mystical bird flying over the wasteland in my dream about my mother, that I gave out a scream.

Leo quickly stepped out from behind a rock, balancing his creation high above his head. "Mother, did I frighten you? Why? Don't you see how beautiful it is?"

"Yes, my dear, it is beautiful," I said, recovering. "But for a moment I thought it was the bird in the dream I told you about, remember?"

"Yes, it's true. It does look a little bit like that. Maybe that's what influenced me. But I built it because some day I want to invent a mechanical bird big enough to carry a man up into the sky." Then, lifting the construction over his head again, he added, "Now, let's see how this one flies by itself!" He gave it a firm push, and the wind promptly caught it, transporting it high up into the sky. With our arms on each other's shoulders, we watched breathlessly as the diaphanous device softly glided back and forth over our valley until it finally settled in a tall tree by the brook.

"Good morning, Donna Caterina. You must be surprised to see me at such an early hour," Messer Ridolfo Ricciardini greeted me one early morning. "I spent the night in Empoli. As you can see, I'm familiar with all the inns around our Tuscan countryside," he said, chuckling. "I heard that they call you 'Monna Lisa of the Flowers.'"

I smiled back at him, holding out my hand. "It's a name I adopted when I used to take my flowers to the small market in Vinci."

"So, you're a floriculturist, too! And where is our young man?"

"Well, a while ago I saw him sitting under a tree. Oh, there he is! Shall I call him?"

"No, no, I want to surprise him. Later, I'd like to see Monna Lisa's famous garden, too," he said wistfully. Though he used a cane, he still seemed to get through the hedges and bushes with the agility of a young man. Leo was lying on his back with pencil and drawing board in hand, sketching the sparrows flying to and from the chestnut tree. "Ah, that's the way you study botany, eh?" cried Ser Ridolfo.

Leo jumped to his feet. "Good morning, *messere*. I'm so glad you didn't come before, for I wasn't able to get away in July as I had hoped."

Ser Ridolfo bent to pick up some of the sheets of paper

spread out on the ground. "So, you turned your attention to the shape of birds' wings, eh? Anyhow, I see that you're good—that's why Andrea snapped you up," he said, placing his hand on Leo's shoulder. "Now tell me: what herbs have you discovered during your long years of study?" Leo hesitated. "Then tell me why you have such a keen interest in birds' wings, if not for drawing them on the backs of angels!"

"No, not only for that, but also because I feel that ... one day man should be able to fly in the air, too," said Leo quite seriously.

"Let's go slowly, young man! We should try to set our feet firmly on the ground first before flying off. There's plenty more to discover on this earth of ours, which is much more important than flying among the clouds. And," he said, pointing to the sky, "beyond that? ... Well, that's not our affair. That's part of the arcanum."

I was amused by Ser Ridolfo's attitude, and as they descended the slope leading down into the green Arno Valley I went back to my work.

"Donna Caterina! Look! He's written my notes on the back of his birds' wings," said Ser Ridolfo when he saw me look out. He was sitting on the bench outside, puffing, while Leo sorted out his drawings on the ground.

"You must be very tired, Ser Ridolfo. Won't you come in? I've prepared a nice vegetable soup that will be good for you both!"

"Ah, very good! Vegetable soup, eh? That's my favorite. I never eat meat. I let animals eat other animals," he said with a laugh.

"Well, my mother feels the same way. To her, flour and vegetables are the only basic ingredients needed for a good meal," Leo commented.

They spent the afternoon sitting under the shade of a tree, Ser Ridolfo on a chair, and Leo on the ground, showing him his drawings of unusual plants he had seen around the valley.

Ser Ridolfo kept coming back every day until he had made sure that both Leo and I had learned the basics of his science as well as its values. He taught me how to save seeds and how to prepare the soil for the next year's crop of herb plants, which could be used to cure all kinds of illnesses.

The following week, Ser Ridolfo presented me with an iron pestle and mortar. "This is for you, Caterina. I'll show you how to powder the dry herbs with this so you can store them in jars for the winter months," he explained.

Leo built a ladder that he placed against the wall of the house in order to climb up to the roof, where Ser Ridolfo had instructed us to leave the herbs to dry away from the dusty ground. We set up a table outdoors on which Ser Ridolfo sorted out the fresh herbs, and I pounded the dry ones in the mortar, mixing them according to his directions. I also learned how to make ointments from those powders, storing them in Rita's glass jars, which until then had served only as ornaments. Then, putting to use my modest knowledge of writing, I was able to label them, indicating the symptoms that could be treated by each mixture.

The following summer, I was anxious to resume our studies with Ser Ridolfo. All through the winter months, my neighbors had come to me with their minor ailments for which he had prescribed various herb tisanes. Even Donna Grazia benefited from this new interest, for one particular tisane, which Leo had mixed, helped her breathe more easily and get through the long winter months with less discomfort. There were many questions, though, I wished to ask Ser Ridolfo now, and I felt confident that after my practical experience his advice would be invaluable.

Leo finally arrived at the beginning of August. As he came to embrace me, there was no doubt he was already a young man, handsome and athletic, but still dressed like a poor art student. After our fond exchanges, he took a small package out of his satchel and offered it to me. I unwrapped a wooden icon that opened like a book the size of my hand. Inside was the image of a Madonna and Child painted in deep colors, muted with such soft highlights that it took my breath away.

"Oh, how beautiful it is!" I said, exhilarated. "You made it, Leo! Didn't you?"

"Yes, it's the first time Maestro Andrea let me use his colors on my own painting!" he exclaimed proudly.

"I thought *you* prepared the colors for *him*."

"Yes, I do that now, but it's still his formula," he specified. "I haven't started to mix my colors yet, but I have them all in my mind."

"You know, Leo," I said, holding up the precious icon, "I always wished I had an outdoor niche overlooking our house and our garden. But I didn't have a sacred image on wood like this one, which could stand all kinds of weather."

"Where would you like to put it?" he asked eagerly.

"I think a good place would be under the tall wild cherry tree on the edge of the slope behind the threshing floor."

"I'll build one for you with its own doors, so you can close them during a storm." I had to get up on my toes to kiss him on the forehead.

The next day, he erected an extraordinary niche on four legs from wood left over from the restoration of the house, and set it in the shade of the cherry tree. Inside the niche, I placed a small oil lamp to keep the lovely holy image always illuminated.

That night, we sat on the low wall to admire the mystical aura the lamp created around the little shrine of our Protectress.

It was as if Ser Ridolfo knew instinctively when to appear that week, and we welcomed him both for his charming good humor and his seemingly endless knowledge, which he continued to impart every year. After yet another summer of training with him the following year, when Leo was fifteen, I turned from a florist into an herbalist—the only one in our hills. Since I also learned how to prepare decoctions for children's coughs, mothers of young children would come knocking on my door, asking me to go and help their ailing little ones, which I often did, sometimes crossing the snowy mountain paths in the middle of the night. Helping the children was my most gratifying experience, because with my cures I brought them love, too—all the love I hadn't been allowed to give my son when he was little. But what made me even happier was to see the thankful mothers bringing their recovered children to visit me. So, thanks to Ser Ridolfo, my life became more fulfilling and my loneliness more bearable, while waiting for Leo to come and spend his summers with me. We usually spent the whole month of August together, when I could finally recount some interesting aspects of my new activity in the surrounding hills, and he would share his discoveries of new herbs. Our common interest seemed to bring us closer together, for a while releasing me from the fear of being totally excluded from Leo's life.

"My dear Caterina, I'm so looking forward to seeing Leonardo this summer," said Donna Grazia one late spring day as we sat on the veranda, "to thank him for that last mixture of herbs he made for me. I've never had such an easy winter in my life since I've been taking this last tisane. I think he should study medicine, rather than just painting."

"He's already so versatile, with his many pursuits, it's a wonder he keeps up with them at all."

Our conversation was cut short by the appearance of the young maid. Before she could say a word, an excited Don Baldo swept past her to announce that he had been able to convince a number of family men in the vicinity to let their women go on the pilgrimage. "This is all due to you, Donna Caterina," he said triumphantly, "to the trust you've gained through your good work."

I rejoiced at the prospect of seeing my son sooner than I expected and perhaps having him as a guide, too—a longtime dream of mine.

It was still early dawn when twelve women and five children over the age of ten waited at the Anchiano crossroads for the vehicle that Ser Giuliano was sending to take them to Florence. Soon the delicious aroma of ripe fruit and fresh-baked loaves filled the big cart pulled by two horses. I followed behind it in my carriage, accompanied by two pretty girls. As the journey progressed and the drab dawn gave way to clear luminous daylight, I made time pass more quickly by proudly pointing out highlights of our beautiful Tuscan countryside along the way.

When we entered the city of Florence, we headed directly to Francesca's tavern. On arrival, the boys jumped off the cart and started to unload their things. One of them, being particularly obliging, came to help us.

"What's your name? Are you here with your mother?" I asked him.

"My name is Mariano, Donna Caterina. I came with my aunt," he said, carrying my baskets inside.

Francesca greeted me with wide-open arms. "What a wonderful surprise, Caterina! Are these children from Anchiano, too?"

"Yes, Francesca. These women are their mothers and aunts."

"You can't imagine how happy I am to meet them! Don't forget, I, too, was born in the hills of Anchiano!" she chirped, as she readied a group of tables for them.

I followed her to the kitchen. "Francesca, I don't know what to do. I have to see my son, but I don't want to disappoint the others, who came here especially to be shown the splendors of the city."

"Listen, I'll have somebody go to the Duomo and get Don Filippo. When he was very young, I put him up here for a time and he never forgot it. I'm sure he'll come right away. He's very nice. He'll be a perfect guide."

Before we finished our meal, Don Filippo rushed in, flushed and out of breath. He was, as I had thought, the young priest I had met at the Duomo on my first visit to Florence. He had put on some weight and had acquired a slightly bolder attitude. On seeing me, he blushed, but I stayed back as the other women crowded around him and kissed his hand. When finally he reached me, with a hint of a smile, he shyly welcomed me back to Florence under his breath.

"My son is studying art here, and I'd like to go and see

him, so I can't join you right away, Don Filippo," I confided with regret.

"That's all right. You can catch up with us at the Duomo. We'll wait for you just inside the main door. You'd better be on your way now," he said, raising his hand to get the group's attention. They all stopped talking and listened, fascinated, to his improvised speech on the churches they were about to visit.

I waved to Francesca, who, slightly puzzled, had been observing us, and slipped out the back door, taking with me only a small bag of sweet *taralli*. At the *bottega* I hesitated for a moment in front of the half-open door until a boy came running out. I stopped him and asked him if he would call Leonardo for me.

"I can't disturb him. He's working with the *maestro* on an important painting. I'm not allowed to interrupt them. If you can wait until I bring back the pigment they told me to get, I'll try to give him your message," he said, running off without even waiting for a reply.

As soon as he was out of sight, I ventured in. A strange silence prevailed. I tiptoed to an arched open doorway and glimpsed Leo from behind working on a large panel. With his brush, he was painstakingly retouching the wing of a kneeling angel. Next to him, standing on a stool, was the *maestro,* painting a dove over the head of a half-naked figure of Christ. The moment Leo caught sight of me, I beat a hasty retreat to the main entrance. Still holding his brush, Leo stealthily caught up with me.

"Mother, how did you get in? Women aren't allowed in here. Especially at a time when I'm working with Maestro Andrea!" he whispered, escorting me into the front garden. Then, looking around, he added, "It's not that I'm not happy to see you."

"I'm sorry, darling. I couldn't find anyone to call you. You know, Leo, we finally made the pilgrimage! I had hoped you could be our guide as you promised, but I see you can't leave now." He just nodded ruefully. "So take these cakes I know you like, and I'll be on my way." His hands were covered with paint, so I slipped the bag of *taralli* into his overall pocket and started to leave.

"Mother, wait! Please, understand! That painting is a very important assignment for me. It's the first time Maestro Andrea's letting me work on one of his projects. He's letting me paint one of the angels. It's an altarpiece representing the baptism of Christ and it's going to be shown at the Academy of Arts to men of prestige!" he exclaimed. "I'm sorry we can't see the works of the great masters together—but you'll enjoy seeing them anyway. You'll see." I smiled and hugged him. "Oh, dear, I got paint on your dress!" he said, kissing my forehead.

"Don't worry, Leo, I'm all right. Go back to your work now!" I murmured, moving toward the street. After a few steps I turned, startled by a young female voice calling: "Leonardo, Leonardo, I'm so glad you're out here."

It was a girl who, with arms outstretched, was running toward Leo. Her long chestnut hair fell down her shoulders covered by a cape flowing over her slender figure dressed in a pastel pink dress.

"Oh Leonardo, if you only knew ..." she cried, hoarsely.

"What happened, darling?" asked Leo, rushing to her.

"They're taking me away! They're marrying me to a complete stranger. A man, I'll never love the way I love you!"

Leo calmingly lifted the curls off her face and gently caressed her rosy cheeks shining with tears. She looked up at him, silently, placing the side of her head in his hand. Her profile, the most beautiful one I had ever seen on a woman's face, reminded me of the profile of the angel Leo had been working on. For a moment, I didn't know if to rejoice at such revelation or be sad about the girl's situation. But, then, I felt a pleasant feeling of affection for both of them in my heart. I swiftly moved on my way, not wanting to intrude any further upon their privacy.

"Ah, you're leaving!" said the boy, bumping into me on his way back from his errand. "Shall I tell him that you were here?" he asked, leaning to pick up some of the small bags filled with colored powders that had fallen from his basket.

"No thank you, young man, I'll come back another time." I said as I headed for the street leading to the Duomo.

At the Duomo, Don Filippo waved to me over the heads of the women and children surrounding him. I knew he had delayed for my benefit. After pointing out the many beautiful things in the Duomo, he took us outside to admire the façade and the tower. Then he went on to tell us about its designer, Giotto di Bondone, whose great artistry, I remembered, Leo had praised so fervently when he was still a child.

From there, we went to the Church of Santa Croce, where, while we viewed Giotto's frescoes, I felt strongly that he must have been Leo's primary inspiration, if not, in fact, his spiritual master. As I gazed in wonder that day at all those exquisite works of art, I considered the many sacrifices their creators must have made in order to be worthy of their God-given gift.

We left the city at dusk, and very soon found ourselves under a deep blue starry sky. The night air was mild, making the journey very pleasurable. The three boys, who on the way out had traveled on the cart, asked to be allowed to sit on the back of my carriage. With this precious load of chattering children, Thunderbolt maintained an easy trot all the way home. At first, the women in the big cart sang church litanies, while we listened. Then I alternated their angelic chanting with my cheerful songs, making up new words as I went along, which amused the children, who joined in so loudly that they soon fell asleep from exhaustion.

When we reached Anchiano, I let the sleepy children go back to their mothers and returned to my solitary existence, still somewhat resentful of the all too brief a time I had with my son.

It was the beginning of another summer when I climbed down the path leading to my *ruscello,* hoping that the sound of the water would lift the heaviness in my head with which I had awakened that morning. I sat with my back against the trunk of the same tree I had grabbed that terrible day when I fell into the torrent and almost drowned, and I wondered if Leo would be able to spend the month of August with me as usual. While I stared down into the water, the gibbering of the cicadas was restful to the point of making me feel lightheaded.

I must have dozed off, for Leo's voice echoed in the valley. I shook my head, thinking I was dreaming, but the echo persisted and I got up. Feeling dizzy, I leaned against the tree again, my sight clouded. Yet I was able to glimpse Leo climbing down the slope. "Mother, stay there! I'm coming down. Wait! Wait there!" he cried, jumping quickly over the bushes. Dressed in a short brown velvet cape with an old-rose silk lining and brown fitted pants that made him look taller, his golden curls falling down in ringlets, he was like the angels I had seen in Florentine paintings. I still thought that I was dreaming, for his short descent seemed to last forever. When he finally reached me, his deep, manly voice gave me quite a turn. "Madama," he announced, "meet Messer Leonardo da Vinci! Member of the Corporation of the Painters of Florence!" I was too dazed to react. He then led me by the hand to the same spot where we had danced when he was a small child and he guided me through the steps of a stately dance. We stopped by the brook, and he scooped up some water, pouring it into my hands. He went back to refill his hands and jubilantly toasted, "Let's drink to the health of Monna Lisa, who was the inspiration for this success!" We both sipped the water from our cupped hands as if savoring a rich wine. "Mother, aren't you well? You look feverish!" he exclaimed, touching my forehead.

"No, my dear. It's the excitement of seeing you and hearing your good news, that's all," I said lightly, although my head still ached badly.

"Let's go back to the house. I'll prepare a brew of herbs for you, while you rest," he said, helping me with the climb.

Back at the house, Leo made me lie down. Meticulously examining all the jars of powdered herbs on the sideboard, he selected a few that he mixed into a terra-cotta bowl. Then he lit the iron stove and put a big pot of water on it. As it came to a boil, he poured the hot water over the powder mixture and stirred it carefully. "This will make you feel better, Mother," he said, offering it to me. "Promise me you'll take it every day until you feel completely recovered!"

"Did you come to Vinci with your uncle?" I asked, as I felt the dark tisane reviving me.

"No, I borrowed a horse. I left it in Thunderbolt's company. But it won't be long before I'll be able to buy a horse of my own. I've been commissioned a great deal of work since I painted that angel." Taking a bow, he added proudly, "Even by Lorenzo de' Medici, himself!"

"Isn't he the son of Cosimo de' Medici, the one they call Pater Patriae?"

"Yes. How did you know that?" he asked with surprise.

"I heard it the first time I went to Florence. It's a long story," I said and started telling him about my experience in the Piazza della Signoria.

He nodded and felt my forehead, seemingly pleased with my improvement. After a while, I noticed he was smiling to himself, so I interrupted my story, saying, "Maybe I like to talk about the past too much. I must be getting old."

He laughed. "No, it's not that at all. You like to talk because you're much better already. Am I right?" He was right, indeed; the herb mixture had done me good. In fact, within a couple of days, I was busy in the garden again.

One morning, he must have climbed out from his window again, because when I stepped outside, I saw him returning on horseback, a bag full of herb plants hanging from his shoulder. "Good morning, Mother. I took Thunderbolt for a nice ride up to Paterno."

"Why so early? It must have been before dawn. I didn't hear you leave."

"I looked for some special herb plants and uprooted them while they were still drenched with dew. I'm going to plant them in your herb garden before the sun comes up," he said, dismounting. "Next summer, I'll try to make the herb picking and drying coincide with the movement of the stars," he said, unrolling a sheet of drawing paper. "I drew something for you, Mother. It's the wisteria tree growing on the side wall of Santa Lucia's church. I'll give it to you after I've painted its tiny violet flowers on a small wooden plate with the paints I brought with me. I want to see if I can capture exactly the same brilliant shade of violet while it's still fresh in my mind," he said with a confident wink.

I don't remember how long he stayed with me this time. Between my recovery and his vigorous activities around the house, it may have seemed shorter than it really was. But I do remember how delighted I was when I saw the wooden plate he had painted placed on the mantelpiece one morning next to the small portrait of me he had given me in Florence. The purple and lilac wisteria clusters seemed to be dripping with real morning dew.

But, alas! It was also the morning of yet another departure. Unable to speak, I watched Leo in his lovely outfit mounting his horse. "Mother, I promise that as soon as I start earning enough money, I'm going to get my own living quarters in Florence, so that you may come and stay with me whenever you please." As he spoke, I forced a smile to hide my tears. "I want you to spend at least the winter months with me, especially if in the future, Donna Grazia really decides to spend hers in town."

During his subsequent visits, I noticed that his flying apparatus was just the first of a series of new constructions he now called "mechanical inventions," which, as he had predicted as a child, could create motion. Among the materials and accessories he brought with him were small indented wheels, different colored wires, and all thicknesses of rope. Using up the pieces of wood and metal left by the masons, he was able to construct his larger inventions right on the bank of the brook. As soon as he was able to test each device, he drew it on paper in great detail, every wheel, every wire and screw. Then he demolished the whole thing, and started building a new one. I had no idea what the purpose was of this unusual exercise, neither did I question him about it, because my only concern was that he should keep healthy and happy, which he did.

One day, though, when I went down to the brook to leave him a basket of food, my curiosity got the better of me. He had just erected a complicated device on two tall beams. I was about to leave to avoid disturbing him when he called me over and asked me to turn a handle. As I did so, a set of wheels started to move, and a heavy rock was lifted by a rope to the top of the beams. Flabbergasted, I marveled at the incredible device, while Leo clapped his hands and jumped up and down like a child. When I let the handle go, the rock fell back to the ground and rolled into the brook, splashing us all over with water. We looked at each other's drenched clothes and suddenly burst out laughing.

From that day, he found it amusing to have me around when he tested a new device. Another one that remained impressed in my memory was built right in the middle of the brook. Its main feature was a shovel attached to the end of a strong beam tied across two poles. By turning some wheels, the shovel was driven into the bottom of the brook and then lifted high up to the top of the beam, where the mechanism of more wheels emptied its contents into a bucket. From the bucket, the wet pebbles were poured into a hollowed tree trunk, down which they slid all the way to the bank.

I gazed in awe at the unusual shiny pebbles scattered all around, selected a few pretty ones and placed them on the grass to dry as Leo studied the excavated matter and added notes to his complex diagrams. Then I busied myself polishing the stones I had set aside, using this as an excuse to linger in his company, for I knew he wouldn't come to the house until late in the day. After a hurried meal, he would sit on the low wall and draw or paint until sunset, his favorite time of day, when he could capture the subtle tones of light he favored so much. I never told him to stop or rest a little anymore, for I saw that he was at his happiest when he was free to express his versatile creativity, a freedom strictly denied him within the austere walls of the *bottega*.

Sometimes, I sat near him, playing my little flute. "Leo,

why didn't you ever learn to play it?" I asked one evening while he was putting away his drawing implements. "I'm sure you would be good at it."

"No, Mother, that's your talent. I do have a musical instrument in mind for me, but I have to construct it first." I looked at him curiously. "It will be an instrument with many strings, at the slightest touch they'll vibrate in a magical way, giving out a most marvelous sound! Its body will have an unusual shape, which will shock people," he said, smiling archly. "I think I'll make it in the shape of a horse's head." He smiled impishly. "Better still, a horse's skull! As for the music I'll play ... ?" he said, stroking his chin. "Well, that's already in my mind, too. You see, Mother, I've learned a lot about tonality by listening to your creative playing."

It was the end of another visit, and we were taking all his surviving mechanical devices to the little room under the old tavern. I stopped as we passed the small window. "You were born during a marvelous dawn right under this window," I said dreamily. Leo turned and smiled. "And this room heard your first cries, darling! That's why I thought it would be a good place to store your inventions. Don't you agree?"

"It's a good *hiding* place for them," he confirmed as we stepped inside. "You know, Mother," he added, "it just occurred to me that if Maestro Andrea even remotely suspected that I was spending so much time on these inventions, he would never let me set foot in his workshop again."

I could scarcely smile, for the thought of his impending departure already weighed heavily on my heart.

15
A CALL FROM THE PAST

I'll never know what prompted such an impulse one morning when I decided to harness Thunderbolt for a drive without any specific destination in mind. At the Anchiano crossroads, my attention was caught by the distant Church of Sant'Amato, standing invitingly way up on the summit of a steep hill towering above the others across the deepest part of the valley.

"I wonder if you could get us up there, Thunderbolt," I said. "If it gets too difficult, we'll just turn back." Once we were on the highway, Thunderbolt kept an unusually slow pace. Boldly cracking my whip the way Giovanni used to, I unintentionally made him break into a fast gallop I was unable to control. Besides losing sight of the church, I realized that we were, instead, heading toward the lower hills. "Thunderbolt! What's the matter with you? We're going the wrong way!" I cried to no avail, for he kept galloping toward a surprisingly barren area, which reminded me of the countryside of my childhood. Ahead of us, in the distance, I saw a tall tree looming over a tiny house, but Thunderbolt suddenly turned away, taking us up a narrow lane. "Stop, Thunderbolt! Please stop! I saw something," I cried at the top of my voice, tugging wildly at the reins, while I tried not to lose sight of the tree, of which only the tip now remained visible.

But when we finally came to a standstill, I saw that we were at the back of the tiny house. When I jumped down to look around, my heart started pounding as I recognized my childhood home. I rushed to the front door, devastated by what I saw. The roof had fallen in, the walls were dilapidated and overgrown with thornbushes, and beams blocked the doorway. It was heartrending to see my dear parents' old stone hut that they loved so much reduced to such a sorry state.

As I looked up at the thick elm tree, I shouted, "The graves! I must find the graves!" I ran over to the tree at the side of the house and stood, trying to remember where they had been dug, but the ground was completely covered with several layers of damp, rotting leaves. I picked up a rusty old shovel leaning against the wall and started poking through the leaves. First, I found the gravestones marking the spot, then under moist soil the wooden crosses Vincenzo had made. I wiped them clean with dry leaves and set them back into the ground behind the gravestones. From the nearby field, I gathered some wildflowers and placed them on the stones. Then I knelt down and meditated on those two loving souls forgotten by the world. I heard the sparrows chirping and reminisced about the happy times I spent, so long ago, entertaining their forefathers with my flute.

Then, remembering the marble slab that had somehow altered the course of my life, I rushed to the front door to see if I could now interpret its mysterious inscription, but the fallen debris made it impossible to see if it was still there. I frantically heaved the rotting beams away from the doorway and brushed off the leaves, dirt, and broken tiles until the slab finally saw the light of day again. The engravings, though, were filled with dirt, so I rushed to the old well and lowered the bucket still hanging on the chain. When I hauled it up, I screamed, letting it fall to the ground, horrified to see large worms writhing inside it. The sight of those creatures crawling out of the bucket and sliding like snakes in the grass turned my stomach and made my head spin.

Pulling myself together, I staggered back to the house. To

my utter amazement, the engravings on the slab now seemed to be quite clean. But try as I could, there was no way for me to unravel the meaning of the inscription.

"I wish Leo were here. He would know what it says!" I cried. I decided to take the slab with me. But when I tried to lift it, I found that it was firmly cemented to the step. Overcome with disappointment, I let myself fall back on the ground. When I looked up again, I was surprised to see the half-open door intact and was tempted to peer inside. While I hesitated, I saw my old father in a chair by the doorstep urging me to go in. So I stood up and stepped into the eerie darkness of the room, strangely unperturbed by his sudden appearance.

The old lamp was still spreading its soft light, which was enough for me to see a newer version of my old mother's favorite bedspread on their bed and her favorite embroidered silk cushion, now brand-new, on her high-backed chair next to the fireplace. Clean, bright terra-cotta bowls adorned the new white cloth on the kitchen table. Somehow I knew that I had entered my old parents' spiritual world. I felt so privileged.

The lamp began to flicker, making the shadows sway across the walls. A small shiny object lying on the trunk where my mother used to keep my baby linens caught my eye. Approaching it slowly, I recognized a pretty pink baby shoe and I wondered why I hadn't seen it on the day I left. As I reached out to touch it, my attention was drawn back to the chair. My mother's white hair seemed to appear gradually against the back of the chair, then her smiling face, and then her whole person. There was a comforting glow about her entire presence. I smiled back at her, hypnotized.

The small light flickered again, suddenly bursting with an overpowering radiance, which brightened the entire room. Squinting through the almost blinding light, I discovered that the room had changed from the pleasant, peaceful nest into a stark and dingy hovel. Gone was its pretty decor, leaving the walls dark and bare. Still shielding my eyes from the piercing light, I peered through my fingers and spied an oblong table in the center of the room on which lay a shining flat object. Getting closer, I noticed that under it were several sheets of parchment.

The oil lamp suddenly went out, and the flat object, which by now I had recognized as the marble slab, started to shimmer. My blood froze as I realized that I had gone back to the time when my parents had found the house. The slab emitted a stream of loud voices, speaking in a strange language, reminding me of the sounds that had emerged from the well. I took it for granted that they were reciting what was written on the slab and on the parchments. The noise was so deafening that I had to cover my ears. Then the room was quiet again.

I reached out to touch the slab with my finger to see if it was real, when a man's powerful voice reverberated in all four corners of the room, making the floor shake. "My girl, you have completed your mission! You are free now, free forever!" I looked around, terrified, as the dazzling light from the slab gradually faded, leaving the room steeped in darkness.

Seeing a ray of daylight coming from the door, I quickly ran outside. The steps cracked under my feet and I fell to the ground. I sat up to look at the door, but my head started to spin again and I closed my eyes. I felt Jasmine's breath on my cheek, and then saw her standing next to me, white as snow. As I tried to touch her, she vanished into thin air. Completely confused now, I looked up at the door again and saw it was still blocked by debris. No longer able to distinguish what was real and what was not, I gave an unearthly shriek, which summoned Thunderbolt from behind the house, pulling the carriage. I went up to him to touch his leg and stroke his neck to make sure he was real. But then I lost control of myself and started hitting his leg hard, unable to restrain my fearful anger at the horse. "Take me away from here, Thunderbolt! Take me away!" I cried, climbing back into the carriage. "Why did you bring me here! Why! What possessed you! I wish you could tell me what made you do it!" Still enraged, I started whipping him violently. Resenting my blows, Thunderbolt broke into a mad gallop along the dangerous curves of the narrow road, skirting the frightening edges of a steep cliff. Almost thrown from my seat, I held firm to the seat rail and shouted, "Thunderbolt, I'm sorry! Please calm down! If you only knew what happened to me there!" I was hoping the horse would sense my anxiety, but he went on regardlessly. Giving up all hope, I shut my eyes and didn't dare open them again until I finally felt the carriage slow down. I breathed a huge sigh of relief like a sob at the sight of the old tavern building.

The memory of those events was never really clear in my mind, maybe because I was afraid to conjure up the same dreadful confusion I had experienced then. Yet, little by little, every day it diminished the vigor and enthusiasm I used to feel in the morning when I set foot in my garden.

For some time, I had noticed a teenage boy near my garden who would hide in a tree whenever he saw me. I paid no attention at first, but one day I recognized him as Mariano, the boy who had been very helpful during the pilgrimage and who had asked to be allowed to sit in my carriage with the other children on the return trip. I asked him what he was doing up in the tree, instead of helping his mother in the field. He did not reply. "Do you like flowers?"

"Yes, very much! When I grow up, I want to have a garden like yours," he exclaimed, his face lighting up.

"Maybe you would like to help me, then?"

"Yes, I would!" he said, scurrying down the tree like a squirrel, his black eyes snapping. He was very agile, but rather thin.

"You haven't answered my first question yet. Your mother is a war widow and you are her oldest son. You should know your duty is to help her in the field. But maybe you're lazy."

"No, I'm not," he protested. "I like to work around beautiful things, that's all. Maybe I'm like the artisans in Florence who spend all night painting. Well, I'd work all night just to grow flowers."

I stroked his dark hair, admiring his enthusiasm. "Very

well, but shouldn't we ask your mother's permission first?" Suddenly elated, he ran toward his home.

When his mother arrived, she couldn't stop thanking me for allowing her son to help tend my garden. "Donna Caterina, my boy wants to work only on things he likes. But he's a good boy, I assure you. My field is so small I can take care of it myself. As for Mariano, I'd like him to learn something better. You understand, Donna Caterina."

From that day on, young Mariano became my assistant, eagerly tending the garden with me. He soon put on some weight, and his olive cheeks took on a rosy hue. As for me, I gradually recovered my former energy.

It was the end of summer when Leo finally arrived on his horse again, looking incredibly handsome in his smart riding outfit. I went to meet him with my arms opened wide. He was now much taller than I, so he almost had to stoop to hug me. "I'm sorry for not coming sooner, Mother, but since the success of my angel, my master insisted I work on all his projects. So the other day, I said, 'Maestro Andrea, I think I need some new drawings of birds' wings,' and he promptly gave me a few days off in the country."

"Didn't Ser Ridolfo say Maestro Andrea was a practical man?" I remarked laughingly. "By the way, is he still unable to walk?"

"Yes, it's so sad! I saw him recently. He was very impressed with the star chart I had devised and was thrilled to hear about my plans to perform the desiccation and mixing of herbs in conjunction with the movement of the sun."

I pointed to Mariano, who was approaching us. "Well, you have a brand-new apprentice now who can't wait to learn all you can teach him on the subject." The boy blushed and then rushed to unharness Leo's horse.

During his stay, Leo spent most of his time working on his new experiments with Mariano, who had a wonderful time following Leo's instructions, often having to climb up and down the ladder to take care of the herbs drying on the roof. I did my share by sorting out the leaves to be powdered and stored in jars, often observing with admiration the way Leo taught his young pupil. It soon became clear to me that not only did he have the makings of a great artist, but also of a great teacher.

At the end of the first workday, we sat on the low wall and watched the sun set, while Leo told me about his future painting projects, which delighted me immensely, for I knew how much he enjoyed the work he was doing. Before it got dark, he took out a silver medallion from his pocket and offered it to me. "This is for you, Mother. I engraved it, using the original method of the renowned old master, Ser Giuliano dei Verrocchi, the founder of our workshop." I held my breath, for it bore a bird's-eye view of the hills of Anchiano surrounding the brook.

"Thank you, my dear. It's beautiful! I'm so proud! You've inherited your grandfather Leonardo's engraving talent, too."

"I engraved it for you in memory of him."

"And you chose the view from here!" I exclaimed, overwhelmed by the precision with which he had fashioned it.

"Well, wasn't it the first landscape view I saw when I was a child?"

At dusk, the melodious whistle of the mysterious nightingale echoed in the air again. When Leo noticed it, too, I realized that it had not been a figment of my imagination. So, when he was about to make a remark, I put my finger on his lips, and we silently listened to its ethereal song until it faded away. "Do you know, Leo, that I still haven't discovered where that nightingale perches?" Then, making myself comfortable, I added, "Leo, I want to tell you about a strange experience I had some weeks ago."

He looked at me with concern. "Mother, was it so bad? You're trembling."

"I really haven't made up my mind whether it was frightening or exhilarating. I only know that it took me several days to feel physically and spiritually normal again." He took my hand to comfort me, and I related to him the disturbing experience I had had at my childhood home.

He held my hand all the time, as if to measure my feelings, until I finished my story. Then, after some consideration, he asked, "When the voice said that your mission was over, what do you think he meant?"

I shrugged, unable to tell him about the mission that had tied me down for all these years. Then, remembering Giovanni's words, I said, "Well, my missions have been many."

He laughed, showing his sparkling white teeth in the dusk. I felt uneasy about the obvious evasiveness of my reply, but turning serious, he said, "I think that when certain special events make a lasting impression on the deep recesses of our memory, sooner or later, they'll come back to haunt us either in our thoughts or in our dreams, or even in the form of a vision. Even if those events were only imagined, while in an unusual state of mind or perhaps while undergoing a stressful period, they could resurface, somehow assuming a real form." He paused for a moment, then, squeezing my hand, he added reassuringly, "But I'm sure, Mother, that it's through these experiences and manifestations that the psyche can unburden itself or, rather, be finally set free."

"How do you know about these things?" I asked, spellbound.

"I don't know. I drew these conclusions while you described what happened to you." I suspected, though, that he had undergone similar experiences in his life, but before I could question him further, I was suddenly overtaken by a violent coughing fit. "The air's turned chilly. Let's go inside, Mother! I'd like you to try a new tisane," he said.

My cough stopped. "No, my dear. I'm all right now, you see?" His thoughtfulness and consideration made me wonder about his personal life. "Leonardo, son, you would make such an ideal companion for a young woman, and a perfect father, too. You have so much love and understanding to offer and so much wisdom to impart to the young," I said, smiling. "I'm sure you've found a girl you really like, haven't you?"

Leo covered his face. I stroked his hand gently, encouraging him to talk to me, but instead he got up as if to stretch his legs and paced back and forth. I realized he was not prepared for such a question. He stopped pacing. "Yes, Mother, I've seen girls that I like, but when I really looked at them, I realized that I was attracted by only one singular exceptional quality. But then I thought it would be unfair to go after a girl who held no interest for me other than that one intriguing quality. No," he said, shaking his head, "I'd be no better than a philanderer, whose only aim is to satisfy his primitive urges." He paused for a moment to look across the valley. "The truth is that I doubt there is a girl with whom I could share my thoughts, a girl who could understand why I have to devote myself to my quest. Besides, if such an ideal woman existed for me, I wouldn't have the time or the patience to look for her." He sat down again. "You see, Mother, it's becoming more and more apparent to me that my fate will not indulge me in that respect." I looked quizzically at him. "Of course, I may be exaggerating. But, you see, I feel I have a mission, too, and that is to pass on to humanity what I am discovering about nature's great resources." I listened, astounded by what I had provoked. He stood up again as he continued. "So, my dear Mother, I'm afraid I'll have to spend a great deal of time withdrawn ... within myself. Of course, I'll have to deal with people ... all my life, but I will have to be able to get away, too, because only in solitude can one be one's own master." I started coughing again, and he promptly took me into the house.

Another Christmas Eve was upon us. This one was going to be much lonelier than usual because of Donna Grazia's unexpected departure. Though her health had improved, her husband's, on the other hand, had deteriorated. I was standing on my doorstep trying to catch the first snowflakes falling gently on the ground. As I looked at them lying in the palm of my hand, I could hardly believe that such delicate flakes could bring about months of inactivity to the entire countryside. Perhaps it was nature's way of giving the earth a rest, I thought.

    I glanced with pride at the friendly lamp in the niche, spreading its soft light over the delicate carpet of snow. It was on a very cold winter night, years earlier, that I had named the Holy Virgin's image inside it 'Santa Maria of the Snow' in thanks for having helped me select the herb mixture that saved the life of a sweet little girl called Marietta.

The sound of footsteps coming from the entrance of the yard aroused my curiosity, and I leaned out to see who was there. My heart leaped to my throat as my Leo, wrapped in a voluminous cape, rushed to greet me. "Leo! My Leo! What a wonderful surprise! On this day, it's a miracle! Ah, you came to spend Christmas with me!" I cried, overjoyed.

"I don't know yet, Mother. I took advantage of my father's coach to come to Vinci and be able to see you, but I had to promise to spend at least tonight there. You see, he brought his new wife to spend Christmas in the old house. But when I saw the snow this morning, there was no holding me back. I left the house while they still slept and walked up here. I've been longing to see the snow falling on these hills again," he said, eyes shining as he looked around.

"My dear, you must spend Christmas Day with me. It'll be our first Christmas together after so many years apart. Who knows when there will be another opportunity?" I pleaded, holding his hands.

"No, Mother. I told you that as soon as I can afford my own house, you'll spend the winters with me. Maybe even next year?" I pulled him inside. "Let me stay outside a little longer, Mother. It's simply wonderful." I let go, and he ran around the threshing floor the way he had when he was a child. As I looked on, the long-past days of his childhood flashed before my eyes.

Happily, he decided to stay, and we spent what turned out to be the best and most memorable Christmas of my life, for it was to be our last Christmas together.

The following Christmas, however, was also different from all the others. I was sitting by the fireplace alone except for Leo's white kitten, now a large cat, who was lying on the floor next to me. We were both watching the flames building up. "I'm glad *you* never left me," I said, stroking it.

A knock at the door made me jump to my feet. "That must be Leo! I knew he'd come to spend Christmas with me again," I cried.

But at the door stood a young man holding out a kind of scroll. "I'm the Vinci dispatcher. Are you Monna Lisa of the Flowers?"

"Yes, I am," I said.

"When I saw this, I knew it must be a Christmas message. So I rushed up here to make sure you got it in time."

"How nice of you, young man. How did you get it?" I asked.

"It was delivered by our Florence courier with the papers for the merchants' headquarters in Vinci. You see, I'm in charge of the local deliveries," he announced proudly.

"How wonderful! It must be from my son. Please come in. I'll get you something warm. You look frozen."

I served him a bowl of soup and sat down to examine the scroll, which was addressed in large letters: "To Monna Lisa of the Flowers." I removed the fine string around it and unrolled it. The message was clear and simple: "Dear Mother, I am not able to come this Christmas as I am working on a new painting of my own. But I look forward to spending Easter with you when I will tell you all about it. You are always in my thoughts and I assure you we'll be spending next Christmas together in my house in Florence. I promise! My warmest embrace to you, Leo." At the bottom of the page, there was a small drawing of a lily blossom inside of which he had drawn a tiny smiling face.

"Young man, if I prepare a message, would you be able to have it delivered to my son, who sent me this one? But I don't have any string or this …"

"Oh, you mean the seal! I can do it for you. At the center, they make us carry sealing wax at all times. Instead of string, why don't you use a ribbon, if you have one?"

I got pencil and paper from Leo's room and, as it would have taken me too long to write a letter, instead I drew a little house with a door on which I wrote Leo's name. On the roof, I wrote, "Lisa waits for you." Then I rolled up the paper, tied a ribbon around it, and proudly handed it to the young man, asking him, "Could you write the address for me, please?"

"Yes," he said, intrigued by the situation. "What's the name?"

"Please write, 'Leonardo da Vinci, Verrocchio's Bottega, Florence.'"

"But, Monna Lisa, I need the name of the street."

"I don't remember it. It's near the River Arno. I assure you, everyone in Florence knows where it is. It's famous."

He started to write, but stopped, puzzled. "This is the name of the son of Ser Piero, the notary. You said he was your son."

"Yes, you're right. But … he … he used to spend his summers here as a child, so I regard him as a son." He accepted my improvised explanation and continued writing. Then he took out a piece of sealing wax, warmed its tip in the fire, and with a coin pressed it on the ribbon. I watched what he did, fascinated.

"If there are any more messages, I'll bring them to you, Monna Lisa," he said as he left.

I thanked him and closed the door quickly, for a sudden feeling of guilt invaded my peace of mind. "Why did I deny my own son, the person I love more than anything in the world?" I asked myself reproachfully.

I started pacing the floor to overcome my agitation, trying to explain why this strange sense of guilt had taken hold of me so unexpectedly. I decided to sit down and examine my entire situation. I thought of how warm and respectful the old countrypeople, who knew my real life story, had been to me all these years. Even the young people growing up in these hills had accepted as fact that I was Giovanni's widow and that I had an artisan son in Florence, who from time to time came to stay with me. Another misconception about Giovanni that I never bothered to correct was that he belonged to a lineage of kilnmen in Vinci also called Accattabriga del Vacca. As for the *catasto* agents making their occasional rounds collecting taxes in our poor hills, they never came looking for me. Maybe I didn't count, because they knew I lived on the humble income from my garden, which happened to be on an estate owned by Florentine monks.

So what was I afraid of? Piero's persecution of me? In the last few years, he had been so preoccupied with finding a wife who could give him an offspring who would follow in his footsteps that Leo's welfare was hardly uppermost in his mind. And since Leo had become independent, my existence no longer posed a threat to his schemes. So why should I worry about keeping my son a secret? Maybe, I concluded, it was simply because I didn't want Leo's life to be tainted with talk of his illegitimate origin.

"Yet you, my dear son, worry so much about this life of mine, in total exile." I sighed, still staring at his thoughtful message. I realized then that there was another guilt tormenting me. Guilt for not sharing his enthusiasm, his dream of living together in his new house! Why this lack of interest? Is it because I've gotten used to being by myself—stuck in my ways? I asked myself, getting up again and briskly pacing the floor. "Oh, Leo! If only we could talk the way we used to. *You* could explain what's happening to me, get me out of this strange apathy that has gotten hold of me!"

I huddled in front of the fire, remembering how my rebellious spirit was sparked by my old anxieties. Now that I had learned resignation, nothing seemed to spur me on to fight for what I wanted any longer. As for Leo, I knew deep down that the world he had created for himself was his own world, in which I really didn't belong. So it seemed that every time I wrestled with my problem I kept coming to the same conclusion—that my presence in this world was really quite superfluous. "Truly," I said, jumping up again, "my existence isn't really necessary anymore!"

"Wait a minute, Caterina. I think you're being inconsiderate. You're not even making an effort to please him," I heard my reproachful voice say. "The truth is that you don't care about him the way you did before."

"That's not true! I still love him with all my being," I rebuffed. "He's still my only reason for living. Oh, God!" I cried. "If only I could tell Leo about these disconcerting thoughts! He'd make me feel that my mission wasn't over, after all."

I sat down in front of the fire again, feverishly grabbing the poker and hitting the logs in the fireplace. They crackled, sending out flames and sparks into the darkness. The dim lamp on the table behind me flickered for a moment, and I winced at the dancing shadows on the walls, which seemed to mock my muddled thoughts.

I sighed deeply as a kind of peace crept over me, mercifully releasing me from my tensions. The warmth of the flames quietly lulled me to sleep, and once again, I felt Giovanni's hand gently guiding me into his celestial garden.

16
LILIUM CANDIDUM!

> Consider the lilies how they grow: they toil not,
> they spin not, and yet I say unto you, that Solomon
> in all his glory was not arrayed like one of these.
>
> LUKE 12: 27

When the following Easter passed by without my seeing Leo, I felt compelled once again to venture a trip to Florence. I could wait no longer to visit him and discuss my conflicting thoughts with him, but most of all to see, at last, one of his finished paintings.

In my garden, the first beautiful lily had bloomed, and I decided to dig up the whole plant, put it in a pot, and take it to the Duomo. So with a large bottle of tisane and some fresh-baked buns, I departed for *la bella Fiorenza* again.

In the cool dawn air, Thunderbolt tried to keep the same steady trot on the highway as when he was a young colt. Every now and then, however, I pulled to the side of the road to give him a little rest. During one of those pauses, I saw again the top of the old tower of my ancestral home. Although I had no wish to revive the memory of that place, I found myself taking the road leading up to it, now overgrown with bushes and weeds. Thunderbolt refused to go ahead, reluctantly stamping his leg. "Thunderbolt, be patient! I have to take another look at that unforgettable place," I said, coaxing him all the way to the iron gate. I got off and tied him to one of its bars. "I won't be long and nothing's going to happen to me, I promise." I squeezed through the narrow opening of the creaking gate, now completely covered with a thick web of creepers. From a distance, I saw the grand old fountain, the only relic still visible. Except for the top of the imposing black tower standing high, the remains of the villa had been engulfed by tall, ugly trees with contorted branches like monstrous claws eager to wipe out any trace of the villa's existence. Even the broken doorway had been entirely blocked by thick, thorny bushes. I wondered if the old cripple who wanted to expiate his sin had ever found any respite from his suffering.

Drawn by the sad, blank gaze of the pretty cherub still balancing on one leg and holding out his empty cornucopia, I stopped in front of the fountain basin, now darker than ever, but filled with clear rainwater. I thought of my mother, Alicia, and a chill ran up my spine. Then, blotting out all morbid thoughts, I gave the forbidding forest one final glance before turning to leave, but a stony rain-washed path running along what must once have been flower beds caught my attention. I followed it, my eyes half-closed, trying to capture anything remaining from a happy time there. As I lingered meditatively, my gaze fell on a delicate bluebell peeping out through a bush. As I plucked it, the whole plant came away in my hand, and on the root hung a shiny thread. It was a gold chain with a small cross. I went to the fountain and rinsed it in the basin. Then I dried it on my skirt and slipped it over my head.

Without looking back, I headed directly to the gate, removed the rock that had held it open for years, and closed the gate for good, letting the creepers continue their silent and tireless weaving.

Back in my carriage, I drove all the way to the city without stopping, keeping one thought in mind, to see Leo even at the cost of provoking his master's anger. Once inside the city, I could hardly wait to enjoy dear Francesca's harboring hospitality. It had been almost four years since I had seen her. Her tavern seemed deserted as I marched straight through to the kitchen, where a strange man who was cleaning the floor barred my way with his broom. When I asked for Francesca, he said she was no longer there. "Where has she gone? I must see her," I insisted.

"She's dead," he stated coldly.

"When?"

"I don't know. I wasn't here," he answered, becoming irritable.

"Good man, could I leave my horse and carriage in the courtyard? I must go to see my son. Francesca always let me stay here."

He shook his head, then after giving me a long vacant look, he said, "All right, but you'll have to take it away soon. Our customers will need the space for the night."

Grief-stricken, I unharnessed Thunderbolt and led him to a manger. There wasn't much time, so I collected the lily plant and hurried down the street.

In my haste, I had forgotten to stop at the Duomo, so I decided to go first to the *bottega*. A boy scrubbing the small white statues in the front garden looked at my plant. "Oh, you brought the lily Maestro Leonardo was looking for!" he exclaimed. "I'll take it to him. He's busy painting a very important church panel."

I hesitated for a moment, then, taking advantage of the situation, said, "No, I must give it to him personally."

"Wait, I'll see." He ran into the building and, moments later, returned. "He can't be disturbed. He's in the conference room with Maestro Andrea. But you can wait for him in the entrance hall." Instead, I followed him all the way to the doorway of the spacious workshop and peeked inside. Several splendid paintings were hanging on the walls and others were propped up on wooden stands. "Is that Maestro Leonardo's painting?" I asked, pointing to one at random.

"No, his painting is hanging on the long wall, but if I let

you in to see it, I've had it! As it is, you shouldn't have come in this far."

"Please let me take a quick look at it. I promise you no one will find out, and when I go to the Duomo, I will pray that one day you'll be as good as Maestro Leonardo."

He looked at me suspiciously, but told me to wait while he went to see if it was safe to let me in. After a moment, he came out into the yard and whispered, "The conference room door is still closed. Come in, but just for a moment. There!" He pointed. "Isn't it marvelous?"

It was breathtaking; an exquisite painting of an angel kneeling before the young Virgin, who looked at him in great wonder! It looked so real!

"See that beautiful lily in the angel's hand?" the boy continued. "Well, Maestro Leonardo isn't satisfied with it. That's why he was looking for a real one." I fell to my knees to thank the Lord for giving me this great satisfaction. "Good woman, you cannot pray in front of an unfinished painting. Besides, it hasn't been blessed yet. Please get up and go back to the courtyard. Don't tell anyone I let you in, or else I'll get thrown out!"

I backed away slowly, my gaze fixed on the holy images of overwhelming beauty. I went outside and sat down on a bench opposite the door, hiding my face behind the lily stalk.

Maestro Andrea was the first to come out. "What a wonderful lily!" he exclaimed. "Leonardo will be delighted. Where do these lilies grow?" I didn't answer, as I had seen Leo coming toward us wrapped in thought. Though my face was still hidden, he recognized me all the same. To avoid complications, I got up, put the plant in his hands, and turned to leave. "Good woman, wait!" cried Maestro Andrea, pointing to the chain I was wearing. "That chain—may I see it? Where did you get it?" he demanded.

I turned to Leo, expecting to be rescued from the embarrassing predicament, but he stood there dumbfounded, holding the lily plant.

So, taking hold of myself, I faced the master and said, "It was given to me by a lady."

could rely on Thunderbolt's good instincts to get us home safely.

When I opened the door of my cozy home, it was like entering paradise. I went directly to the powder jars to look for the herb blend Leo had prepared especially for my cough, but it was empty. I remembered then having given the last of it to a sick little girl. So I lit the fire and boiled some chamomile instead, hoping it would give me some relief. But when my headache got worse and the shaking persisted, I decided to take to my bed.

After a while, I heard a knock at the door. Recognizing Mariano's touch, I asked him to come in. He looked at me wide-eyed. "Donna Caterina, are you sick? Did something happen to you on your trip?"

"I caught a chill … because of the fog. If I stay in bed for a while, I'll be all right," I said, still shaking. "The fire is out. Please light it again, Mariano. It's very cold in here. I'm freezing."

"But it's a very warm day. All right, I'll do it, but then I'll fetch my mother," he said, bustling around the fireplace.

"By the way, Mariano, do you have any of Leo's herb blend for coughs?"

"I don't know. I'll go home and look for it right away," he said, running off. I knew it was just an excuse to get his mother.

In fact, she came back with him, explaining she had never had any of Leo's mixture. She sat at my bedside, putting cold compresses on my forehead, which helped alleviate the pain. Realizing it was serious, I couldn't stand the thought of Leo being so far away, unaware of my condition. Besides, only he would have known what to do. "Nora, you must get word to my son, Leo," I cried out. "He's in Florence at Verrocchio's *bottega*." I stopped, suddenly confused by my fever. "No, he's outside playing with his construction projects. Please, bring my little boy here!"

"But Donna Caterina, you know Maestro Leonardo's a grown man now and he's much too far away for us to get word to him," Nora said, gently mopping my brow.

"Then have Mariano go to call Donna Grazia for me."

"But she's in Empoli, taking care of her sick husband. Remember? Try to rest now, my dear," she insisted. I sank back into my pillow, but my preoccupation about not being able to reach Leo still tormented me as, through the window, I watched the sky getting dark and starry. Then Nora made me sip some more chamomile, and I finally managed to get some sleep.

At the first light of dawn, I woke to the sweet sound of the swallows chirping on the roof. I sat up and called out, "Help me, Nora! Help me get to the old well! I'll feel better if I can watch the sun come up from there! I know I will!" She rushed to my bedside and tried to calm me, holding me down until I gave up struggling.

Suddenly, the door opened wide, and my Leo burst in, filling the room with his overpowering presence. The morning light accentuated his tall, broad frame and frowning face in such a way that I didn't recognize him.

"Maestro Leonardo! Oh, you're here! Donna Caterina is very sick!" I heard Mariano say to the giant stranger, who stopped to talk with Nora.

"Mariano, who is that man? Who is he? He's not my Leo. My Leo is just a child. He's playing outside—call him!" I shouted.

Leo rushed to me and knelt by my bed. "Mother, what happened? It's me, Leo."

As soon as I heard his voice, I recognized him. "Ah, my Leo, it's you! How did you know I was sick?"

"I didn't know. But last night, when I finished drawing your lily and took it to the Duomo, I heard you calling me. I looked around, happy to know you were still in the city, but I couldn't see you anywhere. I ran to the tavern, where they told me you had left the previous day. There were travelers still commenting on the terrible fog that had forced many to turn back that night. So I decided to come and see how you were." He gently felt my forehead. "Nora told me that you've run out of the herb mixture I prepared for you."

"Yes, my dear, I gave it to the sick children. I was well, and with the summer coming, I didn't think I needed it anymore."

"Don't worry, Mother. I'll go out and pick some special herbs that will help you recover," he said, stroking my head.

"No, my dear, don't leave me. Now that you're here, I'll be all right, you'll see! I feel much better already. For a while, I had forgotten you were a grown-up man," I said with a little laugh. The cool touch of his hand relaxed me, and I tried to rest.

I woke up smelling the vinegar-soaked compress a woman was holding on my forehead. I pulled it off. "Who are you? Where's my child?"

"Donna Caterina, I'm Nora, Mariano's mother. Don't you remember me? Master Leonardo went to pick some herbs for you. He'll be back soon."

"When did he arrive? Why didn't he come to me first?"

"He did as soon as he arrived from Florence." Then, hearing footsteps in the yard, she rushed to the door. "Maestro Leonardo, come! Come quickly! Your mother's awake."

I remembered then that Maestro Leonardo was my son, who painted beautifully. He hastily gave the bunch of herbs to Nora, and came over to me. "Leo, did you know I saw your painting of the Annunciation? It's beautiful beyond words! And the lily, too!" Suddenly, I was in total darkness. "Leo, are you there? I can't see you?"

"I'm here, Mother. I'm just going to see if the tisane is ready."

I grabbed his hand. "No, don't leave me, my dear, don't …or I'll get confused again. Before you arrived, I dreamed of Giovanni. Remember him, dear? He said he's waiting for me. Then I saw Alicia, my mother. She was with her Leonardo. They looked so handsome! They all kept calling me, asking me to stay with them, but I want to stay to grow flowers for your drawings. What am I to do, Leo? Is this the end?" I still couldn't see him, so I held on to his hand tightly.

"No, it's not the end! You'll stay with me. You'll get better soon, you'll see. And then I'll be able to explain my stupid behavior at the workshop, so you can forgive me, Mother!"

"Forgive you for what, my dear? What are you saying?"

"In Florence ... at Verrocchio's studio. You came there, remember?"

"Oh, yes, I remember, but it was my fault ... because I was upset, because ... I didn't appreciate your concern...for me. I wanted to tell you about those strange thoughts that had been bothering me lately."

"What thoughts? Now, stay calm! You can tell me later. Please, try to drink some of this," he said, putting a bowl to my lips. But a sudden burst of coughing made me spill it, and I fell back, exhausted.

I felt him touching my eyelids and wondered if he knew I couldn't see anymore. He felt the back of my head as if trying desperately to determine what was wrong with me. Then he put his ear to my chest, squeezing my fingers at the same time. But as a strange force started pulling me away, I felt an urge to reassure him that I was ready and whispered, "Don't worry, my dear. Maybe my time has come. The voice ... the prophet was right, after all, when he told me my mission was over, for ... you belong to the world now ... just as your art ... belongs to the world. You don't need me anymore...."

"That's not true, Mother! Please don't say that! You mustn't leave me. I still need you. You are the source ... the source of all my inspiration!"

"No, my son. Yours is a gift from God—you'll never lose it. But I promise you I will always be thinking of you," I said, trying to touch his cheek in the dark.

"Your portrait, Mother! I still need you to pose for it. I have put aside the perfect board for it."

"Oh, my son, you don't need me for it. You said it was in your mind, remember? Look! The angel agrees with me. He's trying to say that he likes the lily! I see the Virgin Mary. She likes it, too ... the lily in your painting!"

"Yes, they're saying that you're like that lily, pure and inspiring. Yes, you` are—without even knowing it. Yes, Mother, without even—"

"Oh, Leo, see the sparrows in the elm tree by my old home? And there's my old father, too! He says it's all as beautiful as it was in my childhood. He's showing me the flowers in the fields. Please take me there, Leo! I'll play my flute under the elm tree for the baby birds as I did then, and I'll recover. I know I will!"

"But, Mother, I don't know the way," he said hoarsely. "Besides, shouldn't we wait until you're strong enough ... to take a trip?"

"Thunderbolt!" I cried. "He knows the way. He'll take us!"

"All right, Mother. We'll go there, I promise. Now calm down."

I couldn't speak, for suddenly I was sinking into a void, deeper and deeper. I gasped as my whole being seemed to bounce back and I then felt myself being lifted up to the ceiling of my room. Leo, still clutching my hand, seemed to be holding me back with all the strength in his body, imploring me not to let go, but his voice began to fade, mingling with the bubbling sound of my *ruscello*. I knew then that I was outside. Yet Leo's hand continued to grasp mine tightly, and I felt as if I were breaking in two. A sudden snap severed his hold, and I was tossed high into space, where I remained suspended. My head, though, didn't ache anymore, and I could see again. From up there, I could see my *ruscello* the same way I had seen it the time I almost drowned. Thinking that this was the same temporary state I had experienced then, I directed my gaze toward my little white house and, incredibly, was able to see inside.

Leo, his head on my hand, was sobbing convulsively over my inert body. Nora and Mariano stood at the foot of the bed with tears in their eyes as Nora tried to console the wailing boy.

"Why doesn't anyone try to revive me?" I asked. Then I found myself drifting over the hills again, feeling as light as a feather, yet unable to direct myself at will.

The dull pounding of a hammer resounded in the air, drawing me toward the back of the house. Under the faint light of dawn, I was surprised to see Leo finishing the construction of a long box. He looked melancholy and drawn as he stood its lid against the wall. Then he took a brush and started to paint something on it. I wanted so much for him to be aware that I was with him, but I was afraid to disturb his concentration. I watched in awe as he carefully painted a large lily on the lid, and when he finally added a touch of pink inside its petals, I felt a sudden urge to put my hand on his shoulder. But before I could do that, an unseen force pushed me back into the void again.

It was daylight, and I found myself above the courtyard, where I saw the closed box with the lily painted on the lid resting on the ground. I realized then that I had a limited view of anything I looked at, as if it were being seen through a long tube. I saw a priest reciting something that sounded like the last rites and four men placing the box on the back of my carriage. Mariano, in a short black cape, sat on the carriage, solemnly holding the reins as tearful women arranged bunches of flowers on the box. Flowers from my garden, I thought! The next thing I saw was the women consoling their sobbing children. They were the same children whose health I had restored with my herbs! "What is going on?" I cried, but nobody heard me.

When Leo finally came into view, whispering in Thunderbolt's ear, the cause of his marked pallor aroused my immediate concern. But Mariano set the carriage in motion and Leo mounted a magnificent horse, whose gray coat shone like silver under the soft sunlight. This must have been the horse of which he had spoken.

A group of countrypeople followed them on foot as far as the crossroad, where Leo signaled them to stop, instructing Mariano to let Thunderbolt lead the rest of the way. I followed them, curious to see where they were going with that box.

At that moment, as if by magic, the box became transparent. Inside was my body, stretched out, seemingly dead. "I'm alive! Don't you see?" I screamed, but to no avail. I hovered in front of them, hoping they would see me, but as I did so, I was immediately pushed up into space, where nothing was visible.

On my next descent, I was in time to see Thunderbolt

own lesson first in order to ..." Alas, not even these words reached his ears, and I sadly looked away.

An evanescent cloud forming in the distance caught my eye as a group of cherubim, appearing out of nowhere, promptly gathered around it and gently pushed it up high into the sky. I saw their pretty heads turn in my direction, encouraging me to join them.

Enraptured by this delightful sight and eager to explore the wonders of the arcanum, I gladly followed their graceful heavenly trail.

17
LEONARDO'S EPILOGUE

Utterly grieved, I made my return from the saddest trip of my life, following the four-wheeled carriage that had provided my mother with her only recreation during her solitary years. Thunderbolt, the supernatural horse, who so uncannily had taken the makeshift hearse back to her childhood home, now maintained a casual trot.

I watched a downcast Mariano, propped up on his high seat, sullenly driving the empty carriage back to the house, and felt sorry for the boy. I knew that he felt as forlorn as I did, and that he was probably asking himself similar questions to those I asked myself—his being how to face the future without the woman who had become his daily guiding influence, and mine how to accept the sudden loss of the woman who had been my tower of strength since the moment my infant's ear had first captured the beat of her heart. A sudden sense of guilt overtook me for having been too ambitious in my constant quest for knowledge, leaving her alone for such inordinate lengths of time. As I stared at Mariano, envy permeated my surging grief. Mariano had experienced her harboring influence, had enjoyed her company, almost every day of the last few years.

Unaware of what was still in store for us, we reached the

dusty crossroad of Anchiano, where the countryfolk, who in the beginning had formed the funeral train, were still waiting for us. As we approached them, I was startled to see fresh tears streaming down their faces, and wondered if they had been crying since morning. I bowed my head to acknowledge their heartfelt participation and went on my way. Mariano had pulled up as they started to gather around the carriage, anxious to speak to him. He grew agitated, answering their many questions. I let Silver Dart, my horse, trot ahead. There was no need for me to talk to them, too. Silver Dart, like Thunderbolt, seemed to have been aware of the solemnity of the occasion, for during the burial procession, he, too, had kept a slow, reverent pace. I had called him Silver Dart because of his prancing body and shimmering gray coat. He was my first horse. I wanted so much for my mother to see him. I glanced up at the old chestnut trees sheltering the rustic tavern building and noticed that a thick, dark cloud of smoke was rising above them. I thought that someone had lit the kitchen fire to cook something for me, and a pain went through my heart with the reminder that it wasn't my mother waiting for me.

I entered the courtyard with my eyes lowered, not yet ready to face the emptiness waiting there. But when thick smoke started choking me, I leaped off my horse and ran toward the house, where I was witness to a most devastating sight. Rooted to the ground, I watched the last of the black debris burning inside what was once the foundation of the little white house my mother had so cherished.

An indefinable yet overpowering smell, mingled with the nauseating odor of melted candle wax, assailed my nostrils, making me shake my head. Yet I was still unable to move, transfixed by the quiet flames that had reduced to embers my mother's few prized possessions. Nothing was left of the new room she had had built just for me, not even a trace of its foundation. The blaze had destroyed it completely, together with all my childhood constructions, inventions, botany notes and drawings—mementos of my adolescent years.

A few sheets of paper, heavily covered with my experimental paint, caught my eye as the wind lifted and blew them toward the olive grove. I was tempted to run and pick them up to find out what had prevented them from being devoured by the fire, but my legs seemed paralyzed. Looking down at my feet, I saw that the threshing floor was covered with soot. Smashed tiles fallen from the roof were scattered everywhere. As I scanned the surroundings for other damage, I was relieved to see that the wooden altar niche I had built for my mother under the cherry tree had miraculously survived the flames, which had scorched the shrubs around it. Only the bottom of the little doors had been singed slightly, but the flame in the tiny glass chalice that had spread its light for almost seven years was, alas, finally extinguished.

Then I timidly glanced at what was once a magnificent garden and gasped with grief. A black sheet of soot had covered the whole field. Dead blooms hung pitifully from the withered stems. Of the herb garden on the slope next to the house, only some half-burned beams and broken tiles, which had somehow escaped the angry fire and fallen among the rare healing plants, could be discerned.

I was startled by the sudden presence of Mariano standing silently at my side. I observed his adult composure, discreetly withholding his comments for fear of upsetting me even further. I searched vainly for words to console his young spirit. But too deeply distraught with my own grieving to be able to formulate suitable phrases, I, too, remained silent. Then, gnashing his teeth, he sprang into action. He raced into the flower garden, threw himself to the ground and desperately began to blow the soot off the poor blossoms. He began to sweep the layers of soot off the soil with his bare hands. He worked energetically as I looked at him listlessly, still standing on the same stone slab, unable to say or do anything. I felt as if all my spiritual energy had been drained and my body was now sapping my physical strength for survival. Even if I had wanted to torture myself with the thought of my childhood retreat having been destroyed forever, I wouldn't have had the strength to do it. In the same way, if I had felt the urge to cry over the sudden abyss created around me by the loss of my mother, I couldn't even have wrung one single tear from my eyes.

A rumble of wheels suddenly brought me to my senses. It was old Thunderbolt, pulling the carriage into the yard. Mariano had obviously left him back on the road to keep him away from the fire. The poor creature needed to be unharnessed, and although I felt grateful to the brave horse for having kept fit and brisk enough to serve my mother until the very last moment, I still lacked the stimulus to move. My eyes remained fixed on the baleful black smoke as it rose over the charred ruin, twisting grimly in the changing wind as it was swept high above the remains of my mother's most beautiful corner of the world.

A loud sobbing drew my attention back to Mariano, who was kneeling on the ground by the dead plants. A sudden burst of energy revitalized me, and I found myself running to his aid. Compassion for the boy's distress had, at last, brought me back to life. I was further touched to see that he was crying at my mother's lily patch, clasping a seared blossom.

He looked surprised as I tried to help him up. Tears ran down his dirty cheeks, leaving light streaks in the smudges of soot. With the back of his hand, he inadvertently smeared the dirt all over his face. "Mariano," I said with a faint smile, "why don't you clean up now and come back tomorrow? There may still be some rainwater in the tub." I pointed to the corner, where the wooden screen I had built for my mother used to be. "See? The tub's still there." He turned his spent gaze toward it. "Believe it or not, it's not the only thing that has escaped the fire. See the niche? Inside it, the holy image of Santa Maria of the Snow is still intact." He looked at it, too. Then, calling his attention back to the lily patch, I said, "Did you know that the bulbs of those lilies are indestructible? And that they'll grow new stalks, new leaves, and even new blossoms?"

Then he looked at me, obviously wondering how a newly bereaved person could be able to speak so calmly. But I continued, "You should know these things, don't you think?" I hinted another smile just to distract him. "After all, you've had a good teacher ..." At this point, my throat closed up, and I turned away, regretting I had gone so far as to mention her. He touched my arm, looking up at me from under his rumpled, damp hair, but then turned away, bewildered. Perhaps he, too, was searching for the right words of consolation for me.

Thunderbolt neighed loudly, distracting us, and we rushed to unharness him. I asked Mariano if he would like to take care of him from now on. "You know that he's a special horse," I remarked, stroking Thunderbolt affectionately.

"Yes, I know. I would love to take care of him!" he exclaimed, his eyes lighting up. Then he respectfully stepped back as I studied Thunderbolt's perfect frame, his muscles still as firm as when I had drawn them in my first equestrian study and mounted him for the first time before my mother's proud eyes.

Thunderbolt shook his mane, and we both sprang back, bursting out laughing.

"Mariano," I said, suddenly feeling more at ease, "I'll talk to the owners of the estate and ask them to give you time to salvage whatever you can from the garden, bulbs, roots, and seeds, and plant them in your mother's field. But you must promise me never to neglect the cultivation of the healing herbs ..." A lump in my throat once again prevented the flow of words, so I headed silently toward the slope behind the tavern to look for my horse. I passed the little room under the tavern and for a while gazed at its tiny window overlooking the valley of the brook, remembering my mother's words when she pointed to it and said, "You were born on a marvelous morning right under this window!" I started as her voice rang in my ears, almost singing. "And this room heard your first cries, darling!" Before I knew it, I found myself looking over my shoulder, quite forgetting that she had left this world forever.

The minute I came to my senses, I regretted having let my imagination get the better of me. Shaking my head, I started down the valley, remorseful for having indulged in such fancies while her spirit was still adjusting itself to her new unknown existence in eternity. However, I couldn't help thinking how strong a hold memories can have on our psyche.

The high-pitched sound of a flute broke my train of thought. It seemed to be coming from the brook below and was so real that I thought it was a passing shepherd playing. But the tune was much too similar to one my mother used to play. As I glanced around nervously, I glimpsed the slight figure of a woman floating above the green cliff on the opposite side of the valley. I stared in disbelief as suddenly the hem of her gown flapping in the wind sparked the memory of my mother's skirt swaying when as a toddler I used to run along the brook with her. Convinced that I was hallucinating again due to my exhaustion, I shook my head and continued to look for my horse. But the sound of the flute assailed me once more, clearer and more intense than before. Although it was time I went on my way, a sudden impulse pushed me toward the site of the old well.

As I came near to it, through a thin veil of mist, suspended in the air was the portrait of a woman. The mist cleared, and I almost gasped to see that the woman was my mother. It was the portrait I had visualized since my childhood, yet even more stupendous! There she was, poised, between the two columns that supported the delicate-Romanesque arch, her hands gracefully crossed in front of her, the same tender smile. I knew then that that was how she wanted to be remembered, and, with my heart beating wildly and my head burning like fire, I called out to her, "Mother, Mother dear, I know that your devoted spirit will forever cherish these hills of ours, and I promise your memory will continue to live on this earth for centuries to come, for I will see to it that all the joys and the anguish you have harbored in your heart, your great courage and infinite tenderness, the boundless love and devotion with which you have inspired me all my life, will be immortalized in your all-encompassing, transcendent smile."

The painting started to fade, and with arms outstretched, I cried at the top of my voice, "This I promise, Mother: I will continue to work on your portrait until it reaches perfection ... till my dying day!"

I stayed there for a few moments, gazing at the bare well, as the sweet sound of the flute gradually faded away. Then, slowly pulling myself together, I looked around to see if there was anyone in the vicinity who could have overheard me. At that moment, Silver Dart trotted over to me. It seemed he had been my sole witness, for a disquieting silence prevailed all around us. I leaned against the saddle for a moment to steady myself, but before I could review what had really happened, I mounted my horse, took one final sweeping look at the desolate valley, and rode away.

It was getting dark as I galloped through a wild deserted forest, purposely skirting the town of Vinci. Finally, in the dead of night, I found myself on the highway to Florence.

Bathed in the pale yet dazzling light of early dawn, the skyline of the grand city seemed to move forward, intent on taking me back into its powerful grip once more.

18
TOGETHER AT LAST

The years have flown in this enthralling place of learning. I never returned to take on the human form again and found out that, prior to my earthly life, I had existed only as an elemental spirit.

The longing to see my Leo has occasionally been alleviated by strange, but brief, visits, which to him were visions or dreams. This time, though, I feel a momentous anticipation as I make my way back toward him. An unfamiliar landscape is before me. A wide, smooth river flows past a splendid castle. As I contemplate its round, pointed towers, unlike any I have ever seen in Tuscany, I'm suddenly pulled toward a stately but much smaller palace* set in the midst of a glorious countyside. I'm passing by the stables at the back of the building and overhear men's voices whisper in a swift, rhythmical language unknown to me; I know that I'm on a foreign land. Attracted to an open window on the second floor, I enter into a large room. Before me, a wide desk covered with drawing papers, pens, and manuscripts; on one side, several mechanical constructions, similar to the ones I've seen Leo make, but far more complicated. I go past the heavy drapes of a door lead-

---

*Le Clos-Lucé, Leonardo da Vinci's home at Amboise, France.

ing into a smaller room. In a corner is a familiar woman's portrait on a stand. Though I cannot stop as I'm still moving, I feel the eyes of this truly beautiful woman radiating a warm inner as well as outer light. Under the draped canopy of a regal bed is a very old Leonardo lying almost breathless. I smile at him, but his glazed stare seems to darken and his breathing sound stops suddenly. I wait, astounded by the sight of this motionless being. I touch his hand. A glow from his lifeless body begins to take a shape of its own, fast becoming more defined and brighter. A child! My little Leo! His golden curls, his impish eyes, his sweet laugh! He reaches out to me just as he did so many times after those long separations, and I feel him in my arms. What joy! What delight to hold him again! Oh, my little Leo! Together at last!